ALSO BY SUSANNE DUNLAP

Émilie's Voice

Liszt's Kiss

A NOVEL

Susanne Dunlap

A TOUCHSTONE BOOK
Published by Simon & Schuster
New York   London   Toronto   Sydney

TOUCHSTONE
Rockefeller Center
1230 Avenue of the Americas
New York, NY 10020

TOUCHSTONE and colophon are registered trademarks
of Simon & Schuster, Inc.

For information regarding special discounts for bulk purchases,
please contact Simon & Schuster Special Sales at
1-800-456-6798 or business@simonandschuster.com.

Designed by Melissa Isriprashad

Manufactured in the United States of America

10 9 8 7 6 5 4 3 2 1

Library of Congress Cataloging-in-Publication Data
Dunlap, Susanne Emily.
Liszt's kiss : a novel
p.   cm.
"A Touchstone book." Includes bibliographic references.
1. Liszt, Franz, 1811–1886—Fiction. 2. Stern, Daniel, 1805–1876—Fiction.
3. Composers—Fiction. 4. Women pianists—Fiction. 5. Musical fiction.
I. Title.

PS3604.U5525   L57   2007
813'.6   dc22   2006050047

ISBN-13: 978-0-7432-8940-5 (pbk)
ISBN-10:   0-7432-8940-4 (pbk)

For Bruce Dunlap, 1953–2006
Always my biggest fan, and forever my much-missed big brother

Liszt's Kiss

Prologue

July 1830

Anne and her mother had spent all of that beautiful afternoon in July in the ballroom, a room made for music and laughter, playing to each other and singing. Mozart, Schubert, Clementi—the marquise had even danced a mazurka while Anne read through some new sheet music by Monsieur Chopin.

"Your playing is more beautiful than ever," the marquise said.

The praise warmed Anne like a summer afternoon. She looked down at her hands, slender but strong, and itching to play and play until her fingers practically fell off. "I shall never be as accomplished as you."

"Nonsense." The marquise rose from her seat on a silk-covered divan and sat in the gilt chair next to Anne's at the keyboard. "You will surpass me by far. It's in your blood. Perhaps someday soon your father will permit me . . ." Her voice trailed off.

Anne took both her mother's hands in hers. She finished the sentence in her own mind with words she had heard spoken many times before: *Perhaps your father will permit me to take you to a concert, a play, a salon, the opera* . . . instead of only to church, or the cobbler's, or the dressmaker's. She had her lessons at home, with her mother or with carefully chosen tutors, and was not allowed to become friendly with other girls her age. But the world the marquise created for her was a comfortable prison, full of music and beauty, and under the spell of her mother's love, Anne hardly questioned the narrowness of its confines.

The marquise began an accompaniment and Anne joined in with the other part of the duet, one she had learned when her hands were still too small to stretch the distance of a fifth. They shared this secret, that a simple melody could mean so much more than anyone else would ever know.

"Must we stop?" Anne said when the duet ended.

The marquise tucked one of Anne's curls behind her ear. "Your father will be back soon."

As if to prove her right, the crunch of carriage wheels on the gravel-strewn courtyard drew their attention toward the ballroom door. Julien, the footman, had already risen from his stool in the vestibule and opened the old mansion's front door when Anne heard her father's unmistakable approach, heard him climb the three steps from the courtyard one at a time so that he could lean on his walking stick. After he passed into the vestibule, he slammed the door shut behind him so hard she could feel the vibration through the floor.

"Good afternoon, Marquis," said Julien.

He did not reply but continued his step *tap* step *tap* approach. He had used a stick to walk as long as Anne could remember. She was told that his lameness was the result of an injury sustained in the course of his escape during the Terror. He threw open the door to the ballroom.

"I need to speak with you, Sandrine."

"Go. Dress for dinner."

Anne reluctantly obeyed her mother's whispered command and curtseyed on her way past the marquis, who did not look at her. He stepped into the room and closed the ballroom door as soon as she left, and immediately Anne could hear his voice raised and his restless pacing back and forth, his cane tapping against the parquet. He only paced when he was angry.

Instead of continuing up the stairs to her bedroom to change into an evening gown, Anne glanced around to make sure no one was watching her and then pressed her ear to the door. She had learned a great deal this way, about things she knew her parents wanted to keep hidden from her, and this stolen knowledge was enough to make her wonder what went on the rest of the time to cause her mother's stifled tears and her father's morose moods.

"But, darling, surely you won't be left out altogether?" Anne could hear the nervous quake in the marquise's voice.

"It's done. I burned my bridges with the house of Orléans before you were born."

"Can you not appeal to Talleyrand?"

"Hah!" The marquis's bitter laugh was so sharp it rattled the door. "He's dropped me already. The first one, in fact. That man will go where it's best for him, no matter what favors he owes."

Her father approached. Anne fled up the stairs to her room. She wondered if her mother would tell her later what had happened. She knew the marquis would not.

Dinner that night was an unusually silent affair. The marquise made an effort to smile and draw out her husband in conversation, but he simply glowered into his wineglass.

Only when Thérèse, her mother's maid, helped her prepare for bed did Anne discover what had happened.

"The king and his family have all fled. The poor are making barricades in the streets, and demanding a revolution."

"Why?" Anne asked.

"They say King Charles overreached himself, setting up a court like the old days, taking away our rights, that we fought a revolution for in the first place."

And the marquis was a part of that court. Keeper of the seal. Anne had no idea what he did in that position, but clearly, he would be doing it no longer. And that would mean he might have to spend more time at home. "Poor Mama," she murmured as Thérèse brushed out her hair.

One

⧫

Black crape covered the windows of the house. The smells of camphor and death hung in the air. The marquise had died only a few hours ago of cholera, a disease that was supposed to attack the poor who lived in dirty, crowded, airless hovels, not the wealthy who lived in mansions in the faubourg Saint Germain. Anne was too numb to do anything but stare out the long windows of the ballroom at Thérèse, who, her face still streaked with tears, carried a basket full of linens to a corner of the courtyard and poured them in a lump onto a bonfire. Billows of black smoke curled up and merged with the flat, gray sky. It was a precaution, Dr. Magendie said. There was likely no danger to the rest of the household, if everyone took chamomile and wore a camphor sachet.

Anne forced herself to turn away from the window. Just three days ago, the marquise had been seated at the pianoforte in the corner of the room. Her eyes had shone with excitement about the music she had recently heard. The foreign pianists who were in Paris, she said, were the greatest geniuses ever known—especially Monsieur Chopin and Monsieur Liszt. Most of all Liszt, who was quite new to the city. She had promised that the next time he gave a concert, Anne would go with her, despite the marquis's rule to the contrary. *When I was your age, I attended concerts every night.* Her mother's voice still echoed in her ears. It had all been so sudden. One moment she was in the bloom of health. Then as they watched, she grew pale, clutched her stomach, and became violently ill. Although Anne herself had seen the passage from torment to peace in her mother's face not even a day later, when the doctor told them that she had died, Anne did not believe him. She was convinced that each time she rounded a corner or entered a room in the great house, she would see the marquise walking toward her, or sitting in a favorite chair and smiling at her, just as before.

"What are you doing here?"

Anne jumped. She turned to see her father leaning heavily on his cane just inside the open ballroom door. "Papa!" She ran toward him. He had retreated to the silence of his library soon after the doctor left, and she had not seen him since the moment of her mother's death.

He shrank away from her, turning so that his shoulder prevented her embrace, and put his hand up to shield his eyes as if he could not bear to look at her, or bear to let her see his tears. Anne stopped a little away from him and balled her reaching hands into fists.

"Leave this room at once. Don't ever come in here again."

Anne knew that pain lay beneath the anger in his voice, but still his tone stung her. "Please—," she began.

He turned his head to the side and gestured her through the door. Too tired and bewildered to think of disobeying him, Anne left, casting one more glance over her shoulder at the beautiful Pleyel, yearning to run to the instrument and play out her grief.

Since that time, Anne's pain had come and gone in waves. Sleep—other than in fitful dozes—was out of the question. Whenever she closed her eyes, her mother's stricken face floated across the blackness. Anne wished she could picture her happy and well, but even when she managed to think back beyond the time of her illness, the marquise still wore an expression of worried sadness. And yet Anne knew that she had been more often cheerful and lively during her lifetime. Why was it not possible to imagine her thus?

There was something, an event, an explanation, a reason, hidden just out of Anne's sight, behind a curtain across a part of her mind that was beyond her reach. She knew it was there, but she did not have the strength to draw that curtain aside. And what difference would it make? Her mother was no more. She would have to find a way to understand that simple fact.

Pierre Talon pulled the sheet up over the face of the young woman who had been telling him only a few hours ago about her childhood in Bretagne, before she had come to Paris to seek work as a seamstress. With a high, thin voice that breathed through cracked lips, she had begged for water with every other sentence and rambled on and on, clinging to life with a thread of narrative. Her efforts had been futile. She lay there dead now, like the twenty others Pierre had witnessed that evening alone. Evening? It was now morning. Through the high windows in the Hôtel-Dieu he could see the sky softening to a dark gray.

"Come, Pierre, we can do no more here."

Pierre's friend Georges pulled him gently away from the stench and moans of the patients who were still in the grip of cholera. The two of them were only medical students who had come to the University of Paris to study surgery with Andral and Louis. The horrible epidemic promoted them quickly to doctors, as they did their utmost with the rest of the students and physicians to deal with this capricious disease. The authorities had already set up cordons sanitaires, and *officiers hygiéniques* supervised the clearing of garbage and detritus from the streets. And yet still, cholera ravaged the population.

"I don't think I can bear to spend another minute here," Pierre said. It had been three solid days, with only a few stolen hours of sleep.

Georges draped his arm over Pierre's shoulder. "They admitted fewer today. There is word that the epidemic is abating."

Pierre nodded. Together they walked through the deserted streets back to the lodgings they shared on the rue des Bernardins near the university. Just two rooms, with a stove in the corner for heating and cooking. The furnishings were sparse, but Pierre managed to purchase an old square piano, and sometimes he played comic songs to amuse his friends. When he had the apartment to himself, he chose other pieces: sonatas and rondos, arrangements of arias from the opera. He was not very skillful, but he found it soothed his nerves to feel the keys beneath his hands and to fill the air with music.

In this time of disease and death, music was vital.

When they returned that morning, Georges threw himself on the one upholstered chair, and Pierre sat down at the piano. He played some waltzes by Schubert from a book he had purchased two years ago, when he first came to Paris.

Neither of them said a word but listened to the tender melodies until Pierre was too tired to continue.

Anne felt stiff and awkward in her heavy black silk gown, one of her mother's that Thérèse had made over to fit her, which rustled annoyingly whenever she shifted her position. Her father wore clothes she had not seen him in since the death last year of a courtier he had known most of his life. She noted when they climbed into the carriage that there were moth holes in his black felt coat and that the edges of his black armband had started to fray.

There was no time for a proper funeral: the priest had come to the house the day before and told them he could say the requiem by the tomb. Although Anne thought fear of contagion rather than other circumstances made him discourage them from bringing the marquise's coffin to the church, his tears about his lovely parishioner's untimely death were genuine. So too was his shock when he tried to draw father and daughter together and the marquis refused to give him his hand. "The Lord is merciful. He has left Your Excellency the com-

pensation of a daughter to soothe the lonely hours of grieving,"
Father Jean had said in the singsong voice so familiar to Anne from
mass. Her father did not have to say anything for Anne to understand
that he felt her presence there more an insult than a compensation.

The marquis's gloved hands lay in tense stillness on his lap. She
wished he would reach over and take hold of her. Such a simple gesture would bring her back to the world she knew instead of leaving
her suspended somewhere vacant and strange. Anne turned away and
stared out the window of the brougham. They drove in a queue of
carriages through a dreary rain north toward Père Lachaise, the
cemetery that had become the fashionable place to be buried, to lay
the marquise in the family vault. The hearse led the way. Anne and
her father sat in the carriage directly behind, and whenever they
rounded a curve, she could see the black feathers on the horses' bri-
dles bobbing with each step they took.

To reach the cemetery, they had to drive through the poor districts of Paris. Anne raised her camphor sachet to her nose and kept
it there, as much to prevent herself from inhaling the overpowering
odor of dead bodies piled up in the streets as to protect herself from
the disease they were told in pamphlets and in the daily papers could
well up from poisonous miasmas. None of the articles had really
explained what a miasma was, but it was invisible and sounded dangerous. And Anne was quite ready to believe that some mysterious,
unseen force had been at work to make her mother fall ill so suddenly.
Certainly there was no justice in it. The marquise was kind and beautiful, gentle and fair. She alone, of the few people Anne had known in
her life, could make her father's face light up with a tender smile.

The marquis had stayed mostly out of sight ever since his wife
died. Anne saw Julien bring him trays of food in the library and take
them away again hardly touched a short while later. He only emerged
when it was time to go to the cemetery. Anne was too frightened of his
mood to approach him without being summoned. Yet she did not
really know why she feared him. He had never been openly cruel to
her. Aside from making his wishes known in the form of immutable
rules, he simply ignored her most of the time, leaving it to her mother

and Thérèse to see that she had everything she needed and to educate her in all the subjects necessary for a young countess to know. She always kissed his proferred cheek before going to bed, but he accepted the kiss in silence. Special occasions entitled her to a pat on the head when he gave her a gift for her birthday or at Christmas.

When she was little, his silence and obliviousness toward her sometimes provoked her to small acts of rebellion. Once Anne hid his cane under a rug because its sound against the floor frightened her so. When her crime was found out, and her mother punished her by tapping her behind gently with the cane, the marquise's own wretched tears and sobs made the experience so painful for Anne that she vowed never to do such a thing again.

As she grew older, Anne had secretly envied her mother for the look the marquis bestowed on her when he watched her come down to dinner, clothed in luxurious silks and velvets and draped with jewels and furs. Thérèse sometimes allowed Anne to sit on the stairs to spy on her parents' parties through the banisters, and she would see admiration for her mother in other gentlemen's eyes as well. The marquise knew her daughter was there but did not mind. She wanted Anne to hear the music, and those parties remained the experience closest to attending a concert that she had ever had. Apart from the occasional celebrated singer or instrumentalist, the small orchestras they engaged introduced her to the sound of strings and woodwinds and brass. Anne recalled a particularly festive occasion—her mother's birthday, she thought—when the marquis hired some of the members of the Paris Opera to perform several scenes in their ballroom. She had been allowed to wear her best dress, and she sat on the lap of a duchess to watch. The lavish costumes enchanted her. One of the scenes was a storm, and the sudden roll of the tympani made Anne cry. She thought that thunder and lightning had somehow broken into their own home. The performance halted while Thérèse took Anne up to her bedroom.

Most of the time, though, Anne would listen and watch from her perch on the stairs, unnoticed by the guests. She became aware at a very young age of the way her mother drew admiration wherever she went, and she saw that her father kept his eyes on his wife constantly and always found reasons to touch her—when he guided her through to the ballroom, when he handed her a glass of champagne, when he asked her to play the piano for their guests.

"Whoa there!" the coachman called out. Their carriage halted so abruptly that Anne was almost thrown off her seat.

"What's wrong?" she asked, but the marquis sat in unblinking silence. Anne raised her thick veils, lowered the window, and poked her head out. "Merciful heaven!"

From every direction, hearses and mourners streamed toward the cemetery, still about half a mile away. It looked to Anne as if the roads themselves were in mourning, covered with black coaches pulled by black horses and driven by coachmen dressed all in black. So many would never be able to gain access to the cemetery at the same time, and up ahead there was some kind of obstruction. She leaned out farther to look.

To Anne's horror, a hearse had turned a corner too sharply, and the coffin it bore had rolled off the bier. In their haste to bury the dead, undertakers did not use many nails to seal the coffins shut; this one had sprung open when it hit the ground and disgorged a purple and swollen body. A young man standing next to the now empty hearse looked around him sadly, and for an awful moment it seemed that no one would come to his aid. For the briefest second, his eyes met Anne's. She pulled her head in and covered her mouth, struggling not to retch.

Anne chose not to look out again, but somehow or other the problem must have been resolved, because they eventually continued their slow progress to the cemetery gates. They waited their turn, and once the gatekeeper admitted them, the horses plodded along the gravel paths through the rows of vaults and memorials that resembled a miniature, Gothic city clinging to the side of the hill. Every third or fourth memorial showed evidence of recent opening and so many fresh flowers had been trampled under the feet of the horses that the air smelled oddly sweet.

The burial service passed in a fog of incense and stifled tears. A small crowd of people came to pay their respects to the marquise. She had been an only child, and both her parents had died soon after Anne was born. As far as Anne knew, there were no other relatives on either side of the family. Her father's only brother had died when she was very young, and she had been told that shortly after his wife also died giving birth to a stillborn child. Anne knew enough from listening to her parents' conversations at the dinner table to understand how the fall of Charles X had assured their banishment from the higher echelons of society. There only remained some close friends of her mother's to bring them news of court—friends with whom the marquis did not deign to associate. And so the little group of mourners assembled at the Barbier family vault consisted mainly of their servants and a few strangers, perhaps stragglers from other burials, or genteel beggars hoping to be rewarded for their tears with a few sous.

As the priest droned on in Latin, scraps and shreds of thoughts and memories passed through Anne's mind like casual visitors, barely stirring her consciousness. Later, she would remember little of the funeral, except for an engulfing sense of desolation and loss. She would remember little, that is, except for an incident that occurred just as she and her father prepared to climb back into their carriage and retrace their route down the hill, through the outlying districts and back to the familiar luxury of the faubourg Saint Germain.

The doors of the Barbier-Chouant vault had closed with a heavy clunk. The pointy arch of its roofline blurred and swayed before Anne's tear-filled eyes, and she was afraid that she might collapse where she stood. She looked for something, anything, to anchor her to the earth. Her gaze lit upon a tall, slender woman standing apart from the rest of the mourners, wearing a bonnet draped in black chiffon veils that obscured her face. The lady lifted a gloved hand to greet them, then turned and walked away.

"Who is she?" Anne asked.

The marquis had closed his eyes. At the sound of Anne's voice he opened them again, and the vacant expression Anne saw there frightened her. She nodded toward the retreating figure of the woman, who had reached a carriage that had stopped by another grave and was climbing in, assisted by her footman. The marquis turned his eyes slowly in the direction Anne indicated. He flared his nostrils when he saw the lady but did not answer.

Anne let the matter drop. Her father's gray head bowed under the weight of his top hat, and his wrinkled face seemed to close her out more than ever. Yesterday his exclusion took on concrete form when Julien put padlocks on the doors of the ballroom and sealed it shut, giving orders that no one—not even Anne—was permitted to enter. She had not yet summoned the courage to ask her father why.

The only explanation she could think of was that the ballroom with its beautiful pianoforte was so vivid a reminder of the marquise that her father could not bear the thought of anyone crossing its threshold again. But didn't he know that all he need do was ask her not to enter? And she would not—at least not while he was in the house. Anne could stand hardly ever being able to play the piano. But being forbidden altogether?—It was too much. Along with his wife, the marquis buried music. And without music, Anne thought, *He might as well have buried me.*

Two

Eugène Delacroix hid behind a stone statue in the grounds of the château Neuilly-sur-Seine. Just outside the gates, the two horses he and his friend Franz Liszt had ridden through the dark to reach the place where the young princess Clémentine lived waited to convey them back to Paris. The clock in the chapel tolled midnight. *Where is he?* Eugène began to feel that this entire escapade was very ill-judged.

From the direction of the château garden Eugène heard running. Shortly after that a woman's voice yelled out, "Stop him! The black-guard!" and one by one the windows of the château came to life with the glow of candles. Moments later Franz's tall, slender figure burst through a box hedge and stumbled toward him.

"For God's sake, man," he panted, "where are the horses?"

Without a word Eugène took Franz's arm and dragged him toward the gate. Before they reached it, they spotted a guard holding a lantern and looking out at the gloom, searching for them. "We'll have to climb," Eugène said, and they headed for a vine-covered stone wall.

"My hands!" exclaimed Franz in a hoarse whisper.

"You should have thought of them before this!"

The two young men scrambled over the wall, tearing their clothes on the thorny vines, and dropped down on the other side. "This way," Eugène said, and led Franz to the chestnut tree where they had tethered the horses to a low-hanging branch. In an instant they mounted and galloped off in the direction of Paris just as the château gates were opened. The guards fired shots into the woods after them.

They rode without stopping directly to Eugène's studio in Saint Germain, where the two adventurers splashed water on their sweating faces.

"Champagne?" Eugène suggested, because that was all he had at the moment.

"I so nearly managed it, my friend," Franz said in his mellifluous Hungarian accent.

"Managed what, exactly?" Eugène was now cross that he had allowed Franz to persuade him to participate in this foolhardy adventure.

"The princess. I simply wanted to kiss her."

"For heaven's sake, the girl is fifteen!"

Franz shrugged. "True love knows no age."

"And you believe, simply because she smiled and gave you a flower when you played for her uncle, that she is in love with you? What do they feed you fellows in Hungary?"

Franz Liszt's eyes glistened with excitement. "They feed us nectar, and teach us to love, above all else. It is the very soul of art."

Eugène gave a derisive snort.

The next morning, a little bruised and scraped from his escapade the night before, Franz prepared for another day of playing the piano and composing in his two small, dark rooms, tucked in under the roof of a building that, although respectable, was hardly luxurious. Every time he ascended the stairs and put his key in the lock, he was reminded of his current financial embarrassment, a temporary condition he intended to remedy at his earliest convenience. He planned to move to a larger apartment in the building so that his mother, who was away on an extended visit to relatives, might stay with him. After a modest breakfast, Franz took his seat at the square piano Monsieur Erard had given to him in exchange for a promise to perform at his salon. He and some of his friends had manhandled it up the stairs one night after they'd polished off a bottle or two of Bordeaux at Eugène's studio, and it showed signs of damage from its drunken ascent. But the tone was good, it had a full, six-and-a-half-octave keyboard, and the action was solid enough to practice on for hours.

Franz warmed up by playing scales, rushing headlong up and down the keyboard, sometimes with the sustaining pedal pressed to the floor so that the sound became a dissonant roar.

"Quiet!" a voice yelled up from below, accompanied by thumping on the ceiling.

"Philistine!" Franz hollered back, playing even more loudly until he heard a distant door open and slam shut and the sound of footsteps pounding down the stairs and finally leaving the building. He stopped playing and ran his long fingers through his blond hair, which hung down to a soon-to-be-fashionable length of just to the top of his collar. His eye caught sight of an untidy pile of cards and invitations that he had tossed on a wooden stool. They had arrived that morning, as a similar quantity had arrived every morning since his last performance at a salon given by the countess Blavatsky. Franz smiled at the memory of that soiree. Three women had fainted dead away, and that was the occasion upon which he had been presented to the princess. Her blushes and her sweet gesture of giving him a rose had emboldened him to undertake that wild adventure last night. This morning he decided it was not worth the danger to pursue the matter any further.

With his right hand, Franz picked out the tune of "Là ci darem la mano," from Mozart's *Don Giovanni*. The frail Chopin had used the aria as the basis for some lovely variations. But instead of playing the ones the Polish composer wrote, Franz took off on his own, bending the sweet melody, distorting it beyond all recognition. *How did the delicate Pole do it?* he thought. In Paris a little over a year, and already he had a well-established studio of wealthy aspiring pianists, and several editions published. His latest, the studies, were being issued one at a time. Chopin told him he would dedicate them to Liszt himself—a gesture that was at once flattering and annoying.

Franz soon tired of his game and began to open his cards, glancing at them one by one, then tossing them aside into two different piles. *Cher Monsieur Liszt,* so many of them began, and continued with declarations of undying love and, in some cases, open invitations to amorous assignations. One pile consisted of those he considered beneath his notice. The others were invitations to which he would respond. One need never be lonely in Paris, Franz thought.

Preoccupied by his pleasant thoughts, Franz did not at first hear the polite tap at his door. When the knock was repeated and accompanied by a delicate, "Ahem!" he at last looked up from his mail. "Who's there?" he called out, ever in fear of unannounced creditors.

"Monsieur Liszt?"

A girl's voice. Franz rose and covered the space between the piano and the door in three long strides, then opened it.

A slightly plump—but pretty—serving maid stood there, holding an envelope in one hand and a red rose in the other. "My mistress bade me deliver these to you in person." She curtseyed and held out her two burdens to him.

But instead of taking the note and the flower from the girl's hands, Franz grasped her arm and pulled her into the room. "She asked you to deliver them in person?" he said. "Won't you take some refreshment before you go?"

Franz saw the blush spread up from the girl's neck into her face. It intensified the gray of her eyes, and she looked even more attractive.

"No, I mustn't, truly, I must go back—"

"What is your name?" Franz asked her.

"Adèle," she breathed. Then she remembered her errand once again and held out the letter and the flower for Franz to take.

Franz's laugh rang out. "Perhaps I should look at this important message you have brought me?" He took the envelope, tore it open at the end, and pulled out the letter it contained.

Monsieur Liszt,

I would be delighted if you would consent to perform a selection at my salon the day after tomorrow. Please send word back with the bearer of this message. I shall consider my life complete if you would play on my beautiful new Erard.

Amitiés,
Comtesse Marie d'Agoult

"So, your mistress is a countess? I expect she is old and ugly, or she would have come herself."

Adèle bit back a laugh. "Some say she is the most beautiful lady in Paris," she said with pride.

Franz nodded thoughtfully. "Tell your mistress that, *dommage,* I am not free on that evening."

The girl curtseyed. Franz opened the door for her and swept her a deep bow. She blushed again, then rushed away.

"So, he won't come. That is a shame." Marie d'Agoult remained in her seat by the long windows in her parlor that overlooked the Seine. She had not yet dressed for the day. Her hair tumbled in unruly golden blond curls over the shoulders of her loose silk robe. She chewed on one ink-stained finger and used her toe to nudge some crumpled-up pieces of paper that were lying on the floor. If Liszt could not come, she might as well have the party another time. Her note to him had been slightly untruthful. She had not yet actually invited anyone to a salon. "I shall join the children at Croissy tomorrow," she said.

"That would be best, madame." Adèle bent down and picked up the littered papers. "They say many more have died of the cholera here in Saint Germain this week."

Marie said nothing, and her maid crept out of the room with her hands full of the leavings of her mistress's night of sleepless thinking.

Poor Sandrine. Marie dashed away a tear with the heel of her left hand, taking care not to smear ink on her cheek. She had been hoping to assemble all the finest pianists in Paris at a salon in her late friend's honor, but now, for the moment, that was not to be. Sandrine had been older, but ever since Marie came to the city when she was in her teens, the marquise's sensitivity and love of music had drawn them together. When Marie married, they drifted apart. Marie became a lady-in-waiting at Charles X's court, and Sandrine was a bourgeoise, therefore somewhat outside society. Her much-older husband held a court position, yet the marquis kept his distance from Marie, barely acknowledging her with a nod when their paths crossed. Later she found out from Sandrine that he disapproved of the artistic circle she gathered around her.

It had seemed an odd match. Not that the situation had never arisen before, where a much older man at the end of his fortunes seeks to marry someone beneath him for wealth. But why the daughter of a nouveau riche merchant, and why would this luminous beauty in turn settle for little more than a title? Added to that was the fact that their marriage appeared different from the usual business alliances. Sandrine never tried to impose herself on the closed, aristocratic society of which he was a member, and the marquis was not extravagant with his wife's fortune, making no outward changes in his circumstances. If anything, he was more retiring and reclusive than he had been before. They did not lead separate lives, as everyone would have expected. Indeed, the marquis never left his wife's side in public. There had been rumors about his jealousy, but Sandrine had never complained of it. Still, Marie and Sandrine had not seen each other for several years. It was the news of her friend's sudden death that had brought Marie into the city.

At the graveside she saw a young lady with the marquis who must have been their daughter. Marie had not seen her since she was a small child, and the countess—Anne was her name—was too covered with veils for Marie to tell whether she resembled her mother. But she could see even from a distance that the young countess was a child no longer, nearly a woman in fact, and now would have no mother to guide her into society. Sandrine had said the girl was more musical than she was and had a natural gift for the pianoforte. No one had ever heard her, of course. The marquis did not permit his daughter to display herself in public.

Marie took a deep breath, drew a fresh sheet of paper from the quire, and dipped her pen in the inkpot.

Chère Mlle. la Comtesse,

My sympathy is with you. Your mother and I were great friends. She was like an older sister to me when I first came to Paris. Please allow me to return her kindness by performing that same role for you. My door is always open. Come to the quai Malaquais any afternoon for tea after this Friday the 30th, as I will be with my children at Croissy until then.

Avec toutes mes amitiés,

Marie d'Agoult

Marie addressed the envelope to Mademoiselle la Comtesse Anne de Barbier-Chouant at the hôtel Barbier, then put it aside to be posted later.

Most of the notes of condolence from distant acquaintances and strangers had been addressed to the marquis, not even mentioning Anne in their expressions of sadness. She was all the more touched, therefore, by the only letter addressed to her, from the countess d'Agoult. Her name had been linked with everything the marquise loved, with music and art and poetry. She knew she had met the lady once when she was quite young but had no recollection of her. The parties and dinners her parents used to have had gradually dwindled over the years, and Madame d'Agoult, like her mother's other friends, visited less and less often. Since the July Revolution, they had had no guests at all, aside from business acquaintances of the marquis. Nothing in her memory would have connected the person her mother had often spoken of so warmly with the tall, remote figure who had nodded to them at Père Lachaise.

"Father, Madame d'Agoult writes that she would like me to call on her next week." Anne had been sitting at her needlework in the library for two hours after dinner while her father stared without turning the pages at a large book on a stand in front of him. His library, once the envy of many learned men, had been sadly depleted. No one ever mentioned it, but Anne had watched as paintings vanished from the walls, the silver tea service stopped appearing in the afternoon, and her mother wore fewer jewels and last year's dresses. The household staff was at a bare minimum: Thérèse—who now acted as housekeeper as well as personal maid—Julien, a cook, and Victor, the coachman. A daily girl came to help with the menial chores. All but two horses had been sold, and they kept only a small carriage and the threadbare brougham they had used on the day of her mother's burial.

The marquis lifted his eyes slowly and fixed them upon her. "Your mother dead not three days, and you want to go calling on her reprobate friends?"

Anne felt the familiar hardness in her chest that closed in on her whenever her father said something unkind, whether he meant to or not. Perhaps it was unseemly to want to visit so soon. Yet the unvarying pattern of their days, the horrid vacantness of her home without her mother, made her feel more angry than sad. And this undesired anger stole her ability to weep and brought her father's uncongenial temperament into relief. Anne knew she should meekly sit with her taciturn father hour after hour, as if visits of condolence were likely, and as if he really wanted her to be there, but ever since the funeral she had been unaccountably restless.

If her mother had been alive, she would have been able to explain why Anne felt as she did and would have interceded with the marquis, saying "Henri, dearest, it's only natural that Anne should want company at such a time, especially without the pianoforte to play . . . ," and her soft words would have soothed him into granting their daughter whatever she wished. Now, Anne didn't know what to do.

Anne waited until her father again lifted his eyes off the page and stared at something in the middle of the room, then summoned her courage to try again. "She was a great friend of mother's, she says, and I think wishes to talk about her with me. I would like to tell someone about Mama." Despite her best efforts to prevent them, tears collected in the corners of Anne's eyes and trickled down her cheeks. Yet she managed to keep them out of her voice.

"You are too young to visit," the marquis said.

"But she was mother's particular friend, so it wouldn't be like visiting. And I'll soon be eighteen."

"She's not suitable company for you. I'll not have you mixing in that crowd, all artists and musicians."

Anne said nothing more, but instead of making neat little stitches on the cushion cover she had been embroidering for months, she took great, messy ones and covered over the delicate pattern that was the result of hours upon hours of silent work. After a few minutes of this quiet destruction she stood.

"I'm going to bed now, Father." She left the room without bestowing her usual perfunctory kiss on his papery cheek.

Despite the unspoken interdiction against making noise, Anne stomped up the stairs, slammed her bedroom door shut, and threw herself on the silk coverlet that draped her bed. At first, each strangled breath scraped into her, fighting to get to her lungs. When she finally gave in to the physical necessity of grieving, the sobs came freely, and before long her pillow was drenched.

The rest of the house was quiet by the time her storm of tears subsided. Her dry eyes burned, and deep breaths shuddered through her. Although her head ached, Anne felt oddly light and unencumbered. She opened her eyes, sat up, and blew her nose in her damp handkerchief. She was still aware of the gaping hole in her heart that would never again be filled. But she was also aware that her life must continue. She could not hide away in her crumbling home, no matter how much her father wished her to. Anne rose and wobbled a little when she stood. She turned, caught sight of herself in the mirror over her dressing table, and gasped. For the briefest instant, she thought the image in the glass was her own mother. Grief has made me older, Anne thought, and it seemed she had grown taller. She had her mother's light blond hair too, pulled up in a knot at the top of her head with clumps of curls draped fashionably over her ears, now somewhat askew from her bout of hysterics. Although her eyes were a darker blue than her mother's had been—and were quite red at the moment—Anne all at once understood why the sight of his daughter might grieve her father so. If he would not let her have company or visit, and had sealed the ballroom shut so that she could not play the piano and remind him of his wife, well then, Anne thought, *I shall have to find another way to pay a call on the countess, and to practice the piano. Mother would have allowed me to; she would have wanted me to.*

Anne sat at her escritoire and wrote a note to Marie d'Agoult, saying that she would call on her next Monday, if that would suit, sealed it, and decided she would give it to Thérèse to deliver. Poor Thérèse was as sad as anyone in the house, and it would probably do her good to take a walk tomorrow.

For the first time since her mother's illness began, Anne slept deeply. Her dreams, rather than being populated with bloated corpses and gaping graves, were of her mother, her index finger to her lips bidding Anne listen to some great secret that only she should hear.

Three

"Where d'you think you're going?"

Anne had not heard her father open the door of the library, and his voice startled her as she settled her bonnet carefully over her coiffure on Monday afternoooon.

"To confession," she answered, holding up her missal and rosary.

"Victor will take you."

"I'd much prefer to walk. The air will refresh me."

The marquis sucked his breath in through his nose in a petulant sniff but said nothing. He had already started closing the library door behind him when he muttered, "Mind you're back in an hour."

"Yes, Papa," Anne said, more to herself than to her father, who was well out of earshot by that time.

Although she knew the atmosphere at the hôtel Barbier had been strained of late, until she stepped out unescorted into the mild, April sunshine, Anne did not fully realize how much she craved escape. The marquis had remained distant and implacable. Each day he receded further and further into a world that excluded her altogether.

Mealtimes were particularly painful. They had always observed the old custom, having a formal dinner at home every evening if the marquis and marquise were not going out. Her father used to say that he had done without for twenty years and more during the Terror and while Napoléon made exiles of the nobility, and he refused to do so now. When the marquise was there, she would liven up even the dullest evening with chatter and gossip, and she could always make her husband smile.

One of the stories Anne often asked her to tell was how she and Anne's father met, and how they came to be married. It seemed like a fairy tale. What she said never varied. The marquis, reportedly euphoric about the return of the Bourbon monarchy in '14 and eager for an heir to carry on the family title, "was in a mood to be captivated," as she had put it, and fell in love with Sandrine Poitou at the opera. "He did not know who I was," her mother would say, "or he might have let his eyes stray to a different box," referring to her lack of pedigree. She never mentioned whether the marquis was disappointed that the heir he presumably married her to produce never materialized. The marquise compensated for her lack of breeding by bringing a large fortune to the union, however.

Anne paused to get her bearings before turning on the quai Malaquais. Madame d'Agoult had given her the number, but the street was lined with well-kept buildings that looked quite similar to one another. Once she was certain she was going the right direction, she turned her thoughts inward again. A large fortune. Where had it gone? Anne had witnessed the gradual dismantling of the household over the past two years, at first thinking little of it, yet becoming more and more aware of their changed circumstances as time went on. She knew from overhearing her parents' conversation that being out of favor at court had put an end not only to their active social life but also to the generous honorarium the marquis had received. Yet when she thought hard about it, Anne realized that the steady disappearance of objects of value dated not from the July Revolution, but from a time a few months earlier. She remembered, because it had all started with a picture she particularly liked that at one time hung over the mantelpiece in the small sitting room. The lady in the painting wore a beautiful velvet dress, and the lace around her old-fashioned collar had been rendered so meticulously by the artist that Anne could see the delicate knots holding the gossamer threads together. One morning, the portrait was no longer there, and all that day her mother and father seemed nervous and started whenever a servant entered the room or some noise from the street was loud enough to be heard indoors.

Why did I not question my mother at that time? Anne wondered. It seemed so obviously strange now. Objects continued to vanish without explanation after that. Trinkets and knickknacks, familiar to Anne since childhood, would one day no longer occupy this or that shelf or alcove. She had stopped even mentioning them a year ago, though, when her innocent inquiry about a Sèvres shepherdess of which she had been fond provoked her mother to an outburst of tears. Now she doubted anything much of real value remained in the house.

Anne had by this time arrived at the building where Madame d'Agoult lived. A pretty young maid answered her pull on the bell. She handed the girl the missal she had brought with her as an excuse to leave her house, followed by her bonnet, gloves, and wrap. "The mistress is waiting for you in the parlor," the maid said, gesturing toward a door that was slightly ajar.

Madame d'Agoult stood by a grand pianoforte in the corner of the large, airy room, looking over some music. Perhaps it was a trick of the light, but the angle of her head, the way she concentrated on the score she held in her hands, was so like Anne's mother that she had to prevent herself from running to the countess with joy and embracing her. Madame d'Agoult replaced the music on the instrument's desk before approaching Anne with her hands outstretched.

"Dear Anne—may I call you Anne?—you look so like your mother. I saw you, at the cemetery."

So it was Madame d'Agoult she had seen the other day. Now it made sense, that she would have written. For a moment neither of them could say anything else. Anne was surprised to find that the tears she thought had run dry the other night threatened to recommence. Madame d'Agoult's eyes were wide and sad, brimming with old sorrows as well as new, Anne thought.

"Come, sit with me and have some tea. I must get to know all about you. Is it very hard, living with your crotchety father in that great mansion?"

Ever since her mother died, Anne felt as if she had been traveling in a foreign country where no one spoke a language she understood. Her conversation with Marie d'Agoult that afternoon was the first normal interchange with another human being she had had in days. For above an hour, they spoke about the marquise, and about music and poetry, her favorite diversions.

"Some time ago your mama wrote to me and told me how well you play the piano," Marie said, pouring Anne yet another cup of tea. "Perhaps you would play something for me?" She swept her hand in the general direction of her pianoforte.

"May I?" Anne asked. When Marie nodded, she rose and took her place at the keyboard of the Erard, a maker Anne did not know. She played a few chords, waking her hands up from their enforced slumber over the past week. The countess kept the instrument perfectly tuned, and the keys felt familiar and safe under her fingers. She began to play a sonata by Mozart, in B-flat major. The Viennese composer's perfectly proportioned phrases and yearning melodies were like balm to Anne's soul. She closed her eyes. All sense of where she was disappeared, and for those few minutes until the first movement ended, Anne left herself behind and entered a world of pure music. When at last she lifted her hands from the keyboard after the final cadence, she almost expected to see her mother's smiling face looking approvingly at her through the raised lid of the pianoforte. Instead, she saw Marie's bowed head, turned away from her and resting in her hand.

"That was beautiful," Madame d'Agoult said.

Anne rose and curtseyed to her hostess before joining her once more by the tea tray. As she was about to sit down again, the clock chimed five. "Heavens, is that the hour? I must leave right away! My father will be most anxious."

"Whatever for? Is everything all right?"

Anne twisted her hands. She didn't know what to say.

"You did not tell him you were coming here?"

"He's so difficult these days. It's worse since my mother died. He won't let me go anywhere except to church, and I may have no visitors either." Anne didn't dare face the countess, now that she had confessed her lie. Doubtless Madame d'Agoult had invited her thinking that she was not the kind of girl who would deceive her own father.

"I see. Well, we must find a way to remedy that, mustn't we? A pretty, talented young lady like you ought to go out in the world."

Anne met her eyes. They sat like still pools above her smiling face. She was nearly as beautiful as her own mother had been.

Marie stood and pulled the bell rope by the mantelpiece. "There is a concert tomorrow evening, at the Salle Wauxhall. Some very great pianists will perform. I think you would enjoy it. I have taken a box and would be delighted if you would join me in it, if you can contrive to meet me here at eight?"

The maid entered with Anne's things. A concert! It was too wonderful to be true. Her mother had promised that soon she would take Anne to her first public concert. Instead, here was her mother's friend, a much better stand-in than she had ever hoped to find. "Yes, I will manage it," Anne said, silently hoping she would be able either to convince her father to allow it or to go without his knowledge.

Anne walked as fast as she could all the way home, wishing that she could lift her skirts up and run. It would be difficult to explain why she had been gone two full hours to confession. And as for arranging things for the evening to come—perhaps Thérèse would advise her.

When Anne reached the great front door of the hôtel Barbier, she noticed a landaulet drawn by one well-groomed chestnut horse standing in the courtyard. She did not recognize the carriage, and it bore no crest. Anne let herself into the house, hoping not to attract the notice of Julien, who would doubtless tell her father right away what time she had returned.

The hôtel Barbier was laid out in the old-fashioned style, without that clear distinction between public and private spaces of more modern mansions. To the right as one entered lay the ballroom, which extended the entire depth of the building, its door still padlocked shut. To the left was the marquis's library, where he spent most of his day when he was not in his chamber upstairs. The large dining room was behind the library. There was a morning room directly behind the staircase. Anne passed her time in this room when she did not have to sit with her father in his library, and they breakfasted and occasionally supped there as well.

The wide, curved staircase led to the first floor, which held the formal parlor, situated directly above the ballroom. They rarely used this room, even when the marquise had been alive, except for the few times they entertained a large group of people. It was too big to keep adequately heated, and those parties had been timed to coincide with the warm months. Six bedrooms, large enough to receive guests during visiting hours, occupied the rest of the first floor. Doors at one end of each floor led to the servants' wing, which bounded the courtyard on one side, contained the kitchens and smokehouse, and terminated in the carriage house. The attics above were used only for storage, although there was enough space up there to house several families. A high wall enclosed the other side of the courtyard.

To Anne's relief, when she entered the house Julien was not seated in his usual place, on the footman's stool. She was about to creep up to her room when she heard voices behind the door of her father's library and tiptoed over to listen.

"What do you mean I can't do anything with it?" The marquis's voice rose in pitch.

A man whose voice Anne did not recognize responded more calmly. "The marriage contract makes it quite clear, and the will, you see, supports it too. You have an annuity to maintain the house and keep you in tolerable comfort, I think. And once your daughter—"

Anne jumped at the unmistakable crack of her father's cane on the large desk. He never moved so suddenly or violently. He must be exceedingly angry.

"Don't you see that this is a desperate situation!" The marquis paced back and forth in quick, short strides, the sharp tap of his stick on the wood floor interspersed with his footsteps. "What use are you! Get out of my house this instant!"

The visitor approached the door so rapidly that Anne barely had time to avoid being hit by it when it swung open. She hid in the curve of the staircase. Julien emerged from the dining room, where he had been setting out the wines for dinner, and helped the gentleman on with his cloak and hat. Anne hoped he had not seen her cowering there.

"Julien!"

To Anne's relief, her father called the footman into the library. As soon as the door closed behind him, she ran softly up the stairs and reached her chamber before anyone knew she was home. She removed her outdoor things and was about to go in search of Thérèse, when Julien knocked on her door. "The master requests your presence in the library," he said.

Anne knew she could not ignore this summons. Doubtless her father would question her about why she had been out for so long. She had prepared an excuse, that she stayed through the Office, and that a curate took some time to comfort her.

The marquis did not look at her when she entered, but that was not unusual. He leaned on his cane and stared absently into the fire that blazed and crackled in the grate. "Yes, Papa?" she said.

"Did your mother give you any papers to keep? Anything I might not know about?"

"No, Papa," Anne said.

"Did she ever mention a dowry to you? Or talk about her fortune?"

"Only when she told me the story of how she met you."

He paused for a moment and then turned, as if preparing to set off down another avenue of thought. "I think you are old enough . . ."

The marquis stopped speaking and walked to his desk, where he picked up papers one after the other and put them down again.

"Old enough for what, Father?"

When he lifted his eyes, for a moment Anne thought he had finally decided not to close her out any longer. He really looked at her, not simply brushing his gaze past her and frowning. Anne straightened her back and lifted her chin. The glimmer of something close to a smile played across his lips, then it faded as quickly as it came. "You are old enough to marry."

"I . . . I beg your pardon?" Anne wasn't sure she had heard him correctly.

"I must do my duty as your father and find you a match."

"Yes, Papa." The words felt dry on her tongue. Anne waited for the marquis to say something more, but instead he returned to his place by the fire and stared again into the crackling flames. She began to think that he had forgotten she was there. She cleared her throat.

"What is it you want?" the marquis said. The irritated edge had returned to his voice.

"Only . . . may I go?"

He waved his hand in her direction. Anne gave a little dip of a curtsey and hurried from the room.

Once in the safety of her own chamber again, she sat at her dressing table and stared at herself in amazement. How could she think of marriage? Who in the name of heaven would she marry? What had brought the idea to his mind? She had never even gone out into society, to a play, or a concert—although if all went well, that state of affairs would soon be remedied. *And he thinks I'm callous to want to visit!*

Anne rose and walked restlessly around her room, picking up trinkets and moving them from one place to the other. *If only I could play the pianoforte,* she thought. She could always think better at the keyboard. The familiar, patterned arrangement of the notes helped her organize her thoughts. If she could not play, she desperately needed someone to talk to. Anne's eyes came to rest on the little brass bell that sat on her dressing table. She seldom used it, rarely finding herself in the position of needing anything that had not already been placed at her disposal by the thoughtfulness of her mother or Thérèse. After only a moment's hesitation, she grasped the bell and rang it.

A short while later, Thérèse knocked on the door and entered. "Yes, mademoiselle?"

Anne ran to the housekeeper, threw her arms around her neck and sobbed into her shoulder. Thérèse patted her on the back and stroked her hair, not asking any questions, just murmuring soothing endearments.

Four

〜

The cholera epidemic still raged, but on those days when he did not have to care for the sick and dying either in the Hôtel-Dieu or the Hôpital de la Charité, Pierre's life continued more or less as normal. He attended lectures every day and fought the rats, sparrows, and nauseating stench while he dissected human cadavers during his anatomy classes. None of them had been cholera victims, though. Although Pierre suspected that it would not have been wise to open one up, his curiosity about the effects of the disease was in danger of overpowering his common sense.

Today's subject was a man his own age who had suffered an aneurysm of the aorta. These hidden killers distressed Pierre the most, like the cramp colic that had taken the life of his younger sister. She died a painful death in a matter of days. While no one even tried to operate on such diffuse complaints of the abdomen, other dangerous conditions had been cured with immediate surgery by skillful practitioners. Every day, new procedures gave hope for the future of medicine.

"Coming to the café this evening?" Georges asked as together they rinsed their bloody hands off under the pump in the yard.

"No," he answered. "I'm going to a concert."

Georges laughed. "After a day with the knife, I just want to get drunk. I don't understand this obsession of yours with music. Or maybe you're going to meet some mysterious lady."

Pierre splashed his friend's face. "It's to raise money for the victims of cholera. Chopin, Liszt—I think perhaps also Kalkbrenner—will play."

"Well, if you want to amuse yourself afterwards, you know where I'll be."

Georges sauntered off in the direction of the students' favorite café. Pierre watched his stocky figure disappear into the crowd of capped and gowned men. He couldn't imagine a friend more different from himself, and yet he was fond of this fellow he had met the day they both started their university studies. Georges was from Normandy, of short stature, with black hair and a swarthy complexion. Pierre was from Toulouse, was tall and thin, had sandy hair, hazel eyes, and only a few wisps of beard. It should have been the other way around, given their birthplaces.

Pierre had barely time enough to eat some bread and cheese and put on evening dress before the concert. He had saved up his modest allowance from his haberdasher father to buy an elegant, silk tailcoat, a brocade waistcoat, a top hat, and white kid gloves in the latest Parisian style. With what was left after paying his rent and feeding himself as cheaply as possible, he purchased good seats at the opera and in the concert halls. He did not want to stand at the back or sit up near the rafters with the other students. *Someday,* Pierre thought, *I shall be a successful physician and host artists and musicians in my own home.*

Pierre's resources did not extend to hiring a fiacre to take him to the Salle Wauxhall. That meant he faced quite a long walk toward the west and across the river, all the way north to the boulevard Saint Martin near the place de la République. But he did not mind. He enjoyed a walk. And by keeping to the western end of the Île du Palais, and staying on the main roads, he would avoid having to negotiate the still-prevalent evidence of cholera victims.

Carriages choked the streets near the theater. Pierre stood outside for a little while and watched the glittering aristocrats descend from their luxurious vehicles. He could hardly believe they inhabited the same city as the poor, sick people he saw every day when he followed Andral on his rounds at La Charité or volunteered at the Hôtel-Dieu. The smell of camphor emanated from every elegantly clad body. Like a talisman, this herb, they thought, would protect them, and somehow it did. The wealthy did not become sick and die like the poor—at least, not in such frightening numbers.

Pierre entered the theater and gave his ticket to the usher, who showed him to a seat in the middle of the stalls. From there, he had a good view of the stage and the boxes, so that he would be entertained both during the concert and during the pause.

The hall was quite full. Pierre found it hard to imagine a more exciting event. People seemed even happier and more jovial than usual, affirming their continued good health by sheer force of gaiety. Pierre amused himself by scanning the faces in the boxes, trying to match the looks of the patrons with titles or livelihoods. One box was full to the brim with five ladies who were so amply proportioned that they looked like baker's daughters, but to sit in such a place and to be so bedecked with jewels they would have to be, at the very least, the daughters of a wealthy banker. Another box contained several smartly dressed young men, whose attitudes of comfort and ease gave them away as members of the aristocracy. He recognized the marquise La Vayer in another box, and Gisquet, the prefect of police, also occupied a seat behind some other people Pierre did not know.

All of the boxes were full except for the one to his left, nearest the stage on the keyboard side. Pierre hardly thought it possible that a box in such a desirable location would not have been sold long before that day, and so he kept his eye on it to see who entered, thinking perhaps it would be some member of the royal family.

The door to the stage opened and a liveried usher walked sedately across to raise the lid of the piano. The dull roar of the crowd softened to a whisper as everyone waited for the first performer—Monsieur Frédéric Chopin—to walk out on the stage and take his seat. Pierre glanced back at the empty box and was surprised to see that in the few moments he had looked away, a party of two ladies had arrived to fill it. One of them he knew to be the countess Marie d'Agoult, a famous society hostess and patroness of the arts. She was frequently to be seen at concerts and the theater. The lady next to her, however, Pierre did not know, although there was something familiar about her too. She had light blond hair and a long slender neck. Her modest black gown accentuated her pale coloring. That gown, and her hair: something about them was familiar. She looked toward the stage, so Pierre could not see her face, but the edge of her cheek, her delicate chin, and her small nose promised beauty.

Uproarious applause jolted Pierre out of his contemplative state. Monsieur Chopin had walked out and bowed to the audience and now sat at the pianoforte.

Having failed to summon the courage to ask permission of her father for the outing, Anne had been nearly unable to meet Madame d'Agoult as planned. She claimed instead to have a headache so that she would not have to dine as usual, and Thérèse, on the pretext of bringing her a powder to take, helped her dress in the best gown she had that would still observe the proprieties of mourning. When they were certain the marquis was at his dinner with Julien serving, Thérèse opened Anne's bedroom door cautiously and motioned her to follow.

The wide silk skirt with its hoop and several petticoats refused to keep quiet as Anne crept down the hallway toward the servants' quarters with Thérèse behind her, looking over her shoulder. Just as they were about to pass through the door that separated the two wings of the house, they heard footsteps coming up the servants' stairs toward them and quickly stepped into one of the guest bedchambers.

"Says I'm to go and sit with the countess, 'stead of eating my supper . . ."

Anne recognized the voice of the daily girl, who had been hired
when they let go of their live-in housemaid. "Stop her, Thérèse!" she
whispered.

Thérèse slipped out of the room and pretended to have come up
the other stairs. "It's all right, Sylvie, you go and eat. I'll stay with
mademoiselle."

"You sure it's no trouble?"

"Of course not."

To Anne's relief, she heard the maid walk back the way she came
and down the stairs to the kitchen. A moment later, Thérèse returned.

"Quickly now!"

"What if he discovers I'm gone?" Anne was fearful. Her father
had continued to act peculiarly since the moment when he first mentioned marriage to her.

"He won't. Now go!"

Thérèse nudged her into the dark passage in the servants' wing
and then led her to the door that opened on the street. Once she was
out of the house, Anne hurried through the lamplit streets to
Madame d'Agoult's apartment, ignoring as best she could the leers of
the café dwellers and a few beggars who hobbled after her.

She found Marie already in her carriage, waiting. "I'm so sorry, it
was difficult to get away."

Marie smiled. "You walked? Well, no matter! We shall be there
right before the concert begins."

By the time they arrived, empty carriages lined the street outside
the theater, waiting until they were needed again at the end of the
concert. Anne and Marie were quickly admitted and ushered directly
into their seats. The spectacle of all those people in one place so over-
awed Anne that she hardly dared look at any of them and kept her
eyes glued to the pianoforte on the stage.

The first performer was Monsieur Chopin. Anne was eager to see
what this man who had composed such glorious music despite his
young age, and to hear him interpret his own composition. She was

surprised, though, at how frail and small he was, and the audience had to be very quiet to hear him play. Even the loudest moments barely rose above mezzo forte, and during pianissimo passages, he played as if only he and the angels were supposed to hear them. But the music—several mazurkas and waltzes with which Anne was not familiar—enchanted her. Anne soon forgot where she was and leaned forward to rest her elbows on the edge of the box.

When Chopin finished, the audience applauded rapturously, including Anne. "Oh, Madame d'Agoult! I have never heard anything so wonderful in all my life."

Marie touched Anne's cheek. "There is so much more for you to learn of the world, Anne." She looked down at her program. "A new young pianist is next, playing some pieces of his own composition. A Monsieur Franz Liszt."

Before Anne could ask the countess what she knew about this fellow, whose name her mother had mentioned only days before her death, the door to the stage opened. A tall, angular figure strode out in front of the audience and stood in the crook of the piano to take his bow.

For Anne, time stood still. A glow of warmth spread from below her ribs to her fingertips. From where she sat, Anne could see Liszt's noble profile.

He bowed slowly and gracefully, then whirled and sat down on the chair before the keyboard. With his eyes toward the ceiling, he drew off his white kid gloves and laid them on the desk of the pianoforte. He brought no music with him. How could one play without music? Anne thought.

She held her breath. The moment Liszt began to play, she felt herself lifted out of her seat, imagining that she floated like a spirit, held suspended by the sheer quantity of notes that spilled into the air from the pianoforte. The power and brilliance of Liszt's technique could not have been more different from Chopin's. Where the Polish pianist had stayed on the surface, detached from the instrument that seemed too big for him, Liszt dove into the keys and tore the music out of them. At times his fingers moved so fast Anne could hardly see them; at others, they spread out so far over the keyboard that it looked as though he had four hands instead of two. Anne felt herself rise higher into the air with every upward sweep of lightning fast arpeggios and swoop to the ground with every huge chord and gargantuan leap. The ending—a thrilling shift to the major mode at a volume she never imagined a piano capable of—left her breathless. When the performance ended, Liszt lifted his hands from the keys with a flourish and looked up at the audience again. This time, he swept his gaze across the boxes. When his face turned fully in their direction and she thought she saw the smallest glimmer of a smile on it, Anne fainted.

Pierre had been to a concert given by the frail Chopin before, but he was more than a little intrigued to hear Franz Liszt, about whom rumors flew like magpies through the city. When the tall Hungarian fellow strode out as though he owned not only the piano but the stage, the hall, and every member of the audience, Pierre understood a little why the pianist fascinated so many people—especially ladies.

Every pair of eyes in the building gazed at this handsome artist. But Pierre could not help tearing his own away to watch the young lady he had noticed earlier in the box with Madame d'Agoult. He had seen her lean forward in total concentration to listen to Chopin, noticing how her slender arms seemed like twigs in the long, fitted black sleeves that went from under the puffed-out shoulders to her wrists, her hands like white doves perched on the ends of them. She was absorbed in the music, unconscious of her beauty, which drew more than just his own notice, he saw.

While Liszt played, rather than rest her chin dreamily in her hands as she had when she listened to Chopin, the girl sat completely upright and gripped the rail in front of her. Even from where he sat, Pierre could see her eyes glitter. Madame d'Agoult leaned forward a little too, but her interest appeared more impassive, more guarded.

At the end of the brilliant set of variations, the audience roared. Pierre applauded heartily and his bravos mixed in with the rest. Curious to see how the pretty young lady responded to the performance, he glanced once more up to the box.

But she was not there—at least, he could not see her—and the older countess d'Agoult stood and looked around in confusion, bending down to the ground every once in a while and trying to get someone's attention when she stood up again. All at once, Pierre realized that the girl must have swooned. If she had simpered and primped in front of the audience, conscious that she was being admired, he might have laughed and left her to her smelling salts. But the intensity of her response to the performance, her unself-conscious abandonment to the music, convinced him that she might be in actual peril.

"Excuse me . . . I beg your pardon . . . so sorry." Pierre fought his way out from the center of the row while the audience continued to bring Liszt out for bow after bow. Once free of the crowd, he dashed through the side door that led up to the boxes. He headed in the direction of the stage and knocked on the door of the one he presumed was where he would find the two ladies.

Madame d'Agoult let him in immediately. "Thank heavens! I thought no one would hear me in this mayhem."

Pierre did not stop to greet her but went directly to the girl who lay passed out on the floor of the box, her face white, her lips bloodless. He lifted her hand, rubbed her wrist, and gently patted her cheeks.

"She lost her mother recently," Madame d'Agoult said.

"To the cholera?" he asked.

"Alas, yes. The marquise was my friend, and she played the piano—taught her daughter, in fact. I expect the concert was simply too much for her." Madame d'Agoult, who, though older, was herself extremely attractive, spoke to him in tones of hushed urgency. "I blame myself! I insisted she come. Her father does not know she is here."

At that moment, the young girl's eyelids fluttered open and she looked up in confusion. As she brought Pierre's face into focus, her forehead wrinkled slightly as though asking a question, then she turned and looked at Madame d'Agoult. She sat up abruptly.

"Oh! How foolish of me. I'm so sorry," Anne said.

"Countess, don't trouble yourself. I'm only glad you are well now," said the countess d'Agoult, kneeling down next to her.

"Let me help you into your seat," Pierre said, unwilling to let go of her soft hand, so different from the hands of the washerwomen and indigents he tended most days.

"Thank you," she breathed, and looked down. Now a delicate blush rose into her cheeks. "I'm grateful for your help, Monsieur . . . ?"

Pierre, who had not presumed to introduce himself to the countess d'Agoult, looked to her, hoping she would give him permission to tell them his name.

"We are deeply indebted to you," she said, holding out her hand to dismiss him. He stood and bowed over her extended hand politely and let himself out of the box.

By that time, all the box doors were open and elegant people wandered from one to the other to visit and enthuse about the marvelous performances they had just heard. Pierre did not hurry back to his seat, instead stopping an usher on his way past. "Who sits in that first box up there?" he asked, pointing.

"Madame d'Agoult, this evening," he said.

"And her young friend?"

"I know not, monsieur."

The usher nodded to him and went on his way.

Pierre hardly attended to the rest of the concert. Although the box was now empty, his mind was full of the scene he had taken part in. He wished he could have discovered the young girl's name. But he had been brought up too well to force an acquaintance where none was desired, and he resigned himself to having only a pleasant memory to enjoy. Yet something Madame d'Agoult had said to him while he was trying to revive the girl struck a chord with Pierre. She said her mother had died recently of cholera.

All at once, he remembered where he had seen her face before. She had leaned out of a carriage in a funeral train when his friend Estèphe's corpse tumbled so gruesomely out of its coffin on the way to Père Lachaise. How horrid that she would have seen that, he thought. No wonder the girl—the countess, he had heard Madame d'Agoult call her—was in such a susceptible state. Pierre decided to make some inquiries. At least he might discover who she was, even if he never saw her again.

"I'm so ashamed of myself for that silly display," Anne said once they were safely inside Madame d'Agoult's carriage and on their way back to Saint Germain. "It's not at all like me to faint."

"You were simply overwrought. It is nothing to be concerned about."

But Anne felt that the countess was annoyed with her. Marie had insisted they leave before the second half of the concert, despite Anne's assurances that she was fully recovered. "I wish I could write and thank that kind young man who helped me," she said.

Marie turned her serene eyes upon her. "My dear, it is best not to think about the fellow. He will expect no thanks, as he was clearly a gentleman, and it would be improper for you to say anything at all to him without knowing much more about his circumstances."

Anne had not been in company enough to understand the subtleties of etiquette and propriety, and it seemed unkind and unfair to send the young man away without so much as a note of thanks—especially one who had looked upon her with such tender concern in his handsome eyes. But with no mother to advise her, she let herself be guided by Marie.

The carriage stopped at the servants' door to the hôtel Barbier. Anne had been desperate to ask Madame d'Agoult another question before they parted that evening, and hesitated to descend. "Madame," she said, "I cannot thank you enough for this evening."

"Please don't mention it," Marie said. "Your mother would have wanted you to attend the concert."

"There is something else, a favor," Anne said, biting her lower lip. "You see, my father has locked the doors of the ballroom where our pianoforte is kept. He does not want to hear music in the house."

"Ah," Marie said. "I see. My dear Anne, you may come to my apartment whenever you like to play my pianoforte. I shall be going abroad tomorrow and will leave word that you are to be admitted in my absence."

Anne embraced the countess, so grateful to this lady who had taken her to her first concert and now would make it possible—if she could manage to get out of the house—for her to continue playing the pianoforte. After that evening, Anne wanted to do nothing else. Only music mattered, the thread that, more powerfully than anything else, still bound her to the memory of her mother.

Five

The day after the concert, Pierre had no time to concern himself about the pretty young lady he had revived from a swoon.

"Pierre! Come quickly!"

Georges burst into the university library where Pierre was deeply engrossed in consulting a large reference book on the digestive system, the subject of the afternoon's lecture by Magendie.

"*Sshh!*" said Pierre. He took his friend's arm and together they hurried out to the square in front of the ancient building. "What is it?"

"I have heard—it's simply unconscionable—they are blaming us, or the doctors anyway."

It was not until the two of them had downed a glass of claret each at the nearest café that Pierre was able to get Georges to utter a coherent sentence.

"You remember Mordieu." He referred to a well-respected doctor who had come to the university to learn more advanced surgical techniques. "He was walking on the quai de la Féraille when they attacked him. A mob, thirsty for blood."

Pierre could not believe what Georges told him. They had set dogs upon the poor fellow and he was ripped to shreds. After that the mob tied what was left of his body to a plank and threw it in the Seine.

"They think we—the doctors—are poisoning them, that the hospitals are only a trick to lure them in and get rid of the poor."

"How can they?" Pierre stared into the bottom of his glass and shook his head slowly.

"I think it is the symptoms. So like poisoning, really."

Pierre was thoughtful for a moment. "And it is the poor who are becoming sick and dying in droves, while the rich . . ."

"I'm supposed to go to the Hôtel-Dieu and help out tomorrow," Georges said. "I'm not sure I care to now."

Pierre leaned across the little table and laid his hand on his friend's shoulder. "We cannot abandon these poor souls to the disease. Many of them recover, and those who die, well . . ." His voice trailed off. Never had Pierre felt more powerless than in the face of this sickness that overtook and galloped through a body so fast, one hardly had a chance to say the word "cholera."

Georges nodded. They each drifted into their own worlds for a moment. Pierre was not thinking of the poor doctor who had been murdered by the mob, instead having a horrible vision of that lovely young lady whose name he did not know turning blue and pale and shriveling up in the grip of the disease.

Silk-covered cushions in bright colors littered the floor of Eugène Delacroix's studio. In the center was a low table in the Turkish style, upon which sat a hookah, with a golden brown, soft cake of opium in its clay pot slowly reducing to ash. The smoke chamber was full, and when Eugène sucked on the mouthpiece at the end of the snaking hose, the water at the bottom of the chamber bubbled like a lazy fountain. The air in the studio was heavy with the tainted breath exhaled by Eugène and his two friends, Franz Liszt and the poet Alfred de Musset.

"Did you see her, Alfred?" Franz leaned back on the cushions and stretched his arms above his head.

"What I don't understand," Eugène said, "is why you didn't accept her invitation in the first place."

With much effort, Franz sat up. He had the sensation that his limbs were made of rubber. *I must try to remember how this feels,* he thought. *I think I could put it into music.* "But I didn't know then," he answered at last, "who she actually was."

Alfred rolled over on his side and propped his head up on his elbow. "Anyone would have told you, you fool. Everyone knows the magnificent Madame d'Agoult."

"Those eyes. So cool, so remote."

"How could you tell from the stage?" Eugène said. "I have excellent vision, and all I could see from where I was sitting was her coiffure and the cut of her gown."

"When I perform, I am immortal," Franz said. His comment provoked a hearty burst of laughter from the others. Even in his drugged haze, he could feel how foolish he must have sounded to them. They should be forgiven, he thought, for indulging themselves in pleasures like this. The news that a famous poet had succumbed to cholera only that morning—only an acquaintance, but what they heard unnerved them nonetheless—had sent them to the solace of opium.

Alfred, whose dapper clothes were rather rumpled from his lounging posture, shook his head to clear it. "I never laugh when I'm sober," he said. "I know Marie. I could introduce you if you like."

Franz inched closer to Alfred. "You would do that, for me? How kind you are, my friend."

"Trouble is, she's fled Paris with half of polite society. Don't know when she's coming back, but I could pay a call and find out."

"No!" Liszt exclaimed, sitting up a little straighter. "I shall call myself, and leave a card."

Eugène slapped his hand on the floor. "Franz! Really you are too much. I noticed the princess Clémentine did not attend the concert."

"I'm done with royalty," Franz said. "A great brute of a fellow came to my door and threatened to break my hands if I ever so much as glanced at the princess again." Franz recalled how embarrassed he had been by the visit, which had brought all his neighbors to their doors.

Eugène and Alfred nodded in unison.

Slowly, testing his balance on the way, Franz stood up.

"My, you're a very tall fellow," Eugène said, and then laughed again until he started to cough. "Where are you going?"

"To the countess d'Agoult's house."

"Do you know where she lives?" Alfred asked.

Franz scratched his head.

"You can't go now!" said Eugène. "It's one—two o'clock in the morning! Sit down again and Alfred will give you the address of her apartment tomorrow."

Franz plopped back down among the cushions. Before long all three young artists were in semisomnolent states and remained there in Eugène's studio until the sun rose and Eugène's Italian housekeeper marched in and tossed them all out.

It had been a week since the concert and Anne had thus far not managed to figure out a way to go to the countess d'Agoult's apartment to practice the piano. If she said she wanted to go to church, her father would summon Julien and make him instruct the coachman to take her directly to Saint Germain des Prés and back. If she claimed to need a length of ribbon from the haberdasher's, or some new silk thread for her embroidery, he insisted she send the charwoman to run her errand, blaming the danger of cholera for his caution. When Anne's mother was living, she always gave her daughter a modest allowance to spend on books, music, bonnets—whatever she chose. But now the marquis gave Anne nothing at all, unless she told him the exact amount she would need to purchase whatever item she desired. She had taken to exaggerating the amount slightly, so that she would have a little extra money for emergencies.

"Father," she said one morning after the maid had cleared the breakfast tray from the small sitting room, "I cannot stand another moment in this house. I want fresh air. I would like to go for a walk."

"Do you not realize what perils there are outside, in the streets? Have you not listened when I have read you the passages of the *Quotidienne*?"

Anne knew he referred to the horrible reports of mobs overpowering doctors and officials. But the unrest occurred in the east, in Saint Antoine, Les Halles, and the Marais. Saint Germain was quiet and safe. The agitation in his tone far exceeded any real need for alarm. "There is no unrest in the faubourg," Anne said. "I shall be safe."

The marquis stood and leaned heavily on his cane. "No. You will stay here. This evening we have a guest coming to dinner, and I want you to make yourself look pretty. As pretty as a girl in mourning can look, that is."

The remark may not have been meant to wound her, but it did. She clenched her fists at her side. At least, she thought, the tedium of another silent dinner with her father would be relieved. "Who is our guest, Father?" she asked, wondering who would pay a social call on her reclusive papa, whose condolence visits had been limited to one or two ancient members of the Bourbon court.

"I've found someone for you to marry," he said, and before Anne had time to react, he rose and made his way to the library, where he would remain until it was time to dress for dinner.

Anne rang for Thérèse. She paced up and down in front of the windows in the parlor that were kept shuttered against the curiosity of the passing foot traffic, her mouth set and her teeth clenched, while she waited for the housekeeper. The servants always knew more about what was going on in the house than she did. When Thérèse entered, Anne stopped abruptly and faced her, trying to appear calm, thinking of the way her mother used to speak to maids when she wanted to scold them without being unkind. Somehow the marquise managed it in such a way that the guilty party would go away feeling both chastened and praised at the same time. Anne wished she had paid more attention at the time.

She drew herself up tall. "I was surprised to learn from my father that we are to have a guest to dinner this evening. I was even more surprised that, as mistress of the house now that my mother is . . . gone, I was not informed of this fact."

"I am sorry," Thérèse said, and folded her hands in front of her, "but Monsieur le Marquis led us to believe you were acquainted with the fact of Monsieur de Barbier's visit."

Thérèse's sarcasm did not go unnoticed by Anne. All at once she realized that she had offended her one ally. "Well, I—do you know anything about this Monsieur de—you said Barbier?" Barbier was their family name. Anne knew of no one else who shared it.

"He is a distant cousin of your father's."

"A cousin? How old is he?" In her astonishment, Anne forgot all about her annoyance with Thérèse. "Have you ever seen him?" She didn't know whether to be pleased at this sudden knowledge that she had a relative somewhere, or dismayed that her father expected her to marry a cousin she had never even met.

"In truth, mademoiselle, I did not know of his existence until this morning. His name is Armand de Barbier."

If Thérèse had never heard of him, then her mother had not either. Anne had long ago discovered that Thérèse had been her mother's closest confidante. "Thank you," she said, trying to convey with her tone of voice how she wished she had not been unkind to the servant and that she wanted things between them to go back to the way they had been.

"From now on, Mademoiselle Anne, I shall not assume that your father has told you anything." Thérèse smiled, and Anne knew they were on safe ground once again.

Later, in her room, Anne sat at her dressing table in front of her mirror, looking through it, not at it. Ever since the concert the week before, her dreams had been filled with images of the young Hungarian pianist whose command of the instrument had lifted her out of her fog of grief and innocence. She was aware that the thought of him awakened feelings in her that went beyond admiration. The memory of his fingers flying over the keyboard gave her a thrill deep inside, in a part of her body she hardly knew existed. If only she could sit beside him as he played, if only he would take her hand, show her how to make such sounds, Anne felt she could die and know she had truly lived.

Anne placed her hands on the edge of her dressing table as though it were a keyboard and lightly tapped out the notes of a Schubert waltz. She closed her eyes, listening to the music in her head. But before long she stopped. Downstairs in the ballroom sat the piano, massive and mute. If her father would only go out of the house, she could get Thérèse to let her in so that she could play. Or better still, if the marquis were not so vigilant, she could return to Madame d'Agoult's apartment and practice on her lovely pianoforte without worrying that someone would inform him of her actions.

And if she were able to go regularly to Marie's apartment, perhaps one day she would be invited to a salon, and then perhaps at the salon, she would meet Monsieur Liszt.

Anne sighed. What hope would there be, though, of meeting the great Franz Liszt if her father forced her to marry some old cousin? *He must hate the sight of me,* she thought, *and wants to get me out of the house.* Despite the difficulties of her recent life, Anne had too many happy memories to wish to depart altogether from the hôtel Barbier and live elsewhere. At least, not while she could still feel the warmth of her mother in every familiar nook. With luck, she thought, Monsieur de Barbier won't want to marry me.

And then she thought a little more. Perhaps she need not rely solely on luck in that regard. Anne's spirits brightened. *Whatever a man would want in a wife, I shall try to appear the opposite.* Her model of the perfect wife had been her own mother. She was beautiful, smelled sweet all the time, smiled and humored her father, and always tried to put everyone around her at ease. Anne rang the bell for Thérèse.

"Yes, mademoiselle?"

"What would cause a man to like me?" Anne asked.

"You need do nothing, mademoiselle, except sit quietly and smile, to have the world at your feet."

Thérèse's fondness sometimes led her to exaggerate, Anne thought. "But is there nothing in particular that a gentleman desires in a lady?"

The maid pursed her lips. "What is it you ask, Countess?"

Anne sighed. "I need your help. I want my father's cousin to dislike me, so that he will not want to marry me, and I cannot imagine how to go about it."

The maid rested her hands on her hips, threw her head back, and laughed so that the crystals of the bobèches on the mantelpiece tinkled. "Now there is something I never expected to hear from a young lady," she said at last, wiping the tears from her eyes with the back of her hand. "What exactly is the old man thinking?"

"He tells me little. But he said this Barbier is the suitor he has chosen for me."

"The marquis may rule here, but he won't force you into an alliance that is not to your liking as long as I am alive. Your mother would not have wanted it. So, yes, I think I can help you, mademoiselle."

From that moment Anne placed her fate in the hands of Thérèse, whose loyalty, she came to understand, had been transferred to her the moment of her mother's death. Anne sat in docile acceptance at first as the maid brushed the carefully arranged curls out of her hair.

"Now wait here while I fetch a clove of garlic and some olive oil."

Anne craned her neck around to cast a perplexed glance at Thérèse.

"There is nothing men dislike more than a woman who looks and smells as though she never washes."

"And you might also fetch that old brown dress of mine," Anne said, now catching on to Thérèse's plan, "the one I was going to donate to the charity school." It had never suited her and would be just the thing to make her appear awkward and ungainly.

Anne knew she would provoke her father's wrath by embarrassing him in front of this aged cousin. But although she had her mother's beauty and talent, Anne had enough of the marquis's stubbornness and determination to make her a little bolder than was quite proper for a marriageable young lady. This secret alliance with Thérèse added to her courage. From now on, she knew she could count on Thérèse to help her do the things she knew her mother would have wanted her to do but of which her father might not approve. She could have cried with relief to know that in this unexpected way, she was no longer alone in the rambling mansion.

Thérèse summoned Anne when their dinner guest arrived, but before descending, Anne waited until she was certain Monsieur de Barbier and her father would have gone either into the parlor or the library. By the time she reached the bottom of the stairs, Anne could hear them in the library. From behind the door her father's voice carried out loudly and distinctly. Her mother had told her that he was known in his day as an excellent orator.

"So, are you taking your chamomile?" the marquis asked.

Anne could not hear the way his cousin answered. The other voice was too quiet to penetrate the massive door. This was not a good sign. Perhaps he was so old that he could barely speak above a whisper. Best to get the awful moment over with, Anne thought, and she knocked quietly, half hoping her father would not hear her. No sooner had she finished rapping than he yelled out a brusque, "Come!" interrupting his own speech to do so.

Suddenly fear gripped Anne. She looked dreadful, she knew. Thérèse had thought of many other touches to add to the effect, including smearing a little charcoal under her eyes to make her appear tired, and Anne doubted they would ever be able to remove the smell of garlic from that particular dress before she once again consigned it to the poor. Although Anne was not generally faint-hearted, this was the first time in her life she had openly defied her father. She did not know how he would react. Still, there was no turning back now. Anne entered the library and curtseyed without looking at her father or his guest.

When she rose, Anne could not tell which of the three of them was the most shocked and horrified. The marquis had donned his court dress, an old scarlet cutaway coat with gold braid and buttons, lace ruffs at his neck and wrists, and black velvet breeches with white hose that hung in wrinkles on his thin calves. He had powdered his hair and applied rouge to his cheeks. Once he had seemed imposing to her in this ceremonial garb. He was thinner and older now, though, and he looked like a molting parrot caught in a plain wooden cage.

If her father's appearance surprised Anne, Monsieur de Barbier's took her aback completely. He looked to be, if anything, younger than she was, and his black tailcoat and long trousers hung loosely on his underdeveloped frame. He wore his light brown hair straight, which was the current style, and his chin had clearly never felt the touch of a razor. Both Monsieur de Barbier and Anne's father stared at her in her drab clothes, their eyes wide and unbelieving, and Anne thought she saw her father's young cousin recoil at her smell.

The marquis drew himself up with only a stern look in Anne's direction to express his disapproval and made the introductions. Monsieur de Barbier spoke quietly when he spoke at all, which wasn't often, only answering questions put to him directly.

Dinner was an awkward affair. The marquis bore the entire burden of conversation, asking questions and answering them himself. Thérèse and Julien both served, bringing out course after course consisting of four or five different dishes each, complete with little hors d'oeuvres placed on the table between each one. The cook had outdone herself. Their meals had been increasingly plain and meager of late, so the bounty of this feast surprised Anne. She ate heartily, ignoring the marquis's glares as she asked for dishes to be passed and cleaned her plate and drained her glass time and time again.

"You must forgive Anne's silence," the marquis said to their young guest after allowing a particularly lengthy pause in his attempts at conversation, "but her mother's passing has come hard upon her."

"Of course," Monsieur de Barbier muttered.

Eventually, the dinner ended. Before the poor young man departed, however, Anne's father made one final, embarrassing attempt to rescue his plan for the evening. "I understand you are fond of driving in the Bois de Boulogne," he said.

His cousin looked confused and was about to open his mouth to answer when the marquis interrupted him. "Perhaps you would take Anne with you sometime. I often tell her that she must not stay at home and brood so about her mother. A pretty young girl like her should be out enjoying life."

Anne fixed her father with a hard, unflinching stare. He would not meet her eyes.

"I . . . I should be delighted," sputtered Monsieur de Barbier.

"Thank you," Anne said. She held out her garlicky hand for him to kiss and was impressed that he managed not to act too hurried when he performed this duty that politeness required of him.

As soon as the fellow climbed into his chariot and drove away into the cool spring evening, Anne turned to her father, said, "Good night, Papa," and hurried up the stairs to her room. She did not want to give him an opportunity to chastise her. To her relief, he did not send Julien to bring her back to the library. Perhaps, she thought, he too was sick of the smell of garlic.

When Armand discovered that the guardian he had never met had insisted that he leave the Jesuit school that had been his home for the past ten years and take an apartment nearby in the Marais, he did not at first believe it. Within days, however, he found himself installed in his new lodgings, with the use of a chariot and two smart horses and a manservant to care for him. He wondered a little how all this was to be paid for, but assumed that the fortune he knew he possessed but of which he had little concrete knowledge had furnished the means. It was entirely in his guardian's control until he reached the age of twenty-one, and he had always assumed he would remain among the Jesuits until that time.

At first he had no idea what to do. He had become so accustomed to having his days regulated by the prayers and lessons of the Jesuits that the solitary hours stretched out before him in a frightening, unbroken block.

"What do young gentlemen of means do all day long?" he asked Felix, his manservant, on the second morning of his new freedom.

"Do?" the valet responded, as though it had never occurred to him before to wonder.

"Yes. Do they have lessons? Or attend services?"

"Ah, I see, Monsieur Armand. No, I believe a day often commences with a visit to one's tailor, and then a drive through the Bois. After that, luncheon in a café is frequently called for. Then visiting. Although I believe the visiting has been somewhat curtailed of late, owing to the cholera."

Armand had not wanted to seem completely naïve, and so he thanked Felix for the information and spread some preserves on his toast.

"Will monsieur require the chariot this morning?" Felix asked, clearly waiting for some instruction or other before retiring to his small room, where he did heaven knew what when he wasn't waiting on Armand.

"No, not this morning," Armand had replied. "I think I shall go for a walk once I am dressed." All he really wanted to do was to return to Les Jésuites to call on his friends there, particularly Père Jaquin, his tutor. This independence business was quite lonely.

That was why he had been so relieved when he received the invitation to dine at the hôtel Barbier, where he would at last meet his guardian. The invitation had necessitated a visit to a tailor, which took up the better part of a day. His credit was good with the merchants, it seemed, and soon he was outfitted with attire suitable to a Parisian gentleman. Except that, at the age of just seventeen, he hardly felt like a gentleman at all. He did not smoke a pipe and drank only a little wine at dinner. He had never gambled—another activity Felix informed him was quite popular with young men. Armand had hoped that he would be able to ask his guardian some questions, find out about his prospects and what was expected of him. All he knew was that his father had left him a large fortune in trust, to be his when he reached the age of twenty-one. He was all the more surprised, therefore, when his adult life started several years before he had anticipated that it would.

On that beautiful spring evening after the uncomfortable dinner, as he drove back to his apartment through the streets of Paris,

Armand found that he was more perplexed about everything than ever. He had not had the courage to ask the marquis a single question, although he ached to know more about his own parents and his family. He knew, from one or two comments dropped by Père Jaquin while he was still at the college, that there had been a rift, that one branch of the Barbier family remained loyal to the crown through the revolution, and the other cast nobility aside and threw its lot in with the revolutionaries. His branch was the revolutionary one, and his clever grandfather had turned to trade and amassed quite a sum. But he wanted to know more than that. What was his father like? And his mother? Were they lively or taciturn? Intelligent or dull? Attractive or plain? He did not possess so much as a miniature to suggest the merest outlines of their appearance.

And there was the countess Anne, daughter of his guardian. What a spectacle she was! Judging by the marquis's expression, she had clearly acted in defiance of his wishes by taking no pains to make herself agreeable. Armand wondered what had provoked her to such an action. Although his uncle had dropped hints about marriage, he had not taken them as anything more than general comments. Could it be that he had in mind that he and the countess should marry?

Despite her greasy hair, dirty nails, and horrid smell, Armand had noticed that his cousin was, in fact, very pretty. She could not do anything to dull the liveliness of her blue eyes or make her movements less graceful.

He pulled the horses up in front of his apartment on the rue Saint Antoine. Felix, having heard the carriage approach, emerged and instructed the porter to take the horses and chariot around the back to the stables.

"Pleasant evening, monsieur?"

Armand did not reply but went directly to his dressing room and let the valet help him prepare for bed. *Tomorrow,* he thought, *I suppose I shall have to indulge my guardian by taking the countess for a drive. Perhaps she will have bathed.* He sighed and extinguished the candle by his bedside. The matins bells tolled out from Les Jésuites. Their nearness comforted him. He recalled something Père Jaquin had told him when he had declared that he would prefer to stay among the fathers and take the priesthood himself. The priest had said that it would be wiser first to find out if he was meant to do God's business—whatever that might be—by going out into the world. "You are heir to a fortune. You should take it into your own control before deciding to relinquish it," Père Jaquin had said. "If you do not, then your guardian will be able to dispose of it however he wishes. Besides," he continued, "to join the Jesuits one must know the ways of man and be willing to travel far and spread the Word, as well as give up one's worldly possessions."

So far, the ways of man—and woman—were so obscure to Armand that he began to understand what Père Jaquin meant. As to giving up his possessions—the priest had made it clear enough on several occasions that the Jesuit fathers would welcome the resources Armand's fortune would provide, at such time when it would be his to command.

But since he found himself out in the world by chance rather than design, tomorrow he would make an effort to explore it more thoroughly, to take an active role in his own future.

Armand fell asleep composing the invitation to his cousin, wondering if he possessed paper fine enough to suit the purpose.

Six

Although she had bathed before getting into bed the night before, the next morning Anne bathed again and, after a thorough dousing with what was left of a bottle of lavender water, almost managed to eradicate the odor from her skin. It took Thérèse a long time to wash the oil out of her hair and arrange it in its usual curls. When the process was nearly over, the daily girl entered the room with two letters that had just that moment been delivered.

One had a foreign frank. Anne, who had never received a letter from abroad before, recognized with delight the handwriting of Madame d'Agoult. She tore it open.

I return from Geneva Friday, and would very much enjoy your company at a salon on the Tuesday evening following at eight, that the baroness Duvernoy is giving at her villa. Please send a note to the quai Malaquais by return saying whether you are free to come.

Amitiés,
M. d'A.

Anne clutched the letter. A salon! She remembered a time, more than a year ago, when she had awakened in the night to the sound of her mother playing the piano in the ballroom. She had put on her shawl and hurried down to greet her because she knew the marquise had returned from a salon given by a foreign princess—whose name was so strange and unpronounceable that she had long since forgotten it.

No candles had illuminated the ballroom, but Anne could see her mother's jewels sparkling faintly in the light from the vestibule when she opened the door. The marquise stopped playing when she saw her and passed her hand across her eyes, perhaps to shield them from the light, perhaps to wipe away a tear: it was impossible to tell. Anne ran to her and knelt at her feet. She could still recall the soft touch of her mother's hand as the marquise stroked her hair and regaled Anne with stories about all the people who had been there and what they had played or sung or recited. *Yes,* Anne thought, *I remember now: Madame d'Agoult sang.*

Just as she had been about to fall asleep kneeling there, imagining the music and the witty conversation, the door to the ballroom flew open and the marquise stopped speaking suddenly. They had been so involved in talking that neither of them had heard the marquis approach.

"Come to bed, Sandrine." Her father's voice was hard, commanding, a tone with which Anne was very familiar. She could feel her mother's hand tremble the slightest bit.

"Go back to your room, *ma fille,*" the marquise whispered.

Slipping past her glowering father and making a great show of running up the stairs, Anne paused just out of sight on the upper landing so that she could hear their conversation.

"I received another one today," her father said, the edges of his voice quiet and brittle.

"Oh darling! I don't know what to say. I—"

Her mother's exclamation was interrupted by the sharp sound of a slap. Anne put her hand over her mouth and held her breath.

"Sandrine! My dearest! I'm so sorry, I didn't mean it, I didn't . . ." The marquis's breathless words held an unfamiliar quaver behind them. Was he crying? She had never known her father to strike her mother before, nor had she ever witnessed him weep.

"Don't speak of it," her mother replied in a tone no different from the one she normally used to cajole her husband out of a sour mood.

They said nothing more before closing the door of the ballroom.

The next morning, it had been as though the scene had never transpired. Anne could not ask about it without giving away her own disobedience, and so she never learned anything more.

Anne forced herself back to the present time. She now realized that she had put her father's words out of her mind, brooding only on the fact that he had struck her mother and received no rebuke for it. Now the entire scene played out again in her mind. What did he mean, *I received another one today*? The marquis had become increasingly preoccupied and troubled after that time, and long before his wife's death. Now, without the mitigating presence of her mother's love and attention to distract her, Anne recognized the undercurrent of unease that had woven through their days.

She shook her head. She did not want to remember such things. For now, she must focus on the fact that her father intended her to marry his cousin—a most unlikely suitor. What a future that would be, Anne thought. Monsieur de Barbier was hardly the type to attract talented, witty, beautiful people. If she married him, there would be no elegant salons, no tales of famous hostesses and dashing artists.

Anne put Madame d'Agoult's letter aside and picked up the other one that had arrived that morning. The handwriting on it was small and crabbed, and although Anne did not recognize it, she was not surprised to discover that it had come from the same Armand de Barbier about whom she had just been thinking.

Chère Countess Anne,

I would be delighted if you would do me the honor of joining me in my carriage for a drive tomorrow. If two in the afternoon would suit, please answer by return.

With respect and friendship,
Armand de Barbier

At first, Anne was vexed. But after a moment, she realized that Armand's invitation couldn't have been more perfectly timed. This was a coincidence that her father never could have foreseen, and it would allow her to do precisely as she wished without his knowledge.

First, Anne answered her cousin, saying that she would accompany him the next day. After that she penned a brief letter to Marie.

Ma chère Madame d'Agoult,

I find I have no engagements on the evening of the salon you were so kind to invite me to, and therefore accept your invitation. I shall arrive at half past seven.

Respectfully yours,
Anne de B-C.

Anne folded the letters and took two envelopes from the neat stack on her escritoire. One she addressed to Marie, the other to her cousin. She hid Marie's letter beneath her blotter and took the other note in her hand. As she marched downstairs to find her father in the library, she held up her chin, hardly able to suppress a little smile. Having suggested the outing himself the night before, the marquis could certainly not object to her accompanying Monsieur de Barbier. Anne hoped that the young man would be as pliable concerning her demands as he was concerning her father's. She had a momentary pang about using him in this way. But she eased her conscience by blaming the marquis, who had placed both of them in such an awkward position in the first place.

As she had anticipated, Anne's father raised no objection to the drive with Armand. Anne felt sufficiently guilty about her motive for accepting the invitation to take extra care over her appearance for the occasion. She wore a crisp, white linen pelerine edged in Venice lace to dress up her black gabardine day dress, put on her newest kid gloves, and carried a gray, lace-trimmed parasol. Her straw bonnet, although tied on with the requisite black ribbons with a pouf of black netting at the back, allowed her soft, perfumed curls to tumble out becomingly.

When Monsieur de Barbier saw her descend the grand staircase to the vestibule, where he waited with her father, he blushed to the roots of his hair and remained speechless through the entire process of helping her settle in his elegant little chariot pulled by two glossy bay horses.

Anne looked back at her father, who stood in the doorway to watch them circle the courtyard and drive out through the gates. Armand turned the horses a little too sharply and threw Anne against the side of the carriage, and out of the corner of her eye she saw the marquis lift his hand in alarm. She turned away quickly, instantly struck with remorse. If her mother had been alive, Anne would never have deceived her in this way. Yet she probably would have had no cause to do so, either.

"Monsieur de Barbier," Anne said, smiling sweetly once they had safely turned west on the main road, "before we spend any more time in each other's company, it is only right that you should know that my father intends us to marry." Her cousin turned his startled eyes on her and in the process nearly turned the horses into the path of an oncoming cart. Anne shrieked and grasped one of the reins. Together they straightened their course, and Anne felt it was safe to continue.

"Monsieur," she said, "you must not imagine for a moment that I have even the smallest desire to oblige him in his wish."

The young man drew in a deep breath, and to Anne's surprise, words tumbled out of his mouth so fast she was afraid his tongue would be tied into a knot. "I am so happy to hear you say so, cousin!" he said. "I don't know anything about being a suitor. I am sure I don't want to be one, at least not yet. I was living at the Jesuit college, you see, and then I had word from the marquis. As your father is my guardian, I must do as he says."

It was Anne's turn to be dumbfounded. "My father—the marquis—is your guardian?"

"Why, yes. I assumed you knew."

"Monsieur—Armand—I may call you thus?" Armand nodded. "I

did not even know of your existence until my father announced that you would be our guest at dinner the other night." And Anne was fairly certain her mother had not known either, or she would surely have insisted they extend hospitality to this only living Barbier relation long before.

"My grandfather made a lot of money supplying Napoléon's armies with rifles and gunpowder, I am told," Armand explained. "My father was your father's second cousin, I think, or something; I never understood their connection. He died when I was only an infant. I would far rather have known him than have his fortune."

"What about your mother?" Anne asked, hungry for information about another person who was not only close to her own age but who shared a tie of blood with her.

"She died when I was born. I had a governess, and I used to live in a large house, but I couldn't tell you where. I went to school at Les Jésuites when I was very small, ten years ago, and was there until recently."

Anne ran her finger over the shiny, red leather trim of the chariot. For a moment she envied Armand for having sums of money that could turn into smart equipages and newly tailored suits. "Did you not wonder about your guardian?"

"Père Jaquin told me that he would rob me if he could get his hands on my money."

"Surely not!" For all her own ambivalence toward her father, Anne bristled to hear him spoken of so unkindly by someone who did not even know him. "He is a little taciturn but not greedy." At least, not on his own account. It occurred to her that he might covet Armand's inheritance for her.

The horses, not having felt the touch of a whip since the beginning of their drive, had slowed to a leisurely walk. Armand flapped the long reins on their backs, and they jerked the chariot forward, pitching Anne back into the seat so that her bonnet was knocked slightly askew. Armand's face crimsoned, whether because she had clearly been offended by his statement or because he had again demonstrated his inability to drive, Anne could not tell. He responded without looking at her. "I did not imagine until I arrived that the marquis intended us to marry. You see, I had considered entering the priesthood."

Anne smiled at the thought of this awkward young fellow in a priest's cassock chanting mass, hearing confession, distributing alms to the poor. "I myself have no calling for the convent," she said, "but I also have no wish to be married before I am quite ready. Would you be willing," she continued, "to help me for just a little while? There is somewhere else I would much prefer to go than the Bois de Boulogne."

"I am relieved to hear it. I don't know the way there, you see!"

Before that moment, Anne had not noticed the direction they had gone, and now she could see that they were not likely to reach the Bois, having taken quite the wrong road. They laughed together, and Anne asked Armand to drive her to the quai Malaquais so that she could deliver her note accepting Madame d'Agoult's invitation and spend an hour or so playing the countess's magnificent Erard. He agreed to leave her at the door and call back for her later.

He had taken quite a bold step, Pierre realized as he walked from the Pont Neuf to the quai Malaquais, noticing that as he made his way west, evidence of the cholera's ravages gradually disappeared. He felt rather guilty spending so much of his valuable time on an expedition that was entirely personal. Yet ever since the night of the concert the previous week, he had not been able to banish the image of that lovely young creature who had fainted in the countess d'Agoult's box. Her face rose before him at the most inopportune moments: when he had just plunged a sharp knife into a cadaver, when he tended to some poor beggar who would die before the night was out, when he laughed and drank the night away with his friends in the café. He was becoming obsessed, and he decided that the only way to cure this mental sickness was to manufacture some way to gain an introduction to the object of his obsession.

He easily discovered where Madame d'Agoult lived and persuaded himself that it would do no harm to deliver a card to the countess inquiring after the health of her young friend. Pierre also knew that, if he added two little letters to separate his first from his last name, *de*, he might have a better chance of acquiring the information he sought. As to what precisely he would do once he had it—he would decide when it was necessary.

The mid-April sun was unseasonably hot and brought prickles of perspiration to Pierre's face. His most respectable day clothes included a wool frock coat that was much too heavy for the weather. He wished he could have afforded a fiacre, so that he would not look like a laborer when he arrived unannounced at Madame d'Agoult's apartment. Everyone complained about the warm weather, which exacerbated the difficulties arising from so many dead in crowded, filthy streets. All of Paris—even in this neighborhood, Pierre noted, where life seemed to continue much as normal—carried the faintest aroma of rotting flesh.

Pierre wiped his face with his handkerchief before ringing the bell. A valet opened the door.

"I wish to present my compliments to Madame d'Agoult," Pierre said, hoping the fellow could not detect the shake in his voice, "and to leave her this."

The valet took the card Pierre gave him and glanced at the writing. "The countess is abroad and will not return for several days," he said.

"I see," Pierre responded. "All the same, I would be grateful if you would give her this message." He started to bow to the valet but stopped himself in time when he remembered that he was supposed to be much above the fellow in rank.

Pierre could feel the blood mount to his face and his pulse race uncontrollably—despite the fact that he had not even seen Madame d'Agoult, let alone the young countess. He hastened away from the apartment, now glad that only a servant had seen him, and was about to turn the corner to leave the quai Malaquais and wend his way back to the Latin Quarter when a smart new chariot passed him going the opposite direction. He stopped and watched out of idle curiosity to see where the chariot halted. To his surprise, it drew up at the comtesse d'Agoult's apartment, and so he waited a little longer to see what happened next.

When a slim, female figure with pale blond curls beneath a close bonnet trimmed in black stepped out of the chariot and walked to the door, Pierre immediately started back in the direction from which he had just come. But the lady disappeared behind the closed door of the building before he was near enough, and the chariot that brought her trotted off away from him. He had been told that the countess was not at home. How was it that her young friend would be admitted in her absence?

Pierre's heart now thumped in his breast. It could only have been she. She was there, so close to where he had been. If he had only arrived a few minutes later, they might have had to greet one another. As it was, he could do nothing without being so forward that he would prejudice any chance of meeting the lady as an equal.

I'll have to rely on the letter, thought Pierre.

Although he had been brought up to know many of the forms of society, Pierre was entirely unschooled in the art of courtship, having been so preoccupied with preparing for the university that he had not made a study of it. His note to the countess d'Agoult was too plain a declaration of interest to leave her in any doubt of his reasons for inquiring after Anne's health and risked inspiring the countess to keep them apart, if she deemed the acquaintance unsuitable.

Unaware that he could have driven a wedge between himself and his dreams, Pierre was happy that at least he had taken some action toward his goal. And seeing the young lady—even from a distance— was a stroke of good fortune he had not anticipated.

The footman admitted Anne to Marie's apartment without any hesitation. She tore off her bonnet and gloves and dropped them with her parasol on the floor by the door, then hurried immediately into the drawing room. There stood the pianoforte, its lid open, its case dusted, with music spread out on the desk. Perhaps Madame d'Agoult had been playing just before she went away. Anne walked reverently to the instrument, sat on the cushioned chair, and paused for a moment to look up and down the keyboard. Even alone in this unfamiliar apartment a pianoforte put her at ease. She forced herself to start her practice with some slow scales, hearing her mother's gentle admonishments in her head, as if she were there at that moment, guiding her.

Once her fingers were warm, Anne paused to look through the musical scores leaning on the desk and stacked up on the floor nearby and discovered many pieces with which she was unfamiliar. She opened a volume of bound sheet music titled *Beethoven* and randomly chose a sonata, in G major, to read through. The lovely work had a sweet, lyrical melody and enough challenges to keep her from being able just to play it at sight. She soon lost all track of time in the effort to master at least part of it. While she enjoyed the satisfying sensation of working the muscles in her hands, arms, and fingers and filling the air with lovely music, she occasionally let her mind wander back to the concert. How far she was from being able to play like Liszt! Anne pictured herself, for a moment, in a romantic garret studio, with the great Hungarian pianist listening to her play, his chin sunk to his chest, long legs stretched out in front of him and crossed at the ankles. When she finished, in her mind she saw him stand and approach the piano, holding out a rose to her.

"I beg your pardon, Countess."

The footman's voice startled Anne from her reverie.

"A gentleman begs to be admitted to the parlor," he continued.

Anne assumed that Armand had returned for her, that the hour and a half had simply flown by and it was time for her to go back to her semi-imprisonment in her father's house. "Show him in, please," she said.

She gazed lovingly down at the keyboard one last time before making herself stand up to go and so did not at first see the person who walked into the room.

"I humbly beg your pardon, mademoiselle," said a silky, foreign voice.

Anne lifted her eyes, and there before her, to her utter amazement, stood Franz Liszt. At first she thought she might be mistaken, that her desire to meet him had disarranged her mind and she had turned the figure of her young cousin into the object of her fondest dreams. But the longer he remained standing there in the middle of the room, the more she began to believe that it was truly he. Her heart fluttered, and she could feel the blood drain out of her face. She forced herself to breathe normally. "Madame—d'Agoult—I'm not—" She could not string a sentence together.

"So I see," Liszt said. "Forgive me for disturbing you, I had planned to leave a card, but when I heard music, I begged to be admitted."

Now Anne felt the blood rush back into her face. "Oh, I was only—" She closed the volume of Beethoven, and in the process knocked another book off the side of the desk, which in turn sent some sheet music floating to the floor. Liszt rushed forward to help her pick up the scores. Anne had already bent down to do the same thing, and they both reached for the volume that had fallen, which happened to be Kalkbrenner's *Méthode*. Liszt's hand closed over hers. She gasped.

"Please, *permettez-moi*, mademoiselle," Liszt said, gently prying her fingers off the book and helping her stand. He did not let go of her, and they stood there next to the piano.

Anne found herself completely unable to think. She stared at the long, slender thumb that pressed on the back of her hand. "Thank you," she said, so softly that almost no sound came from her throat.

He lifted her hand and kissed it gently. "I will disturb you no longer. It was wrong of me to interrupt the practice of art."

Anne finally forced herself to look up into Liszt's face. His eyes were the dull green of the Seine on a sunny autumn day, his nose was straight, and his lips were full. The blond hair that framed his face caught the light and shimmered. Before she could bring herself to say anything, he stepped back, bowed to her politely, and left the room. Anne was vaguely aware of a door bell jangling, and so it did not surprise her when, a moment later, her young cousin walked in.

"Are you ill, Anne?" he asked and rushed over to her.

She smiled. "No. In fact, I am remarkably well."

The maid brought Anne's bonnet, gloves, and parasol. In a daze, she readied herself to leave and mounted the chariot as though she were stepping onto a cloud.

"Who was that fellow going out as I arrived?" Armand asked.

"That, cousin, was Franz Liszt, the greatest pianist alive."

Armand did not say anything for a while, and Anne was so engrossed in her own fantasies that she didn't even notice. Just before they reached the rue du Barq, the street where Anne lived, Armand said, "Did you go there especially to meet him?"

Anne turned to her cousin, her eyes wide with surprise. He had a frown on his face. "Of course not! I went, as I said, to practice the piano. My father has locked ours away since my mother died." She was a little hurt by the implication that she could have done something quite so brazen. But on reflection she realized how it must have appeared to Armand. And as she had lied to her father, why would he not assume she would lie to him as well? "I simply do not know why Monsieur Liszt arrived at that moment, or why he was admitted to the parlor when Madame d'Agoult was not at home."

"She was not at home?"

Anne put her hand on her cousin's arm, which felt a little more tense than necessary, since he hardly drove the docile horses who thankfully needed only the barest minimum of guidance on the wide streets of Saint Germain. "Please don't tell Father. All I want is to be able to play the pianoforte, and to hear beautiful music. That's how the countess d'Agoult helps me. She said I could practice on her Erard while she was away, and she invites me to concerts and salons."

By the time they returned to the hôtel Barbier, Anne had recovered her wits and felt that she had satisfied her cousin that she had not done anything deliberately immoral in going to the home of the countess in her absence. The marquis came to the door to greet them.

"Until tomorrow, then, at the same time?" Anne said to Armand.

He smiled. "Of course, *ma cousine*."

Anne did not stop to speak to her father but went straight to her bedroom.

Franz strode over the Pont des Arts and paused in the middle to watch the barges plying the dirty river. He had waited over a week to carry out his plan to call on the countess d'Agoult, hoping that perhaps she would have returned from Switzerland by then. When he had approached the address Alfred gave him and heard the sound of a piano being played rather well, his spirits soared. The countess was known to be an accomplished musician, and Franz naturally assumed it would be she. No wonder the footman who answered his pull at the bell looked surprised when he insisted that the countess expected him and that he should be let in to the parlor right away. Since the fellow did not contradict him, Franz deduced that the young lady he found there in place of Madame d'Agoult must also have been a countess.

The first thing he noticed when he walked into the room was that the pianoforte had an excellent tone, like silk, but with the crisp finish of properly made dampers, and that it was being played with a great deal of tender expression. His eyes had only after that sought out the person seated at the instrument, and he quickly realized she was not the lady he had come to see. The girl looked as though she had seen a ghost when she saw him, stumbled in her speech, and gave other indications of being entirely *bouleversée* by his sudden appearance. Clearly, Franz thought, she knew who he was.

While he watched loads of flour sacks and turnips pass beneath the bridge on their way to the quais in one direction, and a barge full of poor, rotting cholera victims float by in another, Franz thought about the young girl he had seen in the place of Madame d'Agoult. She was clearly a close friend, to be there in the countess's absence. And quite a talented artist too, if a trifle untaught. Perhaps Madame d'Agoult was taking care of the girl, bringing her out, as they said.

And he recalled the young lady's clothes, which, although she was in mourning, revealed a trim figure and a graceful air. He began to fit the pieces together and decided that he had inadvertently stumbled upon the naïve young protégée of the woman whose affections he desperately wished to secure, no doubt an orphan or some such, and by her appearance an aristocratic one too.

Such a creature could be highly susceptible, highly impressionable. He had had a notion, something he had been thinking about and trying to expand into a full-blown strategy. Franz's notion was that in his campaign to win the countess, it would be essential to have an ally. At first he had thought of the pretty young Adèle, but servants were notorious gossips. Madame d'Agoult's young lady friend, on the other hand, might have enough refinement to fill that position far more discreetly, if certain circumstances could be brought about. All he had to do now was to think of a way to manage that. It cheered Franz to have such a pleasant solution to his conundrum fall into his hands, and he continued his walk home in excellent spirits.

Seven

On the evening of Madame Duvernoy's salon, Marie sat in her parlor and awaited Anne's arrival. The note Monsieur de Talon had delivered in her absence lay on her escritoire. The young man was evidently quite smitten with Anne. His thinly veiled inquiry after her health did not fool Marie for an instant. His name was unfamiliar to her, but she remembered that he had a pleasant face and behaved with sensitive decorum. Might he be an appropriate suitor for Anne? She would find out more about him, if she could, then decide. Marie was pleased to think she might perform such an important service for Sandrine's daughter. The girl was pretty, intelligent, and quite musical. As to her financial prospects—Marie did not know what remained of her mother's no doubt substantial dowry, or even if things had been left so as to provide for the daughter at all. Her looks and talent could take her far, though, even without a fortune. *The kindest service I could perform,* Marie thought, *would be to introduce her to society, so that she might find a suitable husband who would truly appreciate her qualities.* Very likely Sandrine herself had intended to see to Anne's debut in the near future.

Marie thought wistfully of the days of her youth, in particular of one handsome soldier who had captured her heart. Her parents did not approve her choice and tore them apart. When he was killed a few months later, she thought she would die of sorrow. Life no longer held any joy for her after that, and so she agreed to marry the first candidate her father presented who was not completely repulsive. Charles d'Agoult was a good man, but the marriage had been a terrible mistake. She and Charles spent as little time as possible in each other's company. He took lengthy trips to the country whenever he could. Her only consolation was her two beautiful little daughters, whom Charles seemed content to leave in her care or with Marie's mother at Croissy.

Marie did not want Anne to make such a mistake. If this fellow turned out to be suitable, and Anne and he could be thrown together so that they might fall in love, Sandrine would rest peacefully in her grave.

Sandrine Poitou had chosen unsuitably too, Marie knew, although the event had occurred when Marie was quite young and she was never acquainted with the particulars. It had all been hushed up, and she had never questioned Sandrine about it directly. But one still heard whispers in drawing rooms throughout the city. Although they never spoke of it, this common history of disappointed love brought them together when Marie came to Paris seven years ago. That and their mutual passion for music and the arts.

Pierre de Talon had left an address on his card. He lived near the university—a student, no doubt, who had come from the provinces. He might nonetheless be of good family and have expectations. To matriculate at the university required means and education. That he had attended the concert also proved him to be cultured. There was only one way to find out for certain, though. Marie took a piece of paper and scratched a quick note to Monsieur de Talon asking him to come for tea on Saturday.

No sooner had Marie folded the letter and put it in an envelope than the bell announced Anne's arrival. Her young friend swept into the parlor, hardly recognizable as the mournful, timid young creature she had met before. As it had been almost a month since her mother's death, Anne had put off the heaviest evidence of deep mourning and wore a pearl gray satin evening gown trimmed with black ribbons. No jewelry, yet the countess sparkled all on her own. Her eyes, tinged with bewildered sadness when they last saw one another, now glowed with eager hopefulness.

"You look lovely, Anne," Marie said, not without the faintest pang of envy, and she kissed her protégée on both cheeks.

"I am so grateful to you for allowing me to play your piano, Countess," Anne said. "I came at every opportunity I had while you were away. And the most extraordinary thing happened—"

Marie picked up her gloves. "Tell me about it in the carriage. We must leave immediately or we may miss Chopin."

As they drove through the warm May evening, Anne told Marie how, believing that her young cousin—his ward—was courting Anne, the marquis had significantly relaxed his restrictions upon her. "I simply tell him that Armand has asked me to meet him in a certain place at a certain time, and he sends me off with his blessing. And he has permitted me to purchase new gowns as well, which is particularly remarkable given how our circumstances have been reduced since he lost his position at court."

This behavior of the marquis puzzled Marie. Even at court, he had been known as rather miserly. Only Sandrine provoked him to acts of generosity or munificence, and the marquise had complained to her once or twice that her husband failed to see the necessity of providing education and other advantages for their daughter. Clearly the marquis stood to gain something by a match between Anne and this cousin. "Anne, what do you suppose will happen when your father eventually discovers that you and your cousin have no intention of marrying?"

"Oh, I don't want to think about that now. After all, what could he do?"

Marie did not want to spoil Anne's evening by telling her how many ways her father could make her life miserable if he chose to, especially while she was under the age of twenty-one. "What were you going to tell me?" she asked, suddenly remembering what Anne had said when she arrived.

But the carriage had stopped at the baroness Duvernoy's elegant little villa beyond the Porte Saint Martin and Anne had no chance to answer. In honor of spring, all the serving staff—footmen and maids alike—wore flowers in their hair and on their costumes. In addition, the maids were dressed *à la bergère.* They draped each lady guest with a garland of jonquils and heather as she descended from her carriage, and the footmen placed laurel wreaths on the heads of every gentleman as soon as he removed his hat in the house.

"Trust Madame Duvernoy to overdo things," Marie muttered to Anne as she escorted her through the reception rooms and introduced her to people Anne recognized as intellectuals, artists, and members of the social elite, both bourgeois and noble. Interested glances followed them throughout the villa, especially, Marie noted, from the men.

"Marie!" The hostess bustled over to her. "I hope I may count on you to lend your voice to the quartet," she said, her eyes darting from Marie to Anne and to the rest of her guests. "And this must be the young countess you wrote to me about."

"*Je suis ravie,*" Anne said, but by the time she arose from her curtsey, Madame Duvernoy had turned away from them. "Oh not yet!" she called out and scurried off to send two servants bearing a tray laden with a roasted boar's head back to the kitchens.

Footmen passed around trays of champagne, and the conversation became more and more lively. Marie kept a sharp eye on Anne, steering her away from the groups of young men, who exhibited more than passing interest, and toward the ladies and the more mature poets and artists.

"Madame d'Agoult."

Marie whirled around at the sound of Alfred de Musset's familiar voice. "Alfred! How charming to see you. Have you written any poems about me?" she asked with a coquettish tilt of her head.

"Every poem I write is, in a sense, about you." He bowed gallantly, and then turned to be introduced to Anne.

"Countess," Marie said, "may I present Monsieur de Musset? Alfred, the countess de Barbier-Chouant."

"I had heard that Madame d'Agoult had brought an angel with her to the party, but I assumed everyone spoke figuratively. Now I see that they simply told the truth."

Anne's eyes had already brightened from the champagne, and at Musset's words her face washed over faintly pink. "Pay no attention to him, Anne," Marie said, taking her arm and steering her toward the music room. "He is a poet, and words come easily to him."

"Touché!" Alfred said as he watched them stroll away.

"Ah! Duchess!" she called to an elderly lady who sat in a comfortable chair and fanned herself, an agreeable smile on her wrinkled face. Marie and Anne curtseyed deeply before her. "Shall you come to the music room?"

"I can hear just as well from this chair," the duchess de Montelimart said.

"I wonder that the entertainment has not started yet." Marie glanced around, noticing that the general movement toward the music room was slower than it ought to have been.

"Apparently the baroness has mislaid the parts for the Weber," the duchess whispered to Marie.

This was a difficulty indeed. Marie and the other three singers had been specially asked to perform and were to be the centerpiece of the program. "And so what will she do?"

"A young Hungarian fellow is in the library writing them all out again from memory, apparently." The duchess agitated her fan rapidly after revealing this astonishing fact.

"Liszt!" whispered Anne.

"So you know him?" the duchess asked.

Anne was about to say that she had tried to explain about his unexpected visit to the quai Malaquais, but Marie took hold of her arm to stop her and said, "We were fortunate enough to hear him perform on the third, at the Wauxhall."

*   *   *

Already the salon had turned out to be more wonderful than Anne could ever have imagined. Alfred de Musset had complimented her, and Anne knew that people stared at her wherever she went. While she assumed some were merely curious, she was old enough to understand the expressions she encountered from the gentlemen, who discreetly ran their eyes up and down from her golden curls to her delicate feet.

"Heine is here, Marie. Come and hear him read."

Their hostess, who had solved her difficulties over the food and was no doubt eager to draw attention away from the delayed musical proceedings, pulled them toward a small parlor already crammed with about twenty guests. In its center stood a smooth-faced young man with a slightly hooked nose and small, wide-set, light brown eyes.

"Who is he?" Anne whispered to Marie.

"A poet, from Germany. One of the finest."

Anne prepared herself to hear some German verses read aloud and not to be able to understand a word of them. Instead, the young gentleman declaimed in beautiful French not poetry, but an article from a newspaper.

"Nothing is so horrible as the anger of a mob when it rages for blood and strangles its defenseless prey . . . a dark sea of human beings in which, here and there, workmen in their shirt sleeves seemed like the white caps of a raging sea. . . . On the rue de Vaugirard, a group of old women removed their clogs to smash in the head of a poor soul they suspected of poisoning them. . . . I saw one of the wretches while he was still in the death rattle. He was naked and beaten and bruised, so that his blood flowed; they tore from him not only his clothes, but also his hair and cut off his lips. A man tied a cord around the body's feet and dragged it through the streets, crying, 'Voilà le choléra-morbus!' The final blow was delivered by a very beautiful woman, pale with rage, with bare breasts and bloody hands. She laughed to me and begged for a few francs' reward for her dainty work with which to buy a mourning dress because her mother had died a few hours before of poison."

When the poet finished reading, the guests looked uneasily at one another and applauded politely.

"What a gruesome story!" whispered Anne.

Marie whispered back, "It is no story. They say it truly happened, but a week ago."

"Champagne! Why, your glasses are all empty."

Madame Duvernoy clapped her hands and two servants with trays full of the pale, sparkling liquid entered, immediately relieving the tension. The baroness herself wore an expression everyone understood to say, *That is the price of genius,* and at the same time to imply that the famous Heine had not consulted her before regaling her guests with such horrors. Nervous chatter and laughter started up again, however, and Anne heard more than one person whisper that Monsieur Heine, being a poet, must have exaggerated what he saw.

The story left a hollow spot in Anne's heart. She was angry at Heine for wrenching her out of her pleasant fantasy of being admired, reminding her of the constant shroud of menace from the disease that had claimed her own mother's life, and distracting her from the astounding prospect of seeing Monsieur Liszt close at hand once again. Like those around her, Anne quickly drained her glass and took another one. The bubbles went to her head. Her mood improved very quickly.

Anne and Marie rejoined the flow of guests making its way slowly to the music room. The scent of flowers was so rich that, when combined with the ever-present camphor and the lavender water and rose water everyone had liberally sprinkled on themselves, the atmosphere was cloying. "Excuse me for a moment," Anne said to Madame d'Agoult.

"Are you quite well?" Marie asked.

Anne nodded. "I need a little air."

She pushed her way through the thronging bodies, brushing against ladies and gentlemen alike and smiling her apologies. Seeing a pair of glazed doors that opened onto a little balcony, Anne headed straight toward them, hoping that a little fresh air would revive her and make her feel less queasy. Before she reached them, a door to her right opened and out strode Liszt, clutching sheets of music manuscript in his arms. He stopped abruptly when he saw Anne.

"I beg your pardon, mademoiselle," he said, bowing to her as well as he could with his hands full. When he stood upright again, he opened his mouth to speak to her but changed his mind and simply smiled.

Anne forgot all about her need to breathe. "Not at all, Monsieur Liszt," she replied, somewhat surprised that she had the presence of mind to say anything at all coherent.

"You have the advantage of me," he said, shifting the papers to get a better grip on them. "You know who I am, but although I was fortunate to see you once before, I do not know you."

"I am—" Anne stopped herself. She should not say. One must be introduced to a gentleman by a mutual acquaintance. "I am simply an admirer of your artistry."

Liszt glanced beyond her as if to ensure that they were quite alone. "Whoever you may be, mademoiselle, I must speak to you. There is something, it's about Madame d'Agoult—"

"There you are, Monsieur!"

The hearty voice of the hostess interrupted him and startled them both.

"Thank you for explaining that to me, Monsieur Liszt," Anne said with a nod of her head. She turned away from him and hurried past Madame Duvernoy, hoping her blush was not too apparent.

By the time Anne arrived in the music room, all the guests were seated and there appeared not to be an empty chair anywhere. She caught sight of Marie and was relieved to see that she had saved a seat next to her at the back, although Anne would have much preferred to be right near the pianoforte, where most of the female guests had clustered.

"Are you feeling better?" Marie whispered.

Anne wanted to ask Marie why Franz Liszt might have mentioned her name with such urgency and secrecy, but before she could do more than nod a yes, Liszt himself entered the room with his burden of music, followed closely by Madame Duvernoy. He placed the sheets on a stand at the front and arranged them neatly, and afterward, to Anne's astonishment, picked up a delicate stool and carried it over to where she and Madame d'Agoult sat. Much to the annoyance of those who had positioned themselves to be as near as possible to him, he perched on the stool and flashed a broad smile at Marie, suggesting that they were old friends.

Anne did not know what to think. Would he have been so bold if he and Marie were not acquainted? After all, he had arrived at Madame d'Agoult's apartment unannounced. She was surprised at herself for not suspecting such a thing earlier. She stole a glance at Marie, who drew in her breath and straightened up just slightly in her chair. *No*, Anne thought, *she is as surprised as I am.*

A soprano with a lovely voice filled the music room with an aria by Rossini, accompanied by a chubby, elderly pianist who sweated profusely while he played his simple part. Anne glanced to the side every once in a while to look at Marie's face, and beyond her to Liszt's profile. What had he wanted to tell her that was so important? *Don't faint again,* she repeated over and over to herself, trying instead to focus on the singer, whose vocal flourishes bore a strong resemblance to a bird trilling for a mate.

The audience applauded enthusiastically when the performance ended. Liszt turned to Marie. "Shall you join us for the Weber?" He looked past her to Anne, including her in the question.

"My young friend does not sing," Marie said with a smile.

"However, your young friend—she has a name, I presume?— plays the pianoforte, I believe." Liszt fastened his smoldering eyes on Anne's for the merest instant, once again flashing her an inquiring look, and the color rushed back into her cheeks.

Marie wasn't entirely certain what had just happened. She turned quickly to Anne. How did Liszt know she was a pianist? Before she had a chance to wonder further, Liszt stood and bowed.

"Madame d'Agoult, allow me."

So, he knows who I am, she thought, not certain whether to be flattered or indignant. Despite the fact that his actions had drawn the attention of everyone in the room, she let him lead her up to the front, where the other willing members of the ensemble had already gathered to sing the quartet from Weber's *Oberon*. The sweaty little pianist who had accompanied the soprano cowered at Liszt's approach and without a moment's hesitation relinquished his seat at the keyboard. The singers arranged themselves in a close semicircle.

Over the dark blue waters,
Over the wide, wide sea,
Fairest of Araby's daughters,
Say, wilt thou sail with me!

While the tenor and baritone sang their verse, Marie stole a glance at Monsieur Liszt. She expected to find him concentrating on the sheet music in front of him, but instead, he gazed directly at her and yet somehow managed to play his part faultlessly. More than faultlessly, with exquisite artistry. *He is endowed with such an excess of talent,* Marie thought, *that he needn't concentrate at all on what he is doing.* Was that what gave him such brazen confidence? They had not yet been formally introduced, and he behaved like a comfortable old acquaintance. No, she thought again, not comfortable. He did not make her feel comfortable.

Mademoiselle de Rouy nudged Marie. The ladies' verse of the quartet had begun, and Marie had missed her entrance. She soon found her place, though, and blended her rich, mezzo-soprano voice with Mademoiselle de Rouy's lighter, higher timbre.

Were there no bounds to the water,
No shore to the wide, wide sea,
Still fearless would Araby's daughters
Sail thro' life with thee.

During the tutti portion of the quartet, Marie could not help glancing now and again at Liszt. As far as she could tell, he never took his eyes off her. She wondered how he managed to continue playing so well and feared that even she, who had endured open admiration in awkward settings many times before, might blush under such scrutiny.

The audience received the quartet so warmly that the performers were forced to repeat it. When at last they took their places as audience members themselves once again, Liszt remained where he was. Marie sat next to Anne.

"I did not realize you had such a beautiful voice," Anne whispered to her.

"And I did not realize—"

Marie had no time to finish her thought, because Liszt began to play a spirited rondo. Only then did she notice that the promised Chopin had failed to appear. Altogether, the evening began to irritate Marie. She had taken Anne under her wing, thinking it would be an easy way to honor Sandrine's memory. But now she had a feeling as though she were mounted on a horse that, although it had originally appeared docile, gathered more strength and obstinacy the farther away from its stable it roamed. Anne had done nothing in particular to provoke such an impression, but the combination of the way she received the admiration that followed her throughout the villa and the oddly familiar behavior toward her of Liszt—whom Marie knew had not been properly introduced to Anne—gave the countess an uneasy feeling in the pit of her stomach.

As soon as the handsome pianist finished his performance, while the ladies at the front all practically draped themselves over him to congratulate him, Marie spoke quietly to Anne. "I feel we must make a graceful exit. If, as you say, your father does not know you have come here, it would hardly do for you to remain and quite possibly make an acquaintance that is beneath you."

Marie stood and smiled at Anne, then said more loudly, "Of course, my dear. If you have a headache, we must leave immediately."

Anne found it difficult to stop the protest that leapt to her mouth when she realized that Madame d'Agoult meant them to depart before all the entertainment had quite finished, and before they had a chance to be presented properly to Monsieur Liszt. But she returned Marie's smile and stood. They nodded respectfully to the other guests as they made their way to the door.

Madame Duvernoy rushed up to them as they put on their gloves and shawls. "Are you unwell?" she asked, clearly disturbed that anyone should be able to leave her party before it ended.

"The countess has a slight headache," Marie answered. "She is still in mourning for the death of her mother."

I don't have a headache, Anne thought, and she pressed her lips together.

They had donned their wraps and were about to walk out the door, their hostess protesting all the time, when Monsieur Liszt strode out of the parlor and came directly to them. He stood in the hallway, towering over everyone else.

"Madame, might I be so bold as to claim an introduction to these two ladies?" he said to the hostess, fixing her with a smile that would have melted the alpine snows.

"Why, Monsieur Liszt! I thought—" She stopped and looked back and forth between Anne and Marie, and the pianist. "Madame, mademoiselle, may I present Monsieur Franz Liszt. Monsieur Liszt, the countess d'Agoult and the countess de Barbier-Chouant."

Liszt bowed politely. Anne noticed that Marie did not extend her hand for him to kiss.

"I hope to have another opportunity to become better acquainted with you, Madame d'Agoult. And with you, mademoiselle."

He looked into Anne's eyes when he spoke to her, and she saw that same searching expression she had noticed when they had met accidentally before.

"Another time," Marie said, turning away rather abruptly and pulling Anne with her out to the carriage. Anne smiled in Liszt's direction, but the door had closed behind them. They climbed into Marie's brougham without a word.

Their silence continued as they trotted off toward the east. Anne was glad of the dark. She did not want Marie to see her expression. Although they had left somewhat before Anne would have liked to, the evening had far surpassed her expectations. Now she had been introduced to Liszt and would be able to speak with him the next time she saw him.

If she saw him again, she thought. All at once, Anne began to think about Marie's mood and actions. She had become stiff and silent when Liszt sat by them and had torn her away when the party had hardly begun. She was puzzled too by Liszt's odd expression when they spoke briefly in the corridor, and by the fact that he mentioned Marie's name. And she could not forget Marie's cool reaction when they were all introduced as well. Anne had thought that her dealings with Madame d'Agoult would be less complicated than life with her father, and yet now it appeared that secrets and nuances lay concealed even in the calm, confident smile of her mother's dear friend. Anne's eyes began to sting. For no particular reason, at that moment she missed her mother more intensely than she had since the day they laid her in the tomb.

Anne felt the gentle touch of Marie's hand on her arm. "It was for the best," she said. "I cannot tell you now all that makes me fear an acquaintance with Monsieur Liszt, but you must trust me."

Marie's eyes glistened in the dim light from the street lamps. "Oh, Countess!" Anne said, and laid her head in Madame d'Agoult's lap.

"I think you must tell me, however, how a gentleman to whom you have never been introduced seemed to know you."

Anne sat up. "While you were away . . . I was practicing the piano, and your footman let him in. He thought I was you, you see, and he heard me play."

"Franz Liszt . . . called on me . . ."

"Oh, madame!" Anne cried. "I should so like to have him teach me the pianoforte!"

Although she could not see Marie distinctly, Anne felt her stiffen again.

"I would like to continue to help you, to be, if not a mother, then a kindly aunt to you," Marie said. "Lessons with Monsieur Liszt . . . I shall think on it."

Anne couldn't help feeling that the countess had been about to say something else altogether. Instead, she remained silent for a while.

"Perhaps we may find you a suitable husband, one to whom your father cannot object and who will also satisfy your own desires."

I don't want a husband, Anne said to herself. *I want Liszt. There,* she thought. *I have spoken the words, even if not aloud.*

The carriage stopped outside the gates of the hôtel Barbier. "I shall tell your cousin that you felt unwell and returned home early," Marie said.

Anne felt a little guilty about presuming on Armand's good nature. He had agreed to fetch her at the quai Malaquais at eleven and convey her back to the hôtel Barbier so that her deception would be complete. Now his trip would be in vain. Marie would make things right with him, she thought. She embraced Marie, relieved that the countess was not truly angry with her, and crossed the courtyard to the house.

Julien opened the door for her.

"Tell my father I have gone directly to bed with a headache," she said, and hurried up the stairs.

Franz and Alfred shared a fiacre back to Paris. Alfred had had too much to drink and dozed next to him, snoring gently. Franz thought about the evening, and particularly about Madame d'Agoult and her friend, and realized that what had started as a potentially enjoyable flirtation was fast turning into an obsession. The more the countess d'Agoult pulled away from him, the more he desired her. Her presence had been overpoweringly seductive, her eyes deep wells of mystery, tantalizingly liquid, maddeningly obscure. He was wholly unable to judge how things had truly gone at Madame Duvernoy's party. Although he had been introduced to Marie d'Agoult and her young friend, the lady's reaction to him was quite cool. It seemed that, for the moment, any direct approach would be out of the question. And yet, the younger countess did not close herself off to him, even when he had tried to speak to her privately, without her chaperone in view. Clearly she was not so versed in the ways of the world as the countess d'Agoult. The fact that his attention to her might have given rise to gossip pricked his conscience, but he also knew that wherever he went, gossip would follow, no matter how circumspectly he behaved.

Despite the fact that he had been unable to make any progress with Marie, Franz decided that his original idea, that of using the young lady to reach the true object of his desires, might still be a solution. All that remained was to think of a way to be thrown together with the young countess so that he could enlist her aid.

They had passed through the Porte Saint Martin and were making their way through the thronging streets of Paris. Snatches of conversation from raucous voices pulled him out of his reverie. The carriage had been stopped momentarily by some fracas in the middle of the street. He leaned out to see what was going on.

"Let go of me, you cad!"

A girl, perhaps the daughter of a tradesman, struggled against the unwanted embraces of a large fellow who looked as though he had had too much wine.

"I'll teach you to flirt with other men!" he yelled, and lifted his hand to strike her. Two other burly men burst from the gathering crowd and grabbed on to him before he could land his blow and pulled him away from the girl. She smoothed down her skirt, patted her curls, and tossed her head before whirling around and walking into the alley nearby.

It was a common-enough scene these days. The cholera exaggerated everything. People became desperate for vitality, strong feelings—anything that would assure them that they were still alive. Perhaps that was why the young countess played the piano with such fervor.

The ruffian's voice echoed in Franz's ears. *I'll teach you,* he had said. Of course. He was surprised he hadn't thought of it before. He would offer himself as a teacher to the talented mademoiselle de Barbier-Chouant. It would be only natural, after all. Chopin had an entire bevy of aristocratic lady students. Here was a candidate for his own studio, which was currently peopled with aspiring but unpromising bourgeois pianists. His mother had only recently written to him to urge him to find more influential students.

Franz laughed aloud in sheer delight.

"What?" said Alfred, rousing himself from his drowse.

"Nothing, my friend. And yet, everything."

"Don't talk in riddles. I've had too much champagne." Alfred turned away from Franz and leaned farther into the corner of the carriage.

Franz crossed his arms over his chest and, by the time he reached his apartment, had composed in his head exactly the letter he would send to the countess Marie d'Agoult in the morning.

Eight

Anne and her father sat in silence at the small table in the morning room drinking tea and eating bread and butter. Anne's head was full of dreams and thoughts about the previous evening, and the marquis read his newspaper with a scowl on his face. Anne was about to ask her father's permission to go and dress for the day when Julien entered with a letter on a small, silver tray, which he held out toward her. Anne reached for it, but her father took hold of the valet's arm and drew the tray closer so that he could examine the envelope. His forehead creased in a deep frown for a moment, but after reading the direction on the letter, he settled back in his chair. Anne could have sworn he seemed relieved.

As she took her note, Julien bowed and left so silently Anne hardly noticed him go. She recognized her cousin's handwriting on the envelope immediately. "Might I go to my room now?" Anne asked.

"Eh? That's the way things stand, do they?"

Anne was about to say something sharp to her father but instead rose from her seat and stood silently, waiting for his permission to go.

"Yes, yes. Off with you," the marquis said, and returned to his newspaper.

Once the door to her room shut behind her, Anne opened the envelope. She and Armand had already arranged to meet that afternoon as usual, and Anne had hoped to call on the countess and bring her a bouquet of flowers in thanks for taking her to the salon the night before. A communication from her cousin could, therefore, only mean some hindrance to their plans.

Chère Cousine,
I fear I am unable to call for you this afternoon. I have for some time been troubled with a slight stomach ailment, and I find that today I must remain at home. I hope this does not spoil your plans.

Amitiés,
A. de B.

Anne crushed the letter in her hand. How vexing! Just when everything had arranged itself so perfectly. She immediately felt sorry for thinking only of her own inconvenience and dashed off a note inquiring after Armand's health, assuring him that her sole concern was his full and speedy recovery. Once the letter was sealed, she rang for Thérèse to come and help her dress. Perhaps the maid would be able to think of some way for her to visit Madame d'Agoult so that she could get out of the oppressive hôtel de Barbier without Armand's aid. If only it were possible for her simply to practice on the Pleyel in the ballroom. That would be relief enough from her father's moods. And Anne was eager to sit at that instrument once again. Her memories were fading too fast. She knew that music would bring the image of her mother back to her in an instant. It might make her sad, but it would also comfort her. If her father went out, perhaps she could convince Julien to let her in.

The housekeeper had entered and laid out her gown on the bed.

"Thérèse," she said, "do you think Papa will ever open the ballroom again?"

"*Hmmph,*" she answered. "Last thing I heard him tell Julien was that the day you and Monsieur de Barbier announced your engagement would be the day he would unlock the ballroom doors."

"Do you have the key?"

"No, not I nor Julien either. Best not to think about it."

What, Anne thought, was her father so afraid of that he wouldn't even let her practice when he wasn't at home to hear? For that matter, why should she not be able to visit Madame d'Agoult openly without having to pretend to be interested in her cousin?

These were questions Anne had no hope of being able to answer, and that fact made her unaccountably cross with Thérèse. With no afternoon plans, Anne would now be forced to spend the day at home, either in the little parlor reading or sewing, or in her own room thinking about all the things she would rather be doing. There had been a time when she had not minded spending most of her days at home, when the marquise found so many ways to help them pass pleasantly.

Once Thérèse had put the finishing touches on her coiffure, Anne returned to the morning room, where her workbasket promised if not diversion, at least a way to occupy her hands. To her dismay, her father still sat where she had left him earlier.

"So, Countess," he said, folding his paper in perfect quarters, "would you care to tell me the state of affairs with Monsieur de Barbier?"

His question was awkward and strange. The thought of speaking to her father about anything personal horrified Anne. "I'm afraid I am not very good company at present," she said, choosing not to elaborate.

"I understand your scruples, but I feel it is my duty to point out to you that your actions—riding alone in a carriage with a young gentleman, meeting him in public places unchaperoned—have quite likely damaged your reputation to the point where finding another suitor might prove difficult."

The marquis gazed severely and steadily at Anne. She stared back in disbelief. He himself had encouraged such behavior, had thrown her together with her cousin. It was he, in fact, who had even provided the vehicle that made everything possible—so Armand had told her. Anne felt the blood course through her body, ending in tingling sensations in the tips of her fingers. She had an almost irresistible desire to throw something at her father. How dare he? When she was a little girl, such feelings sometimes resulted in the destruction of a favorite doll. After she became a little older and learned to play the piano, Anne found she could put her ill humor to good use at the keyboard, and would play for hours, making her fingers stronger and stronger. At that moment, she did not know whether she was more cross that her father's observation might have some truth in it, or that he had outmaneuvered her and rendered her own machinations utterly ineffectual. "I see," she said. "And if he does not wish to marry me?" Anne could hear the thin edge of panic in her own voice and wished she could have avoided showing him this weakness.

"I believe I can say with confidence that as things currently stand, he will marry you."

The air crackled with everything Anne wanted to say but didn't.

"You had a letter this morning."

Anne knew he expected her to hear the question implicit in the statement. She wished she could pretend not to understand what he expected of her, but she did not know how to be so openly disrespectful. All she could think to do was to say as quickly and with as little expression as possible, "He writes that he is ill and therefore unable to attend me as arranged."

"Ill?" The marquis drew his unruly eyebrows together so that they met above the bridge of his nose. Before Anne had a chance to assure him that Armand had said nothing about cholera, he hurried away to his library, leaving Anne in possession of the parlor.

The furniture had been moved out of the room, which was crammed with men of all conditions. Among the crowd Pierre noticed the mayor of the Sixth Arrondissement, several uniformed officers from the prefecture of police, a dozen or so merchants, and about twenty artisans, their hands still dirty from tanning or printing or staining or dying—whatever craft they practiced in their tiny shops. The officer of hygienics stood on a chair and addressed them all.

"It is our duty, as citizens of Paris, to do our utmost to contain this disease. Our strongest defense against its ravages is information."

"All your lists and bulletins aren't curing anyone!" yelled an angry voice from the back.

"It is true, we know neither the cause nor the cure. But the statistics you gather will be studied with care, and we will come to understand the form of this dread killer, his habits, his movements, the types he attacks, and those he leaves alone. Only then may we strike with certainty and root him out at last."

"He could start with the doctors, if you ask me," muttered a surly butcher standing next to Pierre.

His comment unnerved the student. The poison riots had been quelled, but still the poor looked upon the hospitals and doctors with suspicion. These local commissions had been formed to involve the community in containing the disease. Some had the responsibility of counting corpses. Others would go from house to house, looking at conditions and trying to spot cholera symptoms that might not have been reported. Still others led bands with kerchiefs tied around their noses and mouths who loaded garbage into horse-drawn *tombereaux* and sent it out to be buried outside the city perimeter—a move that was very unpopular with the ragpickers, whose livelihood depended on being the first ones to get to the refuse.

All the students had been encouraged to join one of the commissions. At first, Pierre thought only that the work would be preferable to spending hours on the cholera wards in the charity hospitals. But when he realized that the volunteers were furnished with detailed lists of houses and apartments with all their occupants, and that he might choose which district to serve in, he thought that there might be a chance that he could find his mysterious young lady. Since he last saw her entering Madame d'Agoult's apartment in Saint Germain, it was to Saint Germain he went.

"This district has seen comparatively few instances of the disease as yet, but the outlying areas, near Montparnasse and the Latin Quarter, are beginning to feel the ravages of cholera morbus." An assistant standing next to the officer handed his superior a sheet of paper. "Already today there have been seventeen deaths from cholera in Saint Germain."

An agitated murmur rose from the listeners.

"You will all be issued camphor amulets, and we now advise also that you wear gloves at all times."

Might as well recite a magical spell over us, Pierre thought. No one knew how cholera spread. The quarantines did not work, and there was no consistent pattern. One side of a street would be annihilated, while the other remained healthy. In one house, everyone died, in the next, only one person became ill. The only reliable predictor was poverty and filth. Perhaps the newspapers were right. Cholera was "the personal tax of the poor."

The meeting ended when they all divided into their various task groups. Pierre's education entitled him to be among those who took the lists of names and addresses and walked from street to street to inspect homes and businesses. He was instructed to visit as many houses as he could before nightfall every day for the next week, and if he finished early, to report to the commissioner of records' office for another list. Pierre scanned the paper a minor functionary handed him and saw that it contained the names exclusively of common folk. Doubtless others with connections had been given the more salubrious streets.

Cholera was a grim business. But that did nothing to dim Pierre's determination to find the fair young lady with the soft hands and the sapphire eyes. If anything, it gave his quest more urgency. All around him was evidence that life was transitory, that death struck arbitrarily and with alarming haste. Who was to say that he—or, God forbid, she—would not be next?

Pierre took his list and went out into the warm afternoon, his camphor sachet dangling around his neck. "Rue du Four," he read, and turned his steps in the direction of the tile makers' enclave.

*   *   *

By the time Pierre dragged himself later that night into the rooms he shared with Georges, fatigue lay across his shoulders like a mantle. He was a strong young man, and once he began his assigned task, he did not stop until he had visited every address on the paper. He had inspected the homes of merchants, lawyers, and doctors living with their servants and well-fed families in commodious, first-floor apartments; shop owners and teachers living in second-floor apartments that provided enough space for a small family and one servant; and artisans and students who occupied small rooms on the third floors like the ones he and Georges shared. Sometimes he found laborers and shop workers in the attics, with hardly space for a straw pallet on the rough floorboards, their children thin and quiet and their infants howling. He discovered two unreported cases of cholera among these last, although he suspected that one of the merchants' sons had had the disease and recovered. He did not, needless to say, find the young lady. *I must have walked miles and climbed a mountain,* he thought, and desired only his bed.

He was about to throw himself on his cot when he noticed a letter propped against his shaving mirror. The handwriting lavishly covered almost the entire surface of the envelope with his name and address. He snatched it up and opened it, realizing that it must have come from the countess d'Agoult in response to his letter to her. Pierre held his breath. It would either be a curt note telling him that the young lady is quite recovered and that there is no need for him to trouble himself about her again, or it would contain some morsel of encouragement. He could hardly bear to read it.

   Cher Monsieur de Talon,

Pierre had forgotten about his deception regarding his name, and instantly regretted it.

Thank you for your kind letter inquiring after the health of my friend, the countess Anne de Barbier-Chouant.

He stopped reading and clutched the letter to him. Her name! He finally had a name.

By your address I see that you must be a student, living near the faculty of medicine at the university. Would you do me the kindness of calling upon me this Saturday to ease my mind about some particulars regarding the cholera epidemic? I shall expect you at three, unless I hear that this is inconvenient for you.

Respectfully,
Madame Marie d'Agoult

An invitation! Even more than Pierre had hoped for. Would she also invite Mademoiselle de Barbier-Chouant?

Pierre lay on his bed with the letter in his hand. He was exhausted, but the agitation of his heart kept him awake well into the small hours of the morning.

Nine

❧

Marie held Liszt's note in her hand. It had produced in her a peculiar mixture of delight and anger. She had received it early in the afternoon on that day after the salon, a day when she expected Anne to arrive as they had arranged. Yet her young friend did not appear, a fact that Marie was uncertain how to interpret. Could she have said something to upset the girl the night before? Might Anne have forgotten the appointment? Neither of those explanations seemed likely, and Marie feared that either Anne's father had discovered how she had been deceiving him, or something had happened to the accommodating cousin and he was unable to convey her to the quai Malaquais.

And now, here was this letter, which she had half expected and half dreaded. Yet it did not contain the message she felt certain it might, judging by the searing glances Liszt had given her the night of the salon. After the usual respectful greetings and expressions of pleasure at having finally made her acquaintance, it veered off in an entirely different direction.

May I be bold, Madame, and ask your assistance in a certain delicate matter? I happen to have encountered your young friend, the countess de Barbier-Chouant, when I called at your apartment while you were abroad. I had hoped to be able to apologize for being unable to accommodate your kind request to perform at your salon. To my surprise, I found your home filled with music despite your absence. Mademoiselle de B-C was playing your pianoforte. I noticed that the girl has considerable talent and would like to help her develop this ability.

Yet I fear that if I present myself to her directly, my motives might be misconstrued. Would you act as intermediary, to see if the countess would welcome my musical guidance for her gift, which is too precious to hide from the world?

Being unacquainted with the young lady's circumstances, I leave it entirely at your discretion how—or whether—to accede to my request.

I remain, etc.,

Franz Liszt

His sentiments were all quite correct. His desire to observe the proprieties surprised Marie a little, bearing in mind his rather provocative actions at the salon. The way he had demanded an introduction, and the bold expression in his eyes. Marie saw her face reflected faintly in the window. Did she look older? Had marriage and motherhood altered her? Could she have misinterpreted his interest in art for interest in something else altogether? Or worse, were the smoldering glances not really meant for her at all, but for—

Marie was a little ashamed of herself for her thoughts. How could she be jealous of a girl who was ten years younger than she? Especially when the man who provoked such a feeling was closer to her protégée's age than her own. And after all, Liszt's letter mentioned only that he wished Anne to become his student. The young countess did not deserve such an ungenerous reaction. She must give the matter serious thought. She had no doubt that Anne would leap at the chance for instruction from Liszt. But what would Sandrine have wanted for her daughter?

She would not, Marie was certain, have wanted Anne to marry a cousin simply to please her father. Nor did Marie. But there was something else that prevented her from hastening to the aid of either of the gentlemen who had recently written to her about Anne, one whose motives were transparent, the other whose motives were somewhat more obscure: if either introduction ended in the development of an unsuitable attachment or, God forbid, an elopement, Marie would bear a heavy burden indeed. She would quite possibly have created circumstances that would lead Anne to the same kind of tragedy her mother had suffered.

She read Liszt's letter again, then laid it aside. There was still no sign of Anne, and the young countess had sent no word of explanation for her absence. Marie rang the little bell that she kept on her escritoire. A moment later the footman entered.

"Please have my carriage brought round in a quarter of an hour."

The fellow bowed and left the room.

Marie had never been to the hôtel Barbier before. When Sandrine was alive, they met at the quai Malaquais, at parties and soirées, or in tea rooms and restaurants. She had encountered the marquis only at court functions that Sandrine attended. He did not often accompany his wife to salons and concerts. Marie briefly wondered if Sandrine had to lie in order to go out without her husband. Whenever she saw them together, he acted with the most vigilant solicitude and took care to prevent her from speaking with gentlemen if at all possible. *At least Charles lets me do as I please*, she thought. In fact, they more often wrote to one another than spoke, so rarely were she and her husband to be found in the same place at the same time. He had fled the unwholesome atmosphere of Paris to visit a cousin in Normandy and was unlikely to return before the summer. She hardly missed him. Her daughters, on the other hand, who were safely out of harm's way at Croissy with her mother, were always on her mind.

When she pulled up to the door of the old mansion tucked in a forgotten corner of Saint Germain, Marie gasped in disbelief. The structure very likely dated from the time of Louis Quatorze, with its mansard roof and ornate stonework—now crumbling in several places. The cherubs that graced the stone pillars through which her carriage passed were barely recognizable. Neither had its head or hands, and only a wing on one and a foot on the other remained to suggest their former beauty. The mansion was shaped like an L on the corner of the street, with its other two sides bounded by high stone walls. One forlorn lilac bush and the remnants of a kitchen garden where some thyme had gone wild and a morning glory vine had crawled up to the eaves were all that relieved the stony courtyard. Even weeds did not grow between the uneven cobbles. More than a century's dirt grimed the façade, and the windows that faced the courtyard were shuttered. If she had not known otherwise, and were it not for the smell of manure emanating from the stable door, Marie would have assumed the building to be unoccupied and ready to be torn down to make way for a more useful residence.

Poor Sandrine, Marie thought. She would have been much more comfortable in a modern apartment, with new stoves for heating in the winter and running water. How had this monstrosity survived the recent furor for tearing down and rebuilding? As a Bourbon loyalist, it was unlikely the marquis had received any special treatment that would have allowed him to retain his family property, especially since he had fled Paris quite early in the Revolution. Someone else in the marquis's family must have had some influence with the officials in the Terror or—God forfend—taken part in it. Or perhaps he had had his property restored to him under Charles X and was one of those to benefit from the practice before the senate had an opportunity to stop it.

Marie descended from the carriage, summoned her courage, walked boldly to the front door, and pulled the bell. A few moments later, an ancient footman with a long, thin face opened the door to her.

"Madame d'Agoult to see the marquis," she said as she gave him her card. The fellow let her into the vestibule and disappeared through a door that led off to the left.

She hardly had time to examine the antique interior before Anne ran out from behind the stairs. "You are here!" she cried, grasping Marie's hands and lowering her voice to a whisper. "I'm so sorry I could not come, but Armand—"

Before she could finish her explanation, the door through which the footman had vanished opened, and the marquis himself walked slowly and purposefully to the center of the entrance hall, stopping a few feet in front of Marie. Several competing emotions flickered across his face. Marie saw surprise, then sorrow, then anger, then suspicion. Like the accomplished courtier he was, he settled his features in the neutral position of mild curiosity.

"Father," Anne said, "may I present the countess Marie d'Agoult?"

He bowed very slightly. "I am acquainted with the countess, from several years ago, at court, I believe?"

Marie curtseyed deeply, in her best lady-in-waiting manner. "I have not had the opportunity to express my deepest condolences to you on the death of your wife, of whom I was very fond."

The marquis said nothing, but Marie noticed that he lowered his eyes slightly.

"Madame d'Agoult, it happens, is acquainted with Armand— Monsieur de Barbier," Anne explained. "We met her in the tea room on one of our afternoons, you see."

Marie noted, briefly, that Anne was quite an accomplished liar. She wondered if she had always been so, or whether the recent necessity for secrecy about her actions had taught her a new skill.

"You wish to speak to me." The marquis paid no attention to his daughter's words but gestured to Marie to precede him into his library without including Anne in the invitation. "Bring some tea for the countess," he instructed Julien.

Books lined the walls of the large, dark room. The marquis took his place at a massive, oak desk situated in the middle of the space, indicating that Marie should sit across from him. *He has granted me an audience,* she thought.

"Marquis," Marie began, "I would like to speak frankly with you about your daughter."

"So, speak." His courtly demeanor changed, becoming rather hard and businesslike.

"I understand from Anne that you wish her to marry her cousin, Monsieur Armand de Barbier."

The marquis shifted his position slightly. "I don't recall giving my daughter permission to discuss our family affairs with strangers."

Marie knew that the marquis's blunt response was intended to throw her off balance—an old courtier's trick. Although she was familiar enough with these tactics, Marie fought against a sensation that she was climbing up a mountain of sand. For the moment she could think of nothing to say in response except, "Indeed," and bought herself a few moments to think by looking down at her hands. When she had regained her composure, she once again lifted her eyes to meet his. "Anne is an innocent, and doubtless did not understand that by confiding in me she would provoke your displeasure. But that is not to the purpose. She has told me, and I believe that if you push her too hard in that direction, you may have a disaster on your hands that you may not have foreseen."

The slightest twitch of the muscles in the marquis's face was the only indication that he even heard what she said. Unwilling to lose her opportunity to speak plainly, Marie continued.

"I too believe that Monsieur de Barbier would be an excellent match for your daughter. However, she has not been enough in the world, she has had too little opportunity to better herself, to make an altogether suitable match for *him*."

A faint smile lifted the corners of the marquis's mouth, but his expression did not change. "She lacks her mother's polish, it is true."

"Precisely." Marie cleared her throat. "I believe that if you do not give Anne a small measure of freedom and let her cultivate some of her distinct gifts and talents, she will end by rebelling utterly, and be lost to society. I imagine your cousin would not be eager to ally himself with such a lady."

Monsieur de Barbier-Chouant leaned forward slightly in a gesture that was more threatening than conspiratorial. "What exactly is your meaning, madame?"

"You and I are both acquainted with certain unfortunate events preceding your marriage. Anne is her mother's daughter. Modesty forbids me to say more."

The marquis's face darkened. "And you, Countess, believe you have the capacity to prevent my daughter's repeating her mother's reputed 'unfortunate events,' as you so nicely put it?"

Marie bristled. "I believe I owe a debt of friendship to the late marquise to help Anne achieve a respectable place in society."

The old man sat back and half lowered his eyelids. *No wonder he was so feared in his day,* Marie thought. The marquis had somehow managed to put her on the defensive even though she had made all the moves. There was nothing left but to press on. To capitulate now would give him an advantage over her that it would be impossible to overturn. She spoke carefully, pausing to consider each sentence before she uttered it and measuring its effect on her auditor as she went. "I am sure you are aware that your daughter is blessed with extraordinary musical talent. I believe much energy and many emotions might profitably be channeled into the cultivation of that gift. I propose that, so that you are not troubled by the constant noise of the piano, Anne spend a large part of her days with me at the quai Malaquais, where she may practice, and where I will secure a suitable teacher to help her develop."

Marie could see the marquis slowly grind his teeth and his breathing become more emphatic. He seemed on the point of saying something, yet he continued silent.

"When Anne is ready, I shall present her at a salon. Her pretty face and accomplished fingers will gain the attention of all the eligible young gentlemen there—including Monsieur de Barbier. There is nothing more likely to stimulate romantic interest than to feel that the object of one's affection is in danger of being secured by another."

The marquis's eyelids flew open and the tiny motion made Marie flinch in spite of herself. A flicker of amusement came and went in his eyes, to be replaced by an expression so veiled that she could not guess his thoughts. What secrets must he have learned to hide, from the time when he had fled for his life in the Revolution. He managed to gaze directly at her without giving anything away and said, "I shall consider carefully what you suggest."

"Sir, I fear Anne's isolation will soon lead to actions on her part that would not have the benefit of a loving hand to guide them." Marie knew she might have pressed him too hard. Still, he appeared to be considering the plan.

"I have no reason to believe that Anne would behave in a manner that would put her reputation in danger," he said. "And yet, I see that to remain here in this house of mourning, with nothing to relieve her sorrow, cannot be wholesome."

He stood, indicating that their conversation was coming to an end. Marie rose as well but did not move. She must force him to a decision. She was not certain why exactly she had decided that Anne's future should be settled that instant, but the more she breathed the atmosphere of grief and bitterness in the hôtel Barbier, the more determined she was to ensure that Sandrine's daughter have a chance at happiness. "So I may assume that you have agreed to permit Anne to attend me every day?" Two could play these diplomatic games, Marie thought.

"I see that it is not to be helped."

He gave in without relinquishing any ground. She smiled warmly at the marquis, ignoring his frostiness, and curtseyed once more down to the floor. On her way back up, she glanced at a pile of official-looking papers on the marquis's desk. Her eye would have swept past them without paying any attention, since she was not accustomed to prying into other people's private affairs, but she noticed familiar handwriting on one of the documents.

"I, Sandrine de Barbier-Chouant . . ."

The sight of those words nearly made her lose her balance as she ascended from her curtsey. Could it be Sandrine's will? Why would it be there, tossed aside with ordinary papers and letters? How she longed to read more! Before she could betray her curiosity, Marie turned away from the marquis and left him in his library.

She emerged to find Anne pacing back and forth across the hall at the foot of the stairs. As soon as she laid eyes on the countess, Anne ran to her and threaded an arm through her friend's so that she could lead Marie to a pleasant parlor at the back of the mansion. This room, unlike the gloomy library, was furnished with taste and elegance. Clearly, this had been Sandrine's influence. They kept their voices low. Marie told Anne briefly about her conversation with the marquis.

"But you must work very hard at your piano studies and try to be a credit to your family." Because, Marie thought, the marquis made no secret of the fact that he believed Marie's influence would corrupt rather than be an example to Anne. "And there is one thing more I must tell you."

Anne's face was a picture of suppressed joy as she paced around the room touching the backs of chairs and clutching her hands together excitedly. If the mere mention of lessons was enough to agitate her so, Marie was curious to see how she would react to the additional news still to be imparted.

"I had a letter from our acquaintance Monsieur Franz Liszt, who expressed an interest in teaching you."

Anne turned pale, and the hand that had lightly brushed the curved back of a brocade-upholstered armchair clutched it for support. "How can it be? Are you certain?"

Marie laughed. "Of course! He is a pianist, and he needs paying students to make his way. I am not surprised he suggested the arrangement. He will come on Monday." For a moment Marie thought Anne might faint again, but the girl managed to regain control of herself. "Come at eleven, to practice the piano and have luncheon. We'll make this our schedule every day. If I am not at home, I shall instruct the servants to show you every courtesy. And now, I must take my leave."

In truth, the interview with the marquis had exhausted her. She had forgotten how difficult it could be to walk that tightrope of saying just enough to gain one's point and not enough to give away information that might be used against one.

There was much to think about on her way back to the quai Malaquais. The place, so oppressive in one way, reminded her keenly of Sandrine. And there was the strange coincidence of having seen her friend's will. Why would it be lying on a desk in full—or almost full—view of anyone? Surely she must have been mistaken. Possibly the old man had been looking at it recently, she thought. Marie was not an inquisitive person by nature, but she longed to know what was in that document. The family's fortune came from the distaff side, that she knew. Many members of the aristocracy had lost all their money during the Revolution and the Empire. She wondered if the marquis's sudden insistence upon Anne's marriage was motivated more by mercenary than dynastic considerations.

How foolish of me to doubt it even for an instant, Marie thought. *Of course marriage is a mercenary affair.* She hoped that the marquis did not intend to sacrifice every chance of happiness for his daughter, as so many others of Marie's close acquaintance had done. The least she could do would be to give Anne the opportunity to discover on her own what love could be.

And she thought how fortunate that she had decided to invite the young doctor to visit. He might be able to perform a service for her that she would not ask of anyone too closely connected with the world in which Sandrine had lived and in which her daughter must find a place. Surely he would forgive her for being so bold.

Ten

Pierre bathed and visited a barber in preparation for his appointment with Madame d'Agoult. He decided against wearing the camphor sachet, which he doubted had any effect whatever on one's susceptibility to cholera. In any case, only isolated parts of the faubourg Saint Germain were hit, as the daily cholera bulletins in the *Moniteur universel* attested. Although he was supposed to perform his health commission duties that day as he had on the two preceding days, he persuaded Georges to act in his stead, with the promise that he would take one of his friend's night shifts at the Hôtel-Dieu.

This time, Pierre hired a fiacre, although he could ill afford the thirty sous. He wanted to make an impression befitting Pierre *de* Talon, and that meant that he should arrive unrumpled and with his shoes still free of mud from the streets.

"I am pleased to make your acquaintance under somewhat less awkward circumstances," Madame d'Agoult said, extending her hand to Pierre as she greeted him in her elegant apartment overlooking the Seine.

"It was my pleasure to be of help," he said. "I only hope that the countess has fully recovered."

"She has indeed. In fact, it is possible that sometime soon you may be able to ascertain for yourself the degree of her improvement. But before I present you to my young friend, I am sure you understand that I wish to know more about you."

Ah, Pierre thought. This was the way of things. Madame d'Agoult acted as gatekeeper. "In that case, I must begin by making a confession. I am simply Pierre Talon of Toulouse, student in the College of Medicine at the University of Paris." He had decided before he came that if the opportunity presented itself, he would give up his subterfuge, which in any case could easily be found out with the simplest of inquiries.

Marie rewarded Pierre's honesty with a bewitching smile. "As I thought. If times were otherwise, I would not necessarily have responded to your letter in quite the same way."

Pierre shifted uncomfortably in his seat. He could not help glancing around him in the manner he had learned in his capacity as health commissioner. The faint odor of the putrid Seine invaded the parlor, although the room looked clean enough. He stopped himself just in time from asking how many people lived in the apartment, and whether any of the inhabitants had had certain symptoms. This was a social call, after all. He turned his attention instead to the grand pianoforte in the corner of the room, a handsome instrument with volumes of music stacked on the floor next to it and sheets propped up on the desk. Madame d'Agoult had said something about the countess and her mother playing the piano. Perhaps her fingers had touched those keys. And despite the fact that his scientific mind knew that if he placed his hands upon them he would not really be any closer to her, his heart made him long to do just that.

"Monsieur Talon?"

Madame d'Agoult's voice punctured his reverie and he colored as if he had been caught without his breeches on. She handed him a delicate porcelain cup filled with hot chamomile tea. "I see that you have read the *instructions populaires,*" he said.

"And I see that you have noticed my piano," she responded. "I presume from your presence at the concert a few weeks ago that you are musical?"

"I play only a little. But I am an appreciative listener."

"You will no doubt be pleased to hear that the countess is an accomplished pianist herself and will commence her studies with the great Franz Liszt on Monday."

Pierre could not help feeling that the countess had dropped that comment like a stone in a pond to see the ripples it would produce. "She is fortunate indeed to have the talent—and the means—to deserve such encouragement." He forced himself to be calm and to appear neutral. Monsieur Liszt had a reputation as an adventurer, but he was in no position to object to such an arrangement.

"She has talent and comes from a good family, but in other ways she is poor indeed." Marie paused to sip her tea before continuing. "You see, as I believe I mentioned when we saw you at the concert, her mother died in March, at the beginning of the cholera epidemic."

"Yes, I remember. But her father?"

"He lives." Madame d'Agoult's face clouded over. "He has taken his wife's death very much to heart, and his daughter resembles my late friend altogether too much, Dr. Talon."

"Not a doctor yet, but I have high expectations of earning a respectable place in the profession."

"Monsieur Talon, the marquis, although no longer a part of the government since the accession of Louis-Philippe, is a formidable gentleman. He fled the Terror and then returned to Paris at the same time as many of us did, to resume his rightful place in society, in politics." Marie leaned toward Pierre. "I have not asked you here simply to determine whether you are worthy of being presented to my young friend," she said. "I have asked you because, as someone with medical knowledge, and access to records and such, you may be able to obtain information that could be vital to Anne's—the countess's—happiness."

Pierre could not imagine what official records could have to do with the countess de Barbier-Chouant's happiness. But he did not want to refuse to help Madame d'Agoult, especially if it increased his chances of meeting Anne. "You have only to ask, and I will do anything."

"Something happened, before Sandrine de Chouant married. I cannot help feeling that these events are at the core of the marquis's strange behavior toward his daughter."

"Strange behavior? Is the countess in any sort of danger?"

"As far as I know at this moment, the only danger she faces is being forced to marry against her wishes, something so common as to be hardly worth commenting upon. But my heart is not easy."

"Countess, what exactly do you want from me?"

"I want you to bring me the record of my late friend's marriage, and her daughter's birth certificate."

Pierre finished his cup of tea in silence. This was not at all what he expected to hear from the countess. She was, in effect, asking him to take advantage of his privileges as a medical professional not only to gain access to information but to steal official documents. Perhaps this was a test? "Could you not simply make the inquiries yourself? I am not unwilling, but what you ask of me is awkward."

"I cannot risk the marquis's finding out that I have sought information pertaining to his family."

Pierre examined the gilded pattern on his teacup. "You desire me to use my position as a salutary commissioner to elicit and then divulge information to you? If this action were ever to be discovered, I might jeopardize my own future."

"Surely these are public documents, available for any citizen to view?"

"To view, perhaps, but why—"

Before he could complete his question, Marie moved to sit next to him on the divan. "Yes, it is true that I might make the requisite inquiries myself, and that simply viewing these papers might provide all the information I need." She placed her hand on his knee and gazed into his eyes. "But I am uneasy. I cannot explain more to you at present. I only know that I must have certain proof of facts about the countess before I proceed."

She spoke with persuasive passion. Yet there was something in the countess's manner of asking that still made him uneasy. "Why do you take such an interest in these matters?" he asked.

"Rather than answer your question directly, perhaps I could ask you one in turn. Is there not some prize, some achievement, that would mean more to you than anything else in the world?" She sat back and leaned away from him. "I believe that Anne is heiress to a considerable fortune."

Pierre stood and strode away from Madame d'Agoult toward the window, his hands thrust into his pockets. How could she think it of him!

She rose and followed him there, standing directly behind his shoulder so that her quiet whisper reached his ears. "I believe, Monsieur Talon, that armed with the information you may acquire for me, I could persuade the marquis to sanction a match between his daughter and yourself. But without the pieces of paper themselves, he could dismiss it all as hearsay."

Pierre turned and looked into the deep, sad eyes of the countess d'Agoult. She remained so close to him that he could smell the complicated combination of scent and light body odor and could see the flecks of brown in her otherwise gray eyes. He began to perspire and knew that he blushed. "Good day, madame," he said hurriedly, then snatched up his hat from the divan and rushed out of the apartment.

Marie guessed that Pierre Talon was a few years younger than she. Quite a handsome fellow, and obviously intelligent and well educated. Not every aspiring doctor took the time to attend concerts. Although his response to her request had not been immediately positive, Marie was confident that, especially once she began to dangle Anne in front of him, he would furnish her with the information she desired. The more she had thought about the way the marquis treated his daughter, and the coincidence of the will having been left out on his desk, the more convinced she was that money was at the root of everything. She had eyes. She could see the paler shapes outlining the places where the portraits used to hang in the stairwell, and she had noticed that the sitting room was only sparsely furnished with those trinkets and baubles that ladies of a certain station liked to collect around them. She had witnessed the same denuding of valuables on other occasions and knew the signs well. The marquis, not accustomed to company, and without a lady's sensitivity to censure by others, had done little to disguise them.

These thoughts continued to go through Marie's mind on Monday, as she sat in the parlor listening to Anne trying to perfect a Beethoven sonata before her first lesson with Liszt. The Hungarian genius was due to arrive at any moment. Marie herself was a little nervous. She imagined that Anne must be beside herself.

In her letter engaging Liszt as Anne's teacher, she had made him agree to maintain complete secrecy about the arrangement—the same promise she had exacted from Anne. When it eventually became known that Anne studied with Liszt, she was never to tell a soul that she had her lessons at the quai Malaquais, nor was Liszt to admit to going there. The lessons were always to be scheduled at times when Marie could chaperone. And Marie had not yet decided whether to invite Liszt when she hosted the planned salon that would introduce Anne to society.

The doorbell jangled and Anne lifted her hands off the keys as if they had suddenly become scalding hot. Her eyes were open and round and she flushed becomingly. She stood rather clumsily from the piano and took a few steps to the middle of the room, where she waited, tense and hardly breathing. Marie remained in her seat.

Liszt entered and made a low bow to Marie before turning to Anne, whom he led by the hand back to the pianoforte. He placed the small portfolio of music he had brought with him on the desk, then pulled up a chair, angling himself so that he could sit near Anne while he taught her and still be visible to Marie. *He knows that this is how he appears most attractive,* she thought. She could see the chiseled outline of his cheekbones and the suggestion of his eyelashes, and his nose, which in direct profile might have been judged a trifle prominent, appeared positively patrician. He faced enough away from her that she could fix her gaze on him unabashedly—which she did. Marie watched every second of the lesson, unable to pay the least attention to the letter she pretended to write.

The more she watched, the more she was persuaded that although Liszt leaned in close to Anne and touched her hands to show her how to achieve certain improvements in her technique, everything he did was not really for the benefit of his pupil but was in some fashion on display for Marie herself: the way he moved, the incline of his head, the frequency with which he smiled or cast a soulful glance at the high ceiling, never turning to look in Marie's direction, yet ensuring that every gesture, every comment, reflected off Anne and shed its light over her.

Anne, by contrast, became so totally absorbed in the lesson that Marie thought she probably forgot that her chaperone was in the same room. At first, the poor girl went pale and flushed deep crimson by turns, but soon her complexion evened out to its usual attractive, rosy hue. Yet whenever Liszt touched her hands, or stopped her by placing his fingers on her arm, Marie could see Anne's tiny intake of breath, too small for anyone to notice who wasn't looking for such a thing.

For Anne, the hour passed much too quickly. As the clock on the mantel chimed three, Liszt concluded the lesson by assigning her a study by Chopin to learn. He had brought the handwritten pages with him; Anne could hardly believe he entrusted her with them.

"It will tax your technique beyond anything you play now," he said, lifting her hand and brushing it lightly with his lips after he had put on his coat in preparation to leave. When he let go of Anne's fingers, he reached into his breast pocket and pulled out a small, leather-bound volume with the word "Byron" stamped in gold on its spine. He paused before giving it to her. Once again, he had that look on his face, the same look he had at Madame Duvernoy's, as if he wanted to say something but did not quite know how. Before the silence became awkward, he spoke. "It's a good translation, I am told. Read the poems, think of them especially as you learn the study. Remember what I told you . . ." He flicked his eyes in Madame d'Agoult's direction. "I would be most interested to have you help me understand them, from your own point of view."

He backed away from her. Marie, who had walked over to the mantelpiece to place several coins there, faced the other way. Anne pointed to the book. Liszt nodded and smiled. At that moment Marie turned toward them again. Liszt bowed politely, scooped the coins up so quickly they hardly noticed his action, and left.

Anne wished she knew what Marie had said to her father. She could hardly believe that he had been persuaded to allow her to spend the better part of most days at the apartment on the quai Malaquais. He didn't seem exactly enthusiastic about it, but he raised no objections. Apparently the marquis knew she would have piano lessons but not the identity of her teacher. Fortunately for Anne, he did not question her closely about the arrangement.

Indeed, he appeared to have forgotten all about Marie's visit by the end of the day, or at least to have ceased caring about it. Perhaps he was distracted by something that happened later in the afternoon, immediately before Anne retired to her room to dress for dinner. The late post arrived, and Anne and her father both happened to meet Julien in the stairwell with it in his hand—she on her way up the stairs, the marquis passing through from the parlor into the library. Without a word, her father took the three letters from Julien. He was about to walk with them into his library when he stopped in midstride, his eyes wide and staring at the face of one of the envelopes.

"What is it, Father?" Anne had asked.

He whirled around to face her. She caught a glimpse of fear in his eyes—something she had never seen in them before—before he settled his expression into his usual scowl. "Nothing," he snapped, then continued and closed the door behind him.

He did not emerge until dinner was placed on the table. Anne had been shocked at the time that he had not even bothered to change, as was his custom.

Anne sat in front of her dressing table mirror letting Thérèse brush out her hair. Soon the memory of her father's odd behavior was driven from her mind as she lingered over every detail of her lesson that afternoon. When she breathed deeply, she could conjure up Liszt's masculine scent of pipe smoke and musty books, and every time Thérèse brushed against her to reach for a different comb or to put a hairpin on the table, Anne imagined Liszt reaching across her to mark a fingering on the page of music propped up on the desk of the piano.

The most exciting moment, however, had been when he demonstrated the way she must change her technique. Anne closed her eyes and relived it for at least the twentieth time since she had returned from the quai Malaquais.

"Show me how you place your hands before you begin," he had said.

Anne had done as she was told, spreading her fingers out straight from the knuckles and angling them down so that her hands looked like upside-down vees from the side.

"Hmm. That does not seem quite natural. Technique should be natural, it should arise from expression, like this."

He nudged her over so that he himself could place his hands on the keyboard. His fingers moved too fast for her to see what he meant.

"Now you try."

Anne did her best to mimic her teacher, but he stopped her right away. "No, that is not it. I cannot explain. Here." Liszt stood behind her and reached around her on both sides, placed his hands over hers, pressed her knuckles down slightly, and curled her fingers so that the ends of them were perpendicular to the keys. The gesture felt like an embrace. "I suggest you practice slowly like that, spend at least an hour on scales and arpeggios every day for the next week. I shall assume you will fix this technical problem on your own so that we may instead use our time together to concentrate on the musical ones."

He let go of her and she attempted the position on her own. "But what about large stretches? If I curl my fingers, I cannot make them."

She played the opening right-hand figure of the sonata, which began with the interval of an octave.

"You'll work it out. It has to feel natural, for the sake of the music."

For another quarter of an hour after that, Liszt had helped Anne with the subtle phrasing of the sonata and showed her how she could use this different technique not only to render passages easier to play, but to give her more control of the musical expression.

She opened her eyes and wiggled her fingers in front of her now, then played a scale on the edge of her dressing table, starting at the imaginary bass and moving to the right toward the treble.

Anne stopped her silent practice when her eye caught the little, leather-bound book Liszt had lent her. She picked it up off the dressing table, ran her fingers over the pebbly morocco, opened it reverently, and turned a few pages.

> *I stood in Venice, on the Bridge of Sighs;*
> *A palace and a prison on each hand:*
> *I saw from out the wave her structures rise*
> *As from the stroke of the enchanter's wand:*
> *A thousand years their cloudy wings expand*
> *Around me, and a dying Glory smiles*
> *O'er the far times, when many a subject land*
> *Look'd to the winged Lion's marble piles,*
> *Where Venice sate in state, thron'd on her hundred isles!*

Liszt had told her that the poems would help her understand the Chopin study. For Anne, the French translation of Byron's English words did not conjure up Chopin's music, though. All she could imagine when she read them was Liszt's voice, and the strange expression he had on his face when he gave her the book. She ached to talk to someone about the way she felt.

"So I understand you are to spend your days with the countess d'Agoult," Thérèse said with a pat on Anne's head to indicate that her brushing was finished.

Anne started. She was so lost in her own thoughts that she had nearly forgotten about Thérèse. "Yes." Anne turned and grasped both the maid's hands in hers. "Isn't it wonderful? She will present me to society." But Thérèse did not look as pleased as Anne thought she should. "Is something the matter?" she asked. "Aren't you happy for me?"

"Of course, *ma fille*," she answered. "But just take care that all she does for you is truly in your interest."

Anne frowned. With no other ally at the hôtel Barbier, she desperately needed Thérèse to share her happiness, not scold her and raise objections. "She was a great comfort and help to Mama."

"She made your mama unhappy. She reminded her of everything her life was not."

"Don't you think Mama knew that already, without Madame d'Agoult's help? I could not imagine marrying someone like my father." She frowned.

"If your face gets stuck in a pout like that, you'll never marry anyone!" Thérèse gave Anne a gentle pinch on the cheek after she laid the hairbrush back on the dressing table. "Remember old Bonnard? The shoemaker?" she continued as she walked across the room to take Anne's nightdress out of the garderobe.

"Of course," Anne said. Why did Thérèse mention the wizened little shoemaker who had provided the whole household with footwear as long as she could remember? When Anne was a child, she always looked forward to seeing him work in his little lean-to shop down an alley in the poorer part of the faubourg.

"He died of cholera today."

There it was again. The cholera. She was sorry about Bonnard, but right now, she did not want to think about death. She preferred to think about music, and about love. The marquise had loved music. Anne loved music, and she also loved . . . "I shall light a candle for his soul when I go to confession," she said.

Thérèse scrunched the nightdress in her hands and held it so that Anne could duck into it like a little child. "I'm not telling you to make you sad, only to warn you. Be on your guard! You're mixing with all sorts, and I think I'd die myself if we lost you too."

Anne was unaccountably cross at Thérèse. The cholera had come and gone in their house, with devastating effect. It was cruelty enough, she thought, to stay alive after such a loss, without having it brought up again and again.

Anne took a deep breath and tried to turn her mind back to her wonderful day. "You're worrying about nothing," she said, and kissed Thérèse lightly on both cheeks. Before she climbed into bed, she ran back to her dressing table to get the book of poetry. She would read until the bedside candle burned low.

Eleven

To reach the Office of Records required passing through the offices of the Prefecture of Police. Pierre noted that fact with dismay when he brought his first weekly report to the commissioner himself. He could have submitted his findings to a local magistrate, but since the records he wished to gain access to resided in the office where the salutary reports were checked and filed, he decided that it would make sense to combine the tasks. He had hoped that it might be a simple matter to gain access to the files he required in order to look up the record of the marquise de Barbier-Chouant's marriage and the countess's birth, as requested by Madame d'Agoult. If all was perfectly straightforward, then he would simply be able to report those facts to the countess and have done nothing but convey knowledge that any member of the public could acquire if he wished. But if there were some irregularity: therein lay the difficulty. In addition to the thorny issue of how to remove the evidence from its lawful location—since the countess had been most insistent that he actually bring her the papers—he was wary of exposing anything untoward about Mademoiselle de Barbier-Chouant's background. Perhaps there was another way to locate the information she requested, one that did not involve the official bureaucratic channels. A small voice in the back of his mind shrieked caution at him, but the countess had piqued his curiosity, and now there was no going back. Every step he took closer to the office where he would make his request committed him more definitely to the enterprise.

And Pierre had ample time to worry about what he intended to do as he followed a clerk through miles of corridors that twisted and turned. He had lost all sense of direction before they finally stopped at a plain door bearing a plaque with the name "Gardive" painted on it. The clerk nodded to Pierre and hurried away, the tap of his polished shoes echoing in the empty hallways. Pierre cleared his throat and then knocked, not too loudly, half hoping no one would answer.

"Come!" answered a businesslike voice on the other side of the door.

Pierre pushed the door open and stepped into a small office, insufficiently illuminated by one tiny window high up, an office whose walls were lined with oak filing cabinets. The commissioner— presumably Monsieur Gardive himself—sat on the other side of an overly large desk, its entire surface covered with papers. Even the sheet upon which he wrote and made notes lay on top of others. Pierre nodded a greeting to the commissioner, who glanced up quickly when he came in, not pausing in his scribbling. After standing immobile and silent a moment longer, Pierre placed the report from his first week as an area health inspector near enough to the commissioner so that it might attract his attention.

With an admirable economy of movement, Gardive pinched one corner of the paper between the fingers of his left hand and slid it so that it now lay uppermost on the pile in front of his face. He commenced scanning it without a word. Pierre pretended simply to look away politely, yet in reality his eyes took in the labels on all the cabinets. In contrast to the chaos in evidence on Gardive's desk, the cabinets were a marvel of organization, divided into two categories. *Atteintes*, the lists of people who had fallen ill, occupied many drawers on one side of the room. On the other, behind the commissioner himself, were slightly fewer drawers labeled *Décès*. Evidently all of the records were of victims of the epidemic, so that the commissioner was surrounded by illness and death. Yet this office had existed before the outbreak and was the repository for all records of birth, death, and marriage in the city. Those not having to do with cholera must be kept elsewhere. He would have to discover their location. While he waited for Gardive to finish checking over his report, Pierre also noticed two other slim doors that led beyond the office: one behind the commissioner, and another to the man's right. Pierre cleared his throat. "With so many dying of cholera, there is no room for other diseases!"

Gardive gave a short laugh and looked up quickly from his scrutiny of Pierre's list. "Yes, although there are those who still prefer to exit this life with a heart attack or apoplexy, to be sure."

"One assumes that even the murderers no longer bother, with cholera morbus to do their work for them."

The fellow, whose brown eyes were glassy and reddish from peering at paperwork that flooded in from all areas of the city, placed his pen down on the desk emphatically. "You think, you part-time health officers, that this difficult task did not exist before March twenty-sixth?" He stood. "Let me show you something."

Gardive stretched his arms over his head. To Pierre's surprise, the previously surly, incommunicative official smiled broadly. "I thank you for giving me an excuse to stand. It is too easy to become obsessed with this vital work." He indicated that Pierre should follow him through the door behind his desk.

The room into which this small door led was surprisingly large—much larger than Gardive's office. More tiny windows placed high up in the walls shed a half-hearted light over the space, which was also crowded with rows upon rows of wooden cabinets with handwritten labels bearing dates. "Here," he said, sweeping his hand, "are all those who have died of other causes since the year 1814. Buried in these drawers and files is information that would tell us a great deal about our city, that might even have prevented this terrible epidemic."

"And those over there?" Pierre asked.

"Births, marriages. But death is much more interesting, don't you agree?"

Pierre nodded. "I have some interest in matters of public health," he said, recognizing the zeal in the beleaguered commissioner's voice.

"Eh, well, we're told to lock all this away. No one's to concern himself with anything but the cholera, and I labor over it from six in the morning until midnight every day." At that he indicated that Pierre should precede him from the room. Once back in his office, the fellow pressed an inked stamp on Pierre's list and placed it in a wooden tray on top of the others.

"I suppose there are earlier records through there," said Pierre, pointing to the door to the commissioner's right. Wanting to know where it led, he could think of no other way to find out.

"Eh? No. According to the world as it now is, no one was born or died before the restoration of the monarchy."

Pierre had to look at his face to discern a trace of expression that indicated he was joking.

"That door allows me to come and go without being set upon by angry citizens, who think that because I collect the information, I must somehow be responsible for the sickness."

Although the look on his face changed not at all, Pierre guessed that Gardive once more spoke in earnest. "Ignorance is a terrible burden," he said. The commissioner resumed his place at his desk. He immediately recommenced his concentrated task and seemed no longer aware of Pierre's presence. "Adieu," Pierre said.

Gardive grunted his reply.

Well, Pierre thought as he did his best to retrace his steps to the front of the Prefecture, at least he had discovered the location of the records. He did not see how he could possibly have a chance to search through them, with the work of the commission so carefully controlled. And Gardive himself occupied the office from early in the morning until late at night.

He stepped out into the late afternoon sun. The weather was mild—which did not bode well for their ability to contain the cholera epidemic. Garbage and corpses would rot more quickly, and conditions that were already unhealthful would worsen. If the files in Gardive's office were not yet full, they soon would be.

As he stood deciding which way to go, whether to take the short route and pass by the putrid Hôtel-Dieu or skirt it and take a longer route home, the kernel of an idea began to take shape in Pierre's mind. He tried to dismiss it from his thoughts, but it kept creeping back in and demanding that he consider it. That other door, the one that let Gardive himself in and out: it must lead to the quai de l'Horloge, he thought. One might, if one took great care, enter the building unnoticed through the door that Gardive used sometime between midnight and six in the morning when the commissioner would not be there, find the necessary records, and leave before anyone knew.

Instead of returning immediately to his rooms, Pierre walked north to the quai de l'Horloge, strolling aimlessly as though enjoying the last rays of the reluctant sun, but all the time looking to see if he could spy another entrance to the Prefecture, hoping to find Gardive's way in, one presumably not guarded by armed officers. To his dismay, two uniformed men flanked every door he saw, and knots of surly citizens clustered around them, shouting at everyone who entered or left. One old lady actually spat on Pierre when he strayed too close to the building.

He was about to abandon his quest when a slight irregularity in the bricks close to the end of one wall caught his eye. He paused, pretending to brush some dirt off his coat while he examined it. There was no doubt that mortar was missing between the bricks in exactly the shape of a small door. Pierre thought he saw an iron ring attached to one side, and it seemed likely that if he pulled that ring, he might well find himself in a hidden corridor that would lead to the commissioner's office.

In a way, Pierre wished he had not made that discovery. It would be much easier to be able to tell Madame d'Agoult that the information she sought was simply not to be had, at least, not without going through official channels and having to explain one's interest in it. But here he was faced with a true choice. He could, if he dared, steal into the Prefecture in the dead of night and rifle through the records. Or at least, he could try.

Pierre's heart beat a little more quickly at the thought of the danger he might face. He also hoped that Madame d'Agoult was prepared to accept the possible consequences of such an action. If they discovered something illegal, or even suspicious, they could be considered criminals for keeping it to themselves—especially if it had any bearing on the disposition of a fortune. Who would ever believe that their motives were not pecuniary?

Pierre hardly knew how he got back to his apartment, his mind had been so occupied with doubts and questions. When he arrived, he found Georges lying down on his bed, his face pale. Pierre's friend had been overzealous in his efforts to care for the cholera victims, and the constant strain and fatigue had begun to tell on him.

"I think you should stay at home tonight. I'll go in your place." Pierre poured a cup of chamomile tea for Georges.

"But you have already worked an extra shift and discharged your debt to me. There is no need for you to undertake something that is my responsibility."

"I do not need to, as you say, but I want to. What good will you do the cholera victims if you yourself contract the disease?" Pierre knew his argument was feeble. There seemed little rhyme or reason in the transmission of cholera, and those who spent days nursing victims seldom became ill with it themselves.

Georges heaved a great sigh. "I confess, I am exhausted. A night off will do me good."

Pierre felt a little guilty about his motives for offering to go in Georges's place. But he was sincere in wanting his friend to rest. The fact that serving on the wards of the Hôtel-Dieu would place him very near the Prefecture of Police, and also give him a reason for being there in the middle of the night, did nothing to diminish his concern over Georges's pallor. "Now, don't go running out to the café as soon as I am gone!" Pierre said, tousling his friend's hair. But in truth, Georges did not look as if he would hurry anywhere, except possibly to the realm of Morpheus.

Georges's shift began at ten in the evening, and Pierre dutifully arrived a little before that hour. By the light of a moon that was a day or two away from being completely full, the ancient walls of the Hôtel-Dieu looked as pale and sickly as its inhabitants. Placard bearers, flower sellers, and fruit sellers cried their politics and their wares, creating a carnival atmosphere around the hospital. A steady stream of carts pulled up to unload the sick into the crowded wards, and Pierre braced himself for the overwhelming stench. If nothing else, the camphor sachet around his neck might ease his own nausea.

Inside, the walls echoed with patients being violently sick and crying out for relief.

"They all want water," said a Benedictine nun whose habit was spattered with vomit and feces. She thrust a bucket and a ladle into Pierre's hands and pushed him in the direction of one of the wards.

Pierre concentrated on dipping the ladle into the water bucket and holding it to the patients' lips, making a distracting game of trying not to spill a single drop, while slaking the sufferers' thirsts as quickly as possible. He could do twelve beds with one bucket of water, then would run outside to the pump, fill his bucket, and run back in to bring water to another twelve. In three hours, he circled the ward no fewer than twenty times and emptied thirty-five buckets of water into the cholera victims' mouths. In that time, half of those who occupied the narrow beds died and were replaced by new victims, while others gradually quieted to something like sleep. These would be the ones to survive. Those who looked as though they would live through the night were, after a time, moved by the nuns, their filthy bodies bathed and their linens changed. Tomorrow they would leave to make room for the newly afflicted.

The bells of Notre Dame tolled two o'clock before Pierre even thought to remember his other task that evening. There seemed to be a slight lull in the severity of the cases on his ward, and so he put his bucket on the floor and stole out to the street.

A few listless beggars leaned against the walls, but the tradespeople and placard bearers had gone. The quiet outside contrasted so sharply with the noise of suffering inside that at first Pierre's ears rang. Before he could lose heart for his daring project, he headed to the quai Desaix and followed it until it became the quai de la Cité and after that the quai de l'Horloge. In the comparative quiet, he could hear the gentle plashing of the river against the shore. Without the clusters of people talking and arguing and doing their daily business, the island in the center of Paris was all dead monuments, tomblike buildings, and churches. The double-towered eminence of Notre Dame cast a long shadow in the moonlight, and an owl hooted its unanswerable question through the lanes. Who would see him? he thought. There was no one about.

Just as he came to believe that he was no more visible than a wraith flitting among the vaults and memorials, a police officer stepped out of the shadow by one of the doors of the Prefecture and called out to him.

"You there! What's your business?"

"I'm . . . a doctor," Pierre reminded himself, as well as informing the officer. "I need air, it's the Hôtel-Dieu." He started to walk toward the guard to prove his point, but the fellow waved him away quickly.

Pierre's arms and legs were so tired from lifting buckets of water and running back and forth to the fountain that he wondered whether he would even have the strength to open a door, let alone climb stairs. He was in such a daze that he almost walked past the hidden entrance, all the way to the place du Pont Neuf. But he stopped himself and, quickly checking to see if anyone was around, approached the irregular bricks he had noticed earlier.

It was as he remembered it. He grasped the ring and pulled. At first, nothing happened. Pierre was afraid for a moment that he had misread the signs, and that this was not a door at all but simply an ancient hitching place. Nonetheless he pulled again, putting all his weight into his effort.

To his mixed relief and dread, the hidden door gradually opened. Once it stood ajar, Pierre could see that it was made not of solid bricks but of only the surfaces of them fixed to boards, a purposeful disguise for a secret entrance.

Unfortunately, this brick-faced panel did not lead immediately into the building. It simply concealed another door, set deep into a frame of time-blackened oak. Pierre tried that door, but it was locked.

He leaned his forehead against the rough planks. How could he be certain, after all, that this entrance led to Gardive's office? He had all but decided to abandon his project when the sound of footsteps and voices reached him from around the side of the building. They were coming too fast for him to step out, close the door, and run away, and so he grasped the inner iron ring and pulled it toward him, squeezing into the space between the two, which was barely deep enough for him to fit.

"I told her if she ever did that again, I'd give her what for," said a low-class voice.

"Women. I wouldn't marry one if you paid me."

The guards laughed as they passed very close by him, and the acrid scent of pipe smoke seeped in around the cracks of the door, threatening to make him sneeze. Pierre tried to put his finger to his nose, but the space was too small. He held his breath instead, his heart thumping in his breast, until the voices faded away around the other side of the building.

Once he believed himself alone again, Pierre pushed the outer door slowly open. He had cracked it only an inch when a small object clattered to the floor at his feet. He opened the door wider so that he could see it by the moonlight.

A key. It must have been on a hook inside the outer door. Quickly, before the guards circled back around, he fitted it in the inner door's lock. The mechanism groaned, but with a little coaxing it gave. Pierre pushed.

The complete obscurity inside the building shouldn't have surprised him. Reluctantly, Pierre closed first the brick-faced door, then the other one, plunging himself into a darkness so profound that he could see phantoms in front of his eyes. He rubbed them and blinked, until he thought he could make out a wall. He put out his hands to feel for it and, to his relief, encountered cold, damp stone. With his hands in constant contact with the wall, Pierre inched forward. In two steps, his foot hit the riser of a stair. He lifted his foot, placed it on the step, then felt with his other foot for the next riser.

Pierre repeated this painstaking process for three flights, until he finally found himself at another door. He could not say for certain whether this door would lead him where he wanted to go, yet he had no choice but to try it. He prayed that the health commissioner—or whoever occupied that office—had left an ember in the grate, or a box of matches and a match-bottle, something so that he could light a candle. Otherwise his stealthy expedition would be for nothing. He felt around for a knob and, when he found it, opened the door.

Pierre's eyes had become so accustomed to struggling to see in the dark that he was at first completely blinded by the glow of the single candle that spread a pool of light over Gardive's desk. He put his hand before his face to shield his eyes.

"I suggest you do not move."

Gardive's voice was precise and hard, and with it Pierre heard the click of metal against metal. He lowererd his hand to see before him the health commissioner surrounded by papers, exactly as he had been that afternoon, only this time aiming a pistol at Pierre's heart.

"Please, let me explain." *What a stupid thing to say,* Pierre thought. What possible explanation could there be for someone to creep up a secret staircase and steal into the office where records of cholera victims were kept?

"I have seen you before. Where?" The commissioner thrust his pistol slightly forward.

"This afternoon. Here." A trickle of sweat traced a path down his spine. "I am a local health inspector. I brought my reports to you, Monsieur Gardive."

The commissioner wrinkled his brow and frowned. "What the devil are you doing here now?"

"Perhaps the same thing you are doing." The possibility that his life would be cut short by violence made Pierre bold. He guessed that the commissioner, although authorized to inhabit this office until midnight, might have stolen in for his own reasons after hours. He noticed that the door to the back room was ajar.

Whatever he had said produced—at least for the moment—the desired effect. Gardive uncocked the pistol and laid it on the desk. "As there is nothing of value to a thief in this room, I'll give you one opportunity to explain yourself, and then I shall ring this little bell here and summon a police officer to throw you in jail."

"It would be a pity to do that to a medical student who, in addition to serving on the Commission of Health, also spends hours tending to patients in the cholera wards."

"Sit," the commissioner ordered, pointing to a wooden chair.

Pierre took the chair and only at that moment realized how exhausted he was. He sat as upright as possible, half afraid he might fall asleep midsentence. "I seek information pertaining to the family of a cholera victim." This was no time to mince words.

"Name?" Gardive stood and approached the filing drawers labeled *Décès*.

"I don't need to examine her death record. It is her earlier history I wish to investigate." Pierre pointed to the room behind the desk.

"I see. And this necessitated an unlawful entry into a public building? Why did you not simply ask me when you were here earlier? Do you have any idea how you have compromised yourself by taking this unwise—illegal—action?"

Pierre felt foolish, now, that he had broken into this small room to gain access to information he might have had for the asking. But something in the way Madame d'Agoult spoke had alarmed him. If there were some dread secret surrounding the late marquise, his interest in the countess gave him a personal stake in its continuing suppression. "I did not ask you because I was afraid of what I might find."

"Now you have aroused my curiosity. Shall we?" Gardive rose, took the candlestick from the desk and reached for the pistol. Before he touched it, he paused and fixed Pierre with a piercing stare.

"Against my own judgment, I have indulged you thus far. I may as well ask you directly whether I need to fear for my own safety."

"I assure you, Commissioner, that I have neither the desire nor the strength at this moment to pose any threat to your person. Indeed, I am deeply sorry—"

Gardive stopped him with a wave of his hand and motioned Pierre to precede him into the record room. He left the pistol behind. "Please remain where I can see you at all times. Date of marriage?"

"August 1814."

"Name?"

Pierre paused. Alas, he could see no way to avoid sharing that information with the commissioner. "The marquise de Barbier-Chouant."

Gardive had already begun searching through the drawer containing the records for the month of the marquise's marriage, but he stopped and looked over his shoulder at Pierre. "Have they paid you to find this information?"

"How dare you suggest—!"

"Well, then, why?"

Whether it was the unreality of the place, shrouded in darkness except for the pool of candlelight that revealed only the commissioner's face and a few cabinets with their neatly inked labels, or his excessive fatigue that affected him, Pierre could not later say. But all at once the tale of his fascination with Anne, the countess de Barbier-Chouant, tumbled out of his mouth.

"So, there is love involved. It's always the way. Either love or money. Sometimes both." Gardive spoke in detached phrases as he looked through the files. "Can you not give me an exact date?" he asked.

"She said the end of August," Pierre said.

"*She* said?" Gardive paused with his hand in the files. "Who is *she*?"

"I . . . I cannot say."

The commissioner turned away and continued his methodical searching through the drawer. "Well, I find no Barbier-Chouant marriage here." He closed the drawer, whose well-waxed runners made this operation nearly silent except for the final click of the catch.

"Perhaps someone put it under the wrong month? Or year?"

"*I* do not make such mistakes," Gardive said. "Perhaps *she* is mistaken in the date."

Pierre looked down in confusion. "I do not believe so."

"That is your belief against my certainty. Neither of these produces the record, however, and it can only mean one of two things."

Pierre waited for him to continue, which Gardive did only after they had both returned to the outer office and he had closed the door behind them.

"It means either the late marquise did not marry or her record is somewhere else."

"But where else would it be?" Pierre dismissed the first suggestion as a jest and was beginning to lose patience with Gardive. Then he remembered that he had no right to complain and in fact should be grateful that the fellow hadn't shot him as soon as he walked through the door.

The commissioner approached the cabinet in his office that was filled with the records of cholera victims. "Date of death?"

"March twenty-sixth."

He soon found the file that corresponded to the date of Sandrine de Barbier-Chouant's death and flipped through it efficiently. Clearly this was something he did not only every day but at least once each hour of every day. "That is strange," he said, pausing before riffling through the file again. "Where did she live?"

"Saint Germain," Pierre answered, although he still did not know the street.

"There is no Barbier, or Barbier-Chouant. Only one record that says 'anonymous' from that district."

"May I see it?" Pierre asked.

Pierre later could not have said at what point Gardive stopped treating him like an intruder and began speaking to him as if he were a colleague with whom he was having a stimulating chat. But the result was that the commissioner brought the entire file out for Pierre to peruse. Midway down the page that listed the names of those who had died in Saint Germain on March 26 was an entry that said, *"Anonyme,"* and gave the address as rue du Barq. The entry was initialed F. M. "Who is F. M.?" Pierre asked.

"That is François Magendie," Gardive answered, with a note of surprise in his voice.

"Dr. Magendie is one of my professors at the faculty of medicine. Surely he would have given a name?"

"It would have been highly irregular not to do so, unless it were some poor wretch whom no one claimed. And in that case, the esteemed professor would be unlikely to have been in attendance." Gardive accompanied his last comment with an ironic arch of one eyebrow.

"Perhaps the birth record of Anne de Barbier-Chouant would solve the mystery," Pierre suggested.

"When was the young lady born?"

"July twenty-sixth, 1815."

Gardive disappeared back into the record room for a while. Pierre could hear drawers opening and closing, papers being sorted through quickly. Soon the commissioner reappeared, his hands empty.

"You are either woefully ill-informed, or you have been sent here to try my patience."

"You found no record of the countess's birth?" Pierre rubbed his eyes to clear his thoughts. "Might I beg your indulgence," he said, "to visit rue du Barq, the street where your unnamed cholera victim was supposed to have lived, and see what I find? I shall bring the information back to you and that way will help to make your records more complete."

The commissioner stood behind his desk, deep in thought. "Very well," he finally said, "although by rights I should have you thrown in jail just to teach you a lesson."

"I . . . I'm terribly sorry. Truly." Pierre looked down at the floor.

"Go," Gardive commanded, but his tone was indulgent rather than stern.

Pierre let himself out the side door and felt his way back down the dark staircase. He stopped and listened for the guards before letting himself out on the quai de l'Horloge. Once safely on the cobbles, he allowed himself to think about what he had discovered that night. There was no record of the marquise's marriage, or of Anne's birth, at least not on the dates Madame d'Agoult had given him. And in the records of cholera victims, the name of the marquise was similarly not to be found.

The bells of Notre Dame struck three. Hours of his shift in the Hôtel-Dieu remained. Pierre trudged back to the hospital and braced himself for the endless task of bringing water to those whose thirst would never be relieved.

Twelve

～⌐∽⌐～

While he was painting, Eugène always fastened his eyes to his brush, whether he used it to mix paints together on the palette or to daub them on the small canvas he had before him. That fine afternoon when Franz stopped in on his way back from teaching Anne at Madame d'Agoult's apartment, Eugène managed to welcome his guest hospitably and carry on a conversation with him without once looking away from his work.

"Day by day, I can feel her desire increasing," Franz said. He still basked in the agreeable glow of unacknowledged passion, in the tantalizing thrill of being in the same room with someone he loved, certain that he and she would one day be together.

"And that makes it all right, what you are doing?"

Franz shifted in his seat so that he could stretch his long legs out in front of him. Eugène always annoyed him when he lectured. For an artist, Delacroix was remarkably level-headed about love. "You act as if I am trying to seduce the young lady, not the beautiful, magnificent woman who acts as her benefactress."

"Well, you give her books of poetry full of romance and tortured souls with little notes hidden in them."

"But the notes are not for her!"

"Are you certain she knows this?"

Franz wished Eugène would face him when they argued, but his friend's attention never strayed from his painting. "Of course I am certain. I as much as told her, on two occasions." Franz was vexed. Although he believed Anne understood his intentions, their circumstances had made it impossible for him to tell her as plainly as he would wish what exactly he expected of her.

"As much as? Well, we'll leave that point aside for the moment. And what of these verses? I wouldn't be surprised if you commission Alfred to supply you with them." Eugène lifted his brush from the canvas, dipped it into two of the viscous colors on his palette, mixed them to create a third, indescribable shade, then dabbed again. "Tell me, are you quite certain your methods will achieve the results you desire? After all, you toy with the affections of one and hope she will docilely help you seduce the other."

"I am not interested in children!"

"Ah! So you are getting even with the world because of the Saint-Cricq business."

"Of course not." Eugène's comment about the countess Franz had tried to elope with when he was only seventeen was too much. It had taken him months to recover from that disappointment, but two years and more had elapsed and he considered himself fully healed now. And compared to his feelings toward the enigmatic countess d'Agoult, his obsession with Mademoiselle de Saint-Cricq had been a pale imitation of love. He strode over to the window. "I must tread very cautiously with Madame d'Agoult. I do not want to send that delicate soul into hiding before I have been able to draw it into my own."

Eugène stood back from his painting and scrutinized it with a frown on his face. "Be careful, Franz. The feminine mind is a veritable trap. And married women are especially dangerous."

Franz scowled at Eugène, then walked over and clapped his hand on his friend's shoulder and peered at the painting. "That's Paganini." He was somewhat surprised at himself for not noticing before.

"I'm glad you recognize him." Eugène waved a brush full of paint in Franz's direction, and the musician moved away quickly. "I intend to do Chopin next."

"Why don't you paint my portrait?" Franz asked, striking a dramatic pose.

"Because," Eugène answered, looking up for the briefest instant, "I expect neither Paganini nor Chopin to live for very long, but you— unless you are murdered on the street by a jealous husband—can wait. Besides, you're much too vain."

"Vain! You're a fine fellow to talk."

Eugène stepped yet farther back from his work, cocked his head this way and that, and at last turned away. He swished his brush in a glass full of solvent, then wiped it on a clean rag, smearing shades of brown in messy lines down the soft, white linen. He repeated the process several times until the streaks faded to nonexistence. When he had finished, he washed his hands in a basin, poured out two glasses of wine from the carafe that the housekeeper had placed on a tray before leaving for the night, and handed one to Franz. "You cannot have them both, you know. And either one will get you in trouble."

"I am not interested in the young countess! Why can you not understand this fact? Our relationship is purely musical, I assure you." Franz raised his glass to Eugène, beginning to doubt a little that he should have said anything at all to his friend about his plans.

"Hah! Those are the most treacherous of all, the ones with artistic pretensions. You give them something to believe in, something that makes them think you're different."

"I gather you have experience in such matters? So what would you do, in my shoes?" Franz stretched out on the divan once more, slopping a little of his wine on the floor in the process.

"First, I would find an excuse to finish the lessons. Hand her off to Chopin; he's harmless enough, and a good teacher, I hear."

Franz dismissed the suggestion with a wave of his slender hand.

"Then I should either declare myself to the countess d'Agoult and commence an affair, or go abroad on an extended tour until I found some wealthy merchant's daughter to marry and got over this unhealthy attraction to older women with husbands." Eugène punctuated his sentence by swallowing down the contents of his glass in one gulp and pouring himself another.

"That really wasn't what I had in mind. In fact, Eugène, I was going to ask a small favor." Franz sat up and leaned toward his friend, who had draped himself over an armchair whose stuffing was about to burst out of its threadbare covering.

"Your favors are never small. What is it this time?"

"If—when—I am able to secure Marie's love, I shall need somewhere to meet her."

"Oh no, no. Not here. The last time you did that, an angry brother slashed one of my paintings. This studio is my livelihood, you know!"

"That won't happen again, I promise. Marie's husband does not care about her, so I have heard." Franz stood and wandered over to the portrait of Paganini that sat drying on the easel. "You've really captured that sickliness of his. He looks like old cholera morbus himself, playing the city to the grave."

"Perhaps that's what has infected you, my friend. Only instead of destroying your body, the sickness has attacked your mind."

"But you will help me," said Franz.

Eugène took a deep breath and whistled it out through his pursed lips. "You are fortunate I value your talent. Just give me plenty of warning if this unlikely event ever comes to pass."

Franz leapt out of his seat, pulled Eugène from his chair, and danced him around the studio.

"What troubles you, my son?"

Armand looked up from his clasped hands to see the gaunt figure of Père Jaquin standing over him, a frown pulling down the corners of his mouth. "Nothing, Father."

"You have confessed three times this week. What sins could weigh on you so, after only a month outside these walls?"

He should have known better than to try to fool the man who had taught him and cared for him for ten years. But Armand did not want to tell Père Jaquin about all the confused feelings that churned his stomach and stole his hours of sleep. He had been warned before he left the school that he would face temptations out in the world, and he had dismissed the possibility, confident that such temptations held no sway over his pure heart.

Yet in the weeks since he had met his pretty cousin, doubts had begun to assail him. First, there was Anne herself. She had initially frightened him with her defiant demeanor the night he went to the hôtel Barbier for dinner. He had thought to discharge his obligation to his guardian by taking her out just once and being done with the matter. Yet when she emerged from the house that next afternoon, her luminous beauty took his breath away. Her smile lit her entire face, and as soon as they were away from the marquis, she spoke to him with intimacy and candor, as if she had known him and trusted him for a long time, and he felt close to her as he had never felt close to another human being.

How could he explain to this celibate priest what emotions tore him apart? Armand knew he had spent his entire life in a cocoon, like the butterflies he had studied the previous year. He would have been content to remain there awhile longer, but his guardian, the marquis, had ripped open the delicate fabric that kept him secure from the world and forced him to crawl blinking into the daylight, afraid to spread his drab wings. It took his cousin Anne to show him how glorious it could be to soar freely in the air.

Sadly, it soon became apparent to Armand that his cousin did not experience a similar awakening in his presence. What at first had seemed like radiant kindness faded into polite self-interest. Her smile lost its spontaneity, and he began to suspect that his chariot and the excuse he provided for her to leave the hôtel Barbier were the sole reasons that the countess had been willing to drive out with him, day after day. Except for lately, when his inquiries had been met with the information that Anne had a daily engagement with the countess d'Agoult, with the blessing of her father. Armand was now completely confused about why there had been such subterfuge in the first place.

Unless he simply did not understand the ways of ladies, and Anne was actually being coy with him because she was in love with him.

Thus his thoughts had circled around, and hour by hour he would change his mind about whether the countess loved him or hated him. This constant fretting made his heart ache almost as much as his belly. His physical pain had grown worse in recent weeks, and in addition to his general confusion about the ways of the world, Armand began to believe God punished him for his impure thoughts about his cousin.

Père Jaquin's strong hand grasping him and shaking him affectionately by the shoulder brought him back to the present, to the tenebrous serenity of Les Jésuites with its perpetual fog of incense.

"Perhaps you should soothe your soul with charitable works," Père Jaquin said. "The Hôtel-Dieu is in desperate need of orderlies to attend to the victims of this scourge."

"I don't know," Armand said, not at all certain that his guardian would wish him to expose himself to such dangers—or even if his new freedom entitled him to make such momentous decisions about his own daily activities.

"Good!" said the priest. "I shall take you there myself and introduce you to the sisters. Shall we say tomorrow morning?"

Armand smiled weakly, vaguely hoping that he would find some excuse not to be able to go to the hospital and face those poor, dying souls. Then, as he remained in the sacred place and prayed, he gradually changed his mind about Père Jaquin's plan. Perhaps demonstrating such courage and sensitivity would do more to recommend him to his musical cousin than a smart equipage and independent means—which so far had impinged little if at all on her sensibilities. He would send Anne a note in the morning telling her about his new purpose in life.

In any case, he would try to find some way to believe it was all to the good. Perhaps he would find a doctor at the Hôtel Dieu who was not too busy to examine him and see what was wrong with his stomach to make it hurt so often.

*   *   *

The volume of Byron that Liszt had given Anne at her first lesson did little to enlighten her concerning the music she was playing. She returned it to her teacher at the end of her second lesson with thanks and was trying to work up the courage to question him as to why exactly the works of the English poet were supposed to have any bearing on the music of Beethoven or Chopin when he gave her another book of poetry, this time by Lamartine. She was about to protest that she wished he would explain a little more what he expected her to gain by it, but something in his expression stopped her. As he pressed the slim volume into her hand, Anne could have sworn that he cast a quick glance in the direction of her benefactress and that, had they been alone in the room, he would have told her something important, something not for the ears of Madame d'Agoult.

In the carriage on the way back from the quai Malaquais she turned the pages of the Lamartine idly, musing over what Liszt could have wanted to tell her, giving free rein to her fantasy in that regard, when she came upon a piece of paper tucked between two pages where a certain phrase had been marked: "Grief knits two hearts in closer bonds than happiness ever can; and common sufferings are far stronger links than common joys."

Having never received such a thing before, Anne did not at first realize that she was in possession of a secret note. She unfolded the paper and read the words written in Liszt's spiky scrawl.

Amie secrète de mon coeur,
I can hardly bear to be so close to you and not be able to tell you what I feel. Dare I hope that, despite your gentle reserve, you return my feelings in some measure? But I must not hope. Only let me express my own desires to you, and I shall be happy for now.

The note went on in that vein for a few more sentences. Anne was dumbfounded, and deeply thrilled. How could it be that her own feelings were mirrored so ardently by Liszt's? No wonder he had looked at her in such an odd way at her lesson.

"Mademoiselle, we have arrived."

Victor's deep voice startled Anne. She dropped the book, only managing to scoop it up off the floor and insert the folded note between its pages before he opened the door of the carriage for her. She tried to act as if nothing extraordinary had happened as she entered the house, praying she would not encounter her father on her way to her room. She needed time to recover from the shock of knowing that the object of her dreams appeared himself to have similar hopes regarding her. He had not asked for an answer, so Anne was spared the difficulty of deciding what she would say. But now she had yet another reason to look forward to her lessons, hardly daring to believe Liszt could hold her in such high regard, but hoping nonetheless that she would find another message hidden in the pages of whatever book of poetry he lent her.

After that first one, there were two more secret letters, and each time he had handed her the book that hid one of the notes, Liszt had done or said something that referred to Madame d'Agoult. If he was so afraid of discovery, Anne thought, why would he take such a risk? Although she knew Marie would be upset if she and Liszt declared their love for one another, surely he would not be the worst match she could make.

Well, she thought, perhaps he would be. She could not imagine trying to convince the marquis to sanction their union. Not with his professed antipathy toward artists and musicians, however famous and talented. But it did not matter. Anne had no desire to think ahead to such boring practicalities as marriage. Her dreams always ended with earnestly clasped hands; deep, tender gazes; and occasionally, a delicate, respectful kiss.

The most recent letter Anne had received pushed the limits of her fantasy, however, by taking matters to another level. Her pleasant daydream of love that made the hours when she was not at Madame d'Agoult's pass so swiftly could no longer remain in the realm of her own mind. This letter had a desperate tone, not only expressing Liszt's feelings in plain language but begging her for a response.

> *My dearest hope,*
> *You must meet me alone, or I shall die. Would you be responsible for such an act? I beg you to give me one word, one indication that I might yet live.*

Even Anne, with her limited experience of worldly matters, knew that she either must answer it or inform Madame d'Agoult of the correspondence and end it.

Anne did not debate for long. She ignored the warning image of her mother that crowded her mind as she took out a sheet of paper and wrote her reply by the light of the bedside candle.

> *Just say where and when. I will contrive to meet you.*

She placed the sheet between the same two pages where the other note had been secreted. The next day she would return the book to Liszt. What would happen after that, Anne could not begin to imagine.

Thirteen

~~~⚬~~~

*Only in the presence of true art can two minds meet. Let ours inter-
mingle as equals this evening. Meet me outside the opera house before
the performance. Wear a mask—it is* Don Giovanni, *Mozart's greatest
work.*

Franz had to rewrite the letter over three times before it lay perfectly
on the page. He found it so much more difficult to express himself in
words than in music. Yet if anyone could make him aspire to poetry,
it would be Marie.

Marie, Marie, Marie!

He wondered if she would ever allow him to call her by her Chris-
tian name. He still did not dare write it on any of the notes he penned
to her in secret, and which he now had proof that his student had successfully delivered to her. Eugène had awakened some doubts in him
and pointed out the flaws in his method of seduction, but Franz had
thought it would be the best way to communicate his feelings without
involving any of the servants—whose gossip would most certainly have
found its way to the wrong ears in time—or to approach Marie directly
and expose her to scandal in that manner. He cared too deeply for
Marie to risk her reputation for anything but the soundest assurance of
her undying love. When he finally received that much-awaited reply, he

tossed it in the fire in his little stove as soon as he finished reading it, despite the fact that he yearned to keep it and treasure it forever.

Now he held in his hands the letter that would not only determine his future happiness but that must be read before this evening, the evening of the opera, if it was to have its desired consequences. Anne's next lesson was not until tomorrow. Franz puzzled over how to deliver his message to Marie. Perhaps now that she had answered him, it would be all right simply to address it to her. The thought of writing her name on the envelope thrilled him. So much had happened since his first, chaste inquiry suggesting the lessons with Mademoiselle de Barbier-Chouant that he was not sure he would be able to hold the pen still enough to do it. Besides, everything had worked so well thus far. Surely there would be a way to continue this filtered seduction. Part of Franz relished the wheels within wheels, the very cleverness of the entire plan, that kept him and the object of his love at a respectful distance until the moment when they would be ready to break through all the boundaries of propriety and etiquette.

"Of course!" Franz exclaimed. Anne, who spent the days between her lessons practicing on the countess's fine pianoforte, would be there even if he was not. He could address the letter to her and put a second note inside explaining what she should do and the importance of ensuring that the enclosed message reached the right hands that same day.

Franz quickly did as he planned, finished dressing, and dashed down the stairs to find some urchin in pursuit of a few sous to deliver his communication.

It should be Mercury himself, on wings of gossamer, flying through the air to carry out the business of the gods.

All Franz could think about was the coming evening. At last to be with Marie!

The morning after she had hidden her own note to Liszt within the pages of a book, Anne descended to the small parlor in a state of such excitement and euphoria that she hardly noticed her father's stern countenance. Although she did not have a lesson that day, and therefore she would be forced to wait before receiving an answer from her teacher, Anne looked forward to a day of happy anticipation practicing the piano at Marie's. She was therefore all the more taken aback when the marquis snapped his newspaper shut and, without even bidding her good morning, said, "We'll visit Monsieur de Barbier on Saturday. He's quite recovered from his illness, he assures me."

Illness? Anne thought. *What illness?* Then she remembered that some indisposition had been his reason for ceasing their daily drives. She instantly felt sorry that she had been too preoccupied by recent events to notice his absence. Once she had written her brief note wishing him well, she had breathed a sigh of relief that his sickness coincided with her changed daily routine and she need not rely upon his generosity to enable her to practice the piano at Marie's. After that, he had written her once or twice to tell her about his daily activities, which included helping out at the Hôtel-Dieu, but had not mentioned again that he continued unwell.

The marquis waved a letter in the air. Anne recognized Armand's tentative handwriting. Of course he would write to his guardian, she thought, feeling a little stupid for not realizing that before, and wondering what he had said about their supposed courtship.

"And I'll wager he'll be pleased to see you look so cheerful. If he has a pianoforte, you can play for him." The marquis stood, preparing to take himself and the missive from his cousin to the library for the day.

"Papa," Anne said, stopping him at the door of the parlor, wanting to beg him please to send Armand their regrets. But she did not know what excuse to offer for her reluctance to visit their cousin, so instead she said, "Won't you let me practice here, on Mama's piano?"

The marquis's face froze for an instant. Anne shrank back, half expecting him to raise his hand and strike her. But instead, he flared his nostrils and looked down at her. "Leave well alone, Mademoiselle."

Anne's father did not need to land a blow with his bony hand. He possessed the remarkable ability to throw an unkind glance at her and hit her squarely in the face, so that she felt it like a slap. Now, by provoking his wrath, she had spoiled her opportunity to dissuade him from insisting on this visit. What if her father put Armand in a position of having to answer a direct question about his feelings toward her? A part of Anne felt rather guilty for having made a liar of him to his guardian. She sensed that, despite his protestations to the contrary, Armand was enough smitten with her to have overlooked the potential consequences of his malleability. And now, Marie's words on the subject came back to her. What would her father do to both of them if he found out things between herself and Armand were never likely to end in matrimony?

Her mind troubled with new worries, Anne climbed into the coach and started toward Marie's as planned. She and her cousin had not spent much time together, yet they had become friends of a sort. She felt especially guilty for ignoring his one hint that his health was not all it should be. And now, she thought as she rocked back and forth in the carriage, she was faced with a dilemma. How could she avoid this undesirable visit? Armand had spoken from time to time about his ambition to enter the priesthood. If her father had any idea about this, it could destroy the delicate balance she had achieved between appearing to acquiesce to her father's wishes and actually behaving precisely as she wanted to. Although he never said it, and Marie did not speak of it, Anne suspected that the only reason the marquis permitted her the freedom and luxury of her days with Madame d'Agoult was because he thought the countess would help her gain accomplishments that would in some way make her more attractive to Armand. The last thing she wanted to be was more attractive to Armand. Arriving with the marquis at his lodgings, got up in her finery, then playing some waltz or mazurka on the piano might succeed only in giving him the idea that she had changed her mind about their relationship. Anne had little desire to torment him by giving him false hopes.

Deciding that there was no time for an exchange of letters on the subject, and that she must find a way to speak with Armand before she and her father descended on him, Anne knocked the handle of her parasol on the ceiling of the carriage. Victor pulled the horses up and leaned over to hear the instructions she called out of the open window.

"The Marais, rue Saint Antoine," she said.

"But Countess," Victor replied, "your father does not want me to convey you anywhere but to the quai Malaquais."

"I am greatly concerned about Monsieur Armand and would like to ascertain that his health has indeed improved." Anne pleaded with her eyes. She knew the old coachman would never refuse her.

"Very well, mademoiselle." He breathed his words out with a heavy sigh.

As soon as they crossed to the Île du Palais, Anne put her scented handkerchief to her nose and did not remove it for the rest of the drive. The odor that hung vaguely in the background of every other scent one inhaled in Saint Germain overpowered her in the neighborhood of the Hôtel-Dieu, and it hardly abated on the other side of the river. All along the sides of the rue Saint Antoine stood carts waiting to take the sick and dying poor to a hospital or to be buried. Even the horses walked with their heads drooping in this neighborhood, as though they too mourned the dead. To her surprise and horror, Anne soon saw the familiar contours of Les Jésuites on her right and gathered that they must be very near Armand's apartment. Could it be that her cousin lived surrounded by death?

Victor pulled up the horses in front of a house opposite the Jesuit church and descended to knock on the door, covering his nose and mouth with his gloved hand. Anne watched out of the window as a servant answered. She could not hear what they said because she did not want to lower the window, but the servant retreated inside the house and shut the door behind him, and Victor returned to the carriage. He tapped on the glass. Anne pulled the window down as little as she could to hear what he had to say.

"Monsieur de Barbier is not at home, and the man does not expect his master to return until after midnight. He stays all day at the Hôtel-Dieu to nurse the sick." Victor paused before continuing, apparently debating whether or not to convey the valet's entire message. "He said if we went there, we might find him. But surely . . ."

Clearly the coachman hoped she would give up the attempt and return to the safer neighborhood of Saint Germain. The countess expected her by now. Anne was sorely tempted to forget her desire to talk to Armand before Saturday and take her chances, but the idea of coming to this neighborhood with her father, having to take tea and be polite when she could barely stand to breathe, distressed her even more than the prospect of a brief visit to the Hôtel-Dieu. "Let us go there, then, and find him. I'll not stay long." She snapped the window up and latched it shut before Victor had a chance to discourage her.

The day after his visit to Gardive, Pierre had walked to the rue du Barq in Saint Germain to see if he could find the house of the anonymous cholera victim. He found it to be a sad old street, and aside from a few abandoned artisans' cottages there had been only a structure that looked like a crumbling convent, or some such relic from the past.

He intended to return and make inquiries in the neighborhood, but he had little time to do so. In addition to keeping up with his studies, Pierre found himself pressed into service night after night at the Hôtel-Dieu. Georges, exhausted from the intensity of the epidemic's worst weeks, had remained sickly. Pierre could only persuade him to stay at home by promising that he would serve in his place. Thus he took night shifts that often stretched into the next morning. He was lucky to steal an hour or two to sleep, and the unreality of his routine had begun to seem disturbingly normal.

"Dr. Talon," said a diminutive monk who was every bit as pale as the sick people he attended, "you are wanted in the chapel."

Normally none of the nurses and doctors had much time to say anything, except to shout out "Dead!" or "Carts!" so when the monk asked for his attention, he gave it immediately. Pierre placed his water bucket on the floor of the ward and signaled to a nun, who was busy mopping up the filth, to take his place. He found after a time that he could bear the smells, and he had developed a sort of routine of running to the pump, filling the bucket, and trying to give as many patients as he could a measure of relief in the form of a drink of water. One night—Pierre counted—sixteen people died in the same bed, one after the other.

This morning, however, was a little quieter. The busy times generally came in waves. He followed the short monk out of the ward and down a corridor. The patients' moans faded as they penetrated deeper into the ancient building. The monk opened the chapel door, and a cloud of incense assaulted Pierre, making him cough and stinging his eyes.

"Please, he is over here."

Only a few votive candles and one long taper illuminated the vaulted space. In the dim light, Pierre could just make out the shape of a man lying on his side on the stone floor. His breathing was rapid and raspy, and his left hand clutched at the smooth paving slabs as though he were trying to pick up the fine layer of dust that covered them. Pierre knelt next to the man, who seemed extremely young. He had a fever, that was clear, but his symptoms were not quite the same as those of the patients in the wards.

"Has he vomited?"

The monk said yes. "But no bloody flux, not like the cholera."

So he too had noticed a difference. Pierre took a closer look at the gentleman. He wore a fine linen shirt and long trousers made of good English wool. This was no vagrant who had wandered off the street. "How did he get here?"

"He works in the wards, like you. Only he collapsed today. I brought him here, thinking he was just tired, but then . . ."

The young man had pulled his right knee toward his chest, and his left hand covered the lower portion of the right side of his abdomen.

Pierre rolled the young man gently onto his back, and the fellow moaned, again pulling his knee up. Pierre ran his hand lightly over the place the gentleman covered. He could feel an unmistakable lump. The poor fellow gave a great cry of pain and sat up, vomiting all over the monk in the process.

It must be hernia inguinalis, *blocking the intestine.* Judging by the extremity of the fellow's suffering, Pierre thought that quite possibly it involved some mortification of the omentum as well as a dropping of the intestines toward the groin. He went through the symptoms and treatments quickly in his mind, as he did when trying to remember the answers for an examination. An entire lecture had been devoted to hernias and how to treat them. When they became this bad, there was only one choice.

Pierre had witnessed an operation that would remove the mortified tissue and replace the intestine. It would be dangerous, but if it succeeded, the gentleman might well recover. "He will die unless someone operates," Pierre said to the monk. "Are any of the surgeons here?"

"Yes, but everyone is busy with the cholera," he said.

Pierre bit his lower lip. "Can't you find someone who could at least take a look at him?"

"There is no one besides you."

If he didn't do something soon, this poor fellow would be beyond aid. Pierre decided he had nothing to lose by acting. "Help me take him to the operating theater."

With some difficulty, Pierre and the monk lifted the writhing gentleman and took him to the room used for surgery. In its center was a high table, and on one wall stood a well-stocked instrument cabinet. Pierre noticed with relief that the hospital was equipped with a good set of round-edged knives, probe scissors, catheters, gorgets, and forceps. The young man's moans became louder and more desperate. They laid him on the table so that his legs bent at the knees and dangled. Pierre removed the soft leather shoes from his patient's feet and placed them by the door, and unlaced his trousers to expose the hernia. *He is hardly a man at all,* he thought, putting his age at sixteen years, no more. The monk restrained the patient with the straps provided for that use. Pierre did not like to think about inflicting pain on this helpless fellow.

After removing his jacket and rolling up the sleeves of his loose shirt, Pierre paused for a moment to collect his thoughts. He believed he could operate, if the monk would stay with him to bring him the instruments he needed. He had a clear image of the procedure in his mind. But cutting into a man who was awake and in pain—he knew it would be a different matter from practicing on a cadaver. "Is there any opium in the hospital?" he asked, not expecting an affirmative reply, but to his surprise, the monk touched the side of his nose with his finger and scurried away. In the meantime, Pierre began a close examination of the area. The hernia was exceedingly inflamed. He prayed that the intestines had not become gangrenous.

The young man was running a high fever and shivered violently. If he did not stop, his trembling would make it difficult to cut neatly. Perhaps some sedation would help. When the monk came back with a little brown cake of opium wrapped in paper, Pierre sent him for a basin of water and a cloth. "Can you understand me?" Pierre said to the gentleman, whose eyes were open but unfocused. "If you can take a bit of this, it will ease your pain." He crumbled up some of the opium and put it in the fellow's mouth. To his relief, the man started to chew slowly and swallowed. It would be difficult to tell if the opium would have enough effect to make the surgery possible, but in the circumstances there was nothing more he could do.

As soon as the monk returned with the basin of water, Pierre readied himself for the task ahead. To his relief, the young man did not shake quite so much since he had taken the opium. "Give him more of this if he starts to scream," Pierre said, handing the packet to the monk.

He took the round-ended knife in his hand, holding it firmly but not gripping it, and, finding a point between the rings of the abdominal muscles above the tumor, made a sure, skillful cut.

The blood surprised him the most. The blood of a cadaver does not flow freely and warm. Pierre started to call out for help but stopped himself in time. With no one to come to his aid, he would only frighten both the monk and his patient. Trying now to stop the shaking of his own hands, Pierre mopped up as best he could to see. Thankfully, although the fellow continued to moan piteously, he did not scream. Before long the concentration required to solve a difficult problem absorbed Pierre, and slowly and steadily, he cut the peritoneum.

As Pierre suspected, the omentum had fallen as well and was necrotic in one place. He called for some thread to make a ligature so that the fellow would not hemorrhage, tied off the intestine, and cut away the mortified flesh before reattaching the vital organs. Then carefully, using his fingers and a blunt probe, Pierre dilated the wound and inserted the intestine back to its proper place. "Sutures, please," Pierre said to the monk, who brought him the needle and some lengths of thread. Breathing deeply and evenly, hoping that his hands would remain steady, Pierre stitched up the dilated wound so that it would contain the intestines. He had found no evidence of gangrene.

All that remained was to close the incision. The monk gave Pierre another threaded needle, and the difficult part of the procedure over, he quickly, methodically made sure he sewed far enough away from the edge of the incision so the skin would not tear, thus closing the wound his knife had created in the gentleman's lower abdomen. To his great relief, the bleeding abated.

"He swooned, Doctor," the monk said.

After Pierre had mopped the closed incision with the now blood-tinged water, he felt the young man's pulse. It had slowed to a normal rate. He gently patted the man's cheek, praying that he would revive and that the stress of the operation would not have killed him.

To Pierre's great relief, the young man's eyes fluttered open.

"Are you in pain still?"

"Yes," he said, "but it's different." He closed his eyes and drifted off once more into a drugged sleep.

Pierre took a deep breath. He had performed his first surgery. The young fellow would have to be closely watched, and there was every possibility of infection. But if the wound healed properly and did not fester, he could count the procedure as successful. The monk smiled at him, and Pierre turned to survey the mess in the theater and help clean it up.

He raised his eyes. The probe he had in his hand clattered noisily to the stone floor when he caught sight of a figure standing in the open doorway.

At first, he shook his head and blinked, certain that the anxiety of performing the operation had created a hallucination. But the person framed in the doorway with her eyes wide and frightened and her hand over her mouth was none other than the countess de Barbier-Chouant.

Fourteen

Victor stopped the coach by the quai and helped Anne down from the carriage. He led her through the mayhem of carts arriving and patients being carried into the wards, where many cots held two or three cholera victims each. They had to walk through one of the congested wards to find someone who looked to be some sort of administrator.

Victor approached the fellow, reaching out a hand but not quite daring to touch him. He settled for clearing his throat rather loudly. When the gentleman looked around, the coachman said, "My mistress is looking for Monsieur de Barbier."

"I don't have time to read all the names of the victims. Look through the wards for yourself," answered the official-looking person, clearly trying to get them out of his way as quickly as possible so he could return to more important tasks.

"Monsieur de Barbier is no victim," Anne said, stepping forward. "He helps on the wards. It is important that I find him." Anne hated herself in that instant for believing her concerns so vital that she would take someone away from helping these desperately ill people, whose screams and moans echoed off the stone walls of the hospital.

It was worse, much worse, than watching all the hearses on the way to the cemetery. One woman screeched out in a way that brought her own mother's sufferings vividly to mind. She closed her eyes. But she had come this far, had taken this step, and felt it necessary to continue until her business was concluded.

A doctor who happened to pass by when she mentioned her cousin's name stopped. "I know Barbier," he said. "He comes every day to be of assistance. I think you'll find him this way."

The doctor led them along a corridor and into another ward. He spoke quietly to someone there, who pointed through a door that led away from the rooms lined with beds where the cholera victims lay. The cloying scent of incense wafted out of a chapel as they passed. Incense normally made Anne queasy, but she found it a welcome relief from the foul odors emanating from the rest of the building.

After walking a bit, they encountered a monk hurrying in the direction of a small wooden door. In his hands he carried a basin of water and a clean cloth.

"Have you seen Barbier?" the doctor asked.

"He's through here," the monk said, jerking his head in the direction of the door, which he passed through himself and then pushed closed immediately behind him.

"What's in that room?" Anne asked.

"It's the operating theater," answered the doctor.

At that moment a nun poked her head out of a door back in the direction from which they had come. "Doctor!" she called, and gestured toward Anne's escort.

He bowed and left them, hurrying away to answer the summons.

What, Anne thought, *would Armand be doing in an operating theater?* He was not a surgeon.

All at once, the perception that her cousin was himself in peril of his life rushed into Anne's heart. Her fear and her distaste for the place vanished, and ignoring Victor's entreaties to remain where she was, Anne dashed forward and opened the door.

The tallow candles gave off a smoky light. Blood dripped into a spreading red puddle from a table that bore the stretched-out body of a young man, his legs bent at the knees and hanging off the end, his lower torso covered by a blood-stained towel. The monk they had seen before wrung out a cloth, which he gave to a tall gentleman in his shirtsleeves who pressed it against the patient's face and said something to him quietly.

The person standing up was too tall to be Armand, which left only one possibility from among those before her. She covered her mouth with her hand just as the doctor turned around.

At first, the fellow froze, letting a metal instrument slip from his grasp. He took a step or two forward toward her, looked at his bloody hands, and stopped.

"Countess," he said. "I—" The doctor, who seemed familiar to her, interrupted himself. He shifted his gaze to over her shoulder, where Anne could feel the protective presence of Victor. "Please take the countess to the chapel. I will meet her there in a moment," he said.

Anne knew she should have been revolted by the scene in front of her, but she could feel nothing, except the sensation of being a visitor from the heavens looking over someone's shoulder, or a spectator at a play. Victor took her to the chapel. She sat in one of the wooden chairs facing the altar. It never even occurred to her to pray.

In a few minutes, the tall doctor came in, bowed to her, and introduced himself as Pierre Talon.

"How do you know my name?" Anne said.

"I saw you on the third of April, at the Salle Wauxhall. You were sitting in Madame d'Agoult's box, and you swooned."

Of course! Anne now recognized the young gentleman who had been so kind to her. He looked different in shirtsleeves and waistcoat. But there were more important matters to discuss than the coincidence of meeting again. "My cousin, Monsieur de Barbier. What did you do to him?"

Now Doctor Talon looked shocked. "That young fellow is your cousin? I confess, it was an emergency, and I did not inquire as to his name."

"Is he dead?" Here, in the chapel, away from the lurid scene of the operating theater, Anne was released from her stupefaction and began to comprehend what she had seen. It had been Armand lying there, bloodied. Her heart raced.

"No, not dead, although he might have been if—"

Doctor Talon stopped short, and Anne understood that he did not want to congratulate himself on saving her cousin's life. "It seems, Doctor Talon, that you make a habit of coming to the rescue of strangers. May I see him?"

"His incision is being dressed now. It may take some time."

Even in the subdued light of the chapel, Anne could see the color seep into the man's cheeks. It made him look much too young to have operated on her cousin. "I'll wait," she said. Talon bowed to her again and left.

"Beg pardon, mademoiselle," Victor said, "but this is no place for a lady." The coachman stood next to her, crushing the brim of his hat in his hands.

"I must stay and see that Monsieur de Barbier is being cared for. You would do me a great kindness if you would go to Madame d'Agoult's apartment and tell her I will not visit today. After that, call back here for me. I'm sure I shall have seen Monsieur de Barbier by then."

Victor was clearly torn between his desire to leave the hospital and his obligation to make sure the countess came to no harm. He hesitated.

"Please, I shall be perfectly well here. Everyone is much too busy to notice me."

Once Victor left her alone in the chapel, Anne leaned her forehead against the back of the chair in front of her and tried to pray.

Soon after the marquis's coachman had given her the news that Anne would not come to her that day, Marie heard the bell again. A moment later, Adèle entered with a letter addressed to Anne. Marie took the letter over to her favorite little desk by the balcony over-looking the river. It was in an envelope but not sealed. The flap of the envelope had simply been tucked in so that the contents would not fall out. She recognized Franz Liszt's handwriting immediately.

She held the letter up to the light. The envelope was of inferior quality, and so she could see the two folded pieces of paper it con-tained. Why would Liszt send Anne a letter when he would see her the next day at a lesson and could easily have conveyed his message to her then? She laid it aside and went back to her own work, finish-ing a long missive to her sister-in-law in Germany. But Marie found herself constantly distracted by the presence of the mysterious note for Anne. Had the countess arrived as originally planned, she would have opened it by now. Perhaps Monsieur Liszt wrote to say that he must cancel tomorrow's lesson. Yet surely he would convey that information directly to Marie herself.

Marie was not given to prying unnecessarily, but she had taken on a heavy responsibility when she convinced the marquis to allow her to groom his daughter for marriage. It was unseemly, in any case, for eli-gible ladies to receive letters from gentlemen—not to mention some-one with Liszt's background and reputation. If it were fifteen years from now and such a letter had arrived for her own daughter, she would not hesitate to open it—or at least, to make her daughter open it in her presence and read it aloud to her.

That, thought Marie, would be the best course of action. When Anne came the next day, she would ask her to do just that.

After she had finished one letter, she wrote another to her mother at Croissy, enclosing two notes for her own little children. Marie planned to visit soon but did not want them to return to Paris until the cholera was no longer a danger. Once all her letters were sealed and placed on the table in the vestibule so that Adèle would take them to be franked later that afternoon, Marie returned to the parlor to fetch the book of Shakespeare plays she had been reading. She was practicing her English. Yet her eye once again caught sight of the troublesome letter for Anne and distracted her. She stood and looked at it for a long while. Then in one quick movement, she took up the envelope, untucked the flap, and removed its contents. A crushed dried flower that had been nested inside one of the pieces of paper tumbled out of its folds and lay at Marie's feet.

Meet me outside the opera house before the performance. Wear a mask . . .

Marie's heart beat hard with indignation. Liszt was making an assignation with his young student! She removed the second note from the envelope and read it as well.

Countess,
I suggest you say that I have instructed you on some detail about your technique that I forgot to mention yesterday. Otherwise, I am confident that you know what to do about the enclosed.

What deception! Marie thought. Recalling Anne's ability to fool her father, she now believed that the girl was not as innocent as she appeared and had been fooling her as well. What had really passed between Anne and Liszt that day when he surprised her in this very parlor, while Marie was abroad? Marie paced up and down, chewing on the sides of her fingers.

Yet she knew herself too well to believe that anger was the only cause of her distress. These notes, although not addressed to her, awakened something in Marie. She could not help but recall the passionate letters of her own youth, the intensity with which she lived each day in expectation of more words of desire and love. How many such secret notes had she opened and read without her parents' knowledge? By comparison, her life since that time had been barren and unfulfilling. Only art held any solace for her.

Marie read the first letter again, this time imagining how it would feel if the pianist's words were addressed to her and not his student. They brought forward feelings she had fought to suppress since before her marriage, opening her heart once more to yearning, longing, but most of all, desire. Not for a man exactly, but for the feeling of love, the desperate, all-consuming ache of believing that one's entire being is dependent on the words, the looks, the touch of that special one, that *him* who fills your dreams with forbidden fantasies. By the time she reached the end of the letter again, she was breathless, and she had decided precisely what she should do. Anne could hardly leave her father's house to meet Liszt, and so she, Marie d'Agoult, would go in her place. He had said to wear a mask. A mask and veils would be perfect, she thought. Marie was a little taller than Anne but equally slim, and beneath a veil, the slightly darker color of her hair would not be apparent. She could accomplish three goals in taking this bold step: she would prevent Anne from compromising herself, discourage the young man from continuing his pursuit, and most of all, she would relive a little of her own, glorious youth, with its tragic, forbidden love.

Although Armand regained consciousness and Anne was able to speak a few words with him, his fever had returned.

"Countess," Talon said, "he must not stay here. There is too much sickness, and the doctors will be unable to care for him."

Anne knew that the young doctor spoke the truth. Yet she did not want to send Armand back to his own apartment, with only a manservant to attend him. She had one choice. He would have to come to the hôtel Barbier. Anne made the decision with a heavy heart. She was certain that, in some way, this change would put an end to the charmed times she had recently enjoyed. Her father would not long remain in a state of ignorance concerning her true feelings, and his hopes of marrying her off to his cousin so that she would no longer be a burden to him would fade. She did not know how this knowledge would affect him and was a little frightened by the thought.

But she could not leave her cousin to languish in pain and peril. "I will take him to the hôtel Barbier, in my carriage," she said. Talon nodded.

As soon as Victor returned from conveying the message to Madame d'Agoult, the doctor and the monk prepared Armand to be transported to her home.

"What must I do?" she said. "How shall I care for Monsieur de Barbier?"

Pierre looked down into Anne's frightened, questioning eyes. His desire to take her in his arms and comfort her was so strong that he put his hands behind his back. But he had decided that the depth of her concern for her cousin indicated more than mere family ties. Doubtless she had feelings for him after all, despite what Madame d'Agoult had said. His disappointment was acute, yet Pierre still glowed with the feeling of power that performing the surgery had given him. "Give your cousin water and broth only at first, for at least a week. Then gradually, as you would if you were introducing a baby to solid food, let him eat what he likes. He should be back to normal, if the incision heals properly, in about eight weeks."

"And his . . . wound. Who shall change his bandages?"

Yes, Pierre thought, it would hardly do for the refined, delicate countess to dress a wound in such an intimate location, even if she were eventually to marry the young gentleman. He looked up at the burly coachman, who shrank back and shifted his eyes away. Clearly the fellow did not feel equal to the task. Before he had a chance to consider the full implication of his words, Pierre said, "I shall come myself, at a time that is convenient for you, and tend to your cousin. I'll show one of the servants how to manage it when I am not there." The look of gratitude on the countess's face once more distracted Pierre from thinking only about the welfare of his patient.

"You would do that? How kind you are!" she said. "I am at home until eleven every morning. Would that be convenient for you?"

Even if it had been the least convenient time in the world, Pierre would have found a way to be there. "The hôtel Barbier: where is it?" he asked.

Anne gave him the address. Rue du Barq. Pierre could hardly believe it. He must have passed by the house when he went there to look for the home of the anonymous cholera victim. The only large structure he had seen with that address was the rather crumbling building behind high walls that he assumed housed nuns or was possibly scheduled to be torn down. That must have been the hôtel Barbier. "You may expect me tomorrow."

They managed to position Barbier in the countess's chariot not too uncomfortably. His patient settled, Pierre stepped away, and the coachman cracked his whip over the horses' backs. The vehicle jolted forward. Pierre winced, imagining how painful such movement would be for Barbier. But it was best to remove him from the hospital, where neglect if not disease might kill him.

Pierre was in such a haze of euphoria that even the cries of the cholera sufferers could not depress him. He spent two more hours helping to remove the dead from the wards and bringing water to those who clung to life, then made his way back to the rue des Bernardins to cheer up Georges.

Fifteen

Thérèse and the daily girl quickly prepared the largest guest room for Monsieur de Barbier. Victor carried him up the stairs and Anne followed after, shedding her bonnet, shawl, and gloves as she went. As soon as she saw Armand settled, she went to her room to change her clothes. All the putrid smells of the hospital clung to her, and she could not get them out of her nostrils. By the time Thérèse came to attend to her, she stood completely naked in the center of her room, shivering.

"You must have a hot bath," Thérèse said, as she reached for Anne's clothes.

"Don't touch them!" Anne snapped. "Bring a basket, wear gloves, burn them."

Thérèse cast a worried glance in Anne's direction. "The marquis would not take kindly to knowing you tossed away the dress he just saw fit to have made for you."

"You mean, especially since he has not yet paid for it? I don't care," Anne said through her now-chattering teeth. She did not feel cold, but the enormity of all that had recently passed, of Armand's delicate state, and of her own temerity in discovering him and bringing him back to the hôtel Barbier, overwhelmed her.

The maid fetched a peignoir from the wardrobe and put it around Anne's shoulders. Once she satisfied herself that Anne was a little warmer, she opened the door to the dressing room and draped the copper tub that sat ready in its midst with towels so that Anne would not scrape herself while she bathed. "I'll send the girl up with water and a basket for the clothes."

Anne hardly remembered how she passed the time before immersing herself in the soothing warmth of the lavender-scented bathwater. She closed her eyes and nearly fell asleep while Thérèse scrubbed her back and scolded her for going to the Hôtel-Dieu, where she might have become ill herself and died.

When her bath was finished, Anne put on her night clothes and climbed into bed. The housemaid had brought up a tray with bread and broth on it, but Anne could not think of eating. She was simply too exhausted to keep her eyes open any longer.

"Your father told me he wanted to see you," Thérèse said, tucking the bedclothes in around her. "I'll tell him you're indisposed. It can easily wait until morning."

"Thérèse," Anne said, stopping the housekeeper on her way to the door. "Please, see that my cousin is resting comfortably."

Anne fell asleep before Thérèse shut the door behind her.

Marie had not been to the opera since before the cholera epidemic. Several of the performers had died, and every night they made last-minute substitutions. It occurred to her only after she was on her way there in her carriage to wonder whether the performance would be any good.

She deliberately arrived a little in advance of the appointed hour so that she could hide herself away and watch for Liszt. Her heart pounded like a schoolgirl's, and she had to keep reminding herself that she should be very angry with the pianist for putting her charge in such a compromising position. As she watched the members of the audience descend from their coaches dressed in their finest, she noted that many had also chosen to mask themselves. It seemed an odd thing to do, but as Marie listened to the snippets of conversation from people who walked past, she began to understand.

"What a clever idea, to have a masked ball during Don Giovanni's party!"

"The performers themselves are supposed to join us."

Ah, Marie thought. So Liszt must have known that, and Anne would have danced with him. He would have held his young student in his arms and whirled her about among revelers made bold by the conceit of a mask. And now, would she stay? It had been her intention to reveal herself to Liszt at an early moment and chastise him for jeopardizing the reputation of an unmarried lady. But Marie was seized with the desire to see how it felt to have those long, delicate fingers curled into the small of her back and feel their warmth holding her hand. Would he, she wondered, notice that his partner was not the countess Anne? How well did he know the contours of his young student's body, how impressed upon his memory was the size and shape of her hand? Most of all, had he received any encouragement from Anne? Clearly the letter had not been his first.

The crowds had thinned. Aside from a few latecomers who hurried through the doors, everyone was inside the theater and there was still no sign of Liszt. Marie began to fear that possibly she had entirely misjudged the Hungarian pianist, and that in addition to his provocative behavior, he had a cruel streak that would entice a young lady to expose herself to censure and then compound her embarrassment by not arriving to meet her as he had promised. She was on the point of leaving, furious at herself for being taken in, when a fiacre pulled up and stopped a few feet from where she waited. She saw the familiar elongated, angular form of Franz Liszt descend. He too was masked, but the black silk band with two holes for his eyes could do little to disguise his distinctive appearance. Marie had no doubt that everyone who saw him would know it was he.

He looked around slowly, obviously trying not to appear to be searching for someone. Could it be that he was not confident his student would be there? Perhaps things had not progressed quite as far as she thought. Marie contemplated slipping away without making her presence known to him. It's not too late, she thought, to back out of her plan. She could stay in her hiding place and Liszt would simply assume that Anne had been either afraid or unable to come for some reason. It would be entirely like him to attend the opera alone.

But as the pianist turned to enter the theater, Marie could not bear the thought of missing this opportunity to examine Liszt at close quarters while concealing her identity from him. She stepped out of the shadows and, without saying a word, placed her gloved hand on his arm.

"Ah! Countess!" he said. "I hardly dared hope—"

Marie put her finger to her lips. She must not speak, or he would surely discover she was not the young countess. Together they entered the theater and took two seats toward the front of the stalls. The concentrated odor of cologne and sweat, her own camphor sachet, and the closeness of her veils made Marie feel a little lightheaded. She was, in some measure, not at all herself that evening.

The orchestra struck up the overture. Although Marie was familiar with the music from looking over the score and from playing through a piano transcription by Mozart himself, she had never attended a performance of that particular work at the opera before. The demonic power of the opening chords shook her, and soon she was deeply involved in the music and barely conscious that Liszt sat by her. She leaned forward in her seat. One moment she let Donna Anna's tortured, passionate music transport her, and in the next was caught up completely in Donna Elvira's ambivalent love. The unrepentant Don Giovanni bore too close a resemblance to Monsieur Liszt, she thought. But, like those of the two ladies Don Giovanni wronged, her own feelings about the pianist were as confused as they could possibly be.

At first Franz was certain Marie would not come. The moment the letter left his hands, he thought of every possible manner in which it could fail to reach its intended recipient or, once received, be treated with disdain. Or perhaps Marie simply had another engagement. In any case, as soon as he stepped out of the carriage and perceived no masked lady who might possibly have been Madame d'Agoult waiting for him, Franz was convinced that all his efforts had been for naught.

Just as he had given up hope, a veiled figure approached him from the shadows. Her lithe shape, her graceful carriage, even the way she stood a little apart at first before approaching him—all these attributes and actions combined to create an unmistakable presence. When she put her finger to her lips to silence the greeting that almost escaped his, he knew that this was she.

As they threaded through the milling crowd to find their seats, the light touch of her hand on his arm sent a shock through him. He could tell even through her glove that her hand was cool. Yet he was convinced that somewhere deep within her lay a burning hot passion.

Liszt had not wanted to call attention to them by sitting in a box where they would be on display and so had chosen seats in the center of the stalls. Since the performance was about to begin, most of the audience was already seated, and they had to clamber past half a row of masked revelers, who all whispered and tittered as they went by. Franz heard his own name more than once, but never that of Marie. He was relieved. Better that she not be exposed to public censure.

The porters snuffed the torches that lit the audience, and the music began. For a moment Franz worried that the performance would not be good. The singers were second-string. The prima donna had been stricken with cholera, and although she survived, she was still too weak to perform, and her understudy had to take the stage. It was rumored that soon the celebrated Giuditta Pasta would come to take her place, but she had not yet arrived. The best tenor had fled to Italy the moment the epidemic began, along with a bevy of costumers and *répétiteurs*. The tenor role was not as important as the two baritones, however, and so he hoped that the performance would at least be passable. If not, the audience around them might become restless and seek to divert themselves by attending to the action in the stalls rather than on the stage. This could spoil his plans.

Thankfully, it soon became clear that the performance would exceed his expectations. Yet Franz gave only half his attention to the drama that unfolded on the stage. The other half was alive to Marie's every nuance of movement, every breath and sigh. Were it not for the music itself, Franz thought he might have been able to hear her heart beat. She, on the other hand, appeared so caught up in the opera that it soon seemed that she had forgotten him. He closed his eyes in an attempt to focus himself anew on the sheer brilliance of Mozart's score.

It was no use. With his eyes closed, Franz became acutely aware of Marie's scent, a delicate fragrance he would never have been able to identify but that instantly conjured up the image of the countess in her sitting room on the quai Malaquais.

Franz passed the first two scenes in a haze of delicious anticipation. When the third scene started, he shifted slightly in his seat so that he could see Marie out of the corner of his eye without having to turn his head. This scene contained the heavenly duettino in which the don seduces the maid, Zerlina. Chopin had used the melody for his variations, the ones that had won him such acclaim when he first came to Paris—although Franz found them a little tame for his taste. Mozart had created a naïvely beautiful tune for a shocking scene. This was the moment, therefore, that Franz had selected to push things a little farther with the countess. He had to know if she would allow it. The idea of it alone sent a thrill to his loins, and he had to banish from his mind an image of the countess which he had—as yet—no right to contemplate. When he calmed himself sufficiently, Franz tensed in preparation for his small action.

> Put your hand in mine,
> Whisper a gentle yes,

The words of the master seducer had begun to work their magic on the coquettish Zerlina. Franz inched his right hand across his lap and onto the countess's, where he touched her left hand, still encased in its white kid evening glove. He felt the slightest impulse as though she would pull away from him, and in response he shifted his position a bit so that if he had to retract, no one would notice. But after that, she did not move, and little by little, he enclosed Marie's hand in his own and drew it smoothly over to his lap. Hardly moving a muscle and trying desperately to resist the temptation to look down as he did so, Franz used the fingers of his other hand to reach inside her glove and gradually work it off, just as Zerlina began her wavering answer to Don Giovanni.

I want to, and yet I don't,
My heart trembles a little,

When he succeeded in removing her glove, Franz gently stroked the countess's bare skin: her fingers, her palm, her wrist. Her hand was smooth but no longer cool. He thought he detected the slightest quickening in her breathing. If she pulled away from him, everyone sitting near them would see that her hand was exposed and guess the rest.

Away, away to enjoy the pleasures
Of an innocent love.

At the final strains of the duet, Franz, pretending to reach for his handkerchief, gently replaced the countess's hand in her own lap, laying her glove on top of it.

Marie could hardly breathe. How dare he! She was certain that Liszt was still under the impression that the lady sitting next to him was the young countess Anne. To have done such a thing to her in full view of an audience at the opera could have earned her protégée a reputation as a flirt. But what was more disturbing was the degree to which his action had unsettled her. She did not want to pull her hand away but rather wanted to lean into him, to let him kiss it, kiss *her*. How could she be so foolish?

The next scene contained the ball, and the ushers had already gathered at the ends of the rows to pull the chairs over to the side so that the audience could dance. Marie decided that this would provide her with the perfect opportunity to leave without making a scene. If the mere touch of his fingers could so unnerve her, she did not trust herself to maintain control when his arms wrapped around her in a dance. As everyone in the stalls stood and chairs were quickly removed, she whirled around and threaded her way through the thronging audience. She could hear the chorus, *"Viva la libertà,"* echoing behind her as she dashed out of the theater.

Marie had sent her carriage away and told the coachman to return when the opera was over. She asked the porter to direct her to the nearest fiacre stand, then picked up her skirts and ran, turning a corner as she heard Liszt's voice call out, "Countess!"

All night, Anne had dreams of blood and sickness, and the faces of her mother, Marie, Liszt, and the young doctor kept appearing in the most unlikely places, on dead bodies, on peasants dragging carts: she even transplanted Marie's head onto her father's bony shoulders.

She awoke when Thérèse opened the curtains in her bedroom to let in the sun. Although she felt somewhat better, Anne dreaded facing the marquis; she pulled the covers up over her face.

"Your cousin's asking for you," Thérèse said.

Armand was awake! Anne threw off her blankets and dressed as quickly as she could. She did not even lace up her shoes but ran down the corridor to the guest room where her cousin lay, with Thérèse calling after her that she would surely trip and be killed.

She found Armand propped up in bed, looking considerably better than he had the day before. "Thank heavens," she said.

Armand smiled. "It hurts abominably, but I think I will be well," he said.

"The doctor is coming later to examine you."

"I hardly remember what happened. Thérèse told me. Thank you, Anne. I . . . you surprised me. I thought you weren't so . . . I guess I misjudged you."

Anne looked down. He hadn't misjudged her. She had only come to see him for her own selfish reasons. The rest was sheer happenstance. Today, rather than dwell on all that had occurred at the hospital, she wanted nothing more than to put the whole thing out of her mind and only concern herself with Marie and her lessons with Liszt. She had every intention of leaving her cousin alone within the hour and returning to Madame d'Agoult's apartment. Yet she knew it would be callous of her to do so.

Although Armand was vastly improved, he was clearly still weak. Anne could tell that, after a few minutes, her company tired him. Not able to put it off any longer, she bid him good day and went downstairs to breakfast.

Anne barely had time to register her father's presence at the round table by the window in the small parlor before he stood and began scolding her.

"Perhaps you would care to explain to me yesterday's extraordinary events?" The marquis's voice was as sharp as a saber. He looked like a narrow, dark blot in the sunny room, and although he hardly blocked the morning light from streaming through the windows, his shadow seemed unnaturally large. She had never seen him so angry.

"I have sent you to the quai Malaquais each day assuming that you went there, because I was assured by . . . that woman . . . that it was the sensible course of action. Now I discover that yesterday you simply chose not to do as you were told. How am I to trust you?" He pressed his lips together in a thin, determined line.

He must have grilled poor Victor. Anne thought quickly. "I was worried about our cousin. It was not like him to stay away, nor was it like him to ask us to make the journey to his arrondissement, especially when the atmosphere there is insalubrious and might injure your health. Besides, I don't see what harm could have come of it."

"What harm . . . I have my reasons."

Anne waited to see if her father would continue, but he remained silent.

"Well, as you see, it is fortunate I acted as I did." She paused for effect. "Perhaps you did not realize it, but I am indeed very fond of Armand—Monsieur de Barbier." Anne tried to bring a little quaver into her voice.

"I suppose we must feed and care for him."

The marquis's voice had lost some of its edge. Anne breathed a quiet sigh. "The doctor, a fellow named Talon, will look in each day until he is quite out of danger."

At that moment, the doorbell jingled somewhere in the depths of the mansion. Both Anne and her father listened without moving, and Anne was not surprised when Julien announced the arrival of the doctor. Without waiting for her father, she hurried to the entry hall to greet the pleasant young man who had saved her cousin's life.

"Dr. Talon," Anne said, extending her hand to him, "how good of you to be so prompt."

"I must correct you, I'm afraid, mademoiselle," he said. "I am not yet a doctor. I am in my final year of medical studies at the university—that is, if I pass the examinations."

For a moment, Anne did not know what to say. A mere student had taken it upon himself to operate on her cousin. Everything appeared to have turned out for the best, and he seemed reliably solid. Nonetheless she was shocked.

"I know what you must think, but doctors are so scarce these days, and speed was of the essence. I had seen the procedure done before," he said, his voice trailing off.

"So, a make-believe doctor has taken my cousin's life into his hands?"

Anne jumped at the sound of her father's voice. She had been so engrossed in Talon's story that she had not heard the marquis approach. "And a good thing he did, if you ask me," Anne said. The desire to oppose her father overcame her scruples concerning Talon's credentials. The student smiled a broad, sincere smile at her that intensified the color of his eyes.

The marquis barely acknowledged Monsieur Talon before entering his library.

"I'll take you to Monsieur de Barbier," Anne said.

If the hôtel Barbier was a wreckage on the outside, its condition was hardly much better within. From the moment he entered, Pierre could see that the mansion was in terrible need of repair, with paint peeling on the banisters, and high above, evidence of water stains where the roof had failed to do its protective duty. Nonetheless, it seemed inconceivable that only the countess, her father, and a few servants lived in this great pile of a building. Once the unpleasant scene with the marquis ended, he followed Mademoiselle Anne up the sweeping staircase to one of the large bedchambers on the floor above. Monsieur de Barbier was asleep when he came in, and Pierre was sorry to wake him, but he would not be able to return later that day.

"He looks much better, don't you think?" the countess whispered.

Barbier stirred at the sound of her voice. His eyes opened. "You must be the doctor," he said.

"Yes, that's right," Pierre said, with a significant look at Mademoiselle de Barbier-Chouant. It would not do for the fellow to think his physician was unqualified to care for him.

"I'll leave you to your patient, Doctor," she said, putting a little extra emphasis on her final word.

Once the door closed behind her, Pierre began his examination. The incision looked tender but not festering. He changed the dressing carefully. "You are more comfortable here than at the Hôtel-Dieu, I imagine," Pierre said.

"I owe you a debt of gratitude," Barbier said.

"Don't be ridiculous."

"What is your fee for such an operation? I'm sure I can afford to pay it." Barbier drew in his breath sharply as Pierre put some salve on the wound.

"I ask no fee. I was at the Hôtel-Dieu, and I did my duty." He finished wrapping the bandage around his patient's lower torso.

Barbier reached out his hand and touched Pierre's sleeve. "I saw the way you looked at her."

Pierre stood upright, his pulse quickening. "I don't know what you mean."

"The marquis means us to marry, my cousin and I," Barbier said. "But I don't think she cares for me in that way."

Pierre opened his mouth to question the young man further but stopped when he heard the unmistakable sound of a cane tapping against a wooden floor outside the door. A moment later the marquis entered the room. Pierre turned to the old man and bowed politely.

"Here," the marquis said, approaching Pierre with a pouch dangling from his hand.

"Oh, no, sir," Pierre said, backing away from him.

"I would be ungrateful if I did not compensate you for the service you have done my family."

Pierre could not refuse the honorarium without insulting the marquis, and so he took it. The purse was surprisingly heavy.

"I should like to look in on Monsieur de Barbier—"

"There is no need. I'll have my own man care for my cousin from now on." He held his arm out in the direction of the door.

Pierre looked back and forth from the marquis to Barbier. Barbier closed his eyes. The marquis barely gave Pierre a look, treating the whole episode as if Talon were a footman, or a merchant who had brought him a length of cloth or an old book to examine. Pierre bowed once more and left the room.

Sixteen

Anne ordered the carriage and left the house before her father had a chance to stop her. She leapt from the vehicle the moment it arrived at the apartment on the quai Malaquais and could hardly wait for the footman to open the door to her. The familiar gentility of Madame d'Agoult's drawing room calmed her. After only the briefest greeting, she sat down at the piano to practice.

Although Anne had always found solace in the physical effort required to play challenging pieces, that day she felt as if all that occurred yesterday had soaked into her muscles, intensifying her practice. She had mastered the Beethoven sonata and now concentrated on polishing the nuances of expression so that she might perform it—if required—at the salon that Madame d'Agoult was going to have. They had not yet agreed on the program, but Anne was eager to test out her ability to acquit herself before an audience. Yet a part of her dreaded the event. Not because she was particularly nervous, but because it would signal the end of her apprenticeship with Marie. Madame d'Agoult had told Anne enough about the agreement she had made with the marquis that Anne understood he had put a time limit on the arrangement.

After a while, she turned to the E-major study by Chopin that Liszt had assigned her. It had not yet actually been published, and if she could play it well enough to perform at the salon, Anne herself would give the premiere—albeit a private one. This was a much more difficult piece than the Beethoven, and Anne struggled not only with its technical aspects but with its musical ones. Its form was so unusual that she could not make sense of it. At first it had seemed quite straightforward: two outer sections and a contrasting middle one. But all was not as it appeared. The piece started out with a lyrical, wistful melody and after a time, without any apparent transition but so logically that it seemed perfectly natural, twisted itself into something dissonant and raucous. Once that was spent, the wistful melody returned—again without anything much to connect the two. The entire piece was beautiful, but it mystified her, and she felt that her teacher was not pleased with her progress.

Anne had not lifted her fingers off the keys for two full hours when Marie cleared her throat politely and suggested that it was time for luncheon. The kitchen maid brought in the tray with cold meats and bread, an aspic, and a pot of tea. Anne could hardly bear to interrupt her practice, but she had eaten little since the day before and found that she was hungry.

"What time will Monsieur Liszt arrive?" Anne asked, so that she could calculate how much more practice she could accomplish before her lesson—and prepare herself for the thrilling possibility that he would conceal a note telling her where they could meet to talk in private.

"Oh, I'm sorry, I neglected to tell you," Marie said, dabbing at her mouth with a linen napkin, "I put him off today and changed the lesson to tomorrow afternoon. I thought that since you had not practiced yesterday, you might be unprepared. And there is another matter I wish to discuss with you before Monsieur Liszt again enters this house."

Anne's heart sank. She had been looking forward to the lesson. And Marie's words reminded her that she had not yet explained her absence of the day before. Quickly she told Madame d'Agoult the entire story.

"How extraordinary," Marie said, more to herself than to Anne.

"How so?"

"Well, that it should have been Monsieur Talon—that gentleman who helped us at the concert—who saved your cousin's life."

"Yes." Anne smiled in spite of herself. It had pleased her to see the young man again.

"I gather you found Monsieur Talon equally appealing upon this occasion as on the last."

Anne was about to protest that she had not given him much thought when she noticed a strange look on Madame d'Agoult's face. "What was it you wished to talk to me about?"

"I would like to ask you something, and I require an honest response."

Marie fixed Anne with a level gaze. *She knows about the notes,* Anne thought. She could not face Madame d'Agoult's serious eyes, and so she looked down at her hands. "Of course." Dozens of possible questions Marie might ask and answers she might give flashed through Anne's mind. She dreaded all of them.

"You mustn't be afraid to confide in me. I understand that there is much you do not know about the world, and especially about—"

At that moment, Adèle entered the drawing room with a letter on a tray. Marie looked as though she was about to scold the maid for interrupting her, but when she saw the letter, which had arrived express, she snatched it up.

"Excuse me," she said.

Marie left Anne alone in the parlor without a word of explanation. Only after her friend was gone did Anne realize that she herself had been clenching her fists so hard that the nails of one hand had etched shallow half moons on her palm. She also realized that she did not want to tell Marie about Liszt. Not yet. She knew that to do so would bring an end not only to the lessons but to her pleasant hours of daydreams about her teacher.

When Marie returned, she had her traveling cloak draped over her arm. "I am so sorry, Anne, but I am called away this instant to Croissy. My mother has taken ill."

Anne stood and prepared to depart, thinking that she could easily walk home.

"Please stay. There is no need for you to leave before your time. I shall return in the morning, I am certain—perhaps even this evening—and will send word if I cannot." Marie hurried out without even taking leave of Anne.

Poor Marie! Anne thought. What if her mother had the cholera? This horrible possibility dampened Anne's relief that Marie had not had time to probe her on the subject of Monsieur Liszt. And her children were there too and could be in danger as well.

Anne returned to the piano. Her heart fluttered and visions of her own mother's violent death flashed before her. *No,* she thought. *I cannot think about that.* She began to play the first thing that came into her head, some lively Schubert dances, letting the exuberance of the music dispel all evil thoughts and consequences. Marie would return tomorrow—everything would be well—and there would be time enough to answer her questions concerning all that had happened.

Without the constraining influence of Marie's quiet presence, Anne felt free to indulge all her fantasies. She imagined the touch of Liszt's hands on her own and wondered if tomorrow would be the day when they would make their assignation. She was not certain where they might meet, or what might pass between them. Doubtless he would know what to do. That is, if Marie did not put a stop to it all before their meeting could take place.

The countess de Flavigny always imagined herself at death's door. Her note to her daughter had expressed the greatest alarm. She had an ache in her stomach and was certain that by the next day she would be dead from the cholera.

Marie knew that her mother was likely to be no more ill than she was, but she could not fail to respond to the summons. She looked forward to seeing her children too, who remained at the château for safety. Six leagues seemed an adequate distance from the disease, which had not spread so much to outlying districts but remained concentrated in the crowded, dirty lanes of Paris. Her husband, Charles, had extended his sojourn in the north, no doubt waiting for news that it was safe to return to Saint Germain.

She intended to see that her mother was well, spend a little time with her children, and come back—with luck, the same day. But when she arrived, she discovered that her mother was, in fact, a trifle poorly. Not seriously, but enough so that the servants had been driven quite mad with the little bell in her room tinkling away every few minutes.

"I see you so rarely, and I worry about you in Paris. Won't you stay here with us for a while?" The countess de Flavigny spoke French with a German accent still. When she whined, Marie found her voice particularly irritating.

"I cannot, Mama," Marie said. "There is much to do in Paris."

"Well, stay the night at least. Spend a little time with the children. They miss you!"

Her mother had said the one thing that could have persuaded Marie to remain more than a few hours. And the fresh air in the country was a pleasant change from the atmosphere of Paris. She had grown so used to the smell of death that she had ceased to notice it. "Very well, I'll stay tonight and leave in the morning." She kissed her mother, then sat and read to her for a while, giving the servants a much-needed respite from the constant demands of their mistress. When her mother nodded off, mouth open and snoring gently, Marie sought out the nursemaid and sat with Louise and Claire while they had their supper and showed her their dolls and the pictures they had drawn.

Later, the countess d'Agoult and the countess de Flavigny dined together at a small table in the bedchamber.

"When do you expect Charles to return?" her mother asked.

"I shall entertain some guests at a salon soon, and he may be back by then."

The comte d'Agoult's comings and goings hardly impinged on Marie's consciousness. She did not miss him at all, although she found it pleasant enough to have his company at those times when he chose to stay in town.

When she finally retired that night, after reading stories to her two little girls and seeing that her mother was comfortable, Marie lay awake for a long time. She did not know what to do about Liszt and Anne. He was as unsuitable a match as could possibly be for the countess, and if something happened to Anne while she was under Marie's protection, the marquis would have every right to be angry.

Worse still, Marie could see that Anne worshipped the Hungarian pianist. Her demeanor toward him, the way she blushed at the slightest accidental touch, and her overzealous application to her piano studies—even the fact that she seldom spoke about him when he was not there—all indicated to Marie that the countess de Barbier-Chouant was highly susceptible to being led dangerously astray. And there had been that business, when Liszt was a little younger, of the countess de Saint-Cricq. The young lady's father had avoided that debacle by marrying her off to a wealthy landowner in the provinces.

Aside from all that, there were her own feelings to consider. She had persuaded herself that the assignation that she had kept in place of Anne had been a duty to her innocent charge. But it had unsettled her, had raised unspeakable possibilities in her mind. And the liberty Liszt had taken with her, thinking that he caressed Anne's ungloved hand, was another cause for concern. It must have been provoked by something between the two of them. What made matters worse was that Marie was certain that the pianist had no intention of actually marrying his student. How could he aspire to such a match? Notwithstanding the marquis, she herself would never permit it.

Therein lay Marie's true difficulty. If she ended the lessons (provided at her own expense) and kept Anne and Liszt apart, then not only would she alienate both of them, but she would place him at an irrevocable distance from herself. She was unwilling to forgo the pleasure of welcoming him into her parlor every few days, and of gazing at him without his knowledge. Although she pretended to read or sew during the lessons, more and more she found herself staring at the two of them, her book open on the desk in front of her. She thought that if she had any talent at drawing, she would be able to re-create every detail of Liszt's face wearing a countless number of expressions.

And his hands . . . Marie could still feel the delicate touch of his fingers on her wrist, on her palm. Several times since the night before, she had imagined those fingers elsewhere on her body. Never, Marie thought, had she desired the touch of a man so intensely.

But it was not I, she reminded herself. His tender gesture was meant not for her but for a girl ten years her junior, whose passions had yet to be awakened by suffering and true love. The pain in her breast was like an invisible hand that wrapped itself around her heart and squeezed it. She had a vision of Anne, writhing in agony and repeating her mother's untimely demise from cholera. She crossed herself. *I do not wish that,* she thought, and yet, how else would Liszt be cured of his infatuation with the young countess?

Or perhaps, Marie thought, she could cure Anne of her adoration of Liszt. The young medical student, the one whom Anne met at the Hôtel-Dieu in the most interesting of circumstances, would be a much more suitable attachment. From her response when they spoke of his heroic deed in saving Anne's cousin, Marie saw that Anne was not indifferent to him. The marquis would not like it, but Marie knew that Armand and Anne would never marry. And these days, doctors were becoming highly respected. Monsieur Talon also had the virtue of being a music lover himself.

She could, if she chose, throw them together again. It might not be the wisest course when she knew so little about the young man, but ever since the opera Marie had found herself slipping further and further away from the safety of social norms, and caring less how low she must stoop to bring about some kind of liaison between herself and Liszt. Disrupting her protégée's infatuation would accomplish two equally desirable goals: Anne would be saved from certain disgrace, and Marie would gain the possibility of fulfillment she had only dreamed of before.

Later on the day after Pierre performed the operation on Monsieur de Barbier, Georges declared himself well enough to return to his duties at the Hôtel-Dieu.

"I don't want them to think you're me," he said, referring to the fact that Pierre had completed the time cards for his service there in Georges's name.

"You still look tired," Pierre said. He noticed that the dark circles beneath his friend's eyes remained, even though Georges had spent a great deal of time recently either sleeping or lying in bed.

"Nonsense!" Georges said. "And besides, now that I know I might have a chance to do something daring and brave, I don't want you stepping in for me again."

Pierre knew that his friend was only teasing, and that he felt guilty for not being able to fulfill his obligation. But Georges insisted, and Pierre was, in truth, relieved not to have to return to that horrible place for a little while.

Once Georges went off to the hospital, Pierre set about to apply himself to his studies, which he had much neglected of late. But try as he might to memorize all the methods of correcting luxations, and of using leeches to the best effect, he could not keep his mind from straying to the countess Anne. He had made mental notes about her surroundings when he attended Monsieur de Barbier that morning, and as a result he learned things about her and her situation that disturbed him deeply. The old marquis was a rather frightening character. After being treated by him with such a strong degree of contempt and scorn, Pierre could easily imagine that Anne's father might wield enough influence to change public records or cause them to be conveniently misfiled.

Pierre had also noticed that the door to his right as he stood in the entrance hall of the mansion waiting to be admitted to see his patient was padlocked shut, with some damage to the ornate brass hardware. It appeared by its carving and its generous dimensions to be the door to some elegant reception room, not a storeroom, and he found it rather strange that such a room would be sealed off from the household. But he had had no opportunity to question anyone about it.

The countess seemed to have recovered quite well from the strain of the previous day, and when she emerged from a room behind the grand staircase, she was a vision of fresh, delicate beauty. She treated him kindly, but Pierre knew that she must have considered him no more than a hireling, someone who was far beneath her in rank, and he had read nothing warmer than gratitude in her eyes. Then he recalled Monsieur de Barbier's cryptic comment about the marquis's desire that he should marry his cousin. Pierre had not had enough time alone with his patient to delve more deeply into the matter.

After an hour or two of pondering the past few days' events, Pierre decided that it was useless to pore over books. Nothing he read made any impression on him, and so he decided instead to visit the commissioner of records and talk to him about recent events, and about his observations of the home where the marquise had lived.

Gardive looked as though he had not moved since the last time Pierre visited him in his office during the daytime. The only change was that the pile of papers in his wooden tray was deeper than it had been, and he appeared, if anything, even more hollow-eyed and intent than before.

"So, you do not visit me in the middle of the night this time," he said, his expression betraying no evidence that he said it in jest.

Pierre felt the blood rise into his face. "No, but I have a little more information for you."

"Sit," he said, his manner softening. "I am weary of counting and tabulating."

The chair was straight-backed and wooden, but the room was so full of papers and files and ledger books that there would not have been space for anything more comfortable.

Pierre cleared his throat. "I visited the home of the marquis de Barbier-Chouant this morning."

"In your capacity as neighborhood commissioner?" Gardive asked.

"No. I now have a rather personal connection with the family, one that arose out of pure coincidence." Pierre explained to the commissioner the events of the day before.

"*Sainte Marie!* The young man is fortunate. Matters might have turned out much differently," Gardive said, referring, no doubt, to Pierre's lack of experience as a surgeon.

"Nevertheless," Pierre continued, "Monsieur de Barbier appears to be convalescing. But there is something strange about the hôtel Barbier."

For the next short while, Pierre tried to describe the marquis and the old mansion with its padlocked reception room.

"The marquis is from the old guard," Gardive remarked, "a breed that was displaced when Louis-Philippe ascended the throne. There are, alas, several such relics in Paris, with no court intrigues on which to exercise their wits and intelligence." Gardive looked as though he was about to dismiss Pierre and go back to his official duties. But instead, he opened a drawer next to him, removed a large envelope containing some papers, and handed them to Pierre. "I too have some information."

Pierre opened the envelope and pulled out several sheets of what looked to be birth records.

"I have often found that if you look only at what is immediately before you, it is possible to be misled. Those who would fool us often assume we will search no further, will cast our net no wider than the inquiries that result directly from the question on the surface."

In his hands Pierre held a list of the infant girls born eighteen years ago in Paris, on the feast of Saint Anne, the twenty-sixth of July, 1814. That being the year of the restoration, when it was once again possible to be a good Catholic, many parents chose to name their daughters after the saint.

"Look where I have marked, in pencil."

Pierre scanned down the records and saw one for a child born in Saint Germain and christened Anne. The entry for her father was left blank. The mother's name was Sandrine P———. Only the first letter of the surname was visible; the rest of it had been scratched away.

"Now look at this."

Gardive gave Pierre another envelope. It contained a baptismal certificate, from Saint Germain de l'Auxerrois, recording the baptism of Anne de Barbier-Chouant on June 16, 1815.

"I ask you," Gardive said, "how it is possible to baptize an infant who has never been born? This paper cost me some amount of difficulty to find, the baptismal records being located elsewhere." He cleared his throat, reached back into the drawer, and took out yet one more piece of paper. "And voilà, my final evidence."

He gave the paper to Pierre. He found himself examining a fair copy of the marriage certificate of the marquis Henri de Barbier-Chouant to Sandrine Poitou on August 26, 1814.

"So you see, with a trip abroad and a wet nurse in the country for the first few years, a bastard becomes legitimate, and the world breathes a sigh of relief."

Gardive sat back in his chair and clasped his hands behind his head. His smile was not exactly self-satisfied, but Pierre saw that the fellow was pleased with his investigations. As for himself, Pierre did not know what to think. The evidence more than suggested that Anne was not, in fact, the daughter of the marquis de Barbier-Chouant. What could have possessed the man, at the age of well over forty and with a prestigious position at court, to consent to such a marriage and such a deception?

"Where did you find these?" Pierre returned the papers to Gardive.

"That I must not say. They were in this building, although misfiled, or rather, filed in a place that would make it less likely that they would be found."

"It would have required a great deal of influence—or money—would it not, to bring about such an occurrence?"

Gardive shrugged. "Who can say? I give you only the records themselves. If you want explanations, I suggest you look for them in the two most basic of human desires: love and money. Now, if you please."

The commissioner ended the interview, and Pierre soon found himself out on the quai de l'Horloge. He stood near the river and watched the barges pass. Before he was born—even before the Revolution—the buildings that weighed down the bridges had been demolished, so that it was possible to look up and down the Seine from any of the banks and have an unimpeded view. Where he stood, near the Prefecture, that view included carts bearing corpses and suffering victims, streaming back and forth on the Pont Notre Dame. He could not imagine the marquise, Anne's mother, being stricken in such a violent way. In thinking of her, Pierre could not help but picture a slightly older version of Anne herself. The vision was too horrible to contemplate.

Gardive had said "love and money." Perhaps Madame d'Agoult could speak on the subject of the former. As to the latter, Pierre had no idea how to go about discovering if there were some baser motive that was hidden along with the records.

He turned his steps to the Latin Quarter. If Georges was back, he might be able to persuade him to pass the evening in the café.

Seventeen

When Franz received the note from Marie postponing Anne's lesson for a day, he wasn't certain how to interpret it. The tone was formal and cool, not at all that of a woman who had agreed to a meeting in disguise and allowed him to caress her hand. That act alone had provided him with ample food for his growing passion, and if he was not mistaken, it had similarly affected Marie.

Why did she draw back now?

Franz played through a composition he had been working on for several weeks that was not falling into place as he would like. He reached the final cadence and left his hands on the keys and his foot on the sustaining pedal so that the sound decayed slowly, the harmonious pitches melding into a soft sea of overtones until he hardly recognized the chord on which his serenade had come to rest.

Of course. That was Marie. Not the bright, vibrant tones anyone with half an ear could hear, but the delicate complexity of a dying sound that only patience would reveal. Someday, Franz thought, he would compose a piece that would capture that quality. He imagined how he would present it to her at some future time. It would be in an exotic, foreign place—Venice, perhaps. He pictured a bedchamber, and the early morning sun slanting through gauzy curtains, touching her tumultuous curls with light as they spread across a silken pillow. He would have arisen early to gaze at her, and as she began to stir, he would pad carefully across the floor, sit at the pianoforte, and play so that his music would be the first sound to fall upon her waking ear.

Franz had no idea how much time he had passed in idle day-dreaming. All he did know was that he would be useless for much of anything until he could bring things to some resolution with Marie. Yet to force some action—already she had pulled away from him. Or perhaps that was simply evidence of her own turmoil?

Tomorrow he would see her again and be able to judge. For now, Franz was too agitated to continue his work, and so he left to find Alfred at the café where the poet spent most afternoons.

Much to Anne's surprise, her father began to take great interest in Armand's treatment and care. He insisted on sitting with him and giving him sips of water and broth. He himself read aloud to his cousin in the afternoon and saw that the strictest silence prevailed in the house so that Monsieur de Barbier might fall asleep in the evening.

Perhaps, Anne thought, her father could be affectionate with other people besides his late wife. It hurt her a little that it should be this comparative stranger who awoke some solicitude in him. Maybe it eased his soul to care for someone who would be more likely to recover, rather than stand helplessly by, as he had when his wife died a horrible death. Anne could think of no other way to account for his behavior.

Although her vanity was piqued by her father's attention to Armand's needs, this new occupation had its advantages for her too. Caring for Monsieur de Barbier took up a great deal of time and prevented the marquis from paying much attention to Anne when she returned from Marie's the day after her cousin's surgery. Anne hoped that he would simply overlook the matter of her disobedience, but her hope was short-lived. The next morning, her father called her into the library, no doubt to scold her. She dreaded this summons.

But instead of flinging bitter recriminations at her as soon as she entered the room, the marquis told Anne in a calm and soothing voice to sit opposite him by the fire. She took her seat, and he continued to speak to her slowly and carefully, testing each unaccustomed word. "I have, perhaps, not been the father I ought to have been during these past weeks following your mother's death." He gazed into the licking flames.

At first, Anne did not believe she had heard him correctly. Had he apologized to her? She could not be certain. *Look at me,* Anne thought. Her father's sentiments were fine and soothed her to hear, but until he lifted his eyes and she could see their expression, she would not know whether to trust him.

"I would like to know—if you would tell me—whether you think you might be able to marry your cousin once he is recovered?"

Ah, thought Anne, *this is why.* Her father acted calm, but he was trying to trick her into telling him everything. "I—I don't know, Father. I am not the only one who must decide, am I? And Monsieur de Barbier is hardly in a state to be contemplating marriage."

She saw his jaw work as it did when he was displeased, yet when he spoke again, his words did not match the agitation in his face.

"But do you think you can *like* him?" he asked.

What could she say? Lying in answer to a direct question was somehow different from not saying where she was going or why and pretending about her cousin. "Father," Anne said, "why does it matter whether Armand and I marry? Surely I shall find another suitor if—"

"Answer my question!" he snapped, his hands gripping the arms of the chair.

Anne blinked her eyes and flinched at the sudden shift in his tone. "You frighten me, Father," she said. He leaned back away from her and again fixed his eyes on the leaping fire. The blaze was too big for this time of year, and Anne grew warm and uncomfortable. "I cannot give you an answer, Papa," she said. "You confuse me. I do not know. Mother would not have forced me like this." She struggled against tears of anger. Anne knew from experience that weeping would do nothing to soften the marquis's mood.

"You do not understand the ways of the world. I suggest we speak again when you can give me a suitable answer," he said, in that same hard tone he had used when he told her to leave the ballroom the day of her mother's death. "I will see you at dinner."

Anne hurried out of the library. As she left, she passed Julien on his way in to the marquis with a card on a silver tray and noticed out of the corner of her eye as she ran up the stairs that there were two gentlemen in dark frock coats waiting in the vestibule. She did not trouble herself about who they were or why they were there, although she thought she had seen them before.

Instead of running into her own room, Anne turned and sought out her cousin. She needed to see him, to make sure that he would not answer her father's questions differently, making some commitment in the extremity of his illness. She did not love him. That Anne knew in her heart. Yet she bore him no ill will. He was family, however distant, and they shared common sorrows.

"Armand?" she whispered. The room was still dark. Thérèse had not yet opened the curtains.

"Who's there?" came her cousin's weak voice.

Assured that he was awake, Anne threw open the curtains before turning to look at Monsieur de Barbier. What she saw made her draw in her breath sharply. "Cousin, are you well?" she said. His bedclothes were twisted around him, and yellowish liquid stained the area near his groin where he had had the surgery. His face was the color of egg custard.

"I'm all right," he said, his voice barely audible.

"No, you're not! Did no one tend you last night? Was my father not with you, or Thérèse?"

"He stayed until I slept. Gave me broth. Such dreams!" Armand tried to move a little and cried out in pain. Anne saw tears flow from the corners of his eyes.

She rang the bell by her cousin's bedside, and soon Thérèse arrived with a tray, which she very nearly dropped as soon as she saw the young man's condition.

"We must get a doctor to come to him," Anne said. "He is much worse."

Anne ran to the door, so intent on finding Victor and telling him to get the coach ready right away that she nearly collided with her father, who stood glowering in the doorway.

"Where are you off to in such a hurry?" he said.

"A doctor," she panted. "Father, Armand is in need of a doctor."

Something in the marquis's eyes halted Anne in her steps. "I'll send for Magendie. Go to your lesson. I must . . ."

His voice trailed off. It was so unlike him to be vague that it took Anne several moments to realize that he did not intend to continue his thought. She wanted to ask him, *Why Magendie?* Why not Talon, who had done such a good job and saved Armand's life? She could not bear the thought of Magendie. He was the doctor who had pronounced the name of her mother's illness and declared her beyond help. Anne looked from Thérèse, to Armand, and back again to the marquis. There was something among them all that she did not understand. She simply wanted her cousin to recover and go back to his apartment, and to have her lesson with Liszt. To return to a routine of any kind, instead of this shifting, unsteady existence she had endured in recent weeks. Even the dangerous thought of Liszt agreeing to meet her somewhere had lost a little of its charm.

Anne let out a short cry of exasperation and ran from the room. She heard Thérèse bustling after her, but she paused only to fetch her gloves and cloak from her bedchamber, pushing past the maid's attempt to intercept her before she descended to the entrance hall. By the time she reached the front door, Victor was already waiting with the carriage. Anne so wanted to tell him to go back to the Hôtel-Dieu and find Talon again, but she dared not. She sat back in her seat, every muscle in her body clenched in anxious worry. She could not make out her father at all. His sudden change of demeanor from the time of their conversation that morning—could it have had anything to do with the two men she noticed in the vestibule, and who had apparently gone by the time she left the house?

Whatever the cause, she wished he would simply ignore her, let her go about her own business. If only Armand had never appeared to disrupt her life. If only—she stopped herself from completing the sentence, even in her imagination. How could she contemplate such a horrible fate for the young man who was her only living relation besides her father?

Yet this wretched thought would not relinquish its hold on her imagination, and Anne wanted nothing more than to tell Madame d'Agoult about it. She would have the wisdom to help her be more calm and accepting.

The footman who answered the door at the quai Malaquais greeted her with the news that the countess had not yet returned from Croissy but that she had left instructions for Anne to come in and make herself at home in the parlor.

That morning, Anne played the piano as though she were clinging to the keyboard for life and sustenance. Her fingers flew. She simply followed them wherever they led her, even when they drew her on to an otherworldly, disembodied state. Time ceased to exist except in relation to the notes succeeding one another in different durations and combinations. She hardly noticed when the kitchen maid brought in the luncheon tray, and when the hours passed and Marie still did not return from visiting her mother. Anne played without resting until the bell announced the arrival of her teacher. She wondered for only a moment whether it would be right to have her lesson without Madame d'Agoult as chaperone. But dismissing the thought as soon as she had it, she bade the footman show Monsieur Liszt into the parlor.

Franz was in a state approaching madness by the time he arrived at the quai Malaquais. His conversation with Alfred had only stirred his emotions to an even greater frenzy. He was determined that he would discover the truth of Marie's feelings toward him that day or throw himself in the Seine on the way home. Even if she told him there was no hope, at least then he could relinquish the smoldering passion that had begun to usurp all his waking thoughts.

He rushed directly into the parlor at the quai Malaquais, ready to greet Madame d'Agoult and read the answer to his all-encompassing question in her eyes. But to his surprise, only Anne was there, seated at the pianoforte. She rose to welcome him. Perhaps it was an illusion, because Marie was not there to serve as a comparison, but the young countess appeared taller. Her eyes met his rather than looking away in embarrassment, and in their clear blueness he thought he saw a question—or was it a tinge of sorrow? Or fear? Franz had always thought Anne pretty, but she seemed such a shadow compared to the magnificent Madame d'Agoult that he had never truly looked at her. He had seen her as the conduit through which his desire for Marie might flow, not as an individual in her own right. Standing before him, waiting for his instruction that afternoon in May, was a young lady—a young woman—with something inside her. At that instant, he thought he understood how to draw it out.

"Let's have the study, without the book," he said. Anne turned her questioning gaze to him. "You cannot truly enter the music if your eyes are fastened to a sheet of paper. Don't be alarmed. You know it in your heart." Then instead of pulling his chair up beside her so that he could watch Anne's hands and correct her, he stood directly behind his student and looked over her shoulder. The lid of the piano was open. He could see the dampers moving up and down inside the case. The opening strains of Chopin's enigmatic étude washed over him as if it were he whose fingers caressed the keyboard. Without even thinking about what he was doing, he bent down so that his head was right next to Mademoiselle Anne's and began speaking quietly into her ear.

The footman had said the countess would return at any moment, and so it hardly seemed at all improper that they should start the lesson before she arrived. Oddly, being alone with Liszt that day made her much less nervous than having Marie in the room watching her. She had the momentary sensation that she and the Hungarian pianist were both children who had escaped their nursemaids for a time and could therefore play as boisterously as they wished without being scolded for ruining their clothes.

Liszt asked her to play the study from memory. She was in just such a mood that Chopin's odd music suited it perfectly, and so she began, eyes closed, to play the notes. He was right. The music came to her, as if she were reading it, only it entered her heart directly. And in the strange, new relationship between them that resulted from their correspondence and from their sudden isolated intimacy, it did not surprise her that, instead of bringing over the chair to sit beside her, Liszt stood immediately behind her and placed his strong, tapered fingers lightly on her shoulders. His touch sent little thrills down her arms to her own fingertips, reaching inside her to guide her hands over the keys. Soon she immersed herself completely in the music. When Liszt began speaking quietly into her ear, his lips so near that she could feel them lightly touch every now and again, it all seemed quite natural.

"Don't be afraid," he whispered. "You are young and innocent. Your thoughts—in this opening section—are pure, but a little bit melancholy. You are in love, seeking, but have yet to find him, the man who will satisfy your innermost desires."

He spoke slowly, timing each phrase with the music so that it seemed to Anne as though he were narrating her own thoughts. The music had split her in two, and one part of her played the piano while the other spoke softly into her ear.

"You see him. Your heart beats faster. You look into each other's eyes, but you are still frightened, and you allow him to leave without confessing your love."

The first section ended. Anne let herself be folded into an embrace of images and half-acknowledged fantasies. Liszt's voice, like his hands, crept inside her, melting into the music. Anne began to understand it as she had never done before. All at once, she saw things, heard things, that transformed the study into something much more than she could possibly have imagined before, freeing it from the need for symmetry and logic that had so impeded her ability to comprehend it. She had little time to marvel at this phenomenon, because the second section, the part that contained the most technical difficulties, had begun.

"You meet again, and you tease him. You hide here and there, but he looks for you and finds you."

Liszt's breath was warm on her ear. She shivered.

"He has you in his arms, but you are uncertain."

At that, the beginning of the major-minor passage, Liszt's hands moved from Anne's shoulders to her upper arms. He touched her gently so that her movement was not hampered, yet with every depression of a key she could feel the soft stroke of his fingers right through her muslin sleeves.

"You pull away, but he clings to you. Your mind and heart are in turmoil."

Liszt dragged his fingers up along Anne's arms and down her back until they came to rest on her ribs. A little shock of pleasure rippled through her. But another voice inside her suggested that his gesture meant nothing, simply allowing her the unrestricted use of her arms to negotiate the difficult double tritones in the coming passage.

"You beg him to leave you in peace, all the time knowing that you are desperate for the feeling of his lips upon yours."

The snaking, contrary-motion diminished fifths and augmented fourths began. Anne started slowly, painfully, and then gathered momentum.

"Your resistance crumbles, moment by moment . . ."

She reached the climactic chords. Liszt's hands had gradually wrapped themselves around her bodice below her breasts. His nose now nuzzled in the curls that draped over her ear. Anne felt the softest touch of his lips on the nape of her neck.

"You give in, you allow your lover to possess you, and passion takes control of you entirely."

These words ushered in the double diminished sevenths. Anne had worked so hard to make them perfect, but now she tumbled down the keyboard, completely unable to concentrate, feeling her teacher's teeth gently nip at her neck, at the tops of her shoulders.

When the passage ended, Anne lifted her hands from the keys. She was breathing hard. Before she knew what happened, she felt Liszt's arms around her, and his mouth closed over hers, not so much kissing as devouring her. She couldn't breathe. At first she resisted, then she let her body relax and reached her arms up around his neck, returning his kiss with every ounce of confused passion in her heart.

After their lips parted, Liszt turned her gently back toward the keyboard, and whispered again in her ear. "But it cannot be. You return to your solitude, only now"—he took Anne's right hand and placed it lightly on the keys—"your melancholy is deeper. It is mixed with joy—and despair."

He straightened himself and turned away from her. He said nothing more but let her finish the piece. To Anne's surprise, her tears dripped on the keyboard. She continued to the end, fingers slipping, her heart aching with pain and sorrow. About her mother, Armand, her father's odd and sometimes cruel ways, her desire for Liszt, and something else, she hardly knew what. Anne kept the keys depressed at the final chord, letting the sounds die away slowly. She did not want to let go of the music.

As soon as she dared lift her eyes from the piano, she sought out those of her teacher. He had taken her away from life for a moment. She longed to be with him again in that other realm where nothing mattered except music, and the closeness of two human beings. She did not need to meet him surreptitiously now. They had been together so completely that Anne could not imagine any exchange between them ever surpassing what had occurred only a few moments before.

But he did not look at her. Instead, Liszt stood as straight as the stem of a quarter note, his eyes fixed on the door to the parlor. Anne followed his gaze. There, still in her bonnet and gloves, stood the countess Marie d'Agoult. She looked questioningly at the two of them.

"What have you done to upset the countess so?" Marie said.

"She was overcome by the beauty of the music," Liszt said, bowing graciously, but Anne thought she detected uncertainty in his voice. "We have just concluded the lesson."

Anne was so confused she could hardly say a word. She gathered up her things, thanked Liszt, curtseyed to Marie, and departed.

Marie had had every intention of arriving at the quai Malaquais in time for Anne's lesson. She felt a little guilty on Anne's account about postponing it one day already and did not want to disappoint the girl again. But her mother had dragged everything out to delay her going, and her own ambivalence about facing Liszt after their rendezvous at the opera also slowed her steps. When the countess de Flavigny asked Marie to read to her, she agreed. Marie waited while her mother wrote notes to her friends, so that she could deliver them in person when she returned to Paris. As she acquiesced to every one of her mother's little demands, she watched the time slip by with increasing anxiety—and dread. It simply would not do to leave Anne and Liszt unchaperoned, and yet she knew she could never look on him with indifference again.

The lesson was to start at two. Marie climbed into her carriage at the last possible moment to arrive on time. But the heavens conspired against her. Right at the entrance to Paris, a refuse cart had been toppled by the ragpickers, who insisted on being permitted to comb through it for treasures. Ten carriages sat unmoving on the road for almost an hour until the dispute was resolved. By the time they lurched into motion again, Marie knew she would never arrive before the lesson began. She wondered, vaguely, whether Anne would have the wits to ask Liszt to come the next day instead. But since she was due to return, she thought it more likely that they would begin, assuming she would join them as soon as possible. Perhaps it would be easier if the lesson were in progress when she returned. That way she would not have to look into Liszt's eyes right away.

Marie arrived at the moment Anne finished playing the climactic chords of the Chopin study. She waited outside the parlor door for a moment, not wanting to interrupt her in the middle of a read-through. But when it appeared that she had stopped playing, Marie opened the door.

The possibility had always existed, buried deep in Marie's imagination, that some scene such as the one she beheld at that moment might come to pass—especially after experiencing Liszt's seductive behavior at the opera house toward someone he thought was Anne. But the reality of it, the sight of Anne and Liszt locked in a passionate embrace, sent her heart leaping into her throat. She wanted to lunge forward and wrench them apart from one another, but instead, she froze. Her response to this event was too important to let her emotions completely overrule her common sense. Marie forced herself back into the role of chaperone. She should be indignant, outraged even. Not devastated and disappointed. It would be better to close the door quietly, make a great deal of noise in the hallway, then enter again. She should let the lesson continue and later write to Liszt, telling him that his services were no longer required. After that, a gentle talk with Anne would be appropriate.

But she could not move. She could not tear her eyes away from the spectacle of that long, lingering kiss. She stayed where she was, watched their lips part gradually, saw Franz Liszt gently release Anne, lower her down to sit on the chair, and place her hands on the keyboard so that she would continue playing the brief remainder of the piece through a rain of silent tears. Each moment twisted Marie's heart in her breast. She struggled to arrange her features in as neutral an expression as possible for the inevitable moment when they would look up and see her standing there.

After the final notes of the study, Liszt raised his eyes, and the expression on his face when they met Marie's passed through bewilderment to shock and dismay. It seemed a lifetime but must have been only a few moments later when Anne, with her dreamy, sad expression, finally gazed at her. They would not have known at what point she had opened the door, and Marie chose, for a while at least, to pretend that she had not seen what passed between them.

The girl departed, with more dignity than Marie expected her to manage in the circumstances. Marie found herself alone and face-to-face with the man whose image had filled her heart with a mixture of unbearable pleasure and pain.

* * *

How much did she see? The question buzzed around in Franz's head as he stood there, completely unable to move. He had become so absorbed in the scene he narrated that he could not say at what point he had ceased to realize that it was the young countess, and not Marie, whose arms he touched, whose ear he breathed into, and whose lips he kissed with all the ardor of concealed desire. When he saw Madame d'Agoult framed in the doorway of her parlor, at first he could not comprehend how she could be in two places at the same time. Then, in an agonizing instant of clarity, Franz understood what he had done.

He hardly noticed when Anne left.

"Do you think your student is ready to perform at a salon? I intend to invite a small group to come next Thursday." Marie's clipped, precise words roused him from his stupor.

"She has made remarkable progress," Franz said, trying to sound as calm as possible, "but she would benefit from a few more weeks of instruction." Perhaps she had entered after the kiss, Franz thought. Perhaps he had not destroyed all his hopes in that stupid, unconscious moment.

But the expression in Marie's eyes was not soft and open as it normally was and as he had hoped it would be. The countess had shut him out. "It is time I presented her to society. A girl so pretty would do well to be married at the earliest possible moment. I cannot wait any longer to do this for her."

She believes I have designs on the countess de Barbier-Chouant! Of course, being alone with her for the lesson, his not having the good sense to insist on returning when the girl was chaperoned, must have led her to that conclusion even if she had witnessed nothing. If nothing else, Anne's tears furnished ample evidence. "I believe she would acquit herself well enough to impress your guests," Liszt answered, wishing that, instead of talking of such meaningless trifles, he could kneel at her feet and beg her forgiveness, confess his love to her, and forget about the talented young lady she had engaged him to teach.

Madame d'Agoult walked slowly to the mantelpiece and tugged twice on the silk rope that made a bell tinkle somewhere else in the house. The footman entered too quickly for Franz to have a chance to say anything more to her in private.

"Show Monsieur Liszt out," Marie commanded. She turned to him. "I shall send you an invitation to the salon."

Franz took his hat and cloak from the footman. He tried to catch Marie's eye so that he could communicate in silence all that had remained unsaid, but she would not look at him.

You fool you fool! he said to himself, as he walked back to his lodgings near the opera house. Nothing had gone as he had planned. The countess did not mention coming to teach Anne again. Once the lessons stopped, he would no longer have an excuse to visit the quai Malaquais without a social invitation. He would have to rely on chance encounters or her own desire to meet him again.

Instead of returning home, Franz changed his mind and made his way to Eugène's studio. His friend would know how he should proceed. Delacroix would be angry, he would scold Franz for behaving so rashly, but would help him in spite of himself.

Eighteen

The look on Thérèse's face when Anne returned from her piano lesson brought her back to the world with a crash. She had never seen the housekeeper appear so distressed, not since the time the marquise first fell ill. Thérèse drew Anne to the privacy of a room in the servants' quarters as soon as Anne walked through the door.

"The marquis is ranting, hollering 'cholera' at the top of his lungs!" the frightened housekeeper said.

"No! It cannot be. Has the doctor come?" She took Thérèse by the shoulders and looked straight into her eyes.

"Yes, but he did not stay long. And there was another visitor too, a clerical gentleman."

"Who?" Anne asked.

"Some Jesuit, saying he was concerned about Armand and asked at the Hôtel-Dieu what had happened to him. He wanted to take your cousin back to the college to be cared for. Your father and he had words, I am afraid."

"Where is my father now?" Anne asked.

"In your cousin's room," Thérèse replied, "but don't you go in there. I've never seen him like this."

Anne had no desire to face her father, especially after their conference that morning, but she had to find out what had happened to Armand. Without saying a word, she left Thérèse and marched back into the main house, through the dining room, across the entrance hall toward the stairs. As she put her foot on the bottom step, her eye caught the door to the library, which stood temptingly ajar. Anne tiptoed over and peered inside. The room was empty but somewhat disordered. She crept in, instinctively drawn toward her father's desk, the mysterious place where all the unseen business of the house was transacted.

The marquis usually kept its surface neat, although cluttered with ever-changing piles of documents and books. But that afternoon, papers were scattered over it in an untidy mess, and an inkwell had tipped over. It spread a dark stain across the beautiful surface of the desk and into the edges of several books. A partially crumpled paper on top of the ink-stained books caught Anne's attention. She picked it up and smoothed it out so that she could read it.

Receipt:
Six silver candelabra
Silver dinner service for twelve
Ruby and diamond necklace
Deed to property known as the hôtel Barbier
Oil portrait
With other items previously impounded, secured against debts in the amount of twenty-five thousand francs for services rendered.

To be held until June 1, 1832, at which time the property shall be forfeit.

MM. Fanjoux et Mérimaux
16, rue du Temple, IVème

So, Anne thought, that was where so many of their accoutrements had gone. But the deed to the house itself? How could her father have done it? And June the first was only a little over a week away! The marquis would never be able to raise such a sum by then. And how had he incurred those debts in the first place? Who were Messieurs Fanjoux et Mérimaux, and what services had they rendered to place her father in their debt? The Barbier-Chouant establishment did not live richly; at least, it had not in recent years. And if the hôtel Barbier were to be seized to pay debts, where would they reside?

"No. Oh no." *I have been so blind,* she thought. Perhaps this was why he wanted her to marry Armand. If she and her cousin were wed, then her father would no longer have to care for her, feed and clothe her, and the costs of running the hôtel Barbier would diminish still further.

But would it be enough? Anne had little sense of how much the food on their table, the wines in their cellar, and the clothes she wore cost. She thought too about the small carriage: he would be able to sell it if she did not need it to drive out in every day. Still, twenty-five thousand francs?

Anne gazed at the paper on her father's desk, and another thought began to form in her mind. Perhaps more than taking away expense, her marriage to Armand might bring money in, and that would solve the financial difficulty. Clearly her cousin had a fortune. Her own mother's—which had been supposed to supply her with a dowry—might have been used up, limiting her prospects of finding a suitable match among her peers. Her father might have seen the existence of a cooperative cousin as a godsend.

Why has he not told me? If only he trusted her, perhaps she would have consented to be married just to solve their problems. But how would it be to spend her life with Armand, with no passion, only duty to keep them together?

On the floor above, a door opened and slammed shut. Anne hurried out of the library, praying that her father would not come down the stairs. But when she reached the entrance hall, she saw no one. She ascended quickly to her cousin's room and tapped on the door, intending to walk in immediately afterward, but her father's brusque "Who is it?" stopped her.

"It's Anne."

He said nothing more for the moment, and Anne turned the knob to let herself in. It was locked. She heard someone inside the room shuffling around, and something fell smashing to the floor. It sounded like glass. Her father cursed under his breath, and then came the familiar sound of his cane-tapping, halting progress in her direction. He unlocked the door from the inside and opened it just far enough so that he could see her, but she could not see past him. "Is it only you?" he asked, peering past her into the corridor.

"Yes, Papa, only me. Did you think there would be someone else?"

"Come in," he said, ignoring her question. "What is it you want?"

"I—I want to speak to Armand. He was so poorly when I left this morning." She begged her father with her eyes.

To her relief, he opened the door wide and motioned her in. Someone had closed the curtains again, and two candles shed a pool of light over Armand, who appeared to be sleeping. A strong smell of camphor barely masked the odor of vomit, which lingered despite the fact that Thérèse must have removed the putrid basin from the room.

"Has the doctor been here?" she asked. Although she already knew the answer, she did not want him to think she had been snooping or getting her information from the servants.

"Magendie. Yes. This morning. He has given me some medicine for our cousin."

"Did he say what is wrong with him?"

"Might be cholera. There are cases that linger, he says. And with care, can be cured."

Armand stirred and groaned in his sleep.

Anne made a move to get closer to the bed. Her father put his arm out to stop her. "Too risky," he said, although he would not meet her eyes. From where Anne stood, Armand looked so pale that he blended in with the bedsheets. She was relieved to see that clean linens covered him, and she guessed that probably his dressing had been changed. Although the camphor and the bitter smell of vomit brought to mind the cholera wards at the Hôtel-Dieu, she did not want to believe that in addition to suffering with his hernia, poor Armand had become ill through tending the very people he had tried to help.

Anne heard her cousin whisper something, she wasn't sure what. She pushed past her father so that she could get closer. "Wa-ter," he said.

"He wants water. Surely there is water!" Anne looked around for a glass. Her father pointed to the floor, where shards of a broken beaker caught the candlelight, and a small puddle spread over the floor. Without hesitation, Anne picked up the little bell on the bedside table and rang it furiously. A moment later the housemaid was at the door. "Get a glass, and a new pitcher of water. Hurry!" Anne commanded, then sat on the edge of her cousin's bed.

"Anne."

She ignored her father's voice. "Someone must care for him!" Anne paid no heed to the possibility that she might provoke her father's wrath. She took hold of Armand's hand, which felt as dry as paper, and hot. The fever was worse, but she did not believe he suffered from cholera.

The marquis moved away from the bed and sat in a chair. It surprised Anne that he had not chastised her for her rude outburst or tried harder to prevent her going to Armand's bedside, and she glanced sideways at him, curious to see his reaction. He sat with his chin sunk to his chest, yet he didn't appear angry or annoyed or cold, but rather, thoughtful, as though he had some idea in the back of his mind that was buried and that he was trying desperately to pull into the light. "Father?" she said.

At that moment Thérèse arrived with a water pitcher and glass. Anne filled the glass, and with one hand raised her cousin's head from the pillow, while with the other she brought the glass to his lips. At the touch of the water Armand's lips trembled, and she tipped the clear, cool liquid into his mouth. He sucked at it greedily, spilling some down his face and onto the pillow.

She repeated the operation three more times. At last Armand grew calmer and drank less desperately. He opened his eyes. "Thank you, Anne," he said, then closed them again and slept.

Anne stood up. Her arms were stiff and sore from holding her cousin's head and the glass. She turned, expecting her father still to be there, but he was gone.

The house was so quiet that Anne fell asleep in the chair by Armand's bed after nursing him until her father and the servants retired for the night. She awoke to the clocks chiming two, stood and stretched, and walked a little away from her cousin's sickbed. He appeared to sleep peacefully now, and his face had lost some of its pallor. Perhaps he was better. If so, tomorrow, she thought, she would have to return to Madame d'Agoult's apartment and face her again. She did not know exactly what the countess had seen, but the puzzled, wounded look on her face haunted Anne. Perhaps it would not be necessary to return right away. She could send word that she was unable to attend the countess because of her cousin's delicate health, that she was needed at home to nurse him. And yet, that would be cowardly. She must, at some moment, return to the apartment of the lady who had been so kind to her.

Liszt's kiss—it was extraordinary. A sensation she had never had before and that, like a drug, she craved again. For a moment, Anne allowed herself to relive it, recalling all those strange tinglings that had awakened every extremity of her body. It did not seem right to have such an unbearably joyous feeling so few weeks after her mother's death, and with her cousin apparently near death as well. Yet all she wanted at that moment was to play the piano, to feel Chopin's glorious, sensual music beneath her hands.

Why, Anne thought, must her father keep the ballroom locked? Surely by now he could bear to hear music. It might even cheer him.

Armand's chest rose and fell in a regular rhythm, and when Anne gently touched his forehead, she could tell that his fever had abated a little. The rest of the house slept too. Only the occasional creak of a settling floorboard disturbed the quiet. Anne took one of the bedside candles and, holding her skirts up so that they would not rustle, tiptoed to the door and let herself out of the room. The hallway was completely dark, except that small part of it that came into view as Anne progressed slowly down the stairs with the taper in her hand.

First, the library. She must look in her father's desk. Having earlier stolen into the room, Anne was not so frightened of this devious step. The door was unlocked, and the hinges had been well oiled so that it swung noiselessly. Anne moved carefully across the floor, staying on the carpeted areas as much as possible. She did not know if her father kept his desk locked, but she had never noticed him with keys. Julien was the one who carried a jangling bunch of them, but only to the wine cellar, the stables, and the front door.

Anne cleared a space for her candle on the desk, set it down amid the papers, and sat in the chair her father normally occupied when he wrote letters. It felt very odd to look out at the room from that position. But she did not tarry over her task. She opened each drawer, relieved to discover that their runners had been waxed to slide easily and noiselessly. Mostly the drawers were full of papers tied into bundles: old letters, bills, receipts. The only item she did not expect to find was a pistol, wrapped in fine cloth in the shallow central drawer. She lifted it. Its cold weight made her shiver. Anne could not imagine it in her father's hands. She replaced it where she found it and continued her search.

As drawer after drawer did not reveal what she had hoped to find, Anne's spirits sank. She was tired. It was time for her to sleep. Only one drawer remained, at the bottom on the right. She pulled it open, and when it too appeared to be filled only with old letters about court life and business, she started to close it again. Something about a particular sheaf of letters, though, stopped her. They were tucked to the side, on their edges, not neatly laid out flat like the others, as if they had been hastily thrust in the drawer to get them out of sight. She grasped one of them and pulled it out.

Henri mon frère,

Yes, I dare to claim it, although you would not have it so. Your star may be rising now, but one day, when your fortunes have changed again and you cannot hide behind your court position and the money that belongs to that whore you call your wife—

Anne gasped. Who would dare call her mother, the sweetest, gentlest creature that ever lived, a whore? She wanted to tear the vile letter up and burn it in the flame of her candle, but she knew that would be unwise. Even if the household was too deeply asleep to smell the burning paper, it would not surprise her if her father knew where every item in his desk was kept and would see immediately that someone had searched through the drawers. Anne knew she should simply put the letter away without reading another of its poisonous words, but her eyes were drawn to the sinuous hand, and despite herself she read it to the end.

. . . that whore you call your wife, I shall reappear in the most unlikely of places, and you and all you hold dear will never be safe again. I cherish the thought of the moment when my vengeance shall be complete.

The letter, written on the coarsest paper, uneven and covered with dark flecks, was not signed. Anne hurriedly tucked it back in its hiding place and riffled through the similar ones around it, noting that the same hand wrote them all on the same cheap paper, and from the few words she read, she saw they all bore the same vile sentiments.

In the dining room an old clock chimed the half hour. Anne had trespassed on her father's library for a long time. She stood up from the desk with the intention of giving up her original purpose and accidentally bumped her knee on a small knob she had not noticed, beneath the drawer where she had found the pistol. She heard a loud *ping* from the opposite side of the desk and held her breath, listening to hear if the noise had awakened anyone else in the house.

Silence. Anne rubbed her knee. She made her way around the

massive piece of furniture. When she reached the other side, she saw that a small, hidden drawer had popped open. The light of her candle revealed that it was empty, except for an iron key, not large enough to belong to the great front door. She said a little prayer that it would turn out to be the key she sought. If not, she would simply go to bed.

Anne wobbled a little from fatigue. Trying her utmost not to make a sound, she crossed the entrance hall, the padlock on the ballroom door drawing her forward like a magnet. The candle nearly tipped over and went out when she placed it on the floor, but she steadied it just in time, stood, and fitted the key into the lock.

Slowly, with a grinding little click, the padlock sprang open. Anne eased the iron loop off the catch and opened the door.

The room smelled musty and old, but the faintest trace of the scent Anne associated with her mother, a delicate mixture of cloves and lavender, lingered in the air. Anne closed her eyes and breathed in deeply. It had been less than two months since her mother's death, and already she found it difficult to remember the exact details of her face. With a sigh Anne opened her eyes again and looked toward the corner where she would find the object of her search, her mother's Pleyel grand pianoforte. She knew she would not be able to press a key and hear its familiar tone, but she wanted to touch it, to imagine sitting there and showing her mother all the wonderful things she had learned during her lessons with Liszt. She walked forward with the candle, bringing different parts of the room into the light as she went. Anne stopped about ten feet away from the far corner of the room. The candle illuminated just enough so that she could see all the way to the walls.

There was no piano. She blinked a few times. But her eyes did not deceive her. How could it have happened? Wouldn't Thérèse have known and told her?

The only time they had all been out of the house was during the marquise's burial. Surely not then, Anne thought, before her body had even been placed in the ground. But lately her father had been acting so strangely that she did not know what to think. The piano was to be hers. Her mother had always said so. He had no right to dispose of it.

The mantel clock struck the three-quarter hour, and Anne realized she must not continue wandering around the quiet house. She hastily left the ballroom, relocked the door, returned the key to the secret drawer in her father's desk, and closed the door to the library behind her. On her way to her room, she looked in to see if Armand was still sleeping. She should stay with him, she thought, but she desperately needed to lie down. She would go to bed just for an hour. Once she was rested, she would return to his bedside and pray that his illness was not the cholera but only some fever from the surgery, and that he would be well again soon.

Pierre was quite surprised to receive another invitation to tea with Marie d'Agoult. He had decided not to tell her of his recent discoveries, thinking that he ought to wait until he was more certain of the facts to share with her the information about the wrong dates on the marriage and birth certificates. He shrank, a little, from revealing that Anne could be an illegitimate child. Although Marie seemed genuinely interested in Anne's welfare, he did not know what use she might make of that information.

But this time, they did not discuss Anne's mother, Madame d'Agoult's late friend.

"I am very concerned about the countess Anne," Marie said, once she and Pierre were seated comfortably in her parlor. "I fear that the lack of a mother has led her to some rather unwise behavior. This recent visit to the Hôtel-Dieu, for example."

"Her motives were quite selfless, I think. And she showed the greatest solicitude for her cousin."

"Were you aware—no, how could you be!—that the marquis intends Anne and Armand to wed?"

Pierre could feel Madame d'Agoult's eyes measuring his reaction. "I heard something of it, from Monsieur de Barbier." He struggled to keep any trace of disappointment out of his voice.

"Don't look so downcast, Monsieur Talon. Anne has no intention of obeying her father in this matter. But I am more interested in how you found things at the hôtel Barbier."

"Have you not visited there?"

"I have been there only once since Sandrine's—the marquise's—death. The marquis did not approve of his wife's friendship with me, and so I was not welcome at their home. Sandrine and I met at parties, at cafés."

"I understood that you and the marquis both served at court together," Pierre said.

"Yes, but we hardly saw one another. The marquis was—is—a shrewd man, who was too busy seeing to his own advancement ever to spare a moment to think about any of the ladies-in-waiting," Marie said.

"He has a certain way about him." Pierre thought about how to describe the old man. "A bit of a curmudgeon."

"How so?" Marie asked.

Pierre told her about how Anne's father had dismissed him when he came to change his patient's dressing. "He seems a rather unkind man. He showed no affection, or even politeness, to the countess," Pierre said. Of course, if the old man knew she was not actually his daughter, as the records suggested, his behavior would be easier to understand.

"Anne has not told me directly, but what you say confirms my fears. This complete lack of feeling for his daughter has left her susceptible, I am afraid, to improper influences." Marie cast Pierre a significant look.

"I don't quite understand you," Pierre said.

"You recall when we first met? At the concert?" Marie proceeded to explain to Pierre what she believed to be the true cause of Anne's swoon. "I admit, it may have been imprudent of me to consent to the lessons with Liszt, but she was so forlorn, so abandoned, and she wanted nothing more in the world."

An infatuation, with the notorious Franz Liszt? From what Pierre had seen of Anne, who, apart from that first encounter, had always exhibited calm sensitivity, he could not believe she would be so weak. Yet Madame d'Agoult presumably knew her better than he. "Countess," said Pierre, leaning forward a little in his seat, "I don't know why exactly, and I do not have enough evidence for it to share with you as yet, but I fear that in addition to this moral danger you say Mademoiselle Anne faces, there may also be physical danger."

"On what do you base your suspicions?" she asked.

"Perhaps I should not have said anything. I have little to support my feeling. Only the way that everyone in the house seems nervous, on edge, as though they are waiting for some terrible event to occur. And the manner in which the marquis dismissed me. I was not even permitted to explain Monsieur de Barbier's care to the housekeeper."

Marie was silent a long while before responding. "I think, Monsieur Talon, that we must work together to ensure the safety of the countess de Barbier-Chouant. I have a plan, but I cannot execute it without your help." She stood and wandered over to the window. "Are you a man of honor?"

"I beg your pardon?"

"You see, if you were a courtier, or an aristocrat, I would know how to exact the strictest secrecy from you. I am afraid I do not know how honor is measured among doctors."

She turned to face him again. If her expression had not been so open and kind, Pierre would have been offended by the question and excused himself immediately from her presence. As it was, he chose instead to believe that she had little experience of people of his class and that she asked an honest question. "I come from a long line of men of business in Toulouse. My father has served as mayor in the city and has been accorded many honors by the guild of haberdashers. I assure you, honor is as important in business and medicine as in any other realm of life."

"Would you, Monsieur Talon, do me the kindness of attending a salon here next Thursday evening?"

"Of course," Pierre said. "But what of this plan?"

"I shall write to you with more details after I have seen the countess. Au revoir, monsieur." She held out her hand. He bent over it politely, then left.

Marie stared at the space where Talon had stood when he agreed to continue helping her. Although he had apparently found out nothing concrete about Sandrine's marriage, she had acquired the information she wished from him, the true state of his feelings. No one who was not deeply besotted with Anne would have risked so much to this point, and still be willing to risk yet more for her sake, without any encouragement from the lady herself. And he clearly came from a good family, if not a noble one. That he was attractive and intelligent made matters all the easier. Although she had no true indication from Anne that she would ever consider the young man as a suitor, she had blushed when they spoke of him and was disposed to think kindly of him for the services he had rendered to her and her family.

Thursday night would bring the matter to a conclusion, one way or the other, Marie thought. She rang for Adèle. She must order the flowers right away. Later she would talk to the cook about refreshments.

Nineteen

Although she had only intended to have the briefest of naps, Anne did not awaken until the sun had been up for some time. When she realized how late it was, she threw a shawl over her nightdress and ran barefoot to the room where Armand lay.

She found Thérèse with him, and the young man was awake. His eyes were more alert than they had been, but he looked frightened.

"So you are a little better this morning," Anne said, rushing to his side.

"Yes, but please do not let the marquis come in."

He spoke quietly and urgently. Anne exchanged a glance with Thérèse. "He will want to see how you are doing," she said.

"But don't leave him alone here. Please!" He looked from one to the other of them in panic.

Anne feared that her cousin would try to leap from his bed if she did not consent to have either Thérèse or herself remain with him at all times. She understood how he felt. The marquis could be a terrifying person. But she had become used to his ways, and he angered more than frightened her now. Anne left Thérèse with Armand while she returned to her own room to dress. She would not go to the quai Malaquais that day. Her cousin needed her at home, and anyway it was not a lesson day. She briefly wondered if she would be able to face Liszt again, to feel quite the same about having him as her teacher. For the moment, she would have to send a note to Marie, and before dressing she did just that, giving it to the daily maid to deliver when she went to market that morning.

As Anne passed the top of the stairs on her way back down the corridor to return to her cousin, she heard her father say something to Julien. She thought she would stop him from making the effort to climb the stairs and try to explain that, in his feverish state, Armand found the marquis's presence disturbing. She had already descended one step when her father's words made her pause.

"Go to Magendie's assistant, and tell him I need the other powder, the one we spoke about. That it is a matter of some urgency. He will know what you mean."

What did the marquis know about medicine that he would suggest treating Armand with some new remedy? Especially when his condition appeared to be improving?

A horrible doubt began to creep into Anne's mind. Surely her father would not deliberately harm his cousin? If he wished Armand ill, why would he have been so insistent upon this marriage, which she deduced must bring with it some enhancement to their fortunes? With her thoughts swirling, she continued to the sickroom, where she found things much as they had been earlier.

"I think we must have some fresh, cool water for Monsieur de Barbier," Anne said, sending Thérèse away so that she could speak to her cousin in private.

As soon as the housekeeper shut the door behind her, Anne drew close to Armand and whispered, "Why are you so frightened of my father, cousin?"

Although he was alert, he was still a little disoriented. His face was red, and his teeth chattered occasionally. "I dont know. Just, when he's here, I feel sicker. And Père Jaquin told me—I mean he always said—"

So that was the real reason: the priest's misinformation. Anne felt a little relieved. "I know he told you my father was wicked, but he is wrong!" She took his hand and pressed it between hers. It was so thin she could feel every bone in it. "Listen to me. My father is only sad and worried about you, and . . . I must just ask you one question. It's important. I'm not prying for my own sake, but for yours."

He turned his glassy eyes upon her, and Anne could read fear in them.

"What is the state of your fortune, and what happens to it if you—if you—" Anne could not bring herself to say the words.

"If I die?" he asked, and something like a smile flitted across his face. "Do you want it, Anne? You too?"

"I too? Who else—but no! Please do not think so. It is only—I'm so confused, and nothing makes any sense."

Armand leaned back on his pillow and closed his eyes. Before Anne could question him further, Thérèse returned with a clean tumbler and a fresh pitcher of water that was covered with a linen cloth weighted at the corners with glass beads. Anne poured the water for her cousin. His hands were still too weak to hold the glass, so she clasped hers around his and helped him raise it to his lips.

She wanted to ask her father about the medicine she had heard him speak of, but she didn't dare. If only Monsieur Talon would come back. She trusted him. After all, it had been he who had saved Armand's life. But short of going to the Hôtel-Dieu to find him, there was nothing she could do to make him return, especially after her father had sent him away. And if by some miracle she were able to convince Talon to attend upon her cousin, the marquis would no doubt throw up every obstacle he could think of. Anne's hopes of having another private moment with Armand were dashed when the marquis himself entered a few moments later.

"How is the patient today?" he asked, his hooded eyes not meeting Anne's.

"I think a little improved, Father," Anne replied.

"You'll be going to your practice soon, I should think," he said, shooing Anne out of her seat at Armand's bedside.

"Did I not tell you?" Anne said. "I sent word to Madame d'Agoult that I could not leave my cousin's side today."

The marquis drew himself up, his silver eyebrows raised in surprise. "I see. You astonish me. I assumed you cared only about your own enjoyment and would be content to leave me and Monsieur de Barbier alone," he said. "I've asked Victor to bring the carriage around."

Anne fought to contain the tears that stung into the backs of her eyes. How could he so misjudge her? Couldn't he tell that she cared very much about Armand's health and would do anything in her power to care for him and hasten his recovery? Yet in her heart, she knew that most of her recent actions might easily appear self-serving. And if she looked to the deepest reaches of her soul, she found that in some fashion they were. Even now, although she was worried about Armand, she could not deny that she welcomed the excuse to leave the hôtel Barbier, to escape to the quai Malaquais and put her concerns about her cousin out of her mind. After all, Armand's fear of her father could be nothing more than the ravings of a fevered mind. The marquis certainly looked solicitous, sitting by his cousin's side pressing a cool, damp cloth to his forehead. She would speak to Thérèse before she left and ask her to watch over Armand.

Anne quietly let herself out of the sickroom and went to fetch her wrap and bonnet. She had not dressed for visiting but did not have the heart to change out of her simple muslin day dress. Madame d'Agoult would have to take her as she was.

If she was still at home, that is. Having sent a note earlier saying that she would not come that day, Anne could not be certain that the countess would not have gone visiting herself. If that turned out to be the case, Anne would simply return immediately to the hôtel Barbier. She knew better than to ask Victor to take her anywhere else. She had seen his expression after her father chastised him the day they brought Armand to the hôtel Barbier. He would lose his position in the household over it the next time, although it occurred to Anne to wonder when his wages had last been paid.

She sat for a moment at her dressing table and, before settling her bonnet over her curls, leaned her aching head in her hands. It hurt from the effort of taking in everything she had seen and heard and felt in the last few days. Although she tried and tried to think of some way to fix all the problems she faced, she was caught. What could she do—with no money, few friends, and only the faintest grasp of the situation? When her mother was alive, life had been comparatively easy. Now, intrigues and half-truths whirled around her, and the horrors of the outside world contaminated the closed circle of her life. Anne reached into her dressing table drawer for the packet of notes she had received from Liszt. Perhaps she could draw some comfort from them. But the memory of Liszt's kiss, and her own part in bringing it about, worked some kind of evil spell on this talisman of her fantasies. She quickly untied the ribbon she had cut off an old bonnet for the purpose of keeping the letters together and read over some of the notes. She wanted to see if there were any hint in them, any clue that would explain what had happened between her and her illustrious teacher and account for some of her present distress and uncertainty.

As she read through the hastily scrawled letters, an awful suspicion began to form in Anne's heart. Not one of them actually addressed her by name. She forced herself to think back to the first time Liszt had hidden a letter in a book of poetry and recalled the expression in his eyes, the way he kept trying to draw her attention to Marie. There was an urgency, a pleading, but nothing that assured her of his love. And at Madame Duvernoy's, he had asked her for her help. Help? Her help in what?

Anne stopped her train of thought abruptly. She did not want to discover something unpleasant or embarrassing, not at that moment. Victor awaited. She was about to retie the letters together in their neat little package to consider later, when the reverse of one of them caught her eye. It said, "F. Liszt, 61, rue de Provence, 7ème." He must have written that note on the back of something that had been sent to him. Now she knew where he lived.

Anne hastily retied the package and hid it in the back of her drawer. She cast an anxious glance toward her cousin's room before descending the stairs. *Perhaps*, she thought, *there is something I can do.* Anything would be preferable to simply standing aside and waiting to see what happened next.

She had passed through the vestibule and was about to climb into the carriage when a man in the simple robe and sandals of a Jesuit priest entered the courtyard. She stopped, thinking to tell him that he had taken a wrong turn, but his purposeful strides toward the door suggested that he intended to call upon the hôtel Barbier. It would be impolite not to greet him. As soon as he was close enough so that their eyes met, she said, "Good morning, Père," with a little bow of her head.

"You must be the countess Anne," the priest said with a broad smile. "I came yesterday to see your cousin, Monsieur de Barbier. I discovered from his manservant that he was being cared for in the home of his guardian, your father."

It seemed that everyone in the world besides herself knew of the relationship between her father and Armand. "Yes, he is here, and rather unwell still, I am afraid. To whom do I have the pleasure of speaking?" Anne did not know why, but the priest's presumptuous, overfriendly manner irked her.

"Forgive me!" he said with a respectful bow. "But Armand has spoken so warmly of you, I felt as if we had already been introduced. I am Père Jaquin, of Les Jésuites. Armand's confessor, tutor—and friend."

He reached out to place his hand on Anne's arm, and she turned away so that he could not reach her without awkwardness, pretending not to have noticed his gesture. The memory of what Armand had said the priest told him about the marquis was still fresh in her mind. How could Armand take the word of this irritating fellow? Yet she could also see that life in the college, with no family or friends from outside, must have been quite lonely. Perhaps she was being unkind to judge this man so harshly and ought to permit Armand the pleasure of a visit from outside the confines of their crumbling mansion. "Julien will see you to my cousin's chamber," she said, and with a dismissive nod, climbed into the vehicle.

As soon as they started toward the quai Malaquais, she put the priest out of her mind and resumed the train of thought that his advent had interrupted. Before long an idea came to her.

"Victor, stop the carriage," she called out, just as they turned onto the quai. "I have been too much indoors of late and need air. I shall walk the remainder of the distance. It is not far. You may fetch me at your usual time."

The coachman was uneasy about doing anything out of the ordinary, especially after the events of the past few days. Despite his hulking size, he cowered at the wrath of his employer. "Don't worry, Victor. No one will know you left me here. See, you can watch me walk toward Madame d'Agoult's apartment." She climbed out and started off to the east along the quai.

Victor sighed, and the little carriage creaked as he shifted his bulky frame in the box. Anne continued to walk without looking back until she heard the coachman's voice say, "Get on!" and his short whip crack in the air over the horses' backs. As soon as Anne thought she was safely out of his sight, she hurried right past Marie's apartment and continued along the quai to the Pont Neuf. She crossed quickly over the tip of the Île du Palais to the opposite bank of the Seine, in the direction of the Seventh Arrondissement. As she drew near to the neighborhood of the opera house, she saw a flower seller on the side of the road. After purchasing a rather wilted bunch of violets from her, Anne asked, "Which way is the rue de Provence?"

The lady pointed out the direction. Anne's heart pounded. Now her decision was made. She did not know how to approach Pierre Talon directly to come to her aid, so she would ask Liszt to intercede, to be an accomplice in her daring enterprise. After that he could make the inquiries she could not to bring the doctor to Armand's bedside. The address on the back of the note was a sign. It was meant to be. Yet what if he was not at home? And if he was, what exactly would she say to him?

By the time she had located number sixty-one, saw that it was an apartment house, and realized that she had no idea which apartment was Liszt's, she comprehended the folly of the step she had just taken. She had already turned away, when all at once, the air on the street was filled with glorious music. From the top floor of the building echoed a sound so powerful that it seemed that not one but ten pianos were being played at once. The structure itself shook. There would be no excuse, Anne thought, for not locating Monsieur Liszt now.

She entered by a door next to the haberdashery on the ground floor and climbed the stairs slowly, gathering her thoughts as she went. She must be calm and not let her emotions take control. She was going to ask him to do something for her because she could not do it for herself. That was all. The stairs became narrower and plainer as she climbed. Liszt's apartment was on the top floor, tucked beneath the mansard roof.

Somewhat breathless by the time she arrived at the plain plank door, Anne paused to wait for a break in the music before knocking.

Franz tortured himself with wishing he could undo his actions of the day before. He had been so absorbed in his own desires that he had insulted the countess's hospitality, possibly damaging his chances not only of winning her but also of being welcomed in that society to which she belonged, and from which his livelihood would continue to spring for the foreseeable future. If his mother ever found out about it, she would be disappointed in him.

At times of suffering and distress, Franz didn't exactly seek refuge in music; it was more that music found a way to feed off the excess emotional charges coursing through him. He had never been more inventive, more inspired. With the constant, tortured thought of Marie keeping him company during his waking hours, and dreams of her inspiring him even as he slept, Franz became intoxicated with creativity. New ideas unrolled themselves before him as he played. Sometimes he created a moment so beautiful he couldn't bear to stop his fingers, and then he would end by straying so far away from his original thought that could not recapture it. But he could afford to squander some of his vast wealth of ideas without regret. That day, he played and played, only stopping when a thought was wholly wrought to lean over the paper he had hastily lined that morning, dip his pen in the inkpot, and dash in the notes as quickly as his hand would allow.

He had paused to write a phrase when he heard a polite, crisp knock on his door. "Come!" he yelled out, without looking around.

A familiar, delicate scent wafted in with the lady, whose petticoats whished gently against the frame of the door as she passed through. Franz unbent from his task and turned.

"Countess," he said, with a deep bow. This he most certainly had not expected. He had no idea that she even knew where he lived.

The sight of Liszt in his shirtsleeves, untied at the neck to reveal his bare chest, almost sent Anne running back down the stairs to seek the safety of the street. But if she did that, he would surely suspect she had sought him out for an entirely different reason than the one she actually had in mind. "I see you are surprised." Anne mustered all the self-control she possessed. "I assure you, I come not to embarrass you with unseemly demands." She could not look at him, instead concentrating on straightening the seam on one of the fingers of her gloves.

"Please, sit down," he said.

"*Non, merci*, I prefer to stand," she said. She hoped he did not notice the slight shake in her voice.

"Mademoiselle, I—"

"Please do not mention the events of yesterday. I have a much more urgent matter to discuss, a matter that involves the health—perhaps even the life—of someone whom I care for." Anne bit the inside of her lower lip while she thought about how to continue, how much of her cousin's story to reveal. She decided Liszt should know as little as possible, just in case. "I presume upon our friendship, because I do not believe you mean me harm, and I require a gentleman's assistance in this matter."

Franz's heart warmed at the sight of this slender young girl, who looked so proud and frightened standing there. If he were not deeply smitten with Marie, he thought, and if he had not already been burned by an association with a young member of the nobility, here would be consolation indeed. He eventually persuaded Anne to sit, and to take a little glass of claret. For the next half hour, she related to him events that formed a confused and menacing picture of life at her father's house. Although he was not certain from what she told him exactly why she felt she must remove her cousin from the marquis's protection, clearly something disturbed her deeply about the situation.

"What would make your father not treat his cousin with all possible care in his illness? Surely he can gain nothing by having the boy's blood on his hands."

Anne turned her eyes away and would not answer him. Nothing he asked her could make her say more. Perhaps, Franz thought, a fortune was involved in the matter.

"Supposing I agree to help you. Would your father not be very angry indeed? And have you no fears for your own safety?"

"Please," Anne said, "I cannot believe my father intends harm. I am unable to explain it. All I know is that he will not permit Monsieur Talon to attend Armand, and so I must take Armand to Monsieur Talon."

"When did you think we might accomplish this abduction, if your father is always at home, as you say?"

"I need a few days to think about it. I wasn't certain . . ."

Franz could well understand that she had not counted on his assistance.

After a moment's thought she continued. "In a few days. Perhaps by Thursday evening I shall have thought of a plan."

"But you will be occupied on Thursday, *non*?" By the puzzled look on her face, Franz saw that she did not know what he was talking about. "The salon, at Madame d'Agoult's. You will perform, naturally. The étude." Franz searched around among the mess of manuscript papers and open books on his table and unearthed the card that had arrived shortly before the countess. He handed it to her. She read it through several times with her forehead creased in a frown, then gave it back to him.

"This may be a stroke of good fortune," she said. "Are you willing, Monsieur Liszt, to place yourself at my disposal upon that evening?"

"I think you had better tell me precisely what you have in mind before I agree to anything."

Anne hoped that the tremor she felt in every part of her body had not been apparent to Liszt during their conversation, in which she described to him the alley by Marie's building where a carriage could wait out of sight, and the door that she knew led there, having seen the maid let in tradesmen through it once or twice when she passed through to the parlor. He had agreed to help her but clearly had some misgivings. Now she must call on Marie. If she was going to perform in less than a week, she would have to practice as much as she possibly could before then. Although she knew that this event had been the purpose of the lessons all along, nonetheless it came as a shock to see her name in writing as giving a debut performance of a new work by the celebrated Monsieur Frédéric Chopin.

Anne took her leave of Liszt, noticing how soft his lips felt on the back of her hand, which he took before she had a chance to put on her gloves, and which he seemed reluctant to release from his grasp. The gesture called to mind the touch of his hands upon hers at her lessons, and that forbidden, unbidden kiss. She looked away when he bowed so that she would not stare at the way his shirt fell open and revealed the outline of his ribs and the dark nipples on his chest. Anne had not allowed herself to look into his eyes after that but left the apartment quickly without a backward glance.

The winding streets of Paris passed by Anne in a haze as she practically floated all the way to the quai Malaquais. She knew that what she had done was as improper as it could possibly be. But now, at least another person—a man—knew of her fears for her cousin's health and would help her put everything to rights. Curiously, her clandestine meeting with Liszt made her less anxious about facing Marie. She had convinced herself that it was unlikely her patroness had witnessed her teacher's brazen behavior the day before. If she had, surely Monsieur Liszt would be more distressed, less sanguine.

Anne pulled the bell and waited to be admitted to Madame d'Agoult's parlor. She found Marie seated at her desk, gazing across the river toward the Tuileries.

"Sit down, Anne," Marie said. "I should like a word with you."

Anne did as she asked.

"You received my note, about the salon?"

Of course, Anne thought. She would have to lie. Yet again. "Yes. That is why I changed my mind and decided to come today. I would like to practice. But there is something else I must ask," she said.

Marie sat without speaking, waiting for Anne to proceed.

"I would like my father to attend this salon." She braced herself for Madame d'Agoult's objections.

But instead, Marie turned her eyes once more to the view from her window as if she had been asked nothing more interesting than whether she would like bread and butter or a cake with her tea. "Very well," she said. "If you can persuade him to come, I shall welcome him."

"What were you going to ask me?" Anne said.

"I simply wondered: has that young man, Monsieur Talon, been to see your cousin recently?"

"He came only once. My father would not let him return. I so wish he would!"

Marie looked back at Anne, this time with a quizzical expression. "For your cousin's sake, or for your own?"

Something in her manner of asking brought a blush to Anne's cheek.

"No matter," Marie said.

Anne longed to protest to Marie that she had misunderstood, and to tell her everything about Liszt and Armand and her father, but she did not know how to begin. Instead, she went to the piano and began practicing with more fervor and dedication than ever. Once her hands touched the keyboard, Anne allowed herself to bask in the thrill of giving her first performance—albeit in front of an invited audience in a private home. She must play to make her mother proud of her. That was reason enough to think of nothing else for the next few hours, and let all the doubts and worries that beset her fade into the background.

Twenty

Pierre stared in disbelief at the letter he had just received from Madame d'Agoult. It had come to him in the same envelope as the invitation to the salon.

Cher Monsieur Talon,

You said you were willing to help me in whatever way I thought would lead to Anne's protection and continued well-being. After some hesitation, I have decided that, before the salon on Thursday, I must ask you to find a way to enter the hôtel Barbier to locate my friend Sandrine de Barbier-Chouant's last will and testament and bring it to me.

When I was there, I chanced to see it in the library, which is to the left as you enter the front door. If you are successful in this errand, please bring the document to me in the greatest secrecy. I would not ask you to do this if I did not believe that it was vital to Anne's safety. Thank you for aiding me in this matter.

How, in the name of heaven, was he to accomplish such a task? He was unlikely to be invited to enter the mansion as a guest. Yet to steal in—that was quite a different matter than finding his way into an official building via a secret entrance. Complicating matters was the fact that the marquis would recognize him if he saw him, and his medical career could be destroyed before it even began. But worse than that, if Anne were to discover him, she would never believe his motives, and he would lose all hope of gaining her favor.

Pierre made a mental note never to agree to something in the future without knowing all the details. He had given his word to the countess, and now he was obliged to do as she requested. Could he enlist the aid of one of the servants? From what he saw, the coachman was too timid, the footman too devoted to his master, and the maid too attached to Anne. He did not even know their names, or whether any of them could read any message he might send.

He rubbed his forehead. He had entered a building in the dead of night once; perhaps it would not be so difficult to do it again. The hôtel Barbier was not likely to be as well guarded as the Prefecture. Yet so much could go amiss. He knew nothing about thievery and would most likely be apprehended and thrown in jail. No, he thought, he must refuse. Or claim that he made the attempt and did not succeed.

Yet that would be dishonorable. And Madame d'Agoult would not have asked him to undertake such a task without excellent reasons. If Anne's safety were truly at stake, he must do his best to comply. Surely there was some other way . . .

Of course! he thought. He must acquire the will, but he need not do it himself. Paris was thick with men desperate to earn a few sous, whom he might hire to perform a robbery and thereby not risk his own involvement. The question was where to find someone who possessed both the skill and the willingness to help him.

Pierre changed into his most worn-out shirt and breeches and donned his old greatcoat with the torn pocket. He left his apartment and headed not for the university or Saint Germain but for the Eighth Arrondissement, north of the Seine and east of the ruins of the Bastille. Deep in the heart of the faubourg Saint Antoine, one of the poorest, filthiest neighborhoods of Paris, was a place known as the Cour des

Miracles. It was to that aptly named quarter that the thieves and vagabonds of the city retired when they were not plying their trade. Blind beggars regained their sight, starving children recovered their health, and epileptics found themselves miraculously cured of that unfortunate affliction—until the next day, when once again they would pour out onto the streets of Paris and beg or thieve from the wealthy. He knew of this place only because it had been mentioned in one of his lectures on civic hygiene as the example of the old, crowded, dirty ways that the authorities were trying to correct through moving people to other neighborhoods, tearing down, and rebuilding. The problem was, so the lecturer said, that no one from any government office could penetrate the Cour des Miracles without risking his life. Pierre decided he would have to try to do something that had stymied more capable men than he. Where else, he thought, could he find someone he could pay to break into a house, steal something, and depart again without raising the alarm? Someone who would have no reason to see him ever again.

Pierre guessed that the number of inhabitants of the Court of Miracles would by now have been substantially depleted by the cholera. He also feared that if they believed he was a doctor, his throat would be cut not ten paces into the maze of tiny alleyways that had been barricaded so effectively during the July Revolution. But without any other knowledge of the underworld, Pierre did not know where else to turn. Better to risk his neck in a setting where no one knew him than bungle an attempt to rob Mademoiselle Anne's home on his own.

Pulling his collar up and keeping his eyes focused downward, Pierre walked rapidly north to the quai de Saint Bernard to cross over the Seine on the Pont d'Austerlitz. The route would take him directly into the Eighth Arrondissement, through the Quinze-Vingts quarter to the faubourg Saint Antoine. Once there, he would have to find his way through the interlacing, twisting streets, many of which had been reduced to dirt when the people dug up the cobbles to build barricades. His goal was the infamous rue de Charenton.

He found the neighborhood easily enough and soon became enmeshed in the winding byways, where little of the daylight filtered down, the buildings creating an unnatural, early twilight. The smell of death and bile was strong, but no piles of corpses littered the streets, which were mostly too narrow to allow a carriage to pass. They must keep them indoors, Pierre thought, and mentally crossed himself. Several times, Pierre approached a bedraggled urchin to ask the way, but as soon as he was within ten feet of the child, he (or she—he found it impossible to tell which) would vanish down some tiny alleyway or into a cleverly hidden doorway. Pierre felt like the scourge of death himself, walking through this godforsaken quarter. He could see people up ahead, dirty rags blending in with the sooty stones of the buildings, and like the rats under the bridges scattering at the light of a torch, as he approached, they would slither into their hovels.

This, thought Pierre, had been a foolish idea. More than once he thought of turning around and fleeing, but a quick glance over his shoulder confirmed what he feared: that he would not easily be able to retrace his steps through the byzantine neighborhood. He began to believe that never again would he return to the genteel dilapidation of the Latin Quarter or visit the sunny, luxurious streets of Saint Germain. He shivered and pulled his coat more closely around him. Compared to this, breaking into the hôtel Barbier himself would have seemed quite simple.

Just as Pierre had decided that, whether he found the same way back or not, he must abandon his dangerous quest, a voice behind him called out, "Monsieur!" He turned and saw lumbering toward him the strangest creature he had ever laid eyes on. His head was overly large for the diminutive body on which it was placed, and short arms pumped furiously while the stumpy legs hurried in Pierre's direction. Had a man his own size pursued him like that, he would have run for his life. Instead, something in the fellow stopped him where he was, and he waited for him to draw near.

At first, Pierre thought this dwarf intended to put out his hand in greeting, but to his horror, at the moment when it would be too late for him to run away, he saw the small dagger the fellow clutched in his hand. With a speed that astonished him, the dwarf grabbed hold of

Pierre's right leg with one hand, and pressed the knife against his testicles with the other.

"I suggest you do not move," the dwarf said, "or you will find yourself most horribly mutilated."

Pierre did not breathe.

"What are you doing here?" The dwarf's voice was oddly high-pitched.

"I—I'm looking for help." Pierre found it difficult to talk because his heart was in his throat.

"Help!" The fellow laughed. "That's rich."

"I have to steal something, and I don't know how." Pierre had taken the measure of this fellow and his ways and decided in that instant that he would never want to introduce such a creature to Anne's home. If anyone were to break into the hôtel Barbier, it would have to be he after all.

The dwarf relaxed his grip on Pierre's leg but did not move the knife from its precarious position. "You? A gent like yourself? How are the mighty fallen," he said.

The turn of phrase surprised Pierre. "You're an educated man?" he inquired.

This resulted in a tiny thrust of the knife. Pierre winced.

"Educated is as educated does. I'll give you half a minute to tell your story, and if I don't like it, I'll cut."

"There's a girl—a lady—who may be in danger. I must steal her mother's will. Her father may have falsified documents. Her mother died of cholera. I'm willing to pay for this help, although I am not a rich man." The phrases tumbled out of Pierre's mouth in no particular order.

The dwarf returned his knife to its hiding place on his person but resumed his grip on Pierre's leg. "You're a fool to come here. We're none too pleased with the bourgeois in this neighborhood." He dragged on Pierre, who was forced to hobble along next to him in a gait that was even more absurd than the dwarf's own.

"What's your name, gent?" the fellow asked.

"Pierre. What's yours?"

This provoked a high-pitched laugh, like a horse's whinny. "Call me Petit."

Pierre's spirits sank as his captor led him deeper into the quarter and eventually pushed him through a doorway that was too small to enter standing upright. He could feel the dripping walls on either side of him in the pitch-black corridor, and eventually they went through another door into a small room. A feeble fire kept the damp at bay here, and a small, dirty window let in barely enough light to see by. A man lay stretched out on a straw pallet over to one side—sick, by the look of him, even in the dim illumination.

"What have you brought me, Petit?" the man said, his voice faint and feeble.

"A job, Captain," Petit answered.

"Speak."

Pierre did not know whether the captain—as Petit called him—wanted him or Petit to explain. "Well, you see—"

"Silence!" the dwarf snapped at Pierre, then addressed the figure lying on the straw. "He's got a break-in. Says he wants to learn how to do it himself, but perhaps we can persuade him to use a hired hand."

"What's the prize?"

This time Pierre was silent.

"Well?" Petit gave him a sharp kick in the ankle. "Who else is going to tell us?"

Pierre shrugged. "I need to find a certain will."

"A will? What value is a will?" The captain shifted a little in the straw. "Does he have any money?" he asked Petit.

Pierre reached into his pocket for the twenty francs he had brought with him, but to his surprise, his money pouch was already in Petit's little hand. The dwarf tossed the leather bag to the captain. "Not much. But maybe there's more to come."

"I—I only meant to ask advice, how to break in, how to avoid getting caught. I didn't—ow!"

Another sharp kick in the ankle silenced Pierre.

"Two hundred francs."

The man on the pallet said the words, but Pierre didn't understand what he meant. He looked at Petit.

"That's what it'll cost ye. For help with the job."

"But I haven't got two hundred francs!" Pierre cried.

"A man who carries twenty with him on the street must have at least ten times as much. And if you don't have it, just steal it. We'll show you how." The captain's voice was slow and precise. When he finished, he and Petit started laughing, and the resulting sound was as peculiar as could be. Petit's shrill whinny combined with a weak, gasped guffaw from the man who lay ill on the pallet. Pierre did not dare inquire into his affliction.

"All right, suppose I can manage to get this sum. How do I know you will help me?"

The dwarf let go at last of Pierre's leg and stood back from him, looking up at his face as if he thought Pierre was completely insane. "You, monsieur, have no choice. We did not ask you to venture into our quarter, but now that you are here, I suggest that you are in no position to bargain."

Pierre recognized the wisdom of Petit's words. "Please, could you not tell me how to go about breaking into an old hôtel, how to move quietly so that no one will awaken and hear me?"

The captain began describing to Pierre the method of stealing into a house in the dead of night. He told him to wrap cloths around his shoes so that he would make no noise, and to try at all costs not to use a candle. He should similarly wrap an iron bar in case he would have to break a window with a minimum of noise.

"But if I have no light, how will I know if I have the document I seek?"

"If you stay long enough in the dark, your eyes will become accustomed." Petit smiled in self-congratulation. Clearly he had had such an experience at more than one time.

To Pierre's surprise, the advice of the sick captain made a great deal of sense. "I think I know what I must do. I'm very grateful for your help. Now I must return to my lodgings, or the fellow I share with will put out the alarm." Pierre gave a polite bow and prepared to leave. But he had not taken two steps when Petit attached himself once again to his leg.

"Not so fast! We need a guarantee, don't we, Captain?"

The captain grunted, but it seemed to Pierre that his illness had made him fall asleep again. All at once there was an overwhelming, acrid aroma of urine. Pierre took in his breath sharply.

"Out!" cried Petit. "I'll find you, Monsieur Pierre. Have no doubt of that! And when I do, it's two hundred francs, or you're done for."

The dwarf propelled him back through the dark corridor and shoved him out the small door. He was about to disappear back inside the hovel when Pierre stopped him. "Wait!"

Petit glowered at Pierre beneath his furry eyebrows.

"What afflicts the captain? Perhaps I may be of help."

The dwarf spat a great globule of mucus that attached itself to the hem of Pierre's frock coat. "Never you mind. It's not cholera, else he'd be dead by now."

Before Pierre could ask which way to go, Petit disappeared back into the house. Pierre looked up and down the little street, which curved so that he could not see far in either direction. He remembered that they had turned right into the door, and so he went to his left. On his way out, he noticed, the dirty, sullen inhabitants did not hide themselves away as they had when he came in. Now they stared at him with open curiosity. One or two little children scurried up to him with their hands out, begging for centimes. He found a couple in a pocket that Petit had not picked.

After about half an hour of wandering toward what he hoped was the south, Pierre broke free of the winding streets and saw the road to the Pont d'Austerlitz. Never before had he been so relieved to see the turbid, green Seine snaking away before him. Yet even after he crossed over the iron bridge into the Latin Quarter, he had an uncomfortable feeling, as of a spider crawling down his back. He was sorry he had gone there, sorry to have witnessed the way those people lived. No wonder there was cholera, he thought. And crime, its own epidemic, flourished in the same conditions.

Pierre hurried back in the direction of his apartment, hoping that Georges would be at home to dispel his gloomy mood. He felt like playing comic songs and drinking champagne, except that he couldn't afford it. The dwarf had relieved him of all that he had managed to save from his small allowance. By tomorrow he must work up the courage to put the captain's advice into practice and secure the will that Madame d'Agoult so desperately wanted. Would he not, then, be a criminal too? Pierre envisioned the notorious detective Vidocq laying a trap for him and carting him off to prison. He had to remind himself that whatever his actions, they were in the interest of exposing perhaps greater crimes and bringing the truth to light. Surely no one would blame him for that.

When he was halfway across the bridge, Pierre changed his mind about his destination. The café, he thought. He would go there directly, where he would be more likely to find Georges in any case. His friend was in the habit of seeking some amusement before taking his night shift at the Hôtel-Dieu. It had been weeks since Pierre had last raised a glass with his colleagues from the faculty of medicine. A little camaraderie would be just the thing, and no doubt someone would stand him a drink.

Pierre could have turned right and walked along the quai to reach the rue des Écoles, but he did not want to be able to see across to the other side of that sinister dividing line. He could not shed the feeling that many eyes watched him from the small windows in the Quinze-Vingts district, and so he continued into the Latin Quarter on the rue de Buffon, then wound through the familiar lanes peopled with students and artists.

"Pierre! Over here!"

The sound of Georges's voice had never been more welcome. He was sitting, as Pierre suspected he would be, with a small group of medical students at two round tables on the street. By the sound of it, they had been heatedly arguing a point and drinking wine while doing so.

"We need you to help us decide this," Georges said, dragging a chair from an empty table nearby so that Pierre could join them.

"Where have you been?" Georges asked, having by then noticed Pierre's drab clothing. "You look like you've seen a ghost."

"Only visiting some poor districts. I didn't want to frighten them by looking too grand." Pierre hoped his explanation would suffice. They all appeared too drunk to care much anyway.

Georges continued, waving his empty glass in the air. "Our debate concerns the criminal mind: does it thrive during a time such as this, when the diseased body becomes a symbol for the depravity of the populace?"

Pierre gratefully downed the glass of red wine another student poured for him. "Why don't you go to the faubourg Saint Antoine and ask the residents there?"

His response provoked hearty laughs all around. Pierre simply smiled and ordered another bottle. He would pay the proprietor next week, when he could draw another installment of his allowance from the bank.

Twenty-One

While Pierre laughed and joked with his friends in the Latin Quarter, Franz and Eugène sat at an indoor table and spoke in low voices in a café on the rue des Beaux Arts, a small street in the faubourg Saint Germain.

"I advise against it. Truly! Remember what happened last time." Eugène's whisper was edged with sarcasm.

Franz frowned at the ruby liquid in the tumbler in front of him. "But this is not the same."

"She's pretty, yes? And a countess, as you said? And virtually an orphan?"

Franz nodded his assent to all Eugène's points.

"I ask you how, pray, is this any different?"

"Let me explain again," Franz said, motioning the waiter to bring another bottle. "We would be going to fetch her cousin, who is ill, she says."

"Hah! I'll not share a carriage with a cholera victim," Eugène said.

"Not cholera, but he is recovering from some operation or other."

"And you believe it would be better to jostle him over the cobbles in a carriage rather than leave him in a comfortable, warm bed? And what will you do with him once you get him out?"

Franz pursed his lips and looked off into the crowd at the café. There were some very beautiful ladies there, he noted, and one eyed him with more than curiosity. He was beginning to wish he had never become involved in the young countess's life. It had been foolish to think that she would be the means to make his feelings known to Marie. "The point is, Eugène, that a lady has asked me for my help." He did not want to tell Eugène about the kiss, the one act that obliged him to come to Anne's aid.

Eugène grasped Franz's arm. "No. I shan't help you. Not this time." He stood and pulled his gloves over his wiggling fingers.

"Where are you going?" Franz asked, shocked.

"To paint. It's how I make the money that pays for all this wine, you know."

Eugène whirled around and threaded his way through the elegant crowd of tea drinkers and Bordeaux sippers exchanging secrets for hours each day.

"But you haven't paid the bill!" Franz called out to him as he went. When the waiter brought him a slip of paper with a list of everything they had consumed that afternoon, Franz said, "Add it to Monsieur Delacroix's account," and before the fellow had a chance to protest, Franz followed his friend out onto the street.

He caught up to him as the artist turned the corner of the lane where his studio was located. "You don't have to go with us," Franz said. "Just come to the salon, and make sure Marie is occupied for an hour while I take care of this matter."

"So you don't want me to hire horses and a carriage for you?"

"Well, there is that. But that is all, I promise."

By now the two friends had climbed the stairs and entered the parlor outside Eugène's studio. "You forget one detail," Eugène said as he removed his gloves and hat and slid his coat off. "I haven't been invited to this soiree."

"That doesn't matter!" Franz said. "You're famous. The countess will be delighted to have you. I'll bring you as my guest."

Eugène stood with his hands on his hips and shook his head at his Hungarian friend. "Give me time to think about it, and I advise you to examine your own feelings as well."

As he left Eugène, Franz had an uneasy feeling in his heart. It seemed that whatever he decided to do, there would be some bad outcome. How did he know, after all, that there really was an ailing cousin? Perhaps the countess wanted to entrap him, to put him in a position where he would have to marry her. It seemed unlikely, knowing Anne, but Eugène's suspicions had poured a good dose of cold water on Franz's desire to be gallant toward his student.

The next afternoon, Anne stood in her father's library holding the invitation to the countess d'Agoult's salon. "You will come, won't you, Papa?" she asked.

He sat at his desk, his eyes fixed at a spot somewhere in the middle of the papers scattered over it. "Our cousin needs care. He must have his medicine."

"Thérèse can do that," Anne said, and added, "if you tell her how. And if you'd let me send for Monsieur Talon—"

"That young fellow again? He's not a doctor."

Anne closed her eyes for a moment. This was not going well. "I'm sure the care you give him, with the help of Dr. Magendie, is sufficient. But this is important. Madame d'Agoult promised she would present me, and if you are not there, people will talk."

The marquis flared his nostrils and sniffed. "I have important business matters to attend to. And this performance nonsense—it is dishonorable."

"Surely the business can wait? And the most exalted people play and sing at these private affairs. Besides, I'm certain there will be people you know there. Marie has many friends from court."

She held her breath until the marquis spoke. "I suppose I must attend. But do not, Countess, ask me to do such a thing again. You do not know what it is you request."

He stood, leaning heavily on his cane. Anne thought her father looked much older, just since her mother had died. "Besides," she said, "I should like you to hear me play."

At that, the marquis raised his eyes to Anne. For the briefest instant, a flicker of something like sorrow passed across them. But soon his face settled into a more familiar expression of bitterness and anger. "We will leave the party immediately following your piece."

Anne could feel her father's gaze burning into the back of her head when she turned and walked out of the library. The salon would take place the next evening. She had spent the afternoon at Marie's piano, knowing now that there was no point in begging her father to open the ballroom, since the Pleyel was no longer there. The countess d'Agoult had acted strangely reserved ever since her last lesson, and Anne became increasingly convinced that she had seen much more than her words since then had indicated.

And now, if her father planned to take her away immediately after her performance, it would be more difficult for her to carry out the plan she had made with Liszt. Unless she could find a way to make her father stay at Marie's, they would never be able to get to the hôtel Barbier quickly enough to accomplish their abduction before the marquis returned.

Armand did not appear to be improving much, although Thérèse said that the wound in his groin had healed nicely. If only her father would allow her to bring back Monsieur Talon! The marquis would let no one aside from himself administer the medicine the doctor prescribed for Pierre, and so Anne could not discover what it was. If she knew that, she thought, she might be able to get word to Talon to ask him about it.

Ever since the day of her visit to the Hôtel-Dieu, Anne had been tortured by disturbing dreams. Dark circles had begun to form under her eyes, and she felt fatigued all the time. She tried to hide the circles with some white powder Thérèse had confiscated from the late marquise's dressing table, but she found it difficult not to yawn, and one day she had almost nodded off at the piano.

Yet as soon as she lay down to sleep at night, her eyes flew open. In the dark of her room, visions of writhing patients rose before her. At one time, she saw a skeleton playing the piano like Liszt, its bony fingers clattering against the keys with great virtuosity. He entertained the dying in an enormous hospital ward, where the inmates retched and clapped by turns and were carted out one by one as they succumbed to their illnesses.

Anne's entire world had changed in the last weeks. Everything she thought she knew had been called into question. Now she was about to do something so daring that her father could, if he chose, have her committed for it. Daughters had been sent away to convents and asylums for less, she knew. But Anne could not bear to watch her cousin fade away without making some attempt to help him.

When she could not sleep, sometimes Anne would try to picture the piano keyboard in her mind and play her pieces on her coverlet. The effort tired her, and after a time she would drift into a disturbed doze. That night, she had finally managed to quiet her mind enough to sink away into semiconsciousness when a noise woke her. She sat upright and fumbled for the candle next to her bed. The floor felt painfully cold against her bare feet, but she stepped across it slowly and quietly and lit the candle with the embers in the heating stove. She drew her shawl over her shoulders and held it tight under her chin, pausing in the middle of her room, listening, unable to decide whether to go back to bed and try to sleep, or stay alert in case something really had awakened her. She did not know exactly why, but she felt the presence of a stranger in the house. Anne blew out her candle and stood in the dark. If she was going to go downstairs to investigate, there was no sense in bringing a light to announce her presence.

Pierre told Georges that he had signed on to work at the Hôpital de la Charité, which was—conveniently—located in Saint Germain, not far from the hôtel Barbier. He took his medical bag with him, but instead of his stethoscope and instruments, he had filled it with a scarf to put over his nose and mouth, a few rags, and some twine to bind the rags around his shoes and the iron bar he brought in case he needed to break a window to gain access to the house. He sat in a café until the church bells tolled midnight, then wandered through the faubourg, walking as though he had business somewhere while he was on the larger streets, or ducking into doorways to avoid being seen when his steps took him through the smaller alleyways. When there seemed to be almost no one around outside anymore, Pierre turned toward the rue du Barq. His heart banged against his ribs. It occurred to him more than once that he was a little insane.

As he approached the dark mass of the hôtel Barbier, Pierre had that odd feeling as of a spider crawling on his neck again. He turned around, thinking perhaps someone had seen him and followed him. But in the dim pools of light from the street lamps, he saw only the cobbles, with an occasional rat slinking past low to the ground. He turned and continued his progress until he arrived at the iron gates, which were shut and locked against just such an eventuality as this.

Pierre knew from his visit here the week before that the family lived in the elegant but crumbling edifice directly opposite the gates. The wing to his left, therefore, had to be the stables and the servants' quarters. He assumed there was a separate entrance to this area within the courtyard and wondered if he could scale the gate, or the wall next to it, to reach it. But the design was such that it would be impossible to reach the top without someone's shoulders to stand on, and so Pierre walked to his left to see if perhaps another door led out to the alley next to the house to allow the servants to come and go unseen.

He was about halfway down the wall in this dark passage when he heard a noise behind him, this time clearly not a rat. He turned, and at the end of the alley, blocking Pierre's exit, stood Petit, his small body silhouetted against the comparative light of the street. Pierre stood utterly still and waited, realizing that he was trapped and could not avoid Petit without grappling with him. He cursed the fact that the tools he had brought to assist his entry into the house were all hidden in his bag and out of immediate reach.

Without making a noise, Petit ran forward. After what had happened the last time the dwarf had run toward him like that, Pierre instinctively crouched into a ball, his medical bag clutched in his arms.

To Pierre's surprise, however, Petit stopped before he reached him and put his finger to his lips, then leaned in close to speak quietly into his ear.

"The captain sent me to protect his investment. You're an easy one to follow," he said, and his shoulders shook with quiet laughter.

Pierre was not certain whether to be dismayed or relieved that he would have help—and expert help, at that—in his delicate enterprise. He did not like the thought of allowing this character from the Court of Miracles into Anne's home in the middle of the night, but there was little he could do about it now.

Petit gestured to Pierre to follow him, and they soon came to a shuttered window set into the stone wall of the house. It was too high for Petit to reach, so Pierre tried to open it, but it had been fastened from the inside. He looked questioningly at the dwarf, who pushed him aside and lifted one foot, indicating that Pierre should hoist him up. He cupped his hands beneath the dwarf's hobnail boot, which dug into his soft palms right through his gloves. He noticed that Petit had not taken the precautions Pierre had learned about the day before, and that for such a small person, he was surprisingly heavy. Soon Pierre's face dripped with sweat.

The dwarf pulled his small dagger out from where he had concealed it in his belt and slipped it between the two shutters, running it up and down until it hit something, then working it gently. To Pierre's surprise, the shutters sprang open.

The window was unglazed. It led into what looked like a pantry. Several fowl hung from the ceiling on iron hooks, and bowls covered with muslin gave off the pungent aroma of fermenting cheese. Pierre and Petit climbed through the window and crept through the small room. They opened a door that led into the main house through an unlit corridor. *This seems too easy,* Pierre thought. If he and the dwarf could enter Anne's house like this, how was it the hôtel Barbier had not been robbed many times before? They did not keep dogs either, he noticed with relief, so there was nothing to raise the alarm at their intrusion.

The dark corridor ended with five steps leading up to another door that opened into the dining room, which was dominated by a long table surrounded by high-backed chairs. The small amount of light that filtered in from the chinks in the drapes revealed a threadbare tapestry hanging on one wall and an antique serving table along another. Petit cast his eye around. "There's no silver!" he whispered. Pierre put his finger to his lips. Now he understood why Petit had come.

They made it into the entrance hall with hardly a sound, despite the fact that the cloths around Pierre's shoes slipped on the polished wood floors. He hoped he would not have to run inside the house. Pierre noticed that the dwarf had mastered the technique of walking silently without using cloths to cushion his footsteps.

To his right was the door that Madame d'Agoult had told him would lead into the library, directly opposite the one that was unaccountably padlocked shut. He tried the library door, found it unlocked, and pushed it open.

The oddly reassuring, musty smell of books was the only proof that they had entered the correct room. The windows must have been not only draped but shuttered, perhaps to protect valuable books from the light. Only a dull glow in the fireplace gave Pierre any idea of the size and shape of the room.

"Well, what are we waiting for?" Petit whispered, so close to Pierre's elbow that he jumped. "Time is our enemy, remember!"

When did they become "we"? Pierre wondered. He felt his way with his feet across the floor until he found the desk, which occupied the middle of the room. To his dismay, it was covered with entirely too many letters and papers for any one of them to stand out. Shuffling around in search of the will would be noisy and time-consuming. Pierre opened the drawers, hoping to find the document he was looking for tucked away, as it was bound to be under normal circumstances. But he found only bills and ordinary letters and papers, nothing on vellum.

In the meantime, Pierre noticed that Petit had come upon a few silver baubles: an inkwell, a pen stand, and a little figure of a Chinaman. These he tucked into the hidden pockets of his coat. Pierre could do nothing to stop him, he thought, without making noise.

He was about to abandon the search in frustration, chastising himself for taking such a risk for nothing, when he spotted a ribbon dangling down the side of the desk and followed it up to where it met the edge of a thick document. He tugged gently on the ribbon and freed the document from the pile. It was definitely vellum. He took it to the hearth to examine in the feeble glow of the embers.

I, Sandrine de Barbier-Chouant . . .

This was the will. He quickly stuffed it inside his coat, the crinkling of the stiff vellum making altogether too much noise, and, now that his eyes had become accustomed to the dark, gestured to Petit to follow him out of the library.

Pierre did not know whether he saw Anne or heard her gasp first. She wore a white nightdress and stood so pale and still on the bottom stair that, if he had not been a man of science, Pierre might have thought she was a ghost. Her hand flew to her mouth. Pierre put his finger to his lips to silence her, but it was too late. Petit came scurrying across the stairwell, his dagger glinting in the subdued light. Pierre hardly remembered moving, but somehow he reached Anne before Petit did, and the blow the dwarf intended for her caught his side, slicing upward through the cloth of his old coat and piercing his skin just below his ribs.

Anne's scream shattered the silence, and soon doors opened and confused voices echoed all over the house.

"This way!" hissed Petit, dragging Pierre, faint with pain and shoes slipping on the polished parquet, back in the direction they had come from. But the sound of running feet from the servants' quarters stopped them. Instead, they dove into the small parlor behind the stairs, and before Pierre knew what happened, Petit smashed a window, clambered through, and scampered off, leaving him to struggle as best he could. It was quite a drop down to the street below, and Pierre wrenched his ankle when he landed. He pressed his hand over the wound in his side, feeling rather than seeing the blood that soaked all the way through his coat. Still he managed to limp into the nearest alley before anyone inside the house reached the parlor window. He prayed that the scarf over his face had disguised him enough so that Anne could not recognize him. Pierre felt his breast pocket. The will was there. He had accomplished his task. Now all that remained was to get back to his apartment, where he had left his medical supplies. The pain in his side was intense, but the blade was short and it had had to pierce several layers of clothing to inflict any damage, so the wound could not have been deep.

That half a league to the rue des Bernardins was the most excruciating walk Pierre had ever taken. He crawled up the steps to his apartment and fainted on the floor before he could dress his wound.

Anne shivered with shock. Thérèse wrapped her in a blanket and sat her down by the library fire, which she had already fed and nursed into a healthy blaze. The marquis lit the candles.

"Seems a lot of trouble to go through for a few silver trinkets," he mused, his eyes wandering over the disheveled desk and around the room. "Probably wanted to frighten us. But why . . ." He did not finish his sentence, instead rubbing his chin thoughtfully. Anne wouldn't have been surprised to discover he no longer recalled that he stood in the middle of his library in the dead of night, wearing his nightclothes. She was too distraught to add to his worry by telling him what she had seen, that someone the size of a child but with a large head had lunged toward her with a knife and would certainly have killed her if the other thief had not thrown himself in the way. It seemed an odd way for a robber to behave.

"Here," Thérèse said, giving Anne a glass of brandy.

The strong drink burned into her throat and warmed her blood.

"Nail some boards over the window in there," the marquis ordered Victor, who had lumbered in after both of the thieves had managed to get away. "Not hurt, are you?" he asked in Anne's general direction.

She shook her head. "Father, surely we should summon the police!"

"No!" the marquis snapped, then modulated his tone. "No, there is no use at this time of the night. Tomorrow morning will be early enough."

His sigh shook his entire frame like the wind rattling an autumn leaf. Anne's heart melted to see her father so weary and vulnerable. If only uncrossable lines had not been drawn between them all those years ago, she might be able to ask him what troubled him, why he could not see the damage he was doing to Armand by not letting the young doctor who had operated on him come back and care for him.

The marquis drew himself up and turned to Thérèse. "I'm going back to bed. Tell Victor to bring Gisquet here at ten."

Once her father had gone and the sound of Victor's hammering ended, Thérèse helped Anne back to her room. As she slipped beneath the covers, Anne whispered, "Go and check on Armand."

"I did already. Poor thing hardly stirred in all the commotion."

Anne's heart sank. She hoped that she and Liszt would not be too late to save her cousin, that he would not perish before help could get here tomorrow night. After he was safe, she would try to discover why her father was so afraid to let anyone near their cousin. She lay down once more, pulling the covers up to her chin. Anne wondered, briefly, if there were any prayer at all that would help in such a case.

The noise and commotion downstairs woke Armand from a fitful sleep. He opened his eyes, gradually bringing into focus the chamber that had become his entire world in the last few days. The fire in the stove had burnt down to embers, and the candle by his bedside was near to extinction. He rolled onto his side to see how much water was left in the carafe.

He had regained enough strength recently to hold a water glass himself. He did not let the marquis know that his health improved but pretended still to be as ill as ever and declining by the hour. That way instead of taking the powders his aging relative prepared for him, he could let them dribble slowly out of the corners of his mouth. They tasted vile, and Armand was aware enough to know that he had healed and become stronger without them.

Père Jaquin had visited him once and spoken something quietly into his ear, but he had been too feverish on that day to understand what he said. Now that he was a little stronger, he remembered. *Heaven will open its arms to the generous-hearted.* What did he mean? Surely he knew that it was impossible for him to do anything about his fortune until he came of age. Armand soon abandoned the effort of puzzling over his tutor's words. Fatigue and weakness still kept him drifting in and out of sleep. He had not looked in a mirror once since he'd been at the hôtel Barbier but could feel that his downy beard had grown long and scraggly. He could hardly ask for a barber to be sent to him when he was supposed to be at the point of death, though. It grieved him terribly for Anne to see him like this, but something kept him from making the effort to regain all his strength—which he felt certain would occur if only he could eat properly. He couldn't really identify what troubled him about the marquis. The old man generally reserved his anger and bitterness for his daughter, always taking care to speak softly and coaxingly to Armand, but there was something in his eyes.

Simply too much went on out of his sight and hearing at that house. All the way through the fog of illness Armand could feel the currents pulling in different directions. Once he had overheard the marquis speaking quietly to Julien at the door of his room.

"Tell them to keep looking," the old man had whispered. "He will bleed me dry. I will lose everything."

But before he could hear any more details, the marquis and the footman had stepped out into the corridor and shut the door behind them. What were they looking for? And who was "he"?

And now, here it was, the most dire hour of the night, and sounds of running footsteps, his cousin's shriek of alarm, and a window breaking set his imagination picturing all manner of horrors. Perhaps "he" had broken into the house to exact some vengeance for a long-ago injury. Perhaps "he" would come and murder Armand where he lay, helpless in bed.

Before too long, however, he heard the calming voice of Thérèse murmuring to Anne as they passed by his door on the way to the countess's own chamber. Armand breathed a slow sigh, something that still pained his groin, but he could not stop it. Anne had not been harmed in whatever strange events had occurred below. He closed his eyes and let feverish fancies and dreams flood into his mind once again. Perhaps tomorrow he would be strong enough to talk to Anne about his fears.

Twenty-Two

Pierre remained passed out on the floor of his rooms until Georges returned from his night shift at the Hôtel-Dieu.

"You are bleeding! What happened?" Georges helped Pierre off the floor and into bed.

"I met a small knife on its way to a different target," he said, wincing as Georges peeled away his now ruined shirt and set about cleaning and dressing his wound. The dwarf's blade had entered at an angle that caused him to bleed more than he had expected. And his side throbbed painfully.

Georges whistled when he saw the cut. "We must send for the police."

"No, no police. The scoundrel only got away with twenty francs. These are desperate times." *And,* thought Pierre, *I am as desperate as anyone in them.* It occurred to him that Petit's theft of the silver baubles was fortuitous in its way. There would be no question as to why anyone broke into the hôtel Barbier, and perhaps he had unwittingly discharged his two-hundred-franc tithe to the thieves.

Georges fetched some water for Pierre, then retired to his own bed. "Call out if you need anything," he said. "I won't sleep."

But the night's work at the hospital had exhausted Georges, and before long his eyes were firmly shut. Pierre waited until his friend's breathing became slow and deep, then gingerly swung his legs over the edge of his bed. Pain shot through his side as soon as he hoisted himself up. Holding on to the furniture, he made his way to the wardrobe where he kept his umbrella. It would do for a walking stick, to lean on if the pain became too strong. There was no time to rest at home. He must reach Madame d'Agoult with the will before the soiree that evening.

Pierre held his side as he stepped gingerly down the stairs. Once he had walked a bit, the pain eased. Pierre's mind cleared, and he realized that, although he had successfully stolen the important document, he had not had a moment to read it. At first he thought perhaps it would be ungentlemanly of him to do so. But then he decided that his actions had earned him the right. He had risked everything: his reputation, possibly his life, and most of all the esteem of a lady who, although he hardly knew her, had inspired him to foolhardy acts of courage. He was either in love or very stupid. He wasn't sure how to tell the difference, but if he were to continue to help Madame d'Agoult protect Anne, he should know what was in the will.

Pierre stopped at a café and ordered a cup of coffee, reached into his coat pocket, unfolded the document, and read.

I, Sandrine de Barbier-Chouant, being of sound mind, do hereby state my last will and testament.

My daughter, Anne, shall have four-fifths of my dowry, an amount equal to one hundred and twenty-five thousand francs, which I brought to my marriage, plus all income accrued on that amount, upon her own marriage or her twenty-first birthday, whichever occurs first. Until that time, should my husband survive me, the income from one-fifth of the capital, twenty-five thousand francs, shall be expended upon anything required for her education and well-being.

Upon my daughter's marriage, should it occur before her twenty-first birthday, my husband the marquis shall receive an amount equal to one-fifth of the capital.

Should my daughter predecease my husband, the entire amount of the dowry, with all income accrued, shall pass to the marquis de Barbier-Chouant. Should the marquis predecease my daughter, then, if she is over the age of eighteen years, all funds shall become her undisputed property.

The will made it quite clear. The marquis would benefit from Anne's early marriage. And if she died, then—surely a father, even a stepfather, if he were proven to be so, would not be so callous as to wish for such an occurrence for the sake of enriching himself. Pierre could not bear to imagine what would happen if Anne were forced to marry poor Monsieur de Barbier, or worse. In that instant, he decided that there was somewhere else he must stop on his way to the quai Malaquais. As soon as he downed his coffee, he set off toward the Prefecture to visit Gardive.

It took him a little longer than usual to cover the distance to the Île du Palais, but he managed to arrive in Gardive's office before noon, when the commissioner normally took his luncheon.

"You are injured, monsieur!" Gardive exclaimed when Pierre entered clutching his side, and he moved some papers so that his guest could sit in the chair.

"Not badly," Pierre said. "I must show you something, but before I do, I ask you for your word that you will not inquire as to how it came to be in my hands."

Gardive hesitated, then nodded. "Agreed."

Pierre drew the will out of his pocket and gave it to the commissioner. He watched Gardive's face closely. The lines on the beleaguered commissioner's forehead deepened as his eyes reached the end of the document.

"How—" He stopped himself. "But this is very suggestive. If, as we suspect, the girl is not the natural daughter of the marquis . . ." His voice trailed off.

"That was precisely my fear, which is why I came to you before I—" Pierre remembered that it would be unwise to mention the countess d'Agoult.

Gardive jerked his head up from perusing the will, alive to Pierre's sudden evasion. "Since you exacted a promise from me, I will not ask you where this document came from, nor why you put yourself to some—trouble—to obtain it, but I received an interesting message this morning." Gardive shuffled some papers and unearthed an official-looking chit, which he handed across to Pierre. "I requested that my friends in the police inform me if they had any information about the marquis de Barbier-Chouant's affairs. It seems that, in the small hours of last night, someone stole some items of silver from the hôtel Barbier, and the marquis has presumed upon his name to summon the prefect himself to begin the investigation—although he shall be attended somewhat later than he originally commanded." He fixed Pierre with a hard stare.

"I—I see," Pierre said. "How unfortunate."

"Unfortunate, in one sense. But perhaps fortunate in another. I suggested to Gisquet that I should accompany him, as the visit would give me an opportunity to inspect the hygienic habits of the household without insult to the marquis—whom I understand can be a difficult fellow."

Pierre returned the paper to Gardive. "As neighborhood inspector myself," he cleared his throat, "perhaps I may . . ."

"Yes, you may accompany me, if you think it wise." His eyes strayed to Pierre's side. Pierre's arm covered it protectively. "I shall meet you there in an hour. I presume you know the way?"

The commissioner helped him rise from his seat. Pierre was under no illusion that the bureaucrat had any doubts about how he had acquired the will, and certainly the commissioner knew that his injury was no coincidence. He wasn't sure exactly why Gardive let him get away with it, except that it had been he, after all, who had brought the entire affair to Gardive's official attention.

An hour would force him to postpone his inevitable visit to Madame d'Agoult if he were to have time to make his halting way to the rue du

Barq. There would be time afterward to get to the quai Malaquais. He hoped that Anne would be out when he arrived. If not, he would soon discover whether she had recognized him the night before.

Anne had insisted upon staying at home to speak to the police. "It was I who saw them, after all!" she said.

"It will tax your nerves unnecessarily. You need not remain here. I'm certain the countess wouldn't object to your coming early."

The marquis had been quite distressed upon discovery that Anne had interrupted a robbery. His concern surprised Anne a little. He insisted that Thérèse bring her a tisane to soothe her nerves, and Thérèse told her the next morning that he would not retire until he was assured that Anne rested comfortably. At moments like that, she thought perhaps he did not mind her so much. But he would soon spoil the impression by saying something hurtful in the next breath and convince her again that he wished it had been she who had perished from cholera, not her mother.

While she awaited the arrival of the police, Anne slipped into Armand's room. He had been sleeping—or unconscious, she could not tell which—since the day before, and Anne feared that the lack of food and water would weaken him still further. She leaned close to him and whispered in his ear, "We shall take you away from here, tonight. We will find Monsieur Talon, who is your friend, and he will examine you and make you better."

Anne was still unwilling to attribute any base motive to her father's failure to treat Armand's illness properly. It would be too horrible to contemplate, and besides, she had seen no evidence of the medicine he had requested from Magendie, nor had she discovered anything about the disposition of Armand's fortune. For all she knew, it would go to the Jesuit college when he died.

Anne heard the bell announce the arrival of the police. The sound of voices in the library reached her as she came down the stairs. She opened the door quietly and crept in so that they would not stop what they were saying because of her presence.

When she saw who was there, Anne stifled a shout for joy. Her father, the prefect Gisquet, and another official whom she did not recognize, were joined by Monsieur Talon. She had no idea how he came to be among the group, but for the moment it did not matter.

The gentlemen heard her little gasp of pleasure and turned their faces toward her, bowing in a group. Anne was a little surprised that Talon, whose modest station in life required the deepest bow of all, only inclined his head in her direction. She felt unaccountably piqued by his lack of courtesy, wondering if she had done anything to offend him.

"Countess, Monsieur le Préfet Gisquet, Monsieur le Commissionaire Gardive, and I believe you are acquainted with Monsieur Talon."

Anne nodded to each of them in turn, noting that her father most pointedly did not address Talon as "Doctor." Gisquet, his hair held in place by overly scented oil and his garments new but poorly cut, removed his watch from his pocket and frowned at it, obviously wishing to be somewhere else at that very instant. Gardive was a more presentable character, neatly turned out and respectful. He lifted an eyebrow and a corner of his mouth, so that it appeared as though half his face smiled while the other half remained serious. And Monsieur Talon, who leaned on the back of a chair, wore an expression that she could not interpret but that suggested he wished to speak to her about something important.

"This small robbery, it's hardly an occasion to warrant the attention of so many gentlemen with more important matters to attend to," she said.

Gisquet took a notebook and a pencil from his pocket. "Countess," he said with an obsequious smile, "can you describe to me the thieves?"

"One was only this tall," she held her hand at her waist, "but he had a large head, and his eyes were like the devil's."

"And the other fellow?"

"Taller. About the size of Monsieur Talon, I would say. But when the small fellow ran at me, the tall one put himself between us and was injured, I believe."

"And Monsieur le Marquis," Gisquet said, turning back to Anne's father, "would you kindly describe the stolen objects in detail?"

The marquis waved his hand impatiently at Gisquet. "A few silver trinkets, that is all. But Anne, you say you were attacked? Why did you not mention this last night?"

"I . . . did not want to trouble you, Papa, and in any case I was not injured." His look of concern touched her. How could she suspect him of wishing her cousin harm? Before she could say anything else to reassure her father, the commissioner spoke.

"*Excusez-moi*, Marquis, but are you certain these are the only items that have gone missing from your house? You have checked every room?"

"Of course, monsieur," the marquis said with a haughty toss of his head.

"I find it difficult, that is all, to imagine that anyone would go to such trouble to break into a house that—if you will excuse my bold-ness—has clearly come upon difficult times and therefore might not be so richly furnished with booty." Gardive glanced in the direction of the blank space over the fireplace where the faint outline of a paint-ing was still visible. "Had you no valuable papers or documents? Per-haps relating to your days at court?"

Monsieur Talon started to cough.

"Who is the officer in charge here?" the marquis asked Gisquet. "Might I have a word with you in private, Gisquet? I'll not have any more time wasted on amateurish speculation."

"I regret that the press of duty prevents me from spending the time to conduct a private conference with you, Monsieur le Mar-quis," Gisquet responded.

Anne saw that her father's words had succeeded in angering both the prefect and the commissioner, and she guessed that the burglary would no longer receive close attention from either.

"*Pardonnez-moi*, mademoiselle," Pierre said, "but how does your cousin?"

Pierre asked the question without moving from where he stood, and all the gentlemen in the library turned to wait for her answer.

"His health improves daily." Anne's father answered before she had a chance to draw breath.

She cast her imploring eyes on Talon and thought she saw a flicker of understanding in them. If only she could take him upstairs to see Armand!

"The prefect has the information he needs. Go prepare for your . . ." The marquis shook his hand in the air. Anne nodded to the entire group but did not make haste to depart. Instead she lingered, hoping to hear something that would ease her mind.

Pierre could not make out whether the marquis was truly distressed about Anne's harrowing experience or not. He wished Gardive would stop needling the old man.

"Has there been illness in this house recently?" Gardive asked.

"Not illness, but a patient. My cousin who is recovering from an operation," the marquis said.

"Is that so?" said Gardive. "And what eminent physician performed this surgery?"

The marquis frowned. "Talon. Damned lucky, if you ask me."

"Indeed!" Gardive turned toward Pierre, his expression of mock surprise causing Pierre to bite his lip to prevent himself from laughing aloud. "And are you pleased with your patient's recovery?" Gardive asked him.

Pierre caught Anne's eye and saw her give the minutest shake of her head. "Yes," he answered.

"And the marquise. Is she out?"

Pierre admired Gardive's sangfroid. He had the courage of a man whose well-being depended not in the slightest upon retaining the good opinion of anyone in the room. Even Gisquet had no control over his appointment.

"My wife, God rest her soul," the marquis crossed himself, "is in the family vault at Père Lachaise."

"Of what did she die?" persisted the commissioner.

"Cholera."

"And there were no other victims in the house? That is unusual."

Gisquet cast a severe look in Gardive's direction, then stepped forward and bowed to the marquis. "We need trouble you no longer. I believe we have all the information we require to commence our investigation."

"Monsieur le Préfet," the marquis began, his tone losing its angry edge. "Please, might I have a word with you?"

He nodded to the others, who bowed to the marquis.

"Go at once, Anne," the marquis said, noticing that she remained in the room.

The countess visibly wilted but obeyed her father's command. Pierre waited until she was out of sight to make his move. He did not want her to guess that he had been injured, fearing that she might at last make the connection between him and the second burglar.

Pierre and Gardive waited for Gisquet in the vestibule with the dour Julien standing guard over them. How he wished he could put his ear to the door of the library and hear what the marquis was saying!

After a short while the prefect emerged, bowed respectfully to the marquis, and walked out into the courtyard with them. Before the footman could shut the ornate doors behind them, the old man called out, "Mind you hang the scoundrels when you catch them!"

For the briefest instant, Pierre had an image of Petit's misshapen little body dangling from a noose in the place de Grève. All it would take was a slight shift in loyalties, and he could find himself swinging up there next to the dwarf.

"Did the old man have any more information about the robber?" Gardive asked the prefect as he climbed into his waiting carriage.

"The marquis," Gisquet corrected pointedly, "has taken me into the strictest confidence. You may leave this investigation in my hands."

How clever, Pierre thought. *Give that glorified bureaucrat a sense of self-importance, and deflect from the case those who might actually be of assistance. The marquis must be hiding something.* He could not bear the thought of leaving Anne alone in that mansion with him.

* * *

The servants had cleared away much of the furniture in Madame d'Agoult's parlor and set up rows of gilt chairs facing the piano. Marie welcomed Pierre in a small sitting room she seldom used; it faced the building immediately behind and let in only filtered light. When she saw that he leaned heavily on his umbrella and was clearly pained by every step he took, she ran to him and supported him herself to a comfortable, upholstered chair.

"Please don't tell me you are hurt because—"

Pierre did not let her finish but handed her the will. "As you see, I succeeded in getting this for you. I will not pretend that I have not read it."

Marie settled a pair of pince-nez on her nose and scanned the document. "It is precisely as I suspected," she said, removing her spectacles and turning her sad eyes on Pierre. "You must act tonight, for Anne's sake. I fear the marquis."

Pierre blinked rapidly. "I'm not sure I understand," he said.

"Monsieur Talon, please do not think me callous, or scheming. But the doubt over the disposition of Anne's fortune will be laid to rest once she is married. The best course for Anne right now would be to marry someone who is capable of protecting her. If she does this, her father will receive his portion of the inheritance, and if anything were to happen to Anne after that, then what remains of the money will pass to her husband, not her father. This would remove all temptation to act in a despicable manner."

Marie's suspicions only reinforced Pierre's own. Yet he was still unwilling to ascribe such base motives to the marquis. "Surely you do not believe that the marquis de Barbier-Chouant would harm his own daughter?"

Marie cocked her head on one side. "You never told me for certain whether you found the birth records."

Pierre looked down. "The documents I saw were inconclusive."

"Inconclusive, but suggestive?"

At that moment, Pierre wanted nothing more than simply to tell Madame d'Agoult all that he knew. But he was afraid, for Anne's sake. "Some inconsistency in the dates of birth and baptism."

"So, you have discovered facts that give substance to my fears. I have long suspected that Anne may not, in fact, be the natural daughter of the marquis," Marie said.

They sat each in absorbed silence until a clock's gentle chime shook them back to the present. "I believe you have some feelings for the countess," Marie said.

She had guessed: it would not have been difficult, Pierre thought, considering the lengths to which he had gone to involve himself in Mademoiselle Anne's affairs. Yet he could not help but recall the pleading expression in her eyes when he asked about the welfare of her cousin. "And what of Monsieur de Barbier?" he asked.

"I know nothing of him or his circumstances. He is ill and frail, so Anne says, and may die. But I cannot help him."

At that moment, the maid entered bearing a tea tray. Pierre was glad of the pause. It gave him time to digest what the countess had said. Did she intend him to elope with Anne? That night?

His confusion must have been apparent, because as soon as the door closed behind the maid, Marie said, "You no doubt think me cavalier with my young friend's honor."

"I should like to know precisely what you propose," he said.

"I believe you are a good man," Marie said, placing her hand on Pierre's arm and giving it a gentle squeeze. "Anne does not know herself yet. She is young and has been through a great deal. And if what you suggest is true, that she was born before her mother's marriage to the marquis, she is not seventeen years old but eighteen—the age at which she may legally contract a marriage without her father's permission. Perhaps I presume too much, but I feel that you, with your sensitivity and education, would make her happy."

Pierre realized the countess flattered him, but to what purpose? "Are you authorized to arrange a match for the countess?" he asked. Even with the tale told by the birth records in the commissioner's office, why would she be willing to ally the countess—a lady whose beauty and fortune would entitle her to much more—to a social inferior?

"If she is inclined to marry, and can prove her father's evil intent, the law will look favorably upon it."

Pierre did not speak. His exhausting night, the pain of his wound, the strange events of the day—everything crowded in upon him. Madame d'Agoult offered him the one fate he hardly dared imagine. Yet he did not want Anne that way, surreptitiously, without even her consent, let alone that of her father—who, whether the marquis was her father in fact as well as in name or not, had raised her from infancy. "If what you are asking is that I carry Anne off, against her will and her father's, I cannot consent to it."

Marie stood and paced back and forth rapidly in the small room. "I had thought," she said, "I had surmised, from your interest in the countess, that nothing would be more welcome to you than to be united with her in the eyes of God and the law."

"You guessed—surmised—correctly. I am indeed truly in love with Mademoiselle Anne. But I know not how she thinks of me. I will not trick her into a marriage—"

"Oh spare me your scruples!" Marie cried. "Do you not see that her future—perhaps even her life—may hang in the balance?"

Her words rang in the silence that followed them.

"Of course," Pierre said, and looked down at his hands. "You have only to tell me what you would like me to do, and I shall comply."

It surprised Marie only a little that Pierre agreed to her plan. She herself thought there was little chance of success in it and had indulged in putting on an act in front of him, posturing and appearing to be more concerned about Anne's safety than she truly felt. A part of her wished he had refused altogether. The plan had been one she thought of in the middle of the previous, sleepless night. She could not rid herself of the vision of Anne and Liszt locked in an embrace at her pianoforte. It was a desperate move, to think of placing Anne in a position where she would either be forced to marry Pierre or be labeled a loose woman and an outcast from society. Marie nearly called Pierre back when he left to tell him that, on second thought, she believed it would be better to wait and see what happened with the marquis. But hesitating too long, she heard the door shut behind her guest.

The poor fellow did look completely done in, Marie thought. She sent him home in her own carriage, which she commanded to wait for him and then bring him back in time for the salon. It seemed possible that he had hurt himself in the process of getting his hands on the will. She did not ask how he managed it, not wanting to be in possession of that particular intelligence. And now that he had agreed to her rash plan, she would be forced to hire a carriage to take him and Anne away that night.

And perhaps, after all, no true harm would come of it. Even if Anne was not aware of Monsieur Talon's qualities, Marie had a sense that they were suited to one another. At least his own feelings were abundantly clear. And it had brought a pain to her heart, to see Sandrine's curving script once more, a hand that had written her so many anguished letters about her love for someone other than her husband, and her hopes for her talented daughter. It would not be so bad for Anne to be the one who had the power and influence in a marriage. She would be able to choose the way she wanted to live, unlike her present life under the marquis's stern rule.

I am doing what is best for Anne, Marie told herself.

And yet, a little stone persisted in rubbing against her conscience. How much of her own interest lay behind her schemes? If she put aside all other considerations, would she, in truth, believe that Talon was the best match Anne could hope for? She was lovely and talented. With her mother's fortune, she would bring a good dowry to whatever marriage she contracted.

The terms of Sandrine's will were most peculiar. It seemed odd that she retained control over her dowry after her marriage. Surely it was more usual for the husband to become the possessor of his wife's fortune in such circumstances, where a title was "bought." Why would the marquis not have insisted upon it? Unless he, himself, had a secret to hide, something Sandrine knew about him that was at least as damning as everything in her own past.

Marie's head ached. She would take a powder before dressing. Tonight would see Anne launched into the society of the artistic elite of Paris. If all went well, Sandrine's daughter would be thrust into the arms of a young man with much to recommend him. At worst, she would have an adventure that would leave her chastened but essentially intact.

Marie did not permit herself the luxury of thinking about how that might leave things between herself and the entrancing Franz Liszt.

Twenty-Three

I'm not the same person at all, Anne thought, staring at herself in the mirror above her dressing table while Thérèse arranged her hair for the salon. She had thought that when her mother died and left her alone with her cold, unapproachable father, life could get no worse. Now, Anne wished for a return to those days before life became so complicated.

Oh, she was grateful to the countess d'Agoult. But what good could possibly come of her surreptitious involvement with Liszt? Once he helped her this evening, she would be deeply in his debt. She hoped he would not expect money and favors, because she certainly could give him neither. And now, everything had changed in her feelings for the pianist. The glow of that kiss had faded in her memory, and all that was left was a feeling of shame.

If only everything were as simple as playing the piano. Despite all else, Anne had begun to realize that she was blessed with a gift beyond what even Madame d'Agoult suspected. She knew the lessons had started as a way to polish her, like a gem to be held up for inspection before purchase. Yet Anne was well aware that for her, music went far beyond a mere accomplishment. Playing the piano had been more than a satisfying diversion for a long time, but in the weeks since the death of her mother it had become the purest element of who she was, the definition of herself. She could not separate her own being from what she played or untease the notes and intervals, chords, modes, and keys from her entire view of life.

Without ever being told directly, Anne understood that this was not how most well-bred young ladies felt about music. No one expected them to be truly devoted to art. What would happen to this gift if she married Armand? Or if she married anyone, for that matter?

"What is wrong, mademoiselle?"

Anne saw in the mirror that a tear had escaped her eye and that she looked desolate—not happy—to be taking part in her first salon. "Oh, I was just thinking of Mama," she answered.

"Let me look at you," Thérèse said.

She stood in front of the tall bevelled mirror on the door of her wardrobe. Her lavender silk gown trimmed with seed pearls was magnificent. It had a bit of décolleté—very much the fashion, but the first time ever for Anne. The ribbons tied around the sleeves were still black, and black lace edged the neckline. It was the smallest token, she thought, of how deeply she felt the loss of her mother. Thérèse herself had made the dress, spending hours over it to get it ready in only a week. Although Anne recognized many of the trimmings from other gowns that had belonged to her mother, she did not know how Thérèse had persuaded the marquis to part with whatever sum the crisp, shiny silk had cost.

Violets and a spray of lilac wound through Anne's fair hair, and she held her gloves and fan in her hand. She looked elegant enough to be going to a ball.

"There is one detail missing," Thérèse said.

The housekeeper crouched down by the side of Anne's bed. From beneath it she pulled a small, ornate wooden box, and brought it to the countess. "Open it," she said.

Anne unlatched the little brass clasp of her mother's jewelry box. Until that moment she had forgotten its existence entirely. "Where did you get this?"

"There's not much left in it. Most of the jewels have been sold in the last two years."

"Didn't my father ask about it?"

"Yes, but I claimed ignorance." Thérèse put her nose in the air.

Anne smiled. "Now he will know, of course. But at least for tonight . . ." Anne fingered the paste pieces, many of which she could picture against her mother's skin, and, after taking them all out and spreading them over her dressing table, found a beautiful suite of crystals: a necklace, a pair of earbobs, two bracelets, and a ring. "But I am in mourning still," she said.

"Your mother would not mind."

She wore the necklace and earrings but decided the bracelets and ring would interfere with her playing and left them aside. "I don't recall Mother ever wearing these," Anne said.

"She never did," said Thérèse, "at least, not after she was married."

Anne understood that perhaps there was a story behind Thérèse's words, but her mind was too full to take in yet another surprise, and she let the matter drop. As Thérèse prepared to lay the box on Anne's dressing table, Anne noticed the small drawer in the bottom of it, where her mama had kept her string of pearls. She did not expect to find the pearls—they were much too valuable to have survived the need for cash—but something drew her to open it nonetheless. Anne grasped the tiny ivory knob in its center between her thumb and first finger and pulled.

As she suspected, there were no pearls. Only some papers. Letters, it appeared, written to the marquise ten years and more ago according to the dates. Anne did not recognize the handwriting. She glanced at the greeting on one.

"My darling Sandrine . . ."

Anne stopped reading and looked up at Thérèse. "You knew about these?"

Thérèse nodded. "I wanted to tell you, but I could not."

My mother had a lover, Anne thought. Did Papa know?

Quickly Anne tucked the letters into her reticule. She would look at them later, think about the questions they raised when she had a quiet moment. There was no time now, and she had to turn her mind to other things—her coming performance, and what Liszt and she must do this evening. Thérèse put her hand on Anne's arm. "She could have left him, you know, but she didn't."

Anne looked down at her satin slippers and traced the grain of the wooden floor with her toe. "You'll stay with Armand, as I asked?"

"Yes, mademoiselle."

As Anne descended the staircase, she recalled that the last time she and her father had dressed in their finery to go somewhere in a carriage together, it was to her mother's funeral. She could not shake the feeling of mourning and kept having to remind herself that their destination was a party, that she would make her musical and social debut, and that they were supposed to enjoy themselves in the midst of lively, intelligent people.

The marquis awaited her in the library. Using his cane for support, he stood when she entered. The sight of his bent form in his ancien régime blue coat and white knee breeches broke Anne's heart. She wanted to love this old man, her father, who had been a part of her life for as long as she could remember, and whom, possibly, her mother had wronged. She knew she would have to read the letters, but her cheeks burned at the idea of it. And if her mother had acted unwisely, what of the marquis? This was still the same man who refused to allow Armand the care he needed and persisted in giving him medicine that seemed to be making him worse, not better.

He approached her without smiling. "It would not do to be late."

She curtseyed to her father and preceded him out to the carriage, not the small one, but the big old brougham. It had last seen use on the day of the burial, which only added to Anne's depression of spirits. The inside of the coach was a little threadbare, but from the outside it would make an impressive arrival. Victor wore his livery suit, now a little tight on him. He made a comical figure on the box all in satin and gold braid, wearing a white wig that sat atop his big, dark head like a pigeon that had decided to nest there. Their two horses had been augmented by two more that were hired for the evening.

They rode the short distance in silence. As they rocked along over the cobbles, the letters Anne had thrust into her reticule began to torment her. What if she had gotten everything wrong? Perhaps everything was the other way around. Her mother, who had been so kind to her, might have been cruel to her husband. And her father—maybe he really was doing everything he could to save their cousin, and if she and Liszt took him away, he would die.

As they waited their turn to draw up in front of the building on the quai Malaquais, the marquis turned to Anne.

"I swore I would never set foot in that woman's apartment. If I could have stayed home tonight without dishonoring the family name, I would have done so," he said, then before Anne had a chance to reply, he stepped down from the carriage.

Pierre changed the dressing on his side before putting on his evening clothes. He added a little extra padding. It would not do to bleed through his best waistcoat. Thank God, he thought, the countess had lent him her carriage. He would never have made the walk. The area around the cut had swelled. Later he would have to pierce it again to let out the fluid that had collected below the skin.

But for now, there were more important matters. He had agreed to Marie's plan to run away with Anne, but he was unwilling to risk retribution—personal or legal—that could end by doing more harm than good, to himself as well as to Anne. The only course, he thought, would be to involve Gardive once more. He would stop at the Prefecture on his way back to Madame d'Agoult's.

By now the officers recognized Pierre and admitted him right away to the commissioner's office.

"You are going to attend a party? Have you miraculously healed?" Gardive's sarcastic tone was quite familiar to Pierre.

"If I could stay at home and rest, I would," Pierre said. "But this evening I have been called upon to do something for which I need your assistance and cooperation."

Pierre explained everything—so far as he dared—to the commissioner. When he had finished, Gardive stood and, without saying a word, retired to the record room. Pierre sat for a while, wondering if he had been dismissed and should depart, or whether the commissioner had gone to fetch some necessary papers and wanted him to wait.

When Gardive returned wearing a cutaway coat and top hat, Pierre was taken aback.

"I spend so little time in my own apartment," the commissioner explained, pulling on one of his elegant, dove gray gloves, "that I keep a change of clothing here, for just such an instance as this. I would not want to be absent from this interesting occasion. Shall we go?"

Together they left the Prefecture, appearing for all the world like old friends out for a night on the town. Gardive assisted Pierre into the carriage, and Madame d'Agoult's coachman clucked his horses to a brisk trot.

Eugène's constant admonitions had begun to work on Franz. He saw that what he had agreed to do that evening could be seen as a serious crime. He also saw that by helping Anne, he would only be affirming whatever suspicions Marie had regarding his feelings toward his student. He had decided that he must tell Anne that he could not participate in her daring adventure. Despite the fact that his kiss had given her a sort of claim on his honor, since no one knew about it, he thought that ultimately it would not matter.

And tonight, Franz thought, he might at last be able to declare his feelings to the countess d'Agoult. To wait any longer, allowing her to assume the worst about his relationship with Anne, risked losing her forever.

The sound of lively voices reached Franz all the way out on the street when he stepped down from the hired carriage. He brought

Eugène along, to act as conscience and help him keep to his altered purpose. The apartment had been decorated with sprays of spring flowers, and as soon as they walked through the door, Marie greeted them graciously, accepting Eugène's presence as a matter of course.

"Come into the dining room," she said. "Refresh yourselves. Hector is here, and Alfred, plus many others whom you might know."

The countess's icy calm drove Franz wild with desire. He wanted to break through that surface, to reach the seething emotions he knew bubbled underneath. But she remained the aloof hostess, introducing and facilitating, orchestrating the flow of servants, guests, and refreshments, and choreographing the conversations, which all revolved around art, music, and poetry. She made anyone who mentioned Louis-Philippe or the cholera pay a forfeit. "I shall send the money to the Hôtel-Dieu tomorrow," she said with a gracious smile.

Eugène was soon deep in conversation with Hector Berlioz, who was rumored to be infatuated with a beautiful English actress. He was supposed to be in Rome studying and composing but had taken unauthorized leave to pursue his lady love. Franz wandered casually from room to room, looking for Mademoiselle Anne so that he could tell her of the change in plans, but she had obviously not yet arrived. He too would perform that evening. Hector's presence gave him the idea to regale the guests with a movement of the *Symphonie fantastique*. He had heard the one titled "Un bal" at a private concert and thought he could play it well enough from memory. Such things always impressed an audience.

The idea of performing impromptu did not make Franz the least bit nervous. It was the thought of Marie that tied his stomach into a knot.

"Monsieur Liszt! I am charmed to see you again."

Madame La Vayer approached him with her hands outstretched. He would have to play the serious artist and flatter all the dowagers and wealthy bourgeoises who would attend. Franz knew he must rely on their generosity and patronage to make him a success.

"Have you heard about Monsieur Erard's new pianos?" the marquise asked.

"No, please tell me," Franz answered, giving her a smile and turning on her the full force of his exotic green eyes.

"Well," she continued, visibly shaken by the unexpected attention, "he claims to have made possible the greatest virtuosity by inventing some kind of mechanism."

Franz listened politely to this old news about the double escapement, a mechanism that at last made it possible to play rapidly repeated notes on the pianoforte, and nodded to acquaintances, accepted introductions and adulation from friends and strangers alike, and all the time his mind was far away, imagining the texture and smell of Marie's white skin beneath her silk gown.

So far, everything was going well. *I know how to do this,* Marie thought, as she greeted her guests, brought people together, made sure glasses were filled and that everyone found the buffet table. She had lined up quite a dazzling array of performers. A famous soprano from the opera had promised to visit briefly and sing one aria. Hugo was going to read, Musset also consented to recite a poem, and Liszt would play as well. Marie had invited Chopin, but he had declined for reasons of ill health. And she must not forget Anne. Despite everything, Marie had to admit that Anne played the étude beautifully.

The one slightly spiteful gesture Marie had allowed herself was to arrange the program so that Anne would perform immediately after Liszt. Not only would she have to sit through everything in a state of nervous anticipation, but the audience would have the performance of the greatest living pianist in their ears when they heard her, a completely unknown ingenue, for the first time. She had no intention of ever telling Anne or Liszt that she had witnessed the fateful kiss, but it soothed her to be able to manage at least a small measure of retribution.

And Marie wondered whether the marquis would attend or not. If he appeared, things could be tricky. Even if she managed to get Anne whisked away in Pierre's carriage, the alarm would be raised almost immediately, increasing the likelihood that they would be apprehended. For a moment she wondered if she had made the right decision in not telling Anne of her plans. Although she thought she detected the possibility of interest whenever she mentioned the young doctor, she was not entirely certain of Anne's feelings, or of the girl's ability to maintain the necessary sangfroid to carry out such a bold scheme under her own father's nose. She came to the conclusion that it would be better if it all happened first, and then Anne would be able to decide afterward whether she wished to ally herself permanently with Monsieur Talon.

"The marquis de Barbier-Chouant and the countess Anne de Barbier-Chouant."

I never thought to see him here, Marie said to herself.

"How kind of you to come, Marquis." She held out her hand to him, but he ignored it and greeted an old acquaintance from court who passed at that moment. Marie turned her gesture into a wave in the general direction of the dining room, where most of the guests were eating and drinking before the entertainment began.

Anne stopped and curtseyed to her. When she stood up, Marie was alarmed by the look in her eyes. She kissed Anne slowly on both cheeks so that she could whisper into her ear. "Are you quite well?"

"Yes, but I must talk to you, Countess, in private."

Several guests wandered through the vestibule toward the parlor. "Of course you may refresh yourself, mademoiselle," Marie said aloud. She took Anne's elbow and steered her toward the back of the apartment, away from the public rooms, to her own dressing room.

She closed the door behind her. "What is it, Anne?"

The young countess paced up and down and could barely stop shaking long enough to open her reticule. She removed from it several folded papers, which she held out toward Marie. They looked like letters. "I haven't read them, I can hardly bear to, but did she? Was she? I mean my mother!"

By now the tears flowed freely down Anne's cheeks. Marie took the letters from her and glanced at them. She read no more than a sentence or two. Even though Sandrine was dead, her private correspondence was no one's business but hers—and possibly her daughter's. Marie did, however, look at the signature. She suspected as much. While Marie's true love had been killed, Sandrine's had lived on, allowing their romance to smolder for years. The marquise and her beloved never saw each other after he went abroad, but had corresponded until the youthful passion eventually spent itself, and the gentleman—a pianist who performed throughout the world to great acclaim—married and settled permanently in Italy.

"He was, perhaps still is, a talented musician, and a kind man. They were very much in love."

"But she wronged my father. She was married!"

"Sshhh!" Marie said, glancing nervously at the closed door. She did not know what to say to Anne. "Your mother was unhappy, as many of us were—are. Surely you must know that?" she said, taking hold of Anne's hands. "Try to put this matter out of your mind. In a short while, you will play glorious music on a beautiful piano. Your mother will be looking down from heaven and smiling."

Anne stopped crying abruptly and sniffed. She lifted her chin, and her eyes flashed. "Or up from hell!"

At that, she held out her hand for the letters.

"No," Marie said, "I shall return them to you later when we have had some time to talk." Anne appeared much more emotional and less stable than Marie had thought she was. Perhaps the plan for the evening was a mistake after all. "I'll leave you to compose yourself," Marie said.

As she reemerged into the reception rooms of her now-crowded apartment, Marie noticed that Talon had arrived, and that he had brought along a rather dour-looking man with a thin mustache.

"Allow me to introduce to you to Monsieur Alaric Gardive," Pierre said.

"Ah, Monsieur Gardive," Marie said, "your work is well-known among my guests. But I warn you, one word about the cholera and I shall fine you fifty centimes!" She could not imagine why the doctor had brought this bureaucrat with him. Perhaps he would act as witness?

After a few minutes Anne joined the others. She appeared to be calm, but every once in a while, Marie noticed, her hand shook as she reached for a glass of wine or a cake. In the circumstances, her fellow guests would put it down to nerves about her coming performance. Another quarter of an hour and Marie must herd them all into the parlor. The countess d'Agoult, who seldom consumed alcoholic drinks at her own parties, took a glass of champagne and drank it down in one gulp.

Twenty-Four

Pierre took a seat at the back of the parlor. He must be ready to hasten away as soon as Anne finished her performance. Marie suggested he should leave the room before Anne's debut, but he refused. She said that was all right, that she had another idea and would find a way to get them both out via the servants' entrance. That was where the carriage would wait for them. Gardive agreed to come along, to act as witness if they indeed married, or as chaperon if it was necessary to return Anne to the hôtel Barbier still a spinster. That way Pierre hoped to avoid sullying her reputation if, as he presumed would be the case, she objected.

The marquis sat over to the side on an upholstered divan and chatted in the ear of an elderly lady, whose stern expression did not vary. Pierre suspected she was deaf. In any case, her impassivity did not seem to matter to the marquis, whose canny eyes took in everything around him, always keeping his daughter in sight. Gardive had actually spoken to Anne's father, although Pierre decided it would be better to avoid him if possible.

To his surprise, Anne approached him in full view of the marquis and took the seat next to him.

"Monsieur Talon, what a pleasure to see you here. I am sorry we were unable to talk when you came to the house earlier today."

"I had hoped to have an opportunity long before tonight to become better acquainted with you," Pierre said. He noticed, again, something behind her expression, and he wished that it meant that she felt the same way he did. He wondered if Madame d'Agoult had warned her about what was to transpire after the salon, or whether it would be as much a surprise to her as to her father. "Have you fully recovered from your ordeal?"

Anne brought her lovely, troubled face close to him and whispered, "Monsieur Talon, if I were able to bring my cousin to you, would you take care of him? Make him well?"

Hadn't he heard the marquis protest only a few hours ago that Monsieur de Barbier was recovering nicely? Pierre had no time to answer Anne, or to ask for an explanation, because at that moment Marie stood beside the piano and quieted her guests.

"I am pleased to introduce our first performer this evening, the soprano whom we have recently heard to great acclaim in Mozart's magnificent *Don Giovanni*. Please welcome, my friends, Signora Giuditta Pasta, who has graciously agreed to appear although she travels tomorrow to her native Italy."

A ripple of subdued excitement greeted the news that the famous Pasta would sing. If it had been any other evening, Pierre thought, he would be thrilled to hear this legendary voice in the intimacy of a drawing room. As it was, he was instead acutely aware of Anne seated next to him, poised as if the slightest disturbance would send her springing off in some direction or other. The arms of their chairs barely touched, but still he could feel her tremble right through the wood. The sensation thrilled him. He had an overwhelming urge to kiss her.

Pierre felt Anne jump and her trembling increase when Liszt quietly took the seat on her other side. The Hungarian pianist lounged in the delicate chair, stretching his long legs out in front of him as far as possible, and angling his torso and head slightly toward Anne. Liszt did not look at her but instead gazed steadfastly at Madame d'Agoult, who had taken a seat over to the side but near the front of the room so that she could act as mistress of ceremonies for the evening. Even from where he sat, Pierre could tell that Liszt's unflinching gaze unsettled the countess.

Gardive did not sit but remained standing at the back of the parlor. He told Pierre that he wished to situate himself so that he could watch the marquis without being seen.

In the midst of Donna Elvira's tormented aria of love and betrayal, the little clock on Marie's mantel chimed softly. *About an hour,* Pierre remembered the countess had said. That was the approximate length of all the performances combined. Anne's subtle scent of spices wafted to him every time she shifted in her seat. An hour? It would be an eternity.

Franz had tried several times to get Anne alone for a moment so that he could tell her he would not go with her to abduct her cousin that evening, that there would be no carriage waiting by the servants' entrance. With the old man there, and Anne's performance at the end of the evening, he was doubly relieved that Eugène had persuaded him to change his mind. The original plan was to take Monsieur de Barbier to the Hôtel-Dieu, to find a Monsieur Talon. Here was another unexpected twist to the evening: Marie introduced him to a fair-haired young gentleman, a budding doctor, by the name of Talon. It was not so common a name. And judging by Anne's reaction to this fellow, and her meaningful glances in Franz's direction, this was the very person she had hoped to find at the Hôtel-Dieu.

By sitting next to Anne, he thought he might be able to steal an opportunity to speak to her as the performers came and went and the guests applauded. But there was Talon, seated on her other side. And she herself was strung as tight as a piano string, ready to pop and do great damage, he feared, if somehow she were released from whatever pins anchored her to the moment.

With nerves so raw, she might deliver an incomparable performance. Or she might freeze and run weeping from the room.

There was nothing else Franz could do about their plan for the time being, and so he indulged himself by watching Madame d'Agoult. She glided to and from her seat like a dancer—or no, an angel—as she introduced the artists one after another, a succession of musicians and poets that would have made any hostess a celebrity. Yet Marie did not exude self-importance. Rather she had that long-limbed grace that was wholly natural, and her wide, gray eyes were at once trustworthy and mysterious. He could feel her not looking at him, and it made him bold. He stared at her openly, noticing that his actions caused several of the older ladies to whisper to each other behind their fans. That would be another way to provoke a response from her, he thought. Let the rumors become so persistent that she would have to publicly deny them, or make them true.

"Monsieur Franz Liszt."

Franz sat up straight, then stood at the sound of applause before he fully realized that it was his turn to perform. What was he playing? Oh yes. "Un bal." There was Hector sunk into a corner, no doubt biting his nails over the response to this movement of his odd and wonderful symphony. No orchestra would touch it for now, so this was as much of a performance as the symphony would get, at least for a while.

Anne quivered with nervous energy. She did not even know herself whether she was frightened or simply agitated. Everything depended upon what happened tonight. Especially now that Pierre Talon was here as well. How she wished she had an opportunity to speak to him privately, to tell him about her plan to remove her cousin from the hôtel Barbier. He could come with them and begin caring for Armand right away. But she dared not. Everywhere she went, Anne could feel her father's eyes upon her.

And the letters to her mother: after speaking with Marie, she ached to read them, hoping to find some vindication in their lines.

She wished she had insisted that Marie give them back to her. Anne knew her mother's marriage had been arranged by the family, despite the romantic picture she had always painted when asked. Marriages usually were, and often young girls would have to marry men much older than they for the sake of some alliance or other. Men were allowed to dally all they chose, even expected to have an "official" mistress. But women must be faithful or risk terrible retribution. How terrible, Anne wondered, might the retribution have been at the marquis's hands if he had discovered that his wife still cherished such a passion? Marie had said Sandrine's lover was a musician. Anne had not looked closely at the signatures on the letters. How would it be, to know who he was?

Once the performances started, Anne struggled to remain calm. She could hardly sit still in her seat, especially since she found herself directly between Monsieur Liszt and Monsieur Talon. She could not help imagining that they were two angels sent to test her. On one side, danger, sensuality, art, music—Liszt. On the other, health, solidity, safety, science—Talon. From one minute to the next she felt herself incline toward one or the other of them. When she caught sight of her father, she wanted Monsieur Talon to enclose her in the secure, protected world of his knowledgeable and capable arms. The sight of Marie, on the other hand, made her long for Liszt's exciting, daring, unmentionably thrilling embrace. When he rose to go to the piano, Anne felt a chilly draft take his place and shivered.

"Are you in some distress, Countess?"

Monsieur Talon whispered directly into her ear. His warm breath reminded her that beside her sat someone capable of putting her fears for Armand to rest. It was maddening that she could not explain everything to him. Instead, she flashed him a quick smile, then turned away and closed her eyes so that she could listen to the curious vision of Monsieur Berlioz's waltz, a single movement from a symphony, apparently. Liszt had a way of making the piano sound like an entire orchestra. Anne did not know how he did it. They were the same felt-covered hammers striking the same taught metal strings, and yet one could hear the violins sigh, the trumpets blare, the drums roll. *I could never play like that,* Anne thought, forgetting that soon enough she would have to take her own seat at the piano and show this elite assemblage what she could do.

Liszt's performance was so astounding that the guests demanded an encore. Anne was relieved. She would perform next. Why, she wondered, had Marie arranged the program that way? Surely it would have made more sense for her to play first, so that the most remarkable artist could be the last one the audience heard before returning to the food, wine, and conversation. That would have made the evening easier for her as well. She could have pled the need to rest after her performance and disappeared to a private room of the apartment and to the back stairs to make everything ready for their flight.

Liszt improvised a brilliant variation on a theme by Paganini and would have been forced to continue with another if Marie had not stepped in.

"Monsieur Liszt has been most generous with his talent this evening. But if he plays much more, none of you will pay to hear him when he next takes the stage at the Wauxhall!"

Everyone laughed.

"And now, as another treat for your musical delectation this evening, I should like to present a young pianist of remarkable gifts. Many of you remember my dear friend Sandrine de Barbier-Chouant, who was herself an accomplished musician."

A few murmurs greeted her remark.

"I have been fortunate indeed to be able to shepherd the artistic development of my late friend's daughter, the countess Anne de Barbier-Chouant, who has inherited her mother's talent. She has spent these last two months under the tutelage of Monsieur Liszt himself."

Anne cast a quick glance at her father. He had never asked the name of her teacher, nor had she volunteered it. Beneath his powder she could see his face grow dark crimson, and his eyes flashed with anger. She prayed that he would not make a scene. It would ruin absolutely everything.

She had no time to dwell on this possibility because Marie held out her hand to her. Anne threaded her way through the chairs that had become disarranged from their neat rows as people clustered together in little groups. She kept her eyes on the piano and gave only the briefest curtsey, her eyes lowered, before taking her seat at the familiar keyboard.

In his preoccupation with events to come, Pierre had nearly forgotten that Anne was to play. He sat forward in his seat and knitted his fingers together. *How awful to have to follow the great Liszt,* he thought. But as soon as the countess put her sensitive fingers on the keys, everyone in the room hardly breathed. The lyrical study, by Monsieur Chopin, cast a tender spell over the audience. At least half the guests closed their eyes, and several showed evidence of tears as the fair countess poured out her young heart before them all. She did not dazzle, like Liszt, yet the notes fell on the ear like pearls, and even the dissonant passages held warmth and roundness, as though she were incapable of creating a harsh sound.

And her face—from the moment she began to play, Anne surrendered herself to the music. Each nuance of feeling was etched on her features. Pierre thought his heart would burst, and he prayed that this lovely creature who embodied the soul of music would consent to be his, forever.

Anne's performance was by no means a disappointment after the great Liszt's. It was a gentle denouement, a wistful coda. When the last, lingering notes died away, no one moved for several seconds. Anne looked up, and Pierre could see the realization of where she was gradually dawn again, and fear—yes, unmistakably fear—creep back into her eyes.

Marie began to clap and said, "Brava, my dear. Brava." But no sooner had everyone else stirred themselves from the enchantment of Anne's playing than the marquis himself stood and with great purpose marched to the front of the room. He took his daughter roughly by the arm. She cowered away. Pierre leaped to his feet.

"That's enough! Enough!" the marquis roared, and there were tears in his eyes.

Marie stood and gently but firmly grasped the marquis's arm, casting a warning glance in Pierre's direction. The rest of the audience were rooted to their seats, stunned. "Monsieur le Marquis, I can understand that you are distressed by how much your daughter brings to mind your late wife. But please, be seated. I have a surprise yet for everyone."

Her words brought the old courtier to his senses. He released Anne and bowed apologetically to Marie. Pierre, who could see the red finger marks on Anne's slender arm from where he was, wanted to rush forward himself and comfort the countess. Anne did not come back to her seat next to him, but Marie took her quietly by the hand and made her stand a little behind her while she spoke.

"Ladies and gentlemen—friends, I should say—it gives me great pleasure to offer you a surprise grand finale. There has been in my home, unbeknownst to you, an artist who more than any other today has captured the imagination of the public. Many of you recently had an opportunity to hear him perform in a benefit concert at the Salle Wauxhall."

Waiting for some signal from her for the commencement of that adventure they had planned, Pierre followed Marie's eyes around the room. He caught sight of Gardive, who raised one eyebrow and inched a little closer to the door.

"Ladies and gentlemen, I give you Paganini!"

The servants, who had been arranged around the room to stand near candles and sconces, at a signal from the countess extinguished them all, plunging the room immediately into complete darkness. From near the door came the strains of a violin. Everyone gasped in surprise as the eerie music moved among them like a ghost.

"Come, Monsieur Talon."

Pierre heard Marie's whisper and the gentlest touch on his sleeve. He followed the sound of swishing petticoats out to the vestibule, which had also been darkened so that no light would flood into the drawing room when the door was opened for the violinist. Before it closed behind them, Pierre saw a footman light one candle on the music stand by the piano, and Paganini's spectral face came into view: its glowing eyes and sunken cheeks looking like death himself.

"Excuse me for a moment, Countess."

It was Anne's voice.

"Anne, wait!" Marie's hoarse whisper followed her, but Anne had opened a door, and Pierre saw her skitter through it in a flash.

"Quickly!" Marie said to him, pushing him in the direction of the door to the back stairs.

"Gardive?" Pierre whispered.

"I'm here," came the commissioner's low, calm voice, and the two of them ran after Anne.

The light in the stairwell dazzled Pierre at first, and his wound stabbed into his side with every step he took, but he did not slow down. Why was she running? Did she know after all?

They soon emerged into the alley next to Marie's apartment building, arriving to see Anne climbing into the waiting carriage. As soon as she closed the door behind her, the driver yelled, "Get on!" and the vehicle lurched into motion.

Pierre turned his confused eyes upon Gardive. "She's leaving without us!" he cried, and he was about to run forward to halt the carriage, when a voice stopped him.

"Where is my daughter?"

Pierre turned, and there, at the servants' entrance, stood the marquis de Barbier-Chouant. He had murder in his eyes and a pistol in his hand, which he aimed at Pierre's heart. The weapon was remarkably steady, considering that the elderly man required the other hand to lean on his walking stick. Necessity had doubtless taught him to use a pistol in his youth.

"Would you care to explain to me how you wounded yourself?" the marquis growled. "You robbed me. The silver was nothing. You took an important piece of paper. And I know more besides!"

Pierre's heart pounded. Fear rooted him in place. *I'm going to die,* he thought.

Twenty-Five

Before Pierre could utter a word, Gardive stepped forward.

"Your daughter, Marquis, has fled in a carriage that was waiting for her here. There is not a moment to lose. We must follow her, or you may never see her again." Gardive reached for the marquis's arm, the one that held the pistol. "Madame d'Agoult told us that grief had made her want to run far away, and now it seems that she has acted on this foolish impulse."

The marquis wrenched his arm free and aimed the gun at Gardive. "You expect me to believe that the countess would do something so foolish? You must have been plotting something together!" The marquis encompassed Pierre and Gardive in his disdainful scowl.

"I suggest," Gardive said, "you put away your weapon. If we hurry, we may yet apprehend her before she has come to any harm."

"Why should I believe a clerk?"

"A clerk, Monsieur le Marquis, with access to all records concerning birth, death, and marriage in the city." Gardive's voice remained even and calm. The marquis flared his nostrils and ground his teeth.

But rather than continue his tirade against them, he uncocked his pistol. Gardive did not hesitate to grab it from him and hand it to Pierre. "Perhaps if you will be so kind as to show us to your carriage?"

Together the three of them went out to the street and found the marquis's brougham. They made an odd group. Gardive looked official and unrumpled, as if not even a typhoon could blow off his hat or muss a hair on his head. Pierre imagined that he was in a frightful state himself, no doubt with his clothes askew, and he'd left his hat in the apartment. And the marquis, so imposing from a distance, was as thin and frail as a little spider beneath his heavy brocade coat.

Pierre was about to speak, but Gardive interrupted him.

"She has too great a start on us to follow her. There is no telling which way she went. We shall return to the hôtel Barbier, Monsieur le Marquis," he said. Gardive put his head out of the window. "Rue du Barq."

The marquis leaned back in the seat. He closed his eyes. A blood vessel in his temple throbbed, and Pierre feared that the old man would have an attack of apoplexy. "I knew I should never have come. Do you have any idea what could happen? The danger . . ." He passed his hand over his forehead.

What danger did the marquis speak of? Pierre had been under the impression that the marquis himself was the source of any danger to Anne or her cousin. Before he could formulate a question, they had reached the hôtel Barbier and pulled into the courtyard. Pierre leaned out in preparation to open the door, and to his shock, he saw the carriage that had been sent to convey himself, Anne, and Gardive to a notary in front of the door, with the housekeeper and the old valet settling a figure wrapped in blankets in it. Before Pierre could say a word, the driver of Anne's carriage urged his horses on around the courtyard.

At that moment, the marquis leaped from his seat and would have jumped out of the moving vehicle if Gardive had not restrained him.

"Let go of me! Don't you see? They are being abducted!"

Before Pierre could say anything, there was a brief moment when the two conveyances were situated so that the occupants of one could see easily into the other. Pierre had a clear view across his companions of Anne, who turned toward them. All three of the gentlemen in the brougham exclaimed aloud, either, "Mademoiselle!" or "Countess!" or "Anne!" when her fear-stricken face peered out the window.

Victor slowed as he pulled up to the main door of the hôtel Barbier. Pierre leaned out and cried, "Don't stop! Go after them! Hurry!"

The horses must have picked up the scent of excitement, because with hardly a whip crack, they took off at a brisk trot and broke into a canter as soon as they were on the street. Victor had to hold them back to prevent their slipping on the cobbles. Pierre kept the window open and hung out of it, pointing and shouting each time the carriage turned ahead of them. Revelers and café dwellers cheered them on as they passed, thinking perhaps two young men had a wager and were racing for a prize. Pierre wanted to question the marquis about what he could mean, why he thought Anne was being abducted, but they were all too intent on the chase to think of anything else.

Anne had climbed into the waiting carriage expecting that Liszt would be inside. When she found herself alone, she hesitated, wondering if she should wait to see if he followed her. But the sound of more than one pair of heavy footsteps hurtling down the stairs behind her gave her no time to consider. "Drive on!" she called to the coachman, who had roused himself with a snort when the carriage rocked, apparently having half fallen asleep on the box. As they started moving, she heard a commotion at the door and looked out the window. Monsieur Talon and Monsieur Gardive had come out into the alley, and Monsieur Talon was pointing at her and waving his arms. She had opened her mouth to call out "Stop!" to the driver, thinking this was a stroke of luck indeed, that Liszt must have told the doctor of their plans and sent him in his place, but then her father appeared behind them. She rapped on the ceiling and yelled out "Hurry!" to the driver.

"Where to, mademoiselle?" he called to her.

"Turn left, rue du Barq," Anne yelled back, wondering that Liszt had not informed the driver of their destination ahead of time as they had planned.

She leaned back and put her hand over her heart, which pounded so hard she could feel it in her ears. How, without Liszt's help and with Monsieur Talon not only at Marie's but in the company of her father, would she ever manage to take her cousin to safety? Now she must count on Julien and Thérèse to help her. They could bring him down to the carriage, at least.

Anne leaped from the fiacre as soon as it stopped, and pounded with the side of her fist on the great wooden door. Julien opened it cautiously but, on seeing Anne, threw it wide. "Please! You must help me. Where is Thérèse?" She pushed past him and ran directly up the stairs.

True to her word, Thérèse had remained at Armand's side. He looked pale and weak, and twitched in a fitful sleep. "Wrap him in blankets, Thérèse," Anne commanded, "and then you and Julien must carry him down to the carriage."

Julien hesitated.

"Do as the mistress says!" Thérèse snapped.

After a quick look over his shoulder, Julien helped the housekeeper gather up the blankets.

Anne reached the carriage first and had already climbed inside when she saw her father's brougham enter the courtyard. "Quickly!" she called.

Julien was old, and he staggered once or twice under his burden; Anne thought her cousin would tumble out of his arms. *Poor Armand,* she thought. She hoped that he had fainted and did not suffer any pain.

They succeeded in getting Armand propped up in the seat, and the driver, now fully understanding that they were meant to be evading the occupants of the other vehicle that had entered the courtyard, cracked his whip loudly. The horses lifted their heads and pranced off. As they rounded the curve directly opposite the other carriage, Anne peeked fearfully out of the window. To her astonishment, she saw Monsieur Talon's profile framed in the window of her father's brougham. Perhaps her father was not inside after all. Perhaps Pierre had come to help her. "Wait!" she yelled to the coachman, who slowed his horses. Anne was about to open the window and tell the young doctor what they were doing when all at once her father's face appeared next to Monsieur Talon's. She heard him scream her name, and with her heart pounding, she cried "Forward!" to the coachman, and slumped back in her seat. How was it that Talon and her father were together?

"Now where?" called the driver as they turned onto the street.

Where? Anne had no idea. This was not at all as she had pictured the rescue of her cousin. She had thought to have the protection of a man as she staged this brash abduction, but now it was just the two of them. "Rue de Provence!" she called up to the coachman. She had little choice. Wherever else she took Armand they might come looking for him. No one would expect her to know the address of Franz Liszt's modest studio. Anne did not think beyond the notion that she must, at all costs, not let her father find Monsieur de Barbier until he was quite out of danger.

To her dismay, she could see through the tiny window behind her that her father's brougham, given added speed by the extra pair of horses they had hired for the night, chased after them for quite a while through the crowded streets. It was not until a carriage crossing from one quai to the other intervened between her vehicle and his that they finally shed their pursuers.

"I think we've lost them, mademoiselle!" yelled the coachman. Anne did not have the strength to comment.

When they finally arrived at Liszt's apartment, and Anne was certain they had not been followed, she turned her attention to Armand. He was in a dead faint. She did not know how she would ever get him up the four flights of stairs to the garret studio.

She lowered the window and put her head out so that she could look up at the box. "Coachman, I need your help."

The fellow climbed down rather unwillingly.

"I shall ring for the concierge while you carry the young gentleman to the door," she said.

"First she wants me to risk my horses's hooves, now this," he grumbled.

"I shall reward you handsomely. After you have helped me carry my cousin up to an apartment on the third floor." The fellow opened the door for her and helped her out. She rang the bell for the concierge, whom she hoped was not yet sleeping, and prayed that the money she had in her reticule—all that she had saved from the small amounts her father had given her in the previous weeks—would be sufficient for what she had requested of the driver.

After a short wait, a groggy-looking fellow in shirtsleeves answered. When Anne told him they needed to bring someone who was ill into Liszt's apartment, he started to close the door in their faces.

"It's not cholera!" Anne said, inserting the toe of her slipper inside the door so that he could not close it without causing her pain. "He has had an operation."

The concierge grudgingly preceded them up the stairs and unlocked the door.

"Where shall I put him?" asked the coachman.

Liszt's parlor was furnished with a couple of upholstered chairs but no divan. Anne entered the bedroom and pointed to Liszt's bed. "Put him there," she said.

Once the coachman had deposited his delicate load, Anne emptied the contents of her purse into his hand and sent him away.

"What shall I say when Monsieur Liszt returns?" asked the concierge, who was now awake enough to notice that a young girl had asked to be admitted in the dead of night to a single gentleman's apartment.

"When Monsieur Liszt returns, I shall depart. I need only stay to care for my cousin, whom I cannot leave alone."

The fellow scratched his head and shrugged, then returned to his own quarters at street level.

Anne knelt by Armand's side and tried to get him to drink some water she had poured for him from the pitcher on a table by the bed. "I won't leave you," she whispered, hoping that her cousin could hear her.

"Anne?"

The word was quiet but unmistakable. Anne leaned in closer to her cousin. "Yes, Armand, you are safe. I shall care for you."

"Where—?"

Armand's voice seemed to come from deep inside his body. Anne continued to give him sips of water, then when he appeared to fall asleep again, she searched in a little cupboard in the parlor for a teapot and some chamomile. There was water in the kettle on the stove. She would make tea so that she could give it to him when he next awoke.

She cast her eye around the austere bachelor apartment. What would everyone think if they could see her now? She dismissed the thought from her mind. All that mattered for the moment was her cousin. *Later,* Anne thought, *I'll find a way to explain all this to Marie, to my father, to Monsieur Talon. When Monsieur Liszt returns, I'll ask him to look for Talon first thing in the morning. He'll understand why I did this.*

Anne was convinced that her actions that evening had saved her cousin's life.

They lost sight of the carriage bearing the countess and her cousin at the Pont Neuf. There was a delay: a cart had to turn around completely and blocked the passage for five minutes. By the time the way was clear, the carriage they had been pursuing was nowhere to be seen.

By now the marquis breathed hard through his open mouth, and beads of sweat gathered on his brow. "We must return Monsieur le Marquis to his home," Pierre whispered to Gardive, who instructed the driver to go back to the rue du Barq.

"They're gone. She'll never forgive me," the marquis breathed. "Never."

When they arrived, Gardive helped the old man down from the brougham and into the house, where Julien stood looking bemused and uncomfortable in the vestibule. "Marquis—," he began, but Pierre stopped him.

"You must see that your master goes to his bed; he is unwell. I recommend a hot brandy and water."

"Where is Thérèse?" the old man grumbled.

"Upstairs, Marquis," Julien said.

"She must know something," he muttered. "I might have known it was she."

Once Julien had helped the marquis mount the grand staircase, Pierre motioned Gardive into the library. His sudden need to sit overcame any scruples he might have had about presuming upon the marquis's hospitality. He certainly felt less of a trespasser that evening than he had the night before, when he had broken in with Petit and stolen the will. "Perhaps when the valet is done with the old man, he'll get us a brandy."

The two men sat on either side of the fireplace and leaned back in their chairs.

"It has long been my experience," Gardive said, "that plans seldom turn out the way they ought to."

Pierre nodded in agreement. The door to the library opened, and Julien cleared his throat softly. "The master says I'm to get you whatever you want."

"Perhaps you'd like to explain what happened here tonight, good man," Gardive said.

Pierre listened absently as the commissioner quizzed the old servant about the events that had occurred before they arrived. None of it interested Pierre particularly. All he cared about was that Anne had gone off heaven knew where with her sick cousin. What would have caused her to take such a precipitate action? She must have been trying to tell him something that evening at Madame d'Agoult's, and he had been so caught up in the idea of the plan with Marie that he had failed to understand her. "If you don't mind, Gardive," Pierre said, interrupting the commissioner's subtle interrogation, "I have no heart for this."

"Of course," he said. "Your injury. We must get you to your bed as well." The two men stood, and Gardive addressed Julien. "Please tell the marquis that I shall call on him tomorrow, if I can bring him news concerning the events of this evening."

Victor had waited in the entrance hall, his hat still in his hands, but Pierre and Gardive declined the offer of a carriage ride back to their own apartments. Pierre said he needed a breath of air, but really he could not bear the thought of once again being enclosed in the brougham, which reeked of the old man's powder and musty clothes.

They found a fiacre at the nearby stand. On their way to drop the commissioner at the Prefecture, where, he assured Pierre, a comfortable cot awaited him, Gardive mused aloud.

"The marquis behaved most peculiarly this evening. Why do you suppose he would have thought both his daughter and his cousin had been abducted?"

"Surely he was only trying to make us believe that they would not purposely run away."

"Perhaps. And yet, there was real anguish in his voice, and he very nearly did himself harm."

They had reached the Prefecture, and Gardive descended. "All I care about is ensuring that Mademoiselle Anne is now safe," Pierre said, as Gardive waited with his hand on the open window frame of the carriage door.

"That, and a good night's sleep, I would wager. Drive on!" he called up to the coachman, who conveyed Pierre the rest of the way to the rue des Bernardins.

Marie had seen Anne disappear down the servants' stairs, followed by Pierre and Gardive. When none of them returned to the party, she assumed that they had escaped as planned. The absence of the marquis worried her a little. She had already rehearsed an explanation for Anne's disappearance that included a headache and the use of Marie's own carriage to return home, but she had no need of it. She chose to believe that the marquis, fatigued by the unaccustomed excitement, had departed immediately after his daughter's performance. He was an old man and had looked tired already when he arrived. In any case, her part in the drama was at an end, and she still had her guests to attend to.

Everyone was enchanted with Paganini's dramatic appearance, as they were by all the performances. Marie received many compliments about Anne's playing and noticed that Liszt was besieged by ladies who were effusive in their praise of his student's as well as his own performance.

Gradually, the apartment emptied. At about midnight, Marie, thinking everyone had gone, entered her disordered parlor and began pulling the hairpins out of her coiffure.

"I beg your pardon, Countess."

Marie gasped and put her hand over her heart. To her astonishment, Franz Liszt was still there, sitting in a comfortable chair by the pianoforte. "Monsieur Liszt, I thought you had gone."

"I would have," he said, rising to join her in the middle of the room, "if I had allowed myself to be drawn into a scheme concocted by my pupil, the countess Anne."

She had never before been alone in a room with Liszt, and the idea that all constraints between them could be done away with made her feel weak. All at once Marie found her legs too tired to bear her weight and lowered herself into one of the gilt chairs near to hand. "Perhaps you had better tell me what you are talking about," she said.

Liszt told her the entire story of Anne's desperate worry over her cousin, and her approach to him to help her remove the young man from the hôtel de Barbier. "I realized, on reflection, that her anxiety must have been the result of an imagination that was overheated by recent loss. I did not want to jeopardize the countess's reputation by being seen to run off with her in the middle of the night."

"You were concerned about her reputation?" Marie could not prevent her sarcastic tone. Yet the look on the pianist's face when she made her comment was so full of sorrow and regret that she wanted to cover his face with kisses and tell him that the behavior she had witnessed did not matter to her. But for all she knew, he still harbored some serious hopes toward Anne.

"I did not intend—I did not mean— Oh, Countess!" Liszt knelt in front of her, grasped her hands in his, and searched her eyes so intently that she had to look away.

"The marquis would never permit you to marry," she said.

"Marry? Who? Anne?"

The surprise in his voice was genuine. Marie looked deep into his eyes. "If you arrange to meet a young lady in a public place, you would be a cad to have any but honorable designs upon her."

Marie had never actually seen someone's jaw drop before, but she could think of no other way to describe the transformation in Liszt's expression in the next instant. He let go of her hands and stood, walking back and forth across her Chinese carpet with his forehead creased in perplexity. "But, my dear Countess," he said after a moment or two, "that was you!"

Marie felt her understanding of the world turn on its head. So he had known! Why did he not say anything? "I thought . . . I wanted to protect Anne."

She stood and Liszt came face-to-face with her. "Surely you understood from my notes," he said.

"Your notes?"

The silence between them lasted long enough for Marie to become aware of the mantel clock's tick.

"You did not receive them, I gather," Liszt said.

Marie shook her head slowly from side to side. "How did you send them?"

"I didn't send them, I gave them to Anne. At her lessons."

"You gave them to Anne. Who clearly did not understand that they were not meant for her and failed to give them to me!" Marie put her hand over her mouth to stifle the laughter she felt was about to erupt from her, whether from astonishment or relief or delight, she could not tell. Suddenly everything made sense. The two notes in the envelope addressed to Anne. Liszt's meaningful glances at her. There was only one thing that still did not fit.

"Countess—Marie—how can I ever explain? I thought when you agreed to meet me that I was in heaven."

"And yet," Marie said, but she stopped herself. Liszt's eyes were liquid with desire. Marie recognized that look, and it made the skin on her neck glow with warmth. How desperately she wanted to give in to the promise of such a passion, the urgent, insane hunger of youth. She could give up everything for this extraordinary man. Everything. Her affluent life, her husband, her friends—only the thought of her children made her pause for the briefest instant. But to do so, she would require more than a furtive affair, whispered about in salons all over Paris. "I think you had better leave now," she said, even as she allowed Liszt to pull her closer. She hardly knew how it happened, but their lips touched. A moment later, his long arms wrapped around her and held her so tightly that the boundaries between them seemed to disappear. Marie closed her eyes and for a moment let herself forget who she was, what she was, where she was.

Yet when the kiss ended, she gently pushed him away. "I think we must not see each other again," she said.

"But we have not even started." Liszt's eyes clouded over in confusion and bewilderment. "Can't you see that I love you!"

Marie smiled sadly at the young pianist's words. She too had once thought that love in itself was enough to overcome everything. "If you truly love me, that love will endure. I believe I must go away on an extended journey to stay with friends in Switzerland. It shall be as though we have never met when I return. After that, when your ardent desire has been blunted by time, if you still wish to claim my friendship, we shall see."

Franz reached out to her but she backed away. He drew himself up tall, and Marie imagined all the tendrils of feeling and fervor he had allowed to escape from him curling back in, being drawn up for safety as though his heart were a separate being inside his body and, having cast its fishing lines out into the world, now reeled them in as quickly as possible. He bowed to her, turned to go, but paused before he closed the parlor door behind him and said, "I may be insane, but I shall wait for you tomorrow night, at Eugène's studio. He will not be there."

Marie turned away. The door shut with a click that went through her like a dagger. She sank down into her chair again, put one hand over her face, and wept.

Twenty-Six

After Marie sent him away, Franz spent hours wandering the streets in a daze. At first he had gone toward a café he knew where he might find friends and a bottle of wine to drown his sorrows. But as he approached its door and heard the raucous, drunken laughter spilling out into the misty night, he continued past without hesitating.

How could he have been so foolish! What made him assume that Anne understood what to do with his ardent letters to Marie? He searched his memory, desperate to find some vindication there, something that would assure him that he had not acted toward the young countess in a way that would have misled her. Unfortunately, everything he recalled rather confirmed her right to assume his sentiments were meant for her. Although he had several times tried to tell her his intentions directly, he had never managed to do more than hint.

His hopes were dashed—and yet at the same time, very much alive. Now he knew for certain that Marie loved him: why else would she have been so hurt by the misunderstanding with Anne? But she would not give in to him. At least, not this evening. And tomorrow?

Franz's thoughts were in turmoil as he strolled aimlessly through arrondissement after arrondissement, barely sensible of putting himself in any danger from the lowlifes that claimed that godforsaken hour of the night for their own. In truth, his tall, angular frame and hollow eyes presented a frightening spectacle in themselves, and those few creatures who roamed the streets with him skittered away when they saw him approach.

Franz was not aware of anything other than his own grief until he stopped in front of the doors of Les Jésuites. The smell of incense and the sound of quiet chanting wafted out to where he stood. *Lauds,* he thought. All at once, the desire to retreat to the comfort and solace of a religious service overcame him. He walked up the steps and entered the lofty dusk of the ancient edifice, took a seat at the back of the nave, and remained with his head bowed and his eyes closed until the Office ended.

The shuffling footsteps of the Jesuits and their students roused Franz from his deep contemplation. An acolyte snuffed the candles one by one, but he dreaded leaving, not wanting to return to the trouble and disappointment of his present life. He drew his breath in and expelled it in a long sigh. When he started to rise from his kneeling position, a hand clapped down on his shoulder from behind. He turned his head to see a priest looking down at him.

"I would hear your confession if that would ease your troubled breast."

It had been some weeks since Franz had confessed. The idea of being able to tell all to someone wholly unconnected with the intrigues and machinations that swirled around him was very appealing. He nodded, followed the priest to the confessional, and knelt on the open side of the ornate wooden cabinet, darkened and worn smooth by centuries of knees. "Forgive me, Father, for I have sinned."

The formulaic phrases came easily to Franz. The priest on the other side of the grille said nothing at first, only punctuating with the occasional *tsk* Franz's account of his attempted seduction of a married woman, and the way he used an innocent young girl to reach her, and the manner in which his attempts had gone so utterly wrong.

"And then, this same girl asked for my help with some dire project—a cousin who is ill, recovering from an operation, who she fears is not being well cared for in her father's house."

"What did she want you to do, my son?"

The question took Franz by surprise. Normally priests only listened or murmured encouragingly.

"To help her abduct him from her home. She was convinced that whether or not he meant him harm, the marquis was damaging the health of his cousin."

"The marquis? Who is this cousin you speak of?"

"I do not recall. But I believe he might have shared the countess's name of Barbier."

Franz could swear he heard something clatter to the floor of the confessional on the other side of the screen. "Absolva te, in nomine patris, filius, et spiritus sanctus, amen," the priest muttered, giving Franz his penance so quickly that the young man wondered if the fellow himself had suddenly taken ill. Before he could rise from his kneeling position, Franz heard the door of the confessional open and shut, and when he stood and looked about him, he saw only the priest's cassock as he disappeared behind the door that led into the living quarters of the college.

When Franz emerged from the church, the fine weather had changed, and Paris was awakening to a chill, gray drizzle. He hurried back to his apartment, now aching for sleep. By the time he reached his door, the lamplighters had extinguished the streetlights, the shopkeepers and artisans had begun to stir, and he was soaked to the skin and delirious with fatigue.

He had already removed his shirt in preparation for sleep when he walked into his bedroom and saw a stranger sleeping in his bed and the countess de Barbier-Chouant, seated on the floor, asleep as well with her head leaning on the edge of the mattress.

"Mon Dieu!" the exclamation escaped his lips before he had a chance to stifle it.

Anne awoke with a start, and the fellow in the bed groaned. Of course, this must be Anne's cousin, the ailing Monsieur de Barbier. So she had been serious. How in heaven's name did she get the fellow here all by herself?

"Monsieur Liszt," Anne said, standing and smoothing down her rumpled evening dress. "Where were you? Why did you not meet me as we arranged?"

"I—" He could not tell her that he had not believed her, that he thought her concerns about her cousin were nothing more than overblown fantasies designed to entrap him into unwise actions. "You cannot remain here."

"I cannot go home either. My father will be so angry."

Poor Anne's face was scarlet with embarrassment, and Franz, remembering that he was half-naked, folded his arms across his chest. "If you would kindly wait in the parlor, I'll dress and then find you a fiacre. You must go to the quai Malaquais. Madame d'Agoult will know what to do."

Anne was so tired that nothing seemed quite real. The events of the night before would not arrange themselves in any kind of sensible order in her mind. All she knew was that Armand was safe. And Monsieur Liszt was right, she could hardly stay there. He assured her he would care for Armand, and that if her cousin appeared to worsen, he would find Monsieur Talon himself, and saw her safely into a fiacre.

It was not yet eight in the morning when Anne arrived at Marie's apartment. She had to wait nearly half an hour in the parlor for the countess to emerge. When she did, Anne saw that her eyes were red rimmed, more as though she had been crying than as though she was simply worn out from a late evening.

"Anne! Where is Monsieur Talon?"

"Monsieur Talon?"

The two ladies stared at each other as though they had come from opposite sides of the earth.

"Please, Anne, this is no time to be mysterious. You and Monsieur Talon and Monsieur Gardive went off in the carriage last night. I simply want to know what happened. I shan't be angry about it, whatever you tell me." Marie rang the bell for tea after she spoke, then sat next to Anne on the divan.

So, Anne thought, the carriage in the alley had not been intended for herself and Monsieur Liszt. *That must have been why he was so surprised to see me.* "Madame d'Agoult, I think there has been some terrible misunderstanding."

Anne braced herself for Marie's disapproval, then related to her the entire story of the plan with Liszt and the events of the night before.

"You mean to say you passed the night in Monsieur Liszt's apartment without a chaperone?"

"Yes, but he was not there. He did not return until about an hour ago, and then he fetched me a fiacre right away, to come here." Anne was by now desperate to know what Marie thought had happened last night. She realized there must have been some other plan that involved her. Instead of speaking, the countess stood, covered her mouth with her hand, and walked over to the window. She remained there for several minutes, not moving until after the maid had brought a breakfast tray and left again. "Please speak to me, madame," Anne said, fatigue and confusion bringing the threat of tears to her voice.

"Oh, Anne, I'm so sorry," Marie said. "But don't you see what a difficult position you are in? To pass the night alone in an unmarried man's apartment—not alone, even, but with a young gentleman whom your father intends you to marry. What can we say to the marquis?"

"Madame," Anne asked, "why did you say you thought Monsieur Talon and I had gone off in a carriage last night? What did you think had happened?"

"I will tell you by and by," Marie said, "but for now we must take some action to preserve your reputation. I shall write to your father, tell him that you fled to me late last night because you feared his wrath. That you simply became alarmed about your cousin's condition and took him to the hospital. I'll ask him to send clothing and your maid so that you may stay here for a while."

Anne took a deep breath to calm her racing heart. She was

relieved. Staying with Marie for a few days meant that she would not have to face her father right away. She had never done anything so openly rebellious before, and she did not know what might happen.

Although Marie still had not told her about Monsieur Talon, Anne was by now too tired to think.

"I must take care of these matters right away," Marie said. "I'll have Adèle put you in the guest room. I suggest you try to sleep for a while. When you have rested, please join me in the parlor for tea. We have much to discuss."

When Armand awoke, he had no idea where he was. He remembered Julien and Thérèse lifting him from his bed at the hôtel Barbier, but the jostling had caused him intense pain around his wound and he had fainted even before descending the stairs. After that, he had surfaced from his swoon once or twice and felt the world around him whirling and jumping. He had noticed the delicate lavender scent of his cousin, and this had reassured him that he was not alone. But he could make no sense of what exactly had happened.

The first thing he apprehended upon opening his eyes was how close to him the ceiling was. He thought for a moment that somehow his bed had been raised on a high platform. He had spent a considerable amount of time gazing up at the crumbling plaster immediately over his head at the hôtel Barbier, and he knew that it used to be many feet higher than it appeared now.

It only took a moment and a slight turn of his head to the side to realize that more than just the height of the ceiling had changed. For another instant, he imagined himself back in the safety and security of the dormitory at Les Jésuites, the room was so sparsely furnished and modestly decorated. Then he saw the soft, blond curls of his cousin draped over the coverlet next to his right arm and knew that they had not entered the college dormitory where he had spent his childhood. Anne's head moved slightly with each even breath, and he could feel her body's warmth. Armand did not want to move, afraid that she would awaken and shift her position away from him.

He was about to let himself drift off to sleep again, not much caring where he was so long as Anne was nearby, when he heard a door opening in another room and the heavy footsteps of a man moving around. He hardly had time to register this intrusion when the door at his feet swung open, and a tall, handsome gentleman stood there, his hair just missing the doorframe. Anne lifted her head off the bed and stood up quickly. Armand felt cold.

Anne and this stranger, apparently a Monsieur Liszt, a name that was familiar to him from some time in the past, spoke in a way that conveyed something beyond their words to Armand. Clearly they were in his lodgings, which was a most unsuitable place for Anne. He heard in his cousin's tremulous voice a breathless nervousness. There was something keyed up about the way she acted with the tall man. It occurred to Armand that his lovely cousin's heart must have quickened at the sight of Monsieur Liszt the way his always did at the sight of her. He closed his eyes, turned his head away, and moaned.

Their talking stopped, and he heard first Anne pass through to the other room, and a short while later, after some shuffling around and opening and shutting of cabinets and drawers, the man followed her. After that he could hear nothing other than the quiet suggestion of a conversation. He supposed they were discussing him, how to get him out of there, or how to get Anne away without ruining her reputation. *I do not care about your reputation,* he thought. *I would take you just as you are, if you would have me.*

Armand decided his health must be improving, because the ache in his heart was now stronger than any other pain he felt.

The next time he woke up, the tall man called Monsieur Liszt sat next to him, his long legs stretched out across the bare, wooden floor. And Armand remembered who he was. He was that pianist Anne had spoken of when they first met. Monsieur Liszt appeared to be sunk deep in his own thoughts.

"Excuse me," Armand said.

"Good!" Liszt exclaimed. "You are awake. Will you take some broth?"

"Where is Anne—the countess?" he asked.

"I hope she is back at home, safe."

"No! If she is at home, she is not safe!"

Armand tried to lift himself up off the bed; the effort sent a searing pain through his abdomen. He cried out.

"Don't upset yourself, man!" Liszt gently pressed him back down on the pillows. "What makes you say Mademoiselle Anne is not safe?"

To Armand's dismay, tears sprang into his eyes and flowed down his cheeks. "I . . . I don't know. I'm not certain, I mean . . . I have nothing to prove it, really—"

Armand started coughing. Liszt sprang from his seat in alarm and fetched a glass of water. "Perhaps I should get a doctor," he said.

"Yes, Dr. Talon, if you please."

Franz had not been introduced to the doctor last night, but Anne had said he might be found near the college of medicine at the university. He grabbed his coat from the back of the chair. "Will you be all right while I'm gone?"

"Yes, I'm mostly tired," Armand answered.

The sooner he could get Talon to come and see the fellow, the better, Liszt thought, as hurtled down the stairs two at a time.

Twenty-Seven

〜

Pierre was aware first of pain when Georges shook him awake at about nine the next morning. His side hurt but not as badly as before. After he had returned last night, he had reopened the wound and drained it, which had proved to be a great relief. There was another pain, though, something pressing hard on his left hip, something on the mattress.

"Wake up, Pierre! There's the most extraordinary fellow looking for you. Speaks with the oddest accent."

Georges continued to shake him, and whatever it was that caused him pain ground into him with each movement.

"Ow! Stop!" he cried, and then sat upright so quickly he hit his head on the wall next to his bed. "What is it?"

"You look terrible," Georges said, concern replacing the fleeting irritation Pierre had noticed on his face as soon as he was awake enough to register anything. "What happened?"

"I can't explain now. Did you say someone was here?"

"Yes, a chap who insists you have to go with him. Wouldn't leave until I woke you."

Pierre felt his side. His hand found the marquis's pistol, which he had tucked in his belt after Gardive handed it to him and never bothered to remove the night before. Doubtless he would have a large bruise. He was about to place the pistol on his nightstand, then thought better of it. "Did he give a name, this fellow?"

"Franz Liszt," Georges said.

All at once Pierre was wide awake. He pulled his coat on over his shirtsleeves and combed his hair with his fingers. What was Liszt doing at his apartment?

Pierre flung open the door to the small reception room, and the pianist unfolded himself from the low upholstered chair. He did not have the same confident demeanor as the night before, even seeming a bit stooped over, as if matters pressed on his shoulders and stopped him from quite straightening his long frame. "I am sorry to trouble you, but the countess Anne bade me find you and bring you to her cousin, Monsieur de Barbier."

"Where is he? Where is she?" Pierre could not imagine how this fellow knew what had happened the night before. He had not seen Liszt, only Anne, remove her cousin from the hôtel Barbier.

"Monsieur de Barbier is at my apartment. He is very ill."

"At your apartment? How—"

"There is no time to explain. You must come with me right away."

"And Anne—the countess—where is she?" Pierre grew hot with suspicion.

"She returned to Madame d'Agoult's apartment early this morning—late last night."

His quick correction did not escape Pierre. "Do you mean to say . . ." It was inconceivable. Yet where else might the countess have stayed the night if she was neither at home nor at Madame d'Agoult's?

"Please do not believe what appears to be an unfortunate circumstance."

"I see no other conclusion possible." Pierre's blood churned.

Georges was by his side in an instant, having hovered just beyond the door of the bedchamber so that he could listen. He took hold of

Pierre's arm. "I am certain that there has been a simple misunderstanding."

"I object most strenuously to this imputation against my honor." Liszt drew himself up to his full height and peered down his aquiline nose at the two students on the other side of the room. "However, it is more important that Monsieur de Barbier receive immediate attention from a doctor. I do not care if it is you or anyone else."

"I am certain my friend is simply overwrought," Georges began, but he was stopped when Pierre gripped his arm. "Ow!"

"Please escort Monsieur Liszt out," Pierre said.

"Are you mad?" Georges whispered to Pierre. "He comes here looking for your help, and you treat him like a criminal!"

"If I am mad," Pierre said, "then . . ." He did not continue, but rudely turned his back on Liszt, who stood in icy shock.

"Come, monsieur," Georges said, taking Liszt's arm and turning him around. "I am at least as qualified as my friend in the practice of medicine. I shall gladly attend upon the gentleman in your apartment."

Pierre heard the door close behind Georges and the pianist. As soon as he knew he was alone, he pounded his fist on the wall and let the bitter tears that had welled up in him wash down his cheeks. Madame d'Agoult was right. Anne had allowed herself to be seduced by Franz Liszt.

But what right had he to judge her, he who had consented to an elopement that was quite possibly against the lady's will? And she was not in the pianist's apartment now. Liszt had said Anne was at the quai Malaquais. Georges would examine Barbier. He, Pierre, must see Anne, talk to her at last of his feelings, discover if there was any hope that he could ever find favor in her eyes—whatever had happened between her and the Hungarian pianist.

Anne tried to rest, but she was far too agitated. She dreaded the moment when she must face her father. She did not know how to tell him that she believed—whether he meant to or not—that his actions, if allowed to continue, might have killed their cousin. She heard the clock chime half past three and was about to freshen up before asking if Marie was free to see her, when Adèle knocked on her door. *Perhaps my things have arrived, and I may change,* Anne thought, and hoped that the marquis had also consented to part with Thérèse. "Come," Anne said, eager for news.

"A messenger from the hôtel Barbier arrived just now with this." Adèle handed Anne a folded note.

Chère Anne,

Please forgive your foolish father for all I have put you through these last weeks. I can only plead grief—which I know you will understand.

So long as Monsieur de Barbier is well, there can be no quarrel between us. Please come back to the hôtel Barbier, and let me try to be a better father to you henceforward—and try to keep you safe from harm. I have instructed Victor to wait for you.

Papa

Anne laid the letter down on the bed and stared at it. Could her father, the same man who barely looked at her when they sat at the dinner table, truly have written such an apologetic note? Or was there some other reason he wanted her to return? She would not tell him where Armand was, if that was what he wanted. Yet how could she remain at Marie's now? He asked so contritely. She had no evidence that he truly meant her harm. "Adèle, please explain to Madame d'Agoult that I have gone to the hôtel Barbier. No, I shall leave her a note."

"Shall I call for the carriage, mademoiselle?"

"There is no need. Victor is waiting for me outside."

Anne scribbled a quick word of explanation, which she propped up on the mantelpiece in the parlor. She would have to see her father eventually. It would be better to get that painful reunion over with right away.

* * *

When she arrived home, Anne expected at least to be greeted by the marquis, but instead Julien intercepted her with the information that he was in his library with a visitor and was not to be disturbed.

No sooner had he uttered the words than her father's raised voice pierced the silence of the mansion. "I tell you, no more! You cannot hurt me, ever again. They are safe, and I shall take steps . . ."

His voice quieted so that Anne could no longer distinguish his words. She ran toward the library, but Julien, in a move that surprised her with its speed, interposed himself between her and the closed door, spreading out his arms to bar her way. Anne knew his loyalty well enough to know that he would never permit her to enter. "The marquis forbids it!" he said, then, in his usual neutral tone, "He requested mademoiselle to retire to your room as soon as you returned."

Anne could not imagine who might be in there, closeted with her father and making him angry. There had been no stranger's chariot in the courtyard. She had hoped that, after all that had passed recently, such mysterious occurrences would end. But Anne was far too tired to think. She decided to go to sleep, and then when she awakened, perhaps she would discover that the last few days had been nothing but a disturbed dream, or that there was some simple explanation for all the mysteries and doubts of the past weeks, and her father would give up his taciturn ways and be a comfort to her at last. At least she need no longer fear for Armand. Without another word, she climbed the stairs. Her nightdress had been laid out for her and a fire lit. There was no sign of Thérèse, but her duties as housekeeper as well as maid often took her to other parts of the house. Anne left her dress in a heap on the floor, pulled her night shift over her head, and climbed into bed.

Exhaustion claimed Pierre soon after Georges and Liszt departed, and he realized that he must have his wits about him when he next spoke to Anne. Despite his agitation, he fell into a deep, dreamless sleep almost as soon as he lay down on top of his coverlet. When he awoke, the sky outside his window was dark. He sat upright so fast he felt dizzy, then bathed and dressed and tried to calm himself sufficiently to be sensible when he confronted Anne. Only after he had completed his preparations did he see the letter, addressed to him, on the table in their small parlor. He did not recognize the handwriting, but when he noticed the official seal at the back, he tore it open. It could only be from Gardive.

I have got my hands on an additional document that I believe you must see. Please attend me at your earliest convenience this morning.

This morning: it was now well into the evening. Pierre snatched his hat and cloak. Without stopping to think, he tucked the marquis's pistol in his belt and ran out of the room, briefly noting that his knife wound did not trouble him nearly so much today. He practically collided with Georges as he dashed down the stairs.

"Where are you going in such a rush?" Georges called. "You won't find him at home!"

Him? Ah, he means Liszt. "I'm off to the Prefecture. I'll explain later."

"Stop a moment!"

The tone of his friend's voice halted Pierre on the stairs. He turned and looked up at Georges, who had planted himself, fists on hips, a few steps above him. "You had it all wrong, you fool."

Despite the urgency of calling on Gardive, Pierre felt compelled to wait and hear what Georges had to say. His friend must have been afraid he would be tempted to challenge the pianist. Georges would not know that his anger had faded, and that all Pierre wanted at that moment was to find out what else Gardive knew and see Anne.

"There is truly nothing amiss. Only Mademoiselle de Barbier-Chouant's desire to help her cousin—who, in the event you wanted to know, is now resting comfortably and will no doubt be well enough to return to his lodgings by morning."

Pierre hung his head, ashamed that he had immediately believed the worst. "I don't know what to say. But I have urgent business and cannot explain anything more to you now." He left without giving Georges a chance to say another word.

*   *   *

Pierre was afraid Gardive might not be available to see him, since he had failed to come in the morning as requested. But the attendant showed him up to the commissioner's office right away.

"I am glad you are here," Gardive greeted him. "I will not waste any time before sharing with you some additional information that I discovered, something I had to request from another office."

He opened a drawer and reached beneath all the papers in it to pull out a document tied together with a faded blue ribbon. Pierre watched, fascinated, as he teased apart the knot with delicate efficiency, taking care not to damage the ribbon, then unfolded the stiff vellum and spread it out over the papers littering his desk. "Come and look," Gardive said. "The marquis is a clever man. No doubt this quality was useful to him in his position at court." He moved over to allow Pierre to read what lay before him. "We have seen Mademoiselle Anne's birth record, her mother's marriage record, and the baptismal certificate. We have drawn certain conclusions from them. But I became intrigued about the sudden appearance of this distant cousin and sought information concerning his relationship to the marquis. Here before you is the wardship agreement. This cousin, as you see, is in fact his nephew, and therefore first cousin to Mademoiselle de Barbier-Chouant."

Pierre leaned closer so that he could read the document. He scanned it several times before raising his eyes.

The marquis de Barbier-Chouant (hereafter referred to as "the guardian") shall have full responsibility for the proper stewardship of the sum of one hundred and fifty thousand francs. This sum and all income accrued shall be remitted to Armand de Barbier (hereafter referred to as "the ward") upon reaching his twenty-first birthday.

Should the ward fail to reach his majority, all income accrued from the proper investment of the capital shall become the sole property of the guardian, and the capital shall be distributed as stipulated in the last will and testament of the ward.

If the ward shall die intestate, then the guardian shall retain all
sums, including capital and accrued income.

"Surely he would not . . . ," Pierre began.

Gardive shrugged. "The marquis disappeared during the Terror
and suddenly reappeared when Louis XVIII ascended the throne.
No one is certain where he went. There were rumors that he was in
exile, but none of the enclaves of nobles and aristocrats who fled the
country at that time had any knowledge of him. The authorities
sought him because he had left many debts behind. But the real question is"—Gardive paused and tapped his index finger against his
nose—"does the young Monsieur de Barbier have a will of his own—
in more sense than one."

"And what is more, the mother's will . . ." Pierre's voice trailed off
as he recalled the words he had read on the document that was now in
Madame d'Agoult's hands.

Should my daughter predecease my husband, the entire amount of
the dowry, with all income accrued, shall pass to the marquis de
Barbier-Chouant.

The commissioner shook his head gravely. "Circumstances could
combine to give the old man every motive indeed to rejoice in the
deaths of both his nephew and his stepdaughter. Perhaps he similarly
rejoiced in the death of his wife."

"I must see Anne immediately. You have been most generous with
your time and efforts. How can I—"

"Say nothing of it. I became fascinated as soon as I discovered the
identity of the young lady. But you—you must take care. With his
cousin removed from his control, the marquis could be desperate
indeed."

Pierre took his leave, assuring Gardive that if he had any cause for
alarm, he would summon the commissioner immediately.

*   *   *

The glow of twilight clung to sky above her, although where Marie stood on the cobblestones was as dark as night. She had left Anne resting at the quai Malaquais, and the servants still tidying up after last night's party. Marie planned to return in time to dine with her protégée and discuss what must be their next course of action. *I have truly taken leave of my senses,* she thought as she stood wrapped in her traveling cloak with her head covered in veils, her hand poised to pull the bell that would alert whoever was in the studio of Eugène Delacroix to her presence on the street below. She prayed that someone would let her in soon, or she would be forced to run home feeling chastened and unwanted. Perhaps Franz had not really meant what he said the night before.

She had tried to keep to her resolve and turn her back on him forever, but the vision of his tormented eyes haunted her all day long. Marie told herself she had only come to make certain he understood that she was serious about what she had said, that they must be strangers to one another again. Already plans were under way to take her and the children to visit her sister-in-law. Charles was on his way back from the north to accompany them.

Marie held her breath at the sound of footsteps clattering down the stairs behind the door. Before she could arrange herself to be greeted, the door was flung open by Franz himself, his hair in disarray and his eyes flashing with barely concealed excitement.

"You are here!" he said, too loudly.

"I wanted to tell you—" Marie could not finish her thought because he had drawn her into the stairwell and caught her up in an embrace that took her breath away. He let go of her only to pull her up the stairs by two hands, stepping backward and tripping, laughing with delight. When they arrived at the top, he kicked the door open, and before she knew it, Marie was enveloped in his arms again, and he kissed her mouth, her eyes, her cheeks right through her veils, then lifted them up over her head and continued kissing her face with his warm, moist lips.

"No . . . you don't . . . understand . . . I . . ." She could barely catch her breath to speak. Before she realized what had happened, he had drawn her into a room where they fell onto a divan, spread invitingly with silk cushions.

I didn't mean to do this, Marie thought.

But that was absurd. If she did not mean this to happen, she should never have come. She was lost. Now, only distance and time could save her.

Twenty-Eight

A noise, loud and sudden, jolted Anne out of her deep sleep. She opened her eyes wide and listened hard, but only silence greeted her at first. After a while, she heard faraway footsteps, perhaps in the servants' wing, perhaps even as far off as the cellars. She did not know how long she had lain there, but it was dark outside, and the candle by her bed had burned down about halfway. She sat up. Thérèse must have come in while she slept and laid a clean evening gown out for her to wear when she awakened. Her brushes and scents were all ranged neatly on her dressing table, and the coverlet had been turned down and folded perfectly at the foot of the bed.

The rest had refreshed her, and Anne rose from her bed, deciding that she should dress and go down to her father. She rang the bell for Thérèse, stepped out of her nightgown, and left it in a white muslin mass on the floor. Since Thérèse would be a few minutes coming, Anne put on a fresh chemise and her corset that hooked at the front, then slipped her gown over her head. It too fastened at the front, but the belt hooked at the back, and so she left it dangling. She sat at the dressing table to see what might be done with her hair while she waited for Thérèse to answer the bell.

Her thoughts turned immediately to Armand. She wondered if Liszt had managed to find Monsieur Talon, and whether her cousin was finally being properly cared for.

Her conscience needled her when she thought about her father. If she had been in his shoes, she would have been distraught to find her ailing relative removed from her care. When she saw him, if he was truly in a mood to forgive and be forgiven, she would explain how she had been mistaken. As soon as Armand was well enough, she would bring him back to the hôtel Barbier.

Thérèse is very long in coming, Anne thought, growing a little cross. She rang the bell again, more loudly this time, and paced around her room. After five more minutes and still no sign of Thérèse, Anne decided to go and look for her. Even if the household was all topsy-turvy, the servants still had their jobs to do. She marched to the door, grasped the handle, and pulled.

It was locked. She tried it again. It would not open. No one had ever locked her in her room before. Why tonight? *I was foolish to believe he had forgiven me,* she thought first. He must intend to punish her. Anne hoped her father would not keep her waiting. She shivered. Surely there was not some more sinister reason that she had been incarcerated like this. *He's afraid I will run away again, perhaps,* she thought. She tried to still the pounding of her heart. Her imagination had run away with her lately, that was all.

The clock on the dressing table chimed eleven. Soon after that, Anne heard sounds outside on the street. The hour was late for anyone to be wandering in that remote corner of Saint Germain. Her windows looked out over the lane behind the hôtel Barbier in one direction, and over the dark alleyway that the servants used in the other. Anne opened the curtains just enough to see what was happening.

The shape was a little indistinct in the dim lamplight, but still it was unmistakable. Anne had to stifle a cry of joy when she saw the familiar form of her mother's grand piano, wrapped in heavy blankets and being hoisted with some difficulty by two burly men through one of the long windows in the ballroom on the floor below.

"Sure we'll get paid for this?" a man's voice said.

"Quiet!" hissed the other. Anne strained to hear his answer and thought she could discern something like "take care of the heirs," or perhaps, "by the heirs," but this made no sense.

He means to open the ballroom! This late-night delivery explained her locked door. The marquis would not want her to come down and see the piano on its way to its resting place, when he believed she assumed it to have remained where it was all along. Perhaps, Anne thought, it had only been away for repairs. Her mother had always complained that the dampers needed to be replaced. She wanted to cry with relief.

Anne sat at her dressing table again and smoothed her hair into a knot at the top of her head. She did not need Thérèse to make her presentable. Once the subdued commotion outside ceased, she would ring the bell again. In all the excitement, doubtless no one had heard her the first time.

At one point, there was a terrible sound as of wood splintering. Anne hoped it was the window, not the piano. But after about a quarter of an hour, all grew quiet. She rang the bell, continuing to ring it for a good while to make sure that someone would hear her.

This time, her ringing brought footsteps to her door. It wasn't Thérèse. It sounded more like Julien. The metallic chink of a key in a lock reassured her that she would soon be free of her temporary constraint, and she stood.

"The marquis would like you to attend him in the ballroom," the valet said. He did not seem particularly cheerful, Anne thought. But Julien always was a dour sort.

Anne hurried happily down the stairs, reaching the ballroom door before Julien could open it for her. She turned the knob with pleasure, noting briefly the damage from the makeshift padlock, and stepped into the room she most associated with her mother, and from which she had been barred almost since the hour of the marquise's death.

Every chandelier and sconce had been lit. Anne shielded her dazzled eyes as she looked for her father. He stood by the piano. Its lid was open, and a chair placed invitingly in front of the keyboard.

"You have rested, child," the marquis said. He still wore the evening clothes he had on the last time she had seen him, but his normally closed and hard expression had subtly changed. There was something tentative about his eyes, even fearful. Anne found this change a little disturbing. "I . . . I must speak with you," he continued. "There are certain facts you should know. But we have a little time. First, I wonder if you would consent to do something for me." He was also pale beneath his powder, and his hand trembled when he lifted it to rub his forehead.

Anne was not accustomed to being asked anything by her father, only to being commanded. She hardly knew what to say. "You know I shall do whatever you wish, Papa."

"Yet you have not obeyed all my requests recently. Perhaps with good reason." He fixed her with a gaze full of emotion. "Yes, you are a good girl. You did not deserve . . . I heard last night how beautifully you play, although you were . . . mischievous not to tell me the name of your teacher."

Anne blushed. She did not want to be reminded, now, of last evening's events. "I wanted you to be proud."

Just before the silence between them became awkward, the marquis cleared his throat. "Will you—could you—play for me now? As your mother used to play?" He gestured for Anne to take her seat at the piano.

His pleading eyes pained her. Could it truly be that he wanted to hear her, now? He, who had always treated her as a shadow of her mother, only worth noticing to oblige his wife. This command performance, Anne thought, was her chance to be the daughter she had always wanted to be, for him. Or at least, to show him the possibility of it. She curtseyed her acquiescence, then slowly, letting her eyes linger over the beautiful, polished wood of the Pleyel's case, walked around the piano, passing close enough by the marquis to smell the camphor in the sachet that hung around his neck, and sat down in front of the keyboard. Before making a sound, she caressed the keys, closing her eyes and enjoying the feeling of the smooth ivory and slightly rougher ebony in their distinctive pattern. With her eyes still closed, she began to play. Not the Chopin study that she had performed the night before, but a sonatina by Clementi that she had learned from her mother and that her father used to ask the marquise to play.

Anne lost all sense of where she was, not even caring that the Pleyel was a little out of tune. She finished the sonatina and immediately played a rondo by Mozart, and after that some variations. Finally, Anne thought, this dark, nightmarish time is coming to an end. All will be well.

Pierre ran to the nearest fiacre stand and hired a carriage to take him to the quai Malaquais. He knew it was late to go calling, but his anxiety was too great not to be sure that Anne was safe at the apartment of Madame d'Agoult.

He found Marie dressed for visiting, writing at her desk in the parlor. Her cloak and hat lay across the divan and her cheeks were flushed. She must recently have returned from somewhere.

"Forgive me for intruding at this hour," Pierre said, nervously passing his hat from one hand to the other, "but I wanted to be certain that Mademoiselle Anne is safe."

"Ah yes," Marie said. "She came back to me. A wise decision. I am sorry things did not turn out as we had planned last night. Perhaps it is all for the best. It seems she had a plan of her own." She stood and offered him a glass of brandy. Pierre declined, and she poured one for herself. Pierre noted that her hands trembled slightly.

"I did not come to talk of that. Might I have a word with Mademoiselle Anne now?"

"Monsieur Talon, it is hardly the hour to visit young ladies!" She smiled. "But in the circumstances, I shall see if she will come."

Marie rang the bell, and a moment later the maid appeared. "Adèle, please ask the countess to attend me in the parlor."

"She is not here, madame," the maid said. "Did you not see her message?"

Adèle walked to the mantelpiece and took a small, folded piece of paper, which must have been propped up originally but had slid down so that it lay flat on the marble surface, and gave it to Marie. The countess opened it, read it quickly, then handed it to Pierre. "It appears that she has gone back to the hôtel Barbier," Marie said. "This is most unexpected."

Pierre froze. He felt as though even his words were weighted with lead, as in a horrible dream where he wished to move quickly to escape some threat but his legs would not consent to be lifted off the ground no matter how furiously he pumped his arms. "Madame," he said, "do you have a piece of paper and a pen?"

In Pierre's state of distress, it seemed that it took her an hour to find a blank sheet, and the inkwell was dry and he had to wait for her to fill it again. When she held out the quill to him, he practically snatched it from her and tore the paper in several places in his hurry to scribble a few words. "Please send someone with this to the Prefecture immediately, and ask for Monsieur Gardive."

Pierre did not stop to say good-bye to Marie but ran from the apartment as soon as she had taken the letter from his hands. He jumped into the waiting carriage. His words tripped over each other while he tried to instruct the driver where to go. Finally he was able to sputter out, "Rue du Barq, and hurry!"

Pierre found himself rocking back and forth in his seat as though his actions could make the horses go faster. When they finally arrived near the mansion, he was as winded as he would have been if he had crawled every inch of the way. Impatient to be under the locomotion of his own legs, he bade the driver stop a little way down the road. It would be safer to approach on foot, he thought. Before leaving the carriage, Pierre picked up the marquis's pistol, which he had placed on the seat next to him so that he could sit more comfortably. He took the small ramrod clipped to the underside of the pistol barrel and gently tapped inside the muzzle to see if the gun was loaded. To his surprise, it was. He put the hammer to half-cocked position and tucked the pistol into the waistband of his trousers, wincing when it knocked against the bruise it had made last night. Funny, he had hardly noticed the knife wound on his other side. Perhaps some pain, even the pain of surgery, might be overcome by simple distraction, he thought.

Making as little noise as possible, he climbed down from the carriage, instructing the fellow to wait for him no matter how long. He said a silent prayer that his note would find Gardive, and help would soon arrive.

As he suspected, the gates were locked shut. Without hesitation, Pierre went to the alleyway on the side next to the servants' quarters where he and Petit had found the wooden shutters that covered an unglazed window. The alley was no less dark, damp, and inhospitable than it had been before, but Pierre was not worried about what would happen if he were caught. His only concern was to enter the hôtel Barbier quietly enough that he would not be discovered before he could find Anne and take her away.

This time he did not have the benefit of the dwarf's little knife to release the latch of the shutters, but there was enough of a gap between them that the ramrod of the pistol fit through, and he accomplished his task. The pantry was dark, as was the corridor outside. As he made his way toward the main house, though, Pierre could see light ahead of him filtering around the edges of the door that led from the servants' wing into the dining room.

Taking care to make as little noise as possible, he eased the pistol out of his waistband and cocked it. Then, slowly, he approached the door, listening for any sign of life beyond it.

All was quiet. Or nearly, anyway. The large table and the threadbare tapestry were as they had been that other night, but rather than the deathly silence of a house wrapped in sleep, Pierre could swear that he heard the faintest sound of a pianoforte. He shook his head. Surely he must be imagining things. He was still overwrought since last night, when Anne's playing had made such an impression upon him. He opened the door of the dining room that led into the entrance hall. It blazed with light from candles everywhere, but there was no one.

Now, however, Pierre definitely heard music. It came from the room opposite the library, which had been padlocked shut the last time he had seen it. Although he had only heard her once, he recognized Anne's sensitive touch. She had reached the finale of a set of variations and, after hardly a break, commenced another piece.

In that brief pause in the music, Pierre heard another faint sound, coming from somewhere nearby. He cupped his ear away from the ballroom and listened. He heard the sound again, from the direction of the stairwell. Moving as noiselessly as possible, he crept around to the side of the curving staircase. The sound issued from behind a panel beneath the stairs. He put his ear right up to the wood. Someone—or something—was in there, no mistaking it. He examined the panel and found a finger-hold only large enough to admit his smallest digit, which he hooked through and used as a probe. The ingenious catch took some working to free, but when he did it, the panel sprang open.

Pierre was greeted by the sight of a Jesuit priest who looked to be of middle age curled up on the floor, his hands and feet bound and his mouth gagged. He nearly exclaimed aloud but for the frightened expression in the fellow's eyes warning him to silence. Instead he lay down his pistol and set to work freeing the priest from his bonds.

"What the . . ."

Once he had use of his hands, the priest put his finger to his lips and gestured toward the ballroom door. Pierre stood, reaching on his way for the pistol he had placed temporarily on the floor. But the priest grabbed it first and tucked it in the back of the rope belt tied around the waist of his cassock, with a stern look at Pierre that suggested he did not approve of violence. They both moved toward the ballroom.

The music stopped as they reached the closed door. Pierre pressed his ear to it.

"Brava, daughter, brava!" the marquis's voice said, sounding nervously jovial. "I think we should celebrate the rebirth of music in this sad house."

Someone in the room rang a bell. Pierre and the priest quickly hid themselves in the curve of the stairs. From the direction of the library they heard the sound of a wheeled cart and a tinkling as of glasses bumping into one another. Soon the cart came into view, pushed by the old footman. It bore a bottle of red wine with two crystal glasses. Julien stopped at the door of the ballroom, scratched on it, and within moments the marquis came to the door but did not let the servant push the cart inside.

"Thank you, Julien," he said, and the footman bowed and walked away.

The two men watched as the marquis poured wine into the glasses, reached into his pocket, and removed a small vial filled with something white. He studied the vial for a moment, then a look of intense pain passed across his face and drained the color out of it. He closed his eyes and breathed deeply, leaning on the cart for support. After a moment he appeared to recover from his spell and put the vial back into his pocket before picking up the glasses and returning to the room, saying, "A toast! To your remarkable talent. You surpass even your late mother. And now, I think it is time for you to know something important, my dear, that I ought to have told you long ago."

All at once Pierre knew he must act. He ran from his hiding place, closely followed by the priest, and burst into the room.

Anne and her father each held a full glass of wine. "Don't believe him, Anne!" Pierre shrieked.

The marquis's look of shock was followed by one of abject fear. He spoke quietly and with forced calmness. "Anne, you must do as I say. Step behind me."

Her eyes jumped back and forth between the marquis and the two other men.

"He means to poison you," Pierre said, "just as he did your cousin."

Anne gasped. "Father?" She began to shake. The glass fell from her fingers and shattered on the parquet floor, red wine flowing like blood toward her feet.

"Anne!" the marquis cried.

She backed away from him.

"That's right, Marquis. You wanted them dead, so you could have all the money to yourself," the priest said, having moved forward and, to Pierre's horror, taken the pistol from his belt. He now leveled it at the marquis, cocked and ready to fire.

"How can you believe I would do such a thing?" the marquis said, his eyes pleading with Anne, although he made no effort to approach her. His face paled. "Don't believe that man. He is not what he seems. He is . . . he is . . ." The old man grimaced. Pierre could not tell whether he was in pain, or whether the words were so distasteful to him that he could not utter them.

"Why not tell them?" the priest said.

"I thought you had died!" the marquis sobbed. "That does not give you the right to blackmail me for their inheritance."

Pierre held his breath. Anne too stood immobile as a porcelain vase, her eyes brimming with tears.

"Julien! Victor!" called the marquis in a hoarse voice, now looking as though he might at any moment collapse.

The two servants must have been waiting outside the door, because they entered as soon as their names were called. The priest stepped back so that they could see the pistol. "Stand aside," he said.

"Bon Père," Pierre said, "what are you doing?" He made a move toward the priest, whose dark eyes shot sparks of anger at everyone around him, but when the Jesuit brought the firearm around to point at him, Pierre backed away again.

"Ask him," the priest growled. "Ask my brother."

A strangled cry erupted from the marquis's throat. At the same moment, Anne yelled out, "Papa!"

"Yes." The marquis shrank into himself. "Although only half a brother—a shameful alliance." He passed his hand over his forehead. "In the Terror, he disappeared. Armand was . . . the son of our other brother, the one who prospered. He made me Armand's ward before his death."

"More lies! You cut me out. You were greedy."

"Not greedy," the marquis said, softening his tone and reaching one bony hand out to Anne, "only blind. Did my best with the money.

Your mother had enough. But soon—after we married, there were demands. I didn't know who, then. I paid to keep him quiet." The old man did not take his eyes off Anne.

"Quiet about what, Papa?"

"About . . . about . . ." The marquis could not speak, although Pierre guessed what he might say.

"I knew that my half brother had a child, but that child was not you. That child has been living among the Jesuit brotherhood these seventeen years. The young Armand, my dear, is a bastard." He smiled as he uttered the words.

Pierre had hoped to be able to spare Anne the hurtful knowledge of her past, but the priest's revelation stopped him dead. Here was something new, another secret, one that he and Gardive had not managed to unearth. He watched understanding dawn in Anne's eyes too. She opened her mouth to speak but said nothing.

"Lies and lies and lies." The marquis shuddered, then held his glass of wine up to the small crowd of stunned spectators that included the priest, who could at any moment have squeezed the trigger of the pistol and sent a bullet into his heart. "A toast. To the truth."

At that moment, from the courtyard Pierre heard the smashing of iron, followed by footsteps running across to the door. "*Au nom de la loi*, open!" Many fists pounded on the old oak door. Julien crept out unnoticed by the priest, who gripped the firearm so hard that his knuckles were white. Pierre was poised to leap at him if he saw the slightest twitch near the trigger.

The marquis lifted his glass to his lips. "Forgive me, Anne. Know that I loved your mother."

Before he could take a sip of the wine, another spell, like the one Pierre had witnessed outside the ballroom, stopped him. This time an even more startling change came over his features. The color drained from his face, and he doubled over as if he had been shot in the stomach, although Jaquin had not fired the pistol. His glass slipped through his fingers, and its ruby contents and shattered slivers intermingled with those of the glass Anne had dropped there moments before. The old man fell to his side, writhing in agony, and then, to Pierre's horror, began to vomit so violently that his face turned blue from lack of air.

"What is it? What's happening?" Anne ran to Pierre, her mouth covered. "Do something! He is ill."

"Anne, don't go near," Pierre said, when he saw that she was about to leave his side and rush to her father, who now lay senseless in a pool of his own vomit. Pierre took hold of her arm, but she shook herself free and ran to the marquis anyway.

"You, fetch some sheets," Pierre ordered Victor, who was too shocked to do anything but obey. Jaquin lowered the pistol and backed toward the ballroom door

"Papa, what is it?" Anne whispered.

"Cholera," Pierre said, one eye on Jaquin, who was about to disappear out the door, the pistol still menacingly cocked.

"I suggest you remain where you are."

Pierre said a silent Ave Maria at the sound of Gardive's smooth, clipped voice and the sight of his impassive face peering over the priest's shoulder. Behind the commissioner stood a cluster of armed police officers, all blocking the way.

"I—I was simply going to retrieve medical help for my—for the marquis," the priest said.

"With a weapon in your hand? And when there is a doctor here already?" Gardive nodded at a tall officer, who took hold of Jaquin and removed the firearm from his grasp.

"How dare you! I shall inform the college. You have no right!" The priest's protestations faded as he was led away.

Gardive walked slowly to Pierre and looked down at the marquis. The old man moaned quietly. Having worked so many nights on the wards at the Hôtel-Dieu, Pierre could discern the futile plea for water in the all-but-unintelligible sound.

"I'm sorry, Countess," Pierre said. She was as white as a holy wafer.

Anne knelt down by her father. "Oh, Papa." Her voice was dry and distant.

"In my pocket. The poison," the marquis whispered.

"It doesn't matter." Anne shushed him and stroked the gray, straggly hair that had been exposed when his wig tumbled off in his fall. "I know it must have been difficult." Her tears fell onto the marquis's cheeks and traced dark lines in the caked powder that covered them.

With great effort the old man lifted his head. "I didn't. Never. It was," he gasped, "it was to be . . . for me."

"Let me in! My poor Mademoiselle Anne!" Thérèse shoved her way through the men standing around the door. Anne ran to her and burst into tears in her arms.

"She was locked in the cellar," said a guard, who entered immediately after Thérèse.

"That priest fellow! Barged in all threats. Before I could call for help, he threw me down the stairs." The housekeeper kept up her nervous tirade as she led Anne out of the room.

Gardive looked at Pierre and jerked his head toward the door. Pierre wanted to run after Anne, to apologize for his terrible mistake, for thinking that the man she knew as her father could have intended to poison her, but he could not refuse to follow Gardive out to the courtyard.

Outside, the fresh breeze dried the beads of perspiration that had gathered on his forehead. "You received my note, I see."

"Yes, but the marquis had already done his work quite well. It seems he spent his last sous to hire agents, who discovered the identity of his blackmailer, the priest, Jaquin, and had taken their report to Gisquet himself."

Pierre had so many questions he did not know where to begin. What brought Jaquin to the hôtel Barbier that evening? Was it the timid Victor, the only one in the household who was strong enough, who had managed to overcome him and secure him in the cupboard beneath the stairs? And who was the marquis's true child? But there was nothing more he could do that night, and his head ached. "Tomorrow," he said.

Gardive bowed. "I'll expect you at noon."

Epilogue

This time, a bright blue sky arched overhead as Anne rode in the carriage behind the hearse, which, instead of her mother's, bore the marquis's body to Père Lachaise. It had been a mere two months since that other death, and yet she felt years older. She had acquired a relative she never knew existed, only to find that they shared not a drop of the same blood. She had thought she discovered what love was only to learn that she had been completely deceived. She had gone from being a sheltered, isolated young lady to being so completely alone in the world that her future was a void, at once thrilling and terrifying. Altogether, she had seen more of the mysteries of life and death than she ever wished to again.

The marquis lingered only twenty-four hours before succumbing to the disease that had taken his wife and spared him the trouble of poisoning himself. Anne had committed to memory the letter Thérèse found when she cleared off the marquis's desk, a letter that explained at least some of the strange goings-on she had witnessed not just since the death of her mother but for several years before that time.

My dear Anne,

If you are reading this letter, then, one way or another, I have achieved my aim of relieving you of the burden of my continued presence on this earth and given you the right to command your own for-

tune, and you undoubtedly know that you are not my daughter. I loved your mother dearly, but I knew that she did not return my feelings. It was enough for me to bask in her reflected light. That is why I stopped myself from becoming too attached to you, who were a belle enfante *when your mother and I married. I always feared that both of you would vanish like the morning mist.*

Yet I possessed a secret as shameful as hers and hid it away as best I could. Armand de Barbier is my heir, my son. My brother married the woman I loved when I was a young man, and in a moment of unguarded passion, I took my revenge upon him by seducing her. Neither your mother nor my brother ever knew of this. But my half brother, the man who styles himself Père Jaquin, who was the result of a liaison between my father and a dancer at the opera, came into possession of certain letters that could have destroyed me. It was he whose demands drained me of money and made me fear for your—and Armand's—safety.

I did not expect Sandrine to die before I did. I had hoped to leave her in possession of the greater part of her fortune when I passed on. That is why, rather than try to gain access to her dowry, I sold my own most valuable possessions.

I beg your forgiveness for trying to make you marry someone the world would assume—if they ever came to know his history and not yours—was your half brother. It was wrong of me. I can excuse it only by saying that I was desperate to find some way to protect you both. I thought that by marrying you to each other, I could put your fortunes beyond Jaquin's reach and therefore make them secure.

God grant that you have not suffered too greatly in your young life. Your gift for music has given me joy, though you did not know it, and even though I cannot claim to have had any influence over it.

I beg you not to judge me too harshly. I grasped what happiness was within my reach. I only wish you more of it than it was my lot to enjoy.

Dieu te protège,
Papa

Armand sat by Anne's side in the carriage. He still felt weak, but he had improved in just a day under the care of Pierre Talon and his friend Georges. It pained him now to think that he had been so deeply mistaken about Père Jaquin, who had turned out to be his estranged uncle. When the commissioner spoke to him about the priest, and Armand confessed that the man he thought of as his friend had more than once tried to convince him to sign his name to a piece of paper that would give his fortune to the Jesuit college under the stewardship of Jaquin himself, they had more than enough evidence to convict the priest of extortion and blackmail.

He had been too ill ever to have a chance to know the man he discovered was in fact his father, the marquis. But now he had the opportunity to know his half sister better, even if he wished they weren't quite so closely related. The old man had acted wrongly in hiding the truth from the family in hopes of bringing about a union with Anne. Armand found it difficult to forgive him for this, but Anne had asked him to set aside his anger. She refused to tell him why, however.

A sigh escaped him involuntarily, and Anne gave his hand a gentle squeeze. Much as he wanted to, Armand still hardly had the energy to return the pressure, and he simply closed his eyes.

Unlike the day they buried her mother, at the height of the epidemic, that morning of the marquis's funeral they were among only a handful of cortèges to climb the long hill to the east of Paris where the wealthy laid their dead to rest.

Monsieur Gardive, the commissioner of records, had told her there was no need to make public the fact that the marquis was not her father. The money, in any case, had been her mother's. And there was enough of it to pay all her stepfather's debts so that Anne could start afresh.

"What will you do now, Anne?" Armand asked.

"I shan't remain at the hôtel Barbier. I intend to sell it as soon as it can be managed." There had been too much sorrow in that old house. Besides, it was in such a bad state of repair that not even her entire fortune would have been sufficient to fix it and maintain it.

Anne marveled that she had not noticed before. She had been blind to so many things. "When I find an apartment, you must visit," Anne said. "I shall have parties and introduce you to society—with Madame d'Agoult's help, of course."

The only items Anne intended to take from her home were the Pleyel and the box of jewelry where she found the letters her real father had written to the marquise after she was married. Everything else she loved was gone already.

Despite their somber destination, Anne had a frisson of pleasure at the thought of what Madame d'Agoult had written to her the day after the marquis's death, about her real father. He had been a great musician, a pianist. Everything made sense. It was at that moment that Anne first had an idea about what she might do in the future. She knew she would have to be brave, but it was her destiny, and it had claimed her even before she was aware of it. She would devote herself to her piano studies and prepare to give a concert. She intended to have students of her own, as well. But the mentor who would shepherd her to the achievement of her dream would not be Monsieur Liszt. Marie had arranged for her to become a student of Chopin's.

Anne felt like such a fool for the confusion over the notes. She and Marie never spoke of it, but Anne was certain the countess knew everything. And as to Liszt himself—she blushed just thinking about him.

"Whoa there!" called Victor's familiar voice. They had arrived at the Barbier vault.

Marie and her husband, Charles, were in the carriage behind Anne and Armand. Charles had a gentle, sympathetic face, but Marie appeared not to like him very much. The four of them plus Thérèse, Victor, and Julien made a small, somber group at the graveside. She was strangely comforted to be there again, in the presence of her mother's spirit.

The priest spoke the same words over the marquis's coffin as he had over Anne's mother's. She watched the oblong wooden box disappear behind the small doors. Despite everything, Anne thought it right that they should lie together in the vault.

Anne looked around one last time before climbing back into the brougham, her gaze straying to the spot where she had first seen Marie's veiled figure a little more than two months ago. She expected the place to be vacant, but to her suprise a gentleman stood there, his hands folded in front of him, his head bowed. When he lifted his hand in greeting, Anne recognized Pierre Talon. He had left the night before last as soon as it was apparent there was nothing to be done for the marquis. After that, everything had happened so quickly, and she was so taken up with matters of life and death, that she had not had time to seek him out and express her gratitude for the concern that had made him take such a risk—even though he had wrongly assumed Anne faced danger from the marquis. "I'll only be a moment," she said to Armand, and walked over to the young medical student.

As she approached, his gaze traveled over her face. She blushed to be so intently scrutinized.

"Monsieur, it was kind of you to come." Anne met his eyes. They were a strange color between blue and green. She judged him to be about twenty-five and noticed that he was strong and straight. *Why did I never see these things before?* Anne thought.

"I felt I owed it to your . . . father, Countess, after being so badly mistaken."

"You couldn't have known." Anne wondered exactly how much Monsieur Talon did know. If he knew that she was an illegitimate child, it was clear from his expression that this fact did not diminish his regard for her. Anne had a pleasant sensation below her ribs. This fellow, this almost-doctor, was in love with her. What was more, she found that she herself could not look at him entirely with indifference. The feeling was not exactly like that desperate infatuation she had felt for Liszt, nor was it quite the same as the fond affection her cousin inspired in her. She blushed and lowered her eyes to the ground. "I shall move to an apartment with Thérèse," she said. "Might I have your address, so that I may invite you to call once I am in my new home?"

Pierre took a small pasteboard card out of his waistcoat pocket and gave it to Anne. "I was going to leave it for you anyway."

Before she could tuck the card in her black reticule, Pierre grasped Anne's hand and brought it to his lips.

"Au revoir," Anne said. She traced an arabesque on the cobblestone with her toe. Pierre kept holding her hand, as if he had something more to say. She was half-afraid he would declare himself right there, by her mother's grave. She hoped he would not. She was not ready for that, yet.

Instead, he said, "When I come, will you play the piano for me?"

She looked into his eyes, which were now lit by a glint of mischief. "Of course!" Anne said, and smiled with relief.

So this is how it starts, she thought.

Acknowledgments

I have so many people to thank for help with the research and writing of this novel that it's hard to know where to start.

First, my gratitude to Robert Bissell, Rita Bleiman, Joan Cenedella, Fran Corriveau, Bill Newman, and Victoria Zackheim—wonderful writers and thoughtful readers who read entire drafts and gave me valuable feedback.

Thanks to Kathy Fable for furnishing me with the means to keep body and soul together during this labor of love, and reminding me that there is a world outside of fiction.

I would also like to thank Tibor Szabo of Music Szalon Pianos for his help with some of the technical aspects of the early Erard.

And special thanks to Peter Bloom, a longtime friend, mentor, and one of the world's foremost experts on Hector Berlioz, who kindly shared his knowledge.

Once again, my editor, Amanda Patten, steered me gently toward making this book the best it could be, copy editor Peg Haller put the green pencil to expert use, and my agent, Adam Chromy, cracked the whip and helped me knock the first draft into shape. I owe a debt of gratitude also to the production team of Simon & Schuster for all they have done to polish the look of this book.

Finally, Charles—my loving thanks for sitting patiently while I read more than one draft out loud to you. You're the best.

Historical Note

The romance between Franz Liszt and Marie d'Agoult was one of the most celebrated of the early Romantic era. Their documented first encounter occurred in December of 1832 (not April), at a salon given by the marquise La Vayer. As reported by Marie in her memoir, that was the occasion of the famous incident with the missing parts of the Weber quartet.

Marie left her husband, Charles d'Agoult, to live openly with Liszt and was denied access to her daughters Louise and Claire because of it. Louise died at the age of six in 1834. Marie bore three children to Franz Liszt (one of whom, Cosima, is famous for later marrying Richard Wagner). Liszt, who frequently left Marie to go on extended concert tours, was the subject of much gossip and was rumored to be a philanderer. Their relationship ended finally in 1844 when the popular press claimed to have discovered a liaison between Liszt and the dancer Lola Montez. Marie went on to become a highly respected journalist in her own right, writing under the pen name of Daniel Stern. She is credited with introducing the French reading public to Ralph Waldo Emerson, Georg Herwegh, and Bettina von Arnim, and her only novel, *Nelida*, published in 1846, was a thinly veiled account of her affair with Liszt. Most of Marie's journalism consisted of political commentary, however, and despite her conservative, royalist youth, she ended up associated with the foremost liberal thinkers of her day, including Hippolyte Carnot, Jules Simon, and Alexis de Tocqueville.

Notwithstanding her considerable personal accomplishments, Marie is chiefly remembered today because of her association with Franz Liszt. She died in 1876 at the age of seventy-one.

After his affair with Marie ended, Franz Liszt left Paris for Weimar, where he formed a long attachment with Carolyne von Sayn-Wittgenstein. They did not have children, but she is often credited with being the true author of many of the writings that were attributed to Liszt himself during his lifetime.

Liszt traveled extensively. In Rome in 1865, he entered the minor orders (doorkeeper, lector, acolyte, and exorcist) and was known as the abbé Liszt from that point on, although he never became a priest.

As a musician, Liszt was very generous with his colleagues and with younger artists. He created piano transcriptions of the Beethoven symphonies so that they could be more widely known, as well as of many Schubert songs. His transcription of Berlioz's *Symphonie fantastique* was for many years the only way the public could hear Berlioz's extraordinary work.

Liszt's generosity of spirit extended to his teaching, and in later years he never charged for lessons. He also accepted all comers, provided they were serious, and taught both amateurs and aspiring professionals. He is credited with inventing the term "master class," which subsequently became the predominant way of teaching solo musicians. Although he never developed a formal method, he taught for his entire life, even up until the last week of his life. Liszt died in Bayreuth in 1886 at the age of seventy-five.

Suggested Reading

Marie d'Agoult, *Nelida*, trans. Lynn Hoggard (New York: SUNY Press, 2003).

Richard Bolster, *Marie d'Agoult: The Rebel Countess* (New Haven, CT: Yale University Press, 2000).

Catherine J. Kudlick, *Cholera in Post-Revolutionary Paris* (University of California Press: Berkeley, 1996).

Memoirs of the Comtesse de Boigne, trans. Anka Muhlstein (New York: Helen Marx Books, 2003).

Michelle Perrot, *A History of Private Life*, trans. Arthur Goldhammer (Cambridge, MA: Harvard University Press, Cambridge, 1990).

Edwin Gile Rich, Vidocq: *The Personal Memoirs of the First Great Detective* (Boston: Houghton Mifflin, 1935).

Phyllis Stock-Morton, *The Life of Marie d'Agoult, alias Daniel Stern* (Baltimore, MD: Johns Hopkins University Press, 2000).

Alan Walker, *Franz Liszt: The Virtuoso Years* (Ithaca, NY: Cornell University Press, 1983).

Liszt's Kiss

1. At the beginning of the novel, Anne is not allowed to go out into society. She is living in a "comfortable prison" (pg. 1) . . . hardly questioning the "narrowness of her confines." (pg. 2) At the same time she is being encouraged by her mother to become an accomplished pianist. Do you think one can become a great artist without knowledge and acquaintance with outside society? Why, or why not? Do you think Anne's experiences in the novel lead her to become a better artist? Does society dilute or enrich her talent, and if so, how? What does Anne gain through her dealings with society, and what does she lose?

2. Music, in general, plays a large part in the novel and in the lives of the characters. What does music mean to Liszt? How is it a means to an end, an art form, a way to express himself and seduce? Why is music so important to Anne? What role does it play in her life? What does music mean to Marie, to Pierre, to Anne's father? How does music bring the characters together in the novel? How does it tear them apart?

3. Intrigue, hidden and ulterior motives, and deceit are part of the world of 1832 Paris. Do you think intrigue is particular to the upper class in the novel? If so, why might that be? Why do the characters choose not to be honest with one another? What do the various characters have to lose by being honest?

4. The novel is set against the backdrop of the cholera epidemic. What does this bring to the story? If one took out the cholera epidemic, how would the story change? In addition, the disease could be viewed as a metaphor in the novel. For what is this a metaphor?

5. Love and money are bound together in the world of the novel. Find examples of this in the lives of the characters. What role does money play in the life of Anne, in the life of her mother? Is love or money more important to the characters? Explain.

6. Liszt tells Delacroix that in Hungary, "They feed us nectar, and teach us to love, above all else. It is the very soul of art." (pg. 15) If this is so for Liszt, how does he manifest this sentiment in the story? What insight does this quote give us into Liszt's dealings with women? What do you think is the relationship between love and music for Liszt? Does this excuse him from the trouble he brings to the other characters whom he involves in dangerous entanglements? Why or why not?

7. Women were known to faint upon hearing Liszt perform. Anne, herself, swoons and faints when she hears him play. Why do you think this happens? To what are the women reacting? Why do you think so many women found Liszt attractive, writing him with "declarations of undying love . . . and invitations to amorous assignations"? (pg.16) Are Anne and Marie attracted to him for the same reasons?

8. Liszt has every opportunity to become involved with Anne, however, it is Marie whom he desires. Why do you think he is more interested in Marie than Anne? What attracts him to Marie?

9. Love and death are major themes in *Liszt's Kiss*. Discuss the relationship between love and death in the novel. How are they similar, different? What is the author trying to say about their relationship?

10. Anne's father does not want her associating with artists and musicians even though it seems that the best in society frequents the salons. Why do you think he wants to keep his daughter away from this circle? Why does he allow her to perform at Marie's salon?

11. Marie d'Agoult takes Anne under her wing. Do you think she helps Anne or hurts her and how? Do you empathize with Marie? Why or why not? Who is the hero in the novel and why? Who is the antagonist and why?

Q&A with Susanne Dunlap

1. *In your historical note at the end of the novel you write that Marie d'Agoult was a true person and had a romantic relationship with Liszt. Is the character of Anne based on any known person or is she a purely fictional character?*

Anne is a purely fictional character. Rather than try to center a story on someone who is very well documented historically, I have taken the approach here of exploring the people history has not recorded, those who might (or might not) have come into contact with famous figures or interacted and been influenced by important events. Anne is the hypothetical "what if" character who inspired the book, in fact. What if a young woman with true talent came across Liszt at a time of his life when he had not yet entirely assumed his mature artistic personality and before he was deeply involved with Marie d'Agoult? What if a young woman of aristocratic birth were a true artist and capable of taking her place among the professionals of her day? What if a woman on the brink of life were touched by tragedy because of a force of nature—in this case the cholera epidemic of 1832?

What I write is not fictionalized history in the manner of Anya Seton or Philippa Gregory (both of whom I love to read), but fiction that builds on actual historical characters and events, introducing nonhistorical characters to round out my imagined world, more in the manner of Sarah Dunant.

2. *Which characters in the novel do you relate to the most and why?*

I relate strongly to Anne, not because I shared her privileged and sheltered upbringing, but because I myself was a pianist, and music and playing the piano were always my refuge and escape when I was younger. But I also empathize with Marie, a woman of learning and spirit who made the wrong choices when she was young, yet who eventually found true love.

3. *This is your second novel in which you bring together music and history. What attracts you to this world? What about music is important to you?*

Making music, making instruments that make music, is a defining human characteristic. Music, whether most people realize it or not, is intertwined with everything that has resulted in the many big, historical events of our modern past, perhaps even longer ago than that. Music has been used for political purposes. Music has been used for religious purposes. Music touches the soul in a way that no other art form does, even literature. In essence it is wordless and imageless, although combining it with words provides an additional layer of meaning and experience. The challenge to me as a writer is to convey the importance of music and its changing aesthetic in a way that somehow communicates not only its place in history, but its emotional and psychic effects on auditors and practitioners.

Besides, I could read music before I could read words, and music still has as much power over me as words, perhaps more in some ways.

4. *How do you decide what you are going to write about? Do the characters find you and then you do your research, or do you research to find your story?*

So far, my ideas have arisen from the research I have done as a musicologist in past years. I find I am obsessed with fitting music into a bigger picture of a society, a culture, even a political milieu. I usually start with a vague idea or principle and do some additional reading. When a story emerges, I start to write. Sometimes the emergence can be gradual, sometimes it just pops into my head. The story evolves through the writing process, and I continue to research as I find the gaps in my knowledge. Once I have identified my story and it starts to take shape, I like to visit the setting, if I can and if I have never been there (or even if I have). The physical characteristics of a place add a lot to my own understanding of it and are very important in creating a believable historical novel.

5. *What do you enjoy most about writing novels?*

Where could I start! Writing novels gives me so much joy and so much pain. I love the challenge of making a story work, of pulling together the pieces of the plot and molding the characters. Usually it's not putting down the first draft that I like best, because that can be excruciating, but taking that initial outpouring and working with it, nurturing it into something that comes close to saying what I hoped to say.

6. *Why did you decide to revolve the story around Anne and not concentrate exclusively on the relationship between Marie and Liszt?*

I didn't want to write a fictionalized treatment of one of the most famous love affairs of the Romantic era, although that would make a wonderful novel. I was more interested in the effect they and their world might have had on a nobody, on an innocent but wounded young woman. I hoped to create a character who could react and respond in a human way to everything around her without being bound by the weight of scholarship that surrounds Franz Liszt and Marie d'Agoult. That scholarship is exceedingly useful and meant that there were many sources on the period available to me. But there is something intoxicating about being able to invent not only a story, but a human being; about making someone literally come to life from nothing on a page.

7. *What would you like the readers to come away from having read Liszt's Kiss? What about the story is most important to you?*

For me, the most important aspect of the story is the power of music to heal and lead one to a greater understanding of oneself. Anne's journey from bereft mourner to self-assured artist is, to me, the center of everything in this novel.

8. *What, from your own experience, did you draw on to write Liszt's Kiss?*

As a pianist, I had a very clear image of how it feels to play the piano, what goes through one's mind and body during practice, during lessons with a teacher one reveres, and during a performance. I found it very rewarding to take my experiences and articulate them in this novel. I have also been fortunate to play several fortepianos from around the period of *Liszt's Kiss* and before. The feeling under the hands and resulting sound is quite different, both from a performer's and a listener's perspective. The double-escapement mechanism that enabled a pianist to play rapidly repeated notes had only recently been invented, and the frames of the instruments were still wooden. This meant that the strings could be of only a certain gauge and length, limiting the volume that could be attained. The tone is also softer and rounder. Today's bright, concert grand timbre would have been quite harsh to early nineteenth-century ears.

9. *There seems to be a growing interest in historical romance novels.*
   Why do you think this might be?

There is a perennial desire to escape to another time and place, one that is not so fraught with the insurmountable problems we hear about on the news every day. While novels set in the present can—and do—certainly take us out of ourselves, our image of the past can have an additional element of escapism. This effect of entering a completely different world has always been a huge attraction to reading for me.

Of course, people who lived then also had to face difficulties and tragedies. Living through them vicariously can put our everyday aggravations into perspective and make us appreciate how comfortably we, in Western society, live today, how the illnesses that claimed many lives centuries ago mostly race through our bodies and leave us none the worse for wear now.

Despite the many and profound differences, I am often surprised when I read well-researched historical fiction at how much emotional connection is possible across time periods. The trick as a writer, of course, is to make those connections without giving characters anachronistic ideas and ways of perceiving their world. Even if it's not completely possible, giving a reader a believable experience of life in another era is always my goal.

10. *What drives you to go back in history rather than tell tales that take*
    place today? What do you think we can learn from looking at the past?

I love history—cultural history, social history, not so much the history that strings together conflicts and dynasties. To be able to imagine what people saw when they walked through the landscape hundreds of years ago, or how their food tasted, or what their garments felt like against their skin helps me understand my own place in the world more clearly. For me, the present is too complicated to work with. A little perspective and emotional distance help me see where the story is. And I love the art, fashions, and literature of those periods, too.

In the end, it may also be my zeal to share my imagining of the past with others that makes me return to these historical subjects. The worst outcome, in my view, would be for us as a society to lose our touch with history. In this digital age where things happen and change so fast, going back to a slower time restores and refreshes me.

ENHANCING YOUR BOOK CLUB:

1. Listen to recordings of Liszt's music and compare them to those of Chopin or Mozart to see what was particular to Liszt's music, the website www.chopin.org may offer resources for an event in your area.

2. Check out from the library a book of paintings from 1832 France to get a sense of how this world looked and how the people in it dressed.

3. Read Ms. Dunlap's first novel, *Emilie's Voice,* to get another glimpse into the world of music and the past.

4. Get more information on Susanne Dunlap by visiting her website at http://www.emiliesvoice.com/.